For our Lexy, who has been a wonderful surprise,
and for Jane and Lisa too. Welcome to the family.

PART ONE

The sudden vanishing of Olive Anderson

1

The woman at the table was one of the most beautiful that Olive had ever seen. She was tall and slim, and her sapphire eyes were ringed in thick black lashes, below brows so perfect they could have been painted on with the finest of brushes. They hadn't been, Olive saw as she drew closer; they were real. Red lips formed a deep Cupid's bow.

In Olive's brief absence from the dining room, the place had filled, become both hotter and louder. Several Christmas parties had arrived. That shouldn't have been a problem, she'd saved herself a seat before nipping out, except . . .

. . . Her seat had been taken by a woman she'd never seen before.

'I think you're at my table,' she said, in a firm voice, one that brooked no nonsense, but smiling as she did so.

The intruder was a little older than Olive, maybe around thirty-eight. Her crew-cut hair was black and looked as though it might curl if allowed to grow; yes, it definitely would, because a few longer strands had formed a perfect circle high on her brow. She wore a sweater the colour of her eyes and, even in midwinter, her skin had the healthy, tanned glow of someone who worked outside. She smelled of cold air. Her eyes met Olive's and two horizontal lines appeared above those exquisite brows.

She said, 'Your table?'

Olive caught a glance flicking her way, someone nearby sensing confrontation, and felt her own chest tighten.

'I left my coat on the seat.' She lowered her eyes to the chair the woman was sitting on. 'That seat.'

The corners of the stranger's mouth drooped as she twisted round. Her movements exaggerated, she leaned out to look at the floor, under the table, giving Olive a chance to see the skintight denim jeans on very long legs and brown leather cowboy boots. She'd be pushing six foot tall when she stood.

She glanced back up at Olive with a sparkle in her eyes, that could have been mischief, or spite, and said, 'Are you sure?'

Fair play, there was no sign of Olive's coat, but she certainly wasn't wearing it and there was no way she'd have crossed the car park from the annexe without it. The bitch had hidden her coat so she could nab the last free table.

'Here you go, madam. Sorry you had to wait so long. I had to fetch a new bottle from the cellar.' The waiter had arrived like vindication from above. Putting a large glass of red wine down, he pulled out the spare chair, gesturing to Olive to sit. 'Allow me,' he said.

Olive allowed him, glad that she'd showered and changed after the drive over, that she looked OK, because the woman across the table oozed confidence like cheese seeping out of a toasted sandwich. As Olive sat, she felt her foot brush one of the cowboy boots and pulled it away sharply.

'And I moved your coat, hope that's OK,' the waiter went on. 'It fell off the chair and I didn't want anyone standing on it. It's hanging beside the bar, I can fetch it if you like.'

'No, that's fine, thank you.' Olive's eyes didn't leave those of the woman across the table. She let her eyebrows rise, waiting for an apology, which didn't come.

'And for you, madam?' the waiter asked.

'Scotch and soda,' the woman replied, her eyes holding fast to Olive's. 'Easy on the ice.'

The waiter either wasn't noticing or choosing to ignore the tension between the two of them. 'Plenty of that outside, I know what you mean,' he said. 'Are you both ready to order?'

Olive noticed then that menus had arrived while she'd been away. Blue-sweater woman picked up the nearest and passed it back to the waiter. 'Rib-eye, please. Rare. Side order of extra chips. No mushrooms, I'm allergic to fungi.'

'Not a problem. And for you, madam?'

'I'm not . . .' Olive began. *I'm not with this woman,* she'd been on the point of saying, but a sudden movement held her back.

The woman opposite had propped her left elbow on the table, cradling the side of her face with her forefinger and thumb, making her wedding band very visible. Her blue eyes seemed to darken, to become the colour of slate, as she glanced down at Olive's left hand, at the ring that, even after six months, Olive was still acutely conscious of, and it could be her imagination, or the wine she'd already drunk in her room, but was there something of a question in the way those blue eyes met hers? Even, perhaps, an invitation?

'. . . I'm not quite sure,' Olive went on. 'What's the vegan option?'

If the waiter was sensing something odd, his voice gave nothing away. 'It's a roasted pumpkin risotto with caramelised onions. Highly recommended.'

Olive wasn't vegan; she wasn't sure why she'd even asked.

'I'll have the rib-eye too, plenty of mushrooms.' She handed back the menu.

'And a large bottle of mineral water,' the woman across the table said. 'My wife has an early start.'

The waiter's eyes flicked from one woman to the other in sudden interest, before he gave a half-smile and walked away.

Silence for a second, then another. Olive opened her mouth to say, *What the hell are you playing at,* and nothing came out.

'So, how was your day?' the woman asked. 'You look tense.'

The mysterious intruder wasn't going to quit the table, that much was obvious. And hadn't Olive left it too late to ask the waiter to find her another? Especially when she'd just allowed herself to be addressed as this woman's wife?

'Everything go as planned?' the woman prompted.

It was unlikely the hotel had another table; there probably wasn't another table in the entire town, not so close to Christmas. She was paying twice the usual price for her room, and she'd been half tempted not to bother, but the thought of another night at home, of another night pretending to be pleased to see Michael, no, that simply wasn't—

'Planet earth to my wife.' The woman with sapphire eyes smiled at her own joke and a dimple appeared in her left cheek.

So, it all came down to this: was a lonely dinner in a crowded, pre-Christmas hotel really what Olive wanted right now?

'Carlisle was nice, as always,' she said. 'Lancaster not so much. The drive over here was pretty hairy. I think the entire north of England might be closed to traffic before the weekend's done.'

She waited for the woman to ask her what she did, to seek details, the customary dance of strangers. Except they weren't strangers, not in this odd game she'd been invited to play. They were married.

'How about you,' she asked, before adding a tentative, 'darling,' for good measure. It sounded odd and forced on her tongue. Her new companion was better at this than she.

That companion sighed, even managed to look bored. 'Hartlepool's a month behind, usual trouble with the lads at Darlington. On the other hand, they passed the health and safety inspection.'

She was in construction, a surveyor or site manager. Assuming, of course, that she was telling the truth.

'The llamas got out again,' she went on. 'I'm going to have to talk to Jim about putting a taller fence up.'

Maybe this whole evening was to be played out in some odd fantasy land. Perhaps Olive herself should pretend to be a brain surgeon or an astronaut, because if you were going to play the game, you might as well play it properly.

A picture flashed into her head: Michael in the study at home, working his way through an endless list of constituency emails, grimacing when a noisy quarrel erupted elsewhere in the house, checking Find My Friends to make sure she'd arrived safely, worried about her being away in such awful weather. One of Michael's pet subjects was the dangers of northern winters.

What on earth was she doing playing games?

Her phone beeped, a message coming in. She glanced down, but it wasn't Michael, only a reminder from her gym that her subscription needed renewing. In the meantime, they were talking – about llamas.

'How far did they get?' Olive asked as the waiter returned with a single shot of whisky on a silver tray.

'Three miles down the road before a motorist called the police. Thanks.' The woman cradled the drink in the palm of her right hand. 'The lads from the farm rounded them up and herded them back.'

So now they were a married couple with pet llamas. Olive felt an unfamiliar tickle in her stomach, the start of an urge to laugh. 'Are they OK?' she asked.

The stranger scratched the back of her head and took a mouthful of Scotch. 'They're fine, let's not talk about the llamas. What are you upset about?'

'I'm not upset.'

The woman leaned closer. Olive caught a whiff of the outdoors again and, beneath it, something like pomegranate, or maybe sandalwood, but faded, as though she'd come straight from work, without showering or changing.

'This is me you're talking to.' The woman put her drink down but missed the coaster because she didn't break eye contact, not even for a split second. 'You're clenching your teeth, your shoulders are up round your ears and you're biting your nails again.'

Olive glanced down; her nails were a mess. As for the rest, well, it was hardly surprising she was uptight given the turn her evening was taking. Maybe it was time to bring this to an end. She could get room service, call Michael, force herself back to normality.

As though sensing her pulling away, the woman leaned in closer until Olive could smell the whisky on her breath. To anyone watching, the interplay would look intimate, familiar, the interaction of two people who knew each other inside out.

'Hey.' The woman's voice was too low to carry beyond the circle of the small table. 'There's only one reason we booked into a hotel so close to home.' She glanced around the noisy room and grimaced. 'This close to Christmas.'

For a second, Olive was on the brink of panic. This woman knew where she lived. No, that was impossible, she'd made a lucky guess based on the trace of north-east in Olive's voice.

'Remind me,' she challenged.

'To talk.' The stranger relaxed back and picked up her glass again. 'Permission to rant, babe. Pretend I'm your best mate. Let me hear it, nothing out of bounds.'

And wasn't this exactly what Olive needed: a rant to a best mate? Except there was no way she could tell her real friends that all their warnings and misgivings had come a hundred-per-cent true, and that, six months into the marriage that everyone had advised against, she'd found herself in an impossible, miserable situation. No, what she needed was to vent to a perfect stranger whom she'd never see again after this evening.

She leaned close, grateful that she'd cleaned her teeth before coming down to dinner. 'Your bloody mother-in-law,' she hissed.

The puzzled frown appeared as expected and Olive waited for the stranger to question what must surely seem an odd choice of words. Instead, she pulled a face, sighed, and nodded her head in silent acknowledgement that, disloyal as it might be to admit it, Olive actually had a point. Bloody hell, she was good at this.

Olive wondered, briefly, if mentioning Gwendoline would act as a salutary reminder, dragging her back into her real life, the one with problems that had to be tackled, and realised she didn't want to go back there, not yet.

'What's she done now?' the woman asked.

A question almost impossible to answer. Being around the mother of Michael's late wife was like death from a thousand small cuts. Little she did was enough to make a legitimate complaint, but her tactic of one microaggression on top of another, day after day, would wear anyone down: speaking over her; leaving her laundry on the line in the rain; losing messages from her friends, even her husband; slamming doors when she was sleeping after a night shift;

disapproving, loudly, of every TV show she chose to watch. So many to choose from.

'She's hiding my mail,' Olive decided upon.

The stranger frowned. 'She's what?'

'When something arrives for me, she hides it, holds on to it for several days and then it magically appears on the doormat as though it was delayed in the post.'

'How do you know it wasn't delayed in the post?'

'Because it's happening too often. Never anything by registered post, because that I could trace. I didn't tell you this, but six of my birthday cards came late. And I know all six people didn't post late. She wanted me to have a miserable day.'

Olive could hear her voice had grown louder; the events of her birthday still rankled. Actually, this was helping, like a bizarre form of therapy; it felt good to offload. She'd been holding too much back the last six months.

'And the girls don't help.' Olive felt a head of steam building, as though now she'd started, it would be hard to stop.

'They're kids,' the woman tried. 'It hasn't been easy for them either.'

Again, a lucky guess. This woman couldn't know her step-daughters' ages.

'I get that. We knew that would be the case. And the girls alone I could deal with. They're not bad kids, of course they're not. But Gwendoline – I don't know – it's like she empowers them. They see her behaving badly and know they can get away with it too.'

The stranger's face was completely serious now, the perfect listener.

'And I've had it. Frankly, I don't want to go home tomorrow.'

And wasn't that the truth?

'So, what do you want to happen?' the woman asked. 'What do you want me to do?'

Olive put her empty glass down. 'There isn't anything you can do, I know that. We're stuck with this. I'm stuck with it.'

The waiter was approaching with their food.

'Rare rib-eye with mushrooms for you, Mrs Anderson.' The waiter had checked the hotel register to learn her name. It was a courteous enough gesture, but it meant the woman across the table now knew her name. 'And without for you, madam.'

'Looks great, thank you.' The fake wife was smiling up at the waiter.

'Anything else I can get you?' The waiter seemed to be lingering longer than was strictly necessary.

'We're good, thanks.'

'Enjoy.' The waiter flashed them both a smile, hovered for a second longer and then walked away.

'OK,' the stranger said.

'OK, what?'

She picked up her fork and speared a chip. 'OK, we'll move out. Whatever you want, you only have to say the word, you should know that.'

Olive felt a mirthless laugh on the brink of slipping out. Like the nightmare her life had become could be fixed that easily.

2

The first man in destroyed the front door. Built like a train, appearing every bit as unstoppable, he shouldered the enforcer and slung it. The crash shattered the silence of the night, and the festive wreath, an intricate spiral of Christmas roses, white thistles and eucalyptus, bounced in protest.

'Armed police!'

'Armed police. Stand clear!'

The enforcer crashed again, then a third time, not quite drowning out the yelling of over a dozen voices. Police raids were noisy affairs.

The oak panelling around the lock shattered and the door swung open. The second man, fully armed, went in like a bullet, knocking the wreath from its hook. He ran left. The third man followed, veering right. The room beyond was well lit, the entrance hall of a wealthy family home. Among those still waiting outside, hearts were thumping, adrenaline surging, every officer in the unit desperate to get in.

Every officer but one.

Noise levels grew.

'Armed police, hands in the air!'

'Armed police, show yourselves now!'

One officer had never done this before; one officer would have given anything to be back on traffic duty right now. He took a deep breath, the night air stinging his nostrils, and had a last look around at the winter night. On the chill breeze, he could detect a hint of salt from the North Sea and woodsmoke from a nearby farm. The house was on high ground, but few lights around him broke up the darkness. The vast expanse of the North York Moors was a stone's throw away.

The fourth man in ran up the carved oak staircase.

The fifth man, the new guy, almost slid on the fallen Christmas wreath. One hand, slick with sweat, gripped the handle of the Heckler & Koch G36. The other held the barrel steady (more or less) as he caught his balance and stepped to one side. His task for the next few minutes was to guard the front door, make sure no one other than his fellow officers left the property.

Simple, he told himself. Nothing to it. Even he couldn't mess this up.

3

An hour after Olive had sat down, the nameless stranger was still exactly that. She hadn't offered her name. Her 'wife' would know it, of course, and if there was a way of subtly finding it out, Olive had yet to think of it.

'Tell me a secret,' that stranger said, when she'd eaten her food, and Olive had managed a little more than half hers, pushing the rest around in a vain attempt to make it look less than it was. Her stomach seemed to be signalling its own disapproval of what she was doing. On the other hand, the wine was slipping down well, so maybe her stomach was as conflicted as the rest of her.

'You know all my secrets,' Olive countered.

'Impossible.'

The woman reached out. Olive saw the hand – freckles breaking up the tan, rough skin around the fingertips – heading towards her face as though in slow motion. She watched it, mesmerised, like a small mammal faced with a swaying snake. Fingers brushed the side of Olive's face and a lock of hair was smoothed behind her ear; they lingered against her neck.

'I like your ears,' the woman said. 'They're sexy. But you know that.'

The room had grown hot, or so it seemed, and the dripping condensation on the dark windows reminded Olive uncomfortably of the rivulets of sweat that would insist on trickling down her back. She'd wanted for some time to take off her jacket but had been wary of the signal it would send. Undressing suggested relaxation, maybe even a desire to show off her body.

Her companion had no such inhibitions; the blue sweater had long since been hung over the back of her chair, revealing a tight black T-shirt. Trying hard not to look, Olive couldn't help but notice the full, high breasts and a small cockleshell tattoo on the woman's right shoulder.

She'd wanted to ask about it, had even come up with a form of words that wouldn't break the rules of the game: *you never did tell me why you chose that particular tattoo?* She held back, because remarking on this woman's body, acknowledging that she'd noticed it, felt like crossing a line.

She'd been deeply shocked to find herself wondering what those breasts would feel like in her hands.

'So, come on,' the stranger prompted. 'A secret.'

The skin of Olive's face and neck was still tingling. She said, 'If I do, will you tell me one of yours?'

The woman shrugged. 'Seems fair. You first.'

Where to begin? 'I hate the boat,' she said.

The woman's eyebrows rose again, feigning surprise, although Olive could have said anything: *I've worked for MI5 for years now, I seduced my maths teacher when I was sixteen,* and this stranger would have no idea whether it was true or not. It was significant, she knew, that she'd chosen to go with something true.

'I've been pretending for months,' she went on. 'Because I know how important it is to you, and how much it means to you that we can enjoy it together, but I'm shaking every time we go out. I feel sick, even when the water's what you call a millpond, and when it tips, when it does that thing you call keeling, or—'

'Heeling,' the stranger corrected, telling Olive that, whoever she was, she knew something about sailing. And also, possibly, that she too disliked it, because her eyes had grown colder and the lines of her jaw had hardened.

'I'm convinced we're going to capsize and that I'll drown, and I hate you then,' Olive went on. 'I hate you for believing me when I say I enjoy it, and I hate the girls for doing it all effortlessly, and I hate Gwen for constantly banging on about how good . . . well, you know.'

She didn't, she couldn't possibly, but – oh God – the relief at putting these feelings into words.

'This feels like something we should have talked about before,' the woman said.

And she was right; Olive had been keeping so much to herself, and her resentment was turning toxic, threatening everything.

'How could I tell you something that would make you love me less?' she said.

The woman opened her mouth to utter some platitude that Olive really didn't want to hear right now.

'Your turn,' she said, to head her off.

The stranger took her time, and Olive had a moment to notice that the Christmas revellers around them were either quietening or drifting away. There was disco music playing somewhere in the hotel and many of the diners had gone in search of it. The room they'd left behind was littered with festive detritus: torn paper hats, streamers lying damp and limp across the paisley-patterned carpet, stained paper napkins, disembowelled crackers and Prosecco corks.

After more than a minute, when Olive was on the verge of prompting, the woman spoke.

'I planned this.'

Olive sat back, feeling her gaze hardening. So, the game was done.

'I saw you, when I came in, sitting alone. I watched you get up, go to the ladies', and I took my chance.'

'Why?' So, it hadn't been an honest mistake, followed by a harmless bit of devilment. This woman had planned it all, for some reason that wasn't yet clear but soon would be. And Olive had drunk far too much wine.

'Because seeing you was like someone had taken hold of my insides and given them a good twist,' the woman replied. 'And the strangest thought sprang into my head.'

Don't ask her what it was. This has gone too far.

'I thought to myself: *There she is. At last.*'

Olive was conscious of movement around them, of staff trying to clear the dining room, but her eyes couldn't leave those of the woman across the table. She waited for the anger to come, for the indignation – who the hell did she think she was dealing with – and waited in vain.

'Can I get you anything else?' Their waiter was back.

Olive couldn't speak. Her companion said, 'Two brandies, please. We'll take them to our room.'

'Not a problem.' The waiter left them.

'Am I out of line?' the woman asked.

Yes, way out of line. She was married, and what she had with Michael was far too important to put at risk now.

And yet, she was so very unhappy. And so very drunk. And this was feeling more and more like something – inevitable.

'I'm in room seven,' Olive said. 'Across the courtyard.'

The other woman stood up. 'I'll get your coat.'

4

The woman who was nameless couldn't help glancing up at the sky as she and Olive stepped out into the sharp darkness. The cold seemed to leap inside her, like knives scraping the inside of her nostrils and the back of her throat. Another inch of snow had fallen while they'd been eating.

Close up, with her arm through Olive's to steady her on the treacherous ground, she could smell her perfume, something rich and sweet; Olive smelled like Christmas.

She couldn't believe how easy it had been. The plan, had Olive remained at her table, had been to approach apologetically, explaining that the restaurant was full, and would she mind terribly sharing. She had a book in her jacket pocket, one she knew – thank you, Facebook – that Olive had read and loved, had planned to pull it out, pretend to be engrossed, establish herself as polite, considerate, the very opposite of a threat.

The conversation would have begun tentatively, uncertainly. She'd have claimed to be a nurse herself, had worked hard on her backstory, to find common ground. Instead, Olive had got up to go to the ladies' and then a waiter had picked up her coat from the floor and removed it.

To the woman who was nameless, it had felt like the fates conspiring in her favour. She'd strode forward without thinking, settling herself in the opposite seat, taking several deep breaths to appear relaxed.

So easy. She'd guessed the Andersons were having problems – well, they would, in the circumstances – but the stuff had come pouring out: bitterness, disappointment, frustration and, beneath it all, a deep loneliness.

She was a little taken aback by how much she was tempted to like Olive. Anderson's wife was gorgeous, of course, but she'd known that. She'd seen plenty of pictures of the two of them together. What she hadn't expected was the luminous quality of her skin, the light in her green eyes, the silky sheen on her hair. Even tired, even distressed, there was a quality about her.

It didn't make any difference. She'd hated Olive Anderson for too long to think of changing course now. Olive would get what was coming to her.

5

The man guarding the mansion's front door – Garry – could feel sweat running into his eyes. Knowing it would look like he was crying, he took one hand off the firearm to wipe it away.

The noise around him was close to deafening: the thunder of boots on stone, men yelling orders, a woman screaming. From outside came a sound like fireworks as distraction explosions went off. A bloke even bigger than he was stumbled on his way into the house and trod briefly on Garry's foot.

Garry didn't swear – he never swore – even hearing bad language made his skin crawl, but he bit his lip hard as real tears filled his eyes. The bloke strode off without apologising, without even looking round, and Garry could taste blood in his mouth.

Blood and tears. Appropriate.

The entire tactical team was inside now, even those who'd come in from the rear. The shouting continued, doors slammed open, the intimidating wall of sound deliberate, to frighten and cower the inhabitants of the house.

Not just the inhabitants.

Garry pressed himself up against the external wall, telling himself it would be over soon, that all he had to do was watch the door, and that nothing, nothing at all, could possibly go wrong.

6

Olive held on to the stranger's arm as they crossed the courtyard. The snow had settled and was already more than an inch deep. From the open window of the bar, a Christmas song blared out, the singer drowned by the drunken warbling of fifty off-key voices. As they passed close by, they walked through a bubble of warm, foetid air. Snowflakes fell into the glass Olive was carrying, melting on contact with the brandy.

She had a sense of events slipping out of her control, of being tossed on the wind of fate. She was drunk, of course, but not so drunk that she'd take a complete stranger to her room unwillingly. This was something else, something she hadn't experienced before. It was scary, and very exciting.

She used her key to open the annexe door and led the way to the end of the corridor. It took fifteen short paces and with each step she told herself it wasn't too late, she could apologise, say she'd changed her mind, had realised that this was the very worst idea in the world.

But Michael, the girls, the life she'd struggled with for six long months had faded in her mind, like a dream that slipped away upon waking, or a dim childhood memory, or an old sepia photograph. It didn't feel real anymore. This was real, the tall woman a half-step behind her, who'd caught her when she'd slipped in the snow just now, so quickly, so deftly, that not even their drinks had spilled.

Her room smelled like the stranger. Olive caught notes of sandal-wood and paused in the doorway. It should be impossible that this woman's scent had leapt ahead of them, to claim the room as her own, just as she was claiming Olive now, coaxing her inside and closing the door, easing off Olive's coat and letting it fall, taking hold of her hair and gently tilting her face up to her own.

'At last,' she murmured, as she bent and kissed her.

So different, was all Olive could think for those first few moments. Michael, who made love like an animal, would have grabbed her the minute they closed the door, pulling her face towards him, ripping clothes off, not caring if he damaged them. Michael would have poured the brandy over her naked body, making sure it slicked its way into all her intimate places, before licking it up. Michael fucked her like a porn star – fiercely, showily – withdrawing several times and manhandling her into yet another impossible position, before eventually, after thirty minutes or so, climaxing noisily.

Michael never cared who might hear him coming, not his daughters, not his late wife's mother, not the cows in the barn or the farmhands who lived half a mile down the lane.

This woman was the very opposite of Michael. She undressed Olive slowly, kissing every inch of skin she uncovered. This woman took her time, stepping back for long seconds to look at her, making Olive feel more than naked under the stranger's gaze.

This woman lifted her, putting her down gently on the bed, before pulling off her own clothes and lying beside her. Still she wanted nothing more than to look, to kiss Olive on the lips, to run her hand over Olive's flesh.

'So submissive,' she murmured into Olive's ear, and it stung. Michael's lovemaking made active participation on Olive's part close to impossible. He never let her take the lead, and somewhere along the line, she'd forgotten how.

This woman gave her plenty of time to change her mind; plenty of time to jump up, grab her coat and run from the room. This woman made it the last thing she wanted to do. By the time her fingers crept inside Olive, as slowly and gently as everything else she'd done, she'd stopped comparing her to Michael.

'Who are you?' she cried once, into the darkened room.

No reply came back.

7

The tactical team were still charging through the eighteenth-century coach house like two-legged rhinos, shiny-black and super-aggressive in full protective gear. Garry could hear boots pounding on the upper floor. The occupants of the house – at least two according to the intel, but it could be more hadn't been found.

The raid on the home of Howie Tricks – younger brother of Stevie Tricks, infamous head of a local gang of organised crime – had been planned for zero four hundred hours the following morning but brought forward after an adverse weather report. By four o'clock the next day, the road outside might not be passable, and Cleveland Police had a tight window to recover several million pounds' worth of stolen bullion and one very, very valuable ruby and diamond necklace recently lifted from Sotheby's – the infamous Ring of Blood and Tears.

Garry glanced at his watch. Eighteen minutes since the operation had begun and it felt like a whole lot longer. He wondered, not for the first time, what in the world had possessed him to train as an Authorised Firearms Officer.

8

The stranger seemed to sleep for a while. Olive lay beside her and waited for the shame to come, as it surely would. The madness was done, the lust sated. Her revenge on her husband, her kick-back at everything her life had become – because that's what it had been, she knew that clearly now – was complete.

Was this shame, this burning feeling in her chest, the sense that she was about to throw up?

Olive eased her way out of bed, fearful of disturbing the woman and at the same time knowing that soon she'd have to wake her and make her leave, because Michael would call early the next morning, and she absolutely could not talk to her husband with a naked woman in her bed. Michael used FaceTime; he would want a virtual tour of the room, demand to know what underwear she'd be wearing that day.

What the hell had she done?

Olive crept her way around discarded clothes, the overnight bag she hadn't properly unpacked, and caught sight of her handbag by the door. She would hide that, in a moment. She couldn't risk this woman finding out anything more about her. She had to remain the anonymous Mrs Anderson. She hadn't even told the woman her first name.

In the bathroom, she used the loo, drank water from the tap, wiped the sweat from her body, but drew the line at the shower. A shower would wake the woman in the bedroom, and besides, the shower was for when she'd gone, when she could wash all trace of her away.

She shivered then, at a sudden flashback to the sex. The sex had been wonderful: soft, teasing, torturously slow, and a tiny, insane voice in her head urged her to slip back into the bedroom, climb between the sheets and have it all again.

Enough. She would wake the woman now, explain that she had to go, that there was no place for her in Olive's life. She'd understand. And she was married too.

She'd forgotten that. The stranger was married; she had as much to lose as Olive did. Relief washed over her.

Wrapping a towel around herself, she pulled the bathroom door open, not trying to be quiet, because it was time to wake up.

The overhead light in the bedroom was on. The woman was awake. Not only awake but fully dressed and zipping up Olive's overnight bag. She turned and seemed to take a deep breath before speaking.

'Get dressed,' she said. 'We're leaving.'

This was a different woman; and yet nothing had changed; she looked exactly the same.

'What?' Olive clutched the towel, grateful that she was wearing something at least. The other woman had even put on shoes, and this was a bit like one of those dreams when you suddenly find yourself naked in public.

Nothing had changed but the woman's eyes, that had grown cold and hard as flint.

And that laptop, open on top of the chest of drawers by the door, that wasn't Olive's. What was going on?

She was suddenly acutely conscious of the inside of her body, and it felt cold and heavy, like sodden clay.

'We're checking out.' The woman's cold eyes had grown shifty. 'Fetch anything you left in the bathroom and get dressed. Now, Olive.'

She'd used her name. Olive hadn't told the stranger her name. She was suddenly deeply afraid.

The woman said, 'I won't tell you again.'

Olive found her voice. 'I'm not going anywhere. Get out of here.'

The woman sighed and took one step to the laptop. She pressed the space bar and the screen sprang to life. A photograph appeared, taken in that very room, of the two of them. Kissing.

No, not a photograph, a video. Olive saw the information bar along the bottom of the screen. A video that was over twenty minutes long.

'Some parts are a bit dark, but it's reasonably clear the woman, naked for most of it, is you and that the person fucking you is not Michael Anderson, member of parliament for Middlesbrough South and East Cleveland.'

The room no longer felt over-bright; it was dimming around the edges.

'Want to see a bit?' the woman asked.

Olive shook her head, but the woman didn't see and it probably wouldn't have made any difference anyway. She fast-forwarded the footage to a little over halfway and pressed play.

The stranger's head was between Olive's legs, her long hands reaching up to cup Olive's breasts. Olive's legs were bent back so that her feet brushed the woman's shoulders; her arms reached up to clutch the bedhead and her mouth was open in a silent cry.

'There were three cameras,' the woman told Olive. 'Above the curtain rail, on the bedhead and behind the lamp on the chest of drawers. I broke into your room when you went down to dinner.'

That's why the room had smelled of her. And she'd even warned Olive. *I planned this.*

'I have you from every conceivable angle, Olive, and I've got to say, congrats on putting on a very good show.'

Olive rushed back into the bathroom, bending double over the loo as everything came pouring out. On her last heave, she realised the woman was right behind her.

'You've got five minutes,' she told Olive. 'Get your clothes on, get every last thing packed and then we check out. At the front desk, we'll explain that we have a family emergency and we have to leave immediately. You'll pay the bill and then we'll get in your car.'

Olive didn't move.

'Five minutes, Olive. Or this tape will be uploaded onto the internet.'

9

The stranger drove. Olive doubted she'd have been capable, even without the amount she'd drunk. Too late, she remembered how little the other woman had consumed herself. Olive had been drunk earlier, the stranger had not.

Olive didn't feel drunk now; trapped in a parallel world where nightmares came true, but stone-cold sober for all that.

Hexham was a small town and they left it behind quickly, heading north into the white night. The stranger drove fast, as though she might outrun the tideline of snow washing ever closer to the centre of the road. She drove aggressively, braking and accelerating hard, upright in the driver's seat, her focus entirely on the road ahead. She drove in silence.

She kept the radio on low, turning up the volume when the frequent traffic alerts sounded. Most of them seemed weather-related: roads blocked, roads being closed for safety reasons, vehicles abandoned or crashed.

As they approached the first village – a tiny, one-pub place called Acomb – Olive forced herself to speak. Just a few words. A simple question.

'Where are we going?'

The stranger didn't take her eyes off the road. 'You'll find out soon enough.'

Olive had no idea whether it was good, or bad, that they didn't have far to go. All she knew was that terror had replaced shame in her head. What the hell had she done, getting into this car?

The clock on the dashboard told her it was twenty minutes

past ten. Michael would have left London, be on his way home, and he always phoned from the car. This woman had taken her phone, though, switching it off and tucking it into an inner pocket of her bag. That bag, and Olive's own, were now in the boot of the car.

She wondered when, if at all, Michael would start to worry about her.

At the edge of the village, they had to slow down as they approached temporary traffic lights. Olive glanced at the door.

'Don't even think about it,' the woman warned, without taking her eyes off the red light ahead.

She had to though, this could be her last chance. Did she dare? Leap from the car and run for the village, scream for help the second she could draw a breath.

She'd made a massive mistake. She hadn't been thinking, back at the hotel. She'd panicked, let herself get dragged into something dangerous. This woman was dangerous. She had to get away from her now.

Her hand slipped down to the seat-belt fastening.

The lights changed to red and amber.

Now. She reached for the door handle.

The stranger pressed her foot down hard on the accelerator. For a second, possibly two, the car danced on the road as the tyres fought for traction and then they shot forward, a moment before the light turned to green.

'Don't make me angry,' the stranger said.

10

Garry knew the answer to his own question, of course. After he'd failed the detective exams twice (and been advised not to bother again), he'd needed a win and had applied to train as an Authorised Firearms Officer. It hadn't even been hard, a simple matter of learning how to use and take care of the equipment, some unarmed close-combat training and a bit of first aid he'd known anyway. He'd excelled at the driving side: the interception tactics, the tactical pursuit driving, and had even proved a half-decent shot, once he'd stopped thinking how he'd cope if faced with a real-life human instead of a target.

It had seemed such a good idea at the time, and he'd finally given his dad something to boast about among his ex-policeman mates down the golf club.

Somewhere in the house, a dog was barking. The Trickses owned two Rottweilers and there'd been talk of them being shot if they proved aggressive. Garry was glad the continued barking, and the fact no gunshots had yet sounded, meant that probably hadn't happened. There would be no prizes for guessing who'd be ordered to deal with any dead dogs.

A crackling sounded over the radio, then, 'We've got Howie Tricks. Howie coming out now.'

The room seemed to fill in seconds. From somewhere close, Garry could hear someone yelling instructions and then Howie Tricks was being led into the room in handcuffs. He was a white bloke in his forties with a winter tan and the gleam of yellow gold on several fingers, both wrists and even around his neck.

In spite of his blinged-up appearance, though, there was something quietly menacing about the man. He didn't struggle but kept his movements deliberately slow. His head swayed this way and that, like a reptile searching out its next meal, as he took in the chaos in his home.

'Where's my wife?' he said, and he didn't need to raise his voice to be heard. 'What have you effing pillocks done with my wife?'

Garry suppressed a shudder; he really hated bad language.

'Tell us where the gold is, Howie,' the op sergeant replied. 'And what about that nice ruby necklace?'

'No idea what you're talking about.'

Howie Tricks had made his fortune buying and selling gold, often – although this had never been proven – from highly dubious sources.

'Get him out of here' the sergeant ordered.

Tricks was led out, but not before he'd caught sight of the man standing to attention by the front door of his home, the man who still had part of the Christmas wreath clinging to his boot.

Garry was in full tactical gear, including helmet and a mask that covered the lower part of his face. Even so, he felt the full force of Tricks' intense gaze. The other man's eyes were a cold, hard blue. Garry tried to suppress a shudder and saw the gleam of satisfaction in the other man's eyes when he failed.

11

The clock on the car dashboard reached ten-thirty. Olive had seen neither moon nor stars, and they'd long since left street lights behind, but the snow seemed to cast a light of its own, softening the darkness. To one side, across a vast white field, a curving line of trees against the grey sky suggested the river was close. They passed through Wall, and the coloured lights of the Christmas tree on the green looked like a symbol of a world she no longer deserved to be part of.

'Who are you?' Olive was surprised at how steady her voice sounded.

'Wrong question.'

Olive opened her mouth to make the obvious retort and caught herself in time; this woman was not going to have it all her own way. Out of the corner of her eye, she saw the stranger glance towards her. More than once.

Eventually, the other woman spoke. 'The right question is: What do I want?'

'I assume this is something to do with my husband,' Olive said.

A soft burst of sound, something between a laugh and a snort.

It had to be about Michael. Most MPs were divisive figures. Plenty disliked their politics, others nursed personal grievances about problems that couldn't be fixed by a stern letter on parliamentary notepaper. Michael, though, had mended more bridges than most. To the extent that it was possible for an MP, he was popular.

Outside the car, the snow was still coming down, thick and fast enough for the windscreen wipers to be on top speed. The edges around the glass were coated in a thick frosting of white and the view of the night landscape was getting smaller by the minute.

On the radio, the music was interrupted by a traffic alert. The A69 northbound was completely blocked and the police were advising people to stay at home if their journey wasn't absolutely essential.

When the announcement was finished, Olive said, 'How did you know I'd be in Hexham tonight? At that hotel?'

Nothing, other than a slight twist of the other woman's lips.

'You planned this. You said as much. You couldn't have been following me for weeks on the off chance.'

Still nothing.

'Someone told you where I'd be.' With that realisation, the churning feeling in Olive's stomach seemed to solidify, to become something that could squeeze the life out of her. 'Who was it?'

The stranger gave a soft laugh. 'What do they say, Olive? Keep your enemies closer?' She glanced across, holding eye contact for a dangerously long time given the speed they were travelling at. 'Looks like you kept yours very close indeed.'

12

The woman who was still nameless could feel the sweat – cold and clammy – between her shoulder blades. Several times already, the car had almost got stuck; either the snowfall had been heavier this far north or the hedgerows had trapped drifts. With each slide of the tyres, each reversal and subsequent struggle to find purchase, she'd felt the rage building. Her hands were clenched – stiff and cold – on the wheel, as though if she removed them, they'd retain their claw-like shape.

'How did you know?' Olive said. It seemed like an age since she'd spoken.

'How did I know what?'

'That I'd let you seduce me.'

The stranger risked taking her eyes off the road to glance Olive's way. Something in the other woman's manner had changed. The rabbit-in-the-headlights look had vanished and instead she looked pissed off. The stranger decided she preferred it; she'd actually been disappointed by how easily Olive had capitulated.

She said, 'I thought it was the other way round.'

'You're a cow.' Olive's voice had hardened too. 'Either way, how did you know it would happen? Suppose I'd told you to fuck off, or moved to another table, or gone back to my room and ordered room service? How did you know I'd be so drunk and stupid and desperate I'd let a creep like you come anywhere near me?'

'Ouch.' Actually, that really did hurt.

'Come on, how?'

'I didn't. You being that easy was a bonus.'

The second the words were out of her mouth she regretted them. 'I apologise,' she said.

'Screw you,' Olive muttered.

'And to answer your question, I had a back-up plan. A couple of benzodiazepines in my jacket pocket. I was planning to slip them into your drink. Five minutes in and I knew it wouldn't be necessary.'

Silence, then Olive said, 'Rohypnol?'

The classic date-rape drug. 'Lucky you drink red wine. The manufacturers put a blue dye in it now, did you know? Easy to spot in a glass of Chardonnay.'

Olive's eyes closed briefly. 'Why? What the hell is this about?'

Something flew in front of the car, startling them both. It was just a bird, but the stranger hadn't counted on being this jumpy.

'Not now, Olive. In case you hadn't noticed, conditions are a bit tricky.'

'Michael phones me. He phones every night I'm away. When he can't get in touch, he'll call the hotel.'

'And what will the hotel tell him, do you think?'

The stranger waited for Olive to catch up. Her silence suggested she probably had. The hotel would tell him that Olive had left with her wife.

13

Tina Tricks, Howie's wife, had been found. Or, rather, had locked herself in an upstairs bathroom, refusing to come out in spite of requests, insistence and finally direct orders from the officers in the hallway outside. In the end, the lock had been broken with a sharp, loud kick. Garry learned all this from snippets of conversation taking place around him. The frantic melee of earlier had calmed now that the team had Howie Tricks and his two associates in custody, none of whom had showed any signs of armed resistance. Having Tina contained as well meant the search could continue in a more orderly fashion.

A tall, slender woman with a thick cloud of dark brown hair, Tina Tricks was led into the hallway in apricot satin pyjamas. Her feet were bare. She clutched a soft toy against her chest with both hands.

'Sit there,' the female officer accompanying her said, before pushing her down onto a padded bench seat directly opposite Garry. 'We need to get you some shoes. Where will we find shoes?'

'Fuck you,' Tina replied, before pulling her feet up onto the bench and curling her body around the soft toy she was holding.

'I'll have a look,' the officer sighed. 'Why don't you have a think about when you last saw that necklace, Tina? I can't believe you didn't try it on.'

The Ring of Blood and Tears, according to the intel, could be anywhere in the house: kitchen fridge, on Tina's person, even around a dog's neck. The necklace was the bigger worry. Bars of bullion would be easy to locate, a piece of jewellery less so.

The op commander strode into the hall and positioned himself directly in front of Garry, effectively blocking most of his view.

'Done the wine cellar, boss.' Another officer, entirely anonymous in full protective gear, approached. 'Nothing. We're moving on to the office buildings next. And I've got a team ready to go into the stables.'

Tina Tricks kept horses – four beautiful animals that were worth the better part of a million quid between them. Directly opposite the stables was another building containing an indoor swimming pool, home gym and offices.

Over his commander's shoulder, Garry could see Tina's eyes fixed on him, as though she found his statue-like stance more threatening than all the officers bustling about. The toy she was holding, he saw now, was a teddy bear. As their eyes met, she clutched it tight again and Garry sensed the strangest feeling creeping over him. Somehow, he knew that teddy was important. Was this the famous policeman's instinct kicking in for him?

Finally?

14

It was almost eleven. In the life Olive had left behind, she'd be alone in a hotel bed, having drunk just enough wine to be able to respond, like with like, to Michael's inevitably raunchy late-night phone call. He'd be telling her he loved her, that he couldn't wait to see her, and she'd say she felt the same, and she'd fall asleep telling herself she could deal with any amount of shit that her new life threw at her because what she stood to gain was worth it.

She couldn't though, she'd more than proven that; drunkenly and stupidly, she'd ruined everything.

Conditions outside were worsening and the wind had picked up as the countryside had become starker. She could hear it keening above the noise of the engine and every few minutes gusts rocked the car.

As the car radio confirmed the hour, the stranger spoke again. 'How much do you know about Michael Anderson?' she asked.

So it was about Michael, but what else could it have been?

'Whirlwind romance? Six months' marriage?' the stranger went on. 'Is that really enough time to get to know someone? To trust someone?'

I trusted you after two hours. Enough to risk throwing my entire life away.

'You've been reading *Hello!* magazine,' Olive said, remembering the photo shoot that Michael had reluctantly agreed to after Gwen had pointed out that the £50K fee would be a welcome boost to the trust fund he'd set up in aid of women's cancer charities. Seven outfit changes, twelve different locations in and around Home Farm, and three embarrassing pages celebrating her marriage to the sexiest man in parliament.

It was thanks to *Hello!* magazine, she realised, that this woman had been able to recognise her so easily. Google Olive Anderson and over a dozen clear images came up.

'I know enough,' she said, and wondered, not for the first time, whether that was really true.

'Do you know he killed his first wife?' the stranger said.

15

Tina Tricks ran for it. One minute she was huddled on the bench seat like a sulky child, the next shooting forward like an arrow, heading for the front door. The officer who'd been her escort grabbed and failed to make contact. No one else was close.

'Mizon, stop her!'

Garry sidestepped, putting himself in the door frame. Tina lowered her head, as though to charge. Seriously? She was half his weight. When she was two paces away, he braced himself for the impact. One hand clutching the teddy, Tina hunched her shoulders, curled her other hand into a fist and thumped him in the balls. As Garry gasped, Tina slipped past him and ran out into the snow.

'Mizon, you wanker. Get after her.'

The snow had continued to fall in the forty-five minutes since the raid had begun. The prints of Tina's bare feet would have made her easy to follow, even if she'd got more than a few metres. Garry watched her dodge round a police van, then leap onto a stretch of lawn. He set off after her. He'd been a runner at school and was pretty certain he could outpace Tina Tricks.

She was surprisingly fast, though. Before Garry was halfway across the lawn, she'd leapt the surrounding wall and was speeding away.

Garry followed, over the wall and onto the verge that edged the road. He reached Tina in seconds, grabbing a handful of her pyjama top. She ran on, stretching the fabric, revealing several inches of her neck and shoulders. She had some sort of tattoo running down her spine. He wrapped an arm around her waist and pinned her against him, hoping back-up was close behind.

'Hands off me, you fucking pervert. Howie will have your balls for this.'

Right now, Howie was welcome; the lads downstairs were still burning from her own assault on them.

'Calm down, Tina,' he gasped, 'or I'll have to cuff you.'

'Don't you fucking touch me.' She kicked his shin; even without shoes, it hurt.

Garry glanced round to see that no one was close. He couldn't lose Tina. Luckily, she was light and thin enough to hold with one arm. Wriggling like a spiked snake, though.

Panting with the effort of holding her, he pulled his cuffs and got the first link around her left wrist. Her right arm was clutched in front of her body. She was still holding that blessed bear. Using more force than felt comfortable – he never liked manhandling women – Garry grabbed her right wrist and pulled it round to join the left behind her back. Giving the sort of scream that might suggest he'd murdered her firstborn, Tina let the teddy fall onto the snow.

Even cuffed, she squirmed and kicked and twisted to get free. Mainly, though, her focus seemed to be on the bear. Thinking it might be hiding a weapon, Garry kicked it some distance away.

'Give me that back, fucker. That's mine.'

She seemed very focused on what appeared to be nothing more than a standard kid's soft toy.

If it was nothing more than a standard kid's toy.

Another officer – finally – came jogging up and took hold of Tina by one arm. 'Come on, let's get you in a car. Nice one, Garry.'

Still, the woman fought; still, her eyes didn't leave the bear.

'Give us a hand, mate? Garry?'

Garry was focused on the bear. Vertically, along the length of its abdomen, the toy had been cut open and sewn back up again with an elaborate blue cross stitch.

Why would anyone do that?

The other officer, twice Tina's weight, was struggling to drag her away.

'Give me that back,' she was yelling. 'That teddy is mine.'

She really was very keen on not letting the bear out of sight. Garry bent and picked it up. It seemed unusually heavy for a kid's soft toy.

And then he knew.

The necklace was inside.

16

Do you know he killed his first wife?

It was the last thing Olive could have predicted. For a moment, it felt like the most bewildering turn of events in a truly remarkable evening and for several seconds no possible response occurred to her.

'That isn't true,' she said at last. 'I was there when Eloise died. Ovarian cancer killed Michael's first wife, and I was her oncology nurse.'

Eloise's death had been a grim reminder of the mortality that no one escapes. Olive had seen many deaths in her time as a nurse, and many of young healthy people during her military service, but there were few things worse, she'd learned, than the ravages inflicted by cancer. Eloise, once so beautiful, had become a sack of loose skin and brittle bone in her final days. Her lovely hair had mostly gone. Through the translucent skin of her face, it had been possible to see the skull that would soon emerge.

'I know,' the stranger replied. 'And maybe you nursed her well, but you didn't save her from her husband.' She glanced into the rear mirror and eased her foot off the accelerator. 'Actually, let's talk. Because I haven't been able to work out exactly how he did it.'

'He didn't do it. Who are you? Some friend of Eloise's, a relative? Because whoever you are, you've been seriously misinformed. She died of natural causes.'

'Pillow over the face is my best guess,' the stranger said, and when she glanced at Olive, the gleam in her eyes had turned cold. 'She'd have been weak by that stage, in no position to fight back.

It would have been over in seconds. Or maybe he switched the machines off.'

Olive took a moment to steady her voice; this woman knew nothing. Nothing at all.

'There were no machines,' she said. 'None keeping her alive, at any rate. She was weeks away from death, possibly even days.'

She was still dangerous. Getting in the car with her had been a terrible mistake.

'No post-mortem, is that right?' the stranger said.

'That's standard procedure for someone in hospital, someone that ill.'

'And her remains cremated, so we'll never know for sure. You don't think that's convenient?'

Olive took a deep breath. 'No, it's entirely normal. Most people are cremated. Eloise was terminally ill. You think medical records can be faked? In a leading NHS hospital?'

The stranger scowled and seemed for a moment to be unsure of herself. When she spoke again, something in her voice had changed.

'So, assuming you're telling the truth now, and you were with Eloise when she took her last breath, were you with her for several hours beforehand? Can you say, hand on heart, that no one, and I'm thinking Michael Anderson now, slipped her a heavy extra dose of morphine?'

'Yes, I absolutely can.' Olive told herself to remain calm, to keep the rising panic under control. 'It isn't possible. Morphine is very strictly controlled. It's kept in a locked drugs cabinet and each consignment is signed out and checked by two nurses. Both witness the drug being administered and then the box is put back in the cabinet. There was no way Michael could have given Eloise extra morphine.'

'Something else then, something he could have brought in, that would make her quietly slip away.'

The woman was delusional, maybe worse than that. Maybe insane. 'Eloise was dying.' How could she make this clearer? 'She probably had two weeks left, at most. Why on earth would Michael, anyone, take the risk of killing someone who was so close to death?'

'Oh, that bit's easy.'

'It is?'

'Yes. He killed her to stop her talking.'

17

Garry had never been more sure of anything in his life before. The Ring of Blood and Tears was sewn inside the bear. It was brilliant, or might have been, if Tina had only had the brains to leave it on her bed, instead of drawing so much attention to it.

Jeepers creepers.

This would make up for everything that had gone wrong for him since he'd joined the force. He'd be the man who found a necklace worth nearly two million pounds. His mum would die of pride. He found the small pocketknife he was never without and released the blade.

Nearly ten metres away, Tina saw him and screamed. 'What the fuck are you doing? Don't you dare touch that.'

Her outrage had stepped up a notch. Even the officer trying to drag her away looked taken aback.

Holding eye contact with the woman in cuffs, Garry shook the bear. Something rattled.

'I'm warning you, you are dead,' Tina yelled at him. 'I will fucking rip your throat out with my bare hands.'

He was feeling cocky now. Who'd have thought the raid would turn out to be – well, fun? 'What you hiding in here then, Tina?'

Garry Mizon had never enjoyed being a police officer more than at that moment, with a teddy aloft in one hand, a knife in the other, and the look of horror on the face of the woman who was going down for being an accessory to a major heist. Come to think of it, he'd never enjoyed being a police officer before. Seventeen years of misery had led him to this. His moment.

He slipped the tip of the knife into the bear's soft belly. It met resistance. Hard resistance. This bear wasn't just full of stuffing.

One by one, to the soundtrack of Tina's agonised wailing, and the sort of cursing that would have made his skin itch like he'd fallen in a bed of nettles in different circumstances, Garry slit open the stiches. Out of the corner of his eye, he saw the female officer, the one who'd been looking after Tina earlier and who'd gone to find shoes, appear in the doorway. She saw what Garry was about to do and set off at a run.

No, she wasn't muscling in, this was his moment. He cut the last stitch and turned the bear belly down, pulling apart the two pieces of fur fabric. The ruby necklace was going to look beautiful in the snow.

What fell out of the bear's innards wasn't jewellery, priceless or otherwise. It was ash. A lot of ash. And bits of bone.

Tina had broken free of the man holding her. She dropped to her knees in the snow and was staring aghast at the mess on the ground. The female officer stopped running, just as a gust of wind swept by and blew the ashes, small pieces of bone included, into the air. Most of the ash hadn't been dampened by the snow; it flew up into the air and dispersed.

'Me mammy!' Tina wailed. 'Me dead mammy! You've spilled me mammy's ashes.'

The female officer approached. 'It's a memory bear,' she told Garry. 'People put their loved ones' cremation ashes inside so they can keep them close. You've just tipped out Howie Tricks' dead mother-in-law.'

The other officer, once again holding a weeping Tina, was looking over Garry's shoulder. 'Most of her's halfway across the North Sea by now. Nice one, Garry.'

18

Olive let several seconds go by, then said, 'Are you completely mad?'

'Help me out here, Olive. I know Michael killed his first wife, and I know he did it to stop her dishing the dirt before she went to meet her maker. What I'm less sure about is whether you had a hand in it too.'

The trembling in Olive's body had gone, replaced by a cold, hard stillness; she was actually being accused of murder.

'You worked the night shift the week she died,' the stranger went on. 'Wards are quiet at night. You're a very experienced nurse. You, of all people, would know how to end the life of someone already terminally ill, in a way no one would suspect.'

Oh, dear God.

'So, did you do it? Or did he, with your knowledge? Or did the two of you do it together? He'd have to marry you then, wouldn't he, Olive? He'd have to keep you close, knowing what you did about him.'

Olive had run out of arguments. 'No,' she managed. The idea that Michael had married her because they were partners in a terrible crime was . . . it was almost funny.

'Maybe you knew nothing until it was over. In which case, this is your chance. Help me bring him down and you might just get out of this unscathed.'

'This is insane. You're insane.'

The stranger took one hand from the steering wheel, only to bang it back down hard. 'Don't play games with me.' Her voice had risen in volume. 'I saw Eloise days before she died. I told her what I knew and I could see it in her eyes. She was on the verge of talking.

I knew she'd break sooner or later, but when I tried to go back, you'd increased security. I couldn't get in.'

Olive remembered Eloise complaining about a troublesome stranger showing up on the ward, making a nuisance of herself. She'd claimed, though, that it had been a disgruntled constituent.

'That was two years ago,' Olive said. 'Eloise died two years ago. You've been planning this for two years?'

'Oh, longer than that,' said the stranger.

The car came to a sudden halt as they hit a snowdrift and the impact threw Olive forward. As the stranger changed gear and revved the engine, Olive quietly unclipped her seat belt.

The stranger didn't notice. She was leaning forward, over the steering wheel, then lowering the driver's-side window to see out.

As the wheels fought for traction, Olive pushed open her door and leapt from the car. The cold hit her like a slap in the face and she sank knee-deep into snow. She heard a cry of outrage as she set off back towards the village they'd just passed through. Two hundred metres, maybe, to the nearest house, but with every step, she sank deeper. Snow tugged at her boots, threatening to pull them clean off her feet. After only a few paces, her thighs were aching; it was like running through water.

'Olive!' The stranger was close behind.

Ahead, on the road, headlights. Olive got ready to scream, wave her arms, stand in the middle of the road and force the oncoming car to stop. And was thrown forward by an unstoppable force. She came down in a pile of snow and the stranger's full weight crashed down on top of her.

She became aware of a biting cold beneath her naked face, of a sharper, more intense pain in her right cheek. The stranger didn't move, and her weight was impossible to shift. Olive could hear the other woman panting, feel the frantic up-and-down movement of her chest. She, on the other hand, could not breathe. Her face was pressed into the snow, it was in her eyes, mouth and nose. She managed a squeal.

'Shut the fuck up.' Hands were in her hair. They tightened their grip on either side of her head as Olive heard the engine of the other car. It had a throaty, rattly sound that reminded her of Gwen's Land Rover.

Slow down, please, slow down. See us. Help me.

The stranger pushed Olive's head deeper into the snow as the sound of the engine passed by, became fainter and died away. Then the weight crushing her shifted. For several seconds, all she could do was gulp. Then her hair was grasped again and a voice hissed in her ear.

'You're coming back to the car, quietly and quickly. Try anything and I will kill you. Do you understand me?'

Olive couldn't speak; she could barely breathe. Her head was tugged upwards.

'Do you understand?'

Still, she couldn't speak.

Her head was banged down onto the snow again and something needle-sharp dug into her face. 'Do you?'

'Yes,' she managed.

'Up.'

The stranger tugged Olive up by her hair. In the distance, she could see the retreating rear lights of the Land Rover that hadn't seen them. She was half dragged, half carried back to the car and manhandled around to the passenger door. The stranger hit her, once, a vicious slap of the hand across her face, and then pushed her into the passenger seat.

They drove on and the smoke-grey twilight claimed them once more.

'You shouldn't have made me do that,' the stranger said, after a few minutes. 'I warned you what would happen.'

Olive became aware of something clinging to the side of her head and put up her hand to find a twig from a hawthorn bush. One of its thorns was embedded in her cheek. She reached forward and pulled down the passenger-side mirror to get it out. She felt, rather than saw, the other woman glance her way.

And then the car left the road.

19

The car left the road. It was as simple and as catastrophic as that. One minute, they were making progress, in spite of the setback, with not much further to go; the next, the car was in free fall.

They were a little over two miles out of a village called Wark; Olive hadn't spoken since they'd resumed driving and, finally, the nameless stranger could feel herself starting to calm down. Her breathing was too fast and her heart still thumping against her chest, but she no longer had the urge to swipe sideways with her left fist, to connect with Olive's face over and over again, to take hold of her hair and shake her head till its insides rattled.

She hated resorting to violence – why the hell did some women have to make it so difficult – and knew she'd let herself down when she'd hit Olive. It hadn't been necessary. Hitting Olive had been about temper and that was something that should be under control. Unlike the fucking weather.

A blackness on the horizon told her that the dense tree coverage of Kielder was getting closer. There were trees on both sides of the road now; still deciduous, unlike the evergreen varieties that grew in the forest, but they were holding back a lot of the snow. She risked speeding up.

The skid took her by surprise. One second, she was heading for a narrow stone bridge that took the road over the river, knowing she'd need some revs to get up the short but steep side; the next, the car was sliding sideways. Instinct kicked in and she steered into the skid. The car righted itself.

'Black ice.' She was speaking to herself rather than Olive, knowing she should have expected it. The snowfall had been lighter this far north, it might even have been raining or sleeting earlier, and the road was damp. A drop in temperature would leave a thin, invisible sheen of ice across the road.

She revved again and the car cleared the crest. The second patch of ice was waiting on the downward slope and, again, she wasn't ready. The car lost traction and slid from the road like an out-of-control speed skater. For a second, she thought they'd hit the bridge; they missed it by inches.

The fence at the side of the road crumpled like straw and the ground beyond simply wasn't there. They were tipping. As the car upended, she found herself staring into Olive's terrified face. Then they hit the ground, they were upside down and tumbling. Her head struck something hard. The very last thing she heard, after Olive's scream, was the voice of the weather forecaster telling them that much more snow was on its way.

20

Garry Mizon had been born of a long line of police officers, all of them good ones, until he came along. Family lore had it that his great-great-grandfather had been the Police Constable Mizon mentioned in dispatches during the hunt for the Victorian serial killer Jack the Ripper. *We hunted the ripper*, the family liked to toast themselves, and Garry never quite had the nerve to point out that no one – Mizon or otherwise – had actually caught the blighter.

Garry's grandfather, Stanley Mizon, had reached the rank of superintendent before he'd retired from Cleveland Police, and was held in such esteem that the town mayor had held a reception in his honour. Peter Mizon, Garry's dad, had excelled in CID. Commended on twelve occasions, he'd led the op in '82 that put local gangster Richie Tricks behind bars for thirty years. Even Garry's mum, Janet, had been a detective sergeant, although she'd allowed her own career to take a back seat when Garry came along, so that she could better look after him and his dad.

When Garry had finished school with decent A levels, there had been no question of the course his life would take and the day of his graduation had been, easily, the happiest and proudest of his life. His grandad wore his service medals and even his great-grandad, at eighty-four, stood proudly outside his retirement home, saluting, as Garry and the family drove by on their way to the ceremony.

It had taken five years or more for Garry to realise he'd made a terrible mistake, that he didn't enjoy police work, that the violence sickened and frightened him and that, time after time, when judgement was needed, he made the wrong call. By that time, though, his grandfather had been diagnosed with terminal cancer and Garry couldn't bring himself to darken Gramps' last days.

When Garry had failed the detectives' exams twice and was advised not to apply again, he'd considered the dog unit, only to learn he wasn't tough enough to put the animals through the necessary intensive training, and a mild claustrophobia meant the underwater search unit was out of the question. The one skill he did have was an ability to drive well, fast but safely in all road conditions, and that inevitably meant spending most of his working hours dealing with motoring offences, handling motorway pile-ups and road accidents, and managing traffic during times of road stress. It was 90 per cent dull, 10 per cent dreadful, but it seemed to be his lot in life. When all was said and done, a police career ended at age sixty with a decent pension. In the meantime – well, it wasn't like he had any grand plans he was putting off.

On the night of the raid on Howie Tricks' Georgian mansion, Garry was seventeen years into his service and, more by luck than good judgement, it was his first disaster. A significant one, though, and one he knew would dog his career until its bitter end.

After the gutting of the teddy, he wasn't remotely surprised to be sent back to the station. He made himself a brew and leaned against the kitchen fridge, grateful that the ongoing Tricks op meant the place was relatively quiet. In a few hours, he'd be off duty for four days. Maybe the worst of the fallout would be over before he was back.

The duty sergeant poked his head round the door.

'Garry, we've a possible missing person. High-profile individual. Detective Sergeant Thomas has been assigned, but her car's not up to the trip in the snow. I need you to drive her up there.' His face twisted into what Garry interpreted as a sneer. 'Can you manage that, do you think?'

Garry agreed that he probably could and collected the keys of one of the Range Rovers. It would take him, he guessed, around forty minutes to reach the rural, hard-to-access home of Michael Anderson, member of parliament for Middlesbrough South and East Cleveland, who seemed to have misplaced his wife.

He set off with mixed feelings. The prospect of being away from the station over the next few hours was more than offset by hearing who he'd be chauffeuring around. DS Lexy Thomas was a twenty-nine-year-old criminology graduate who'd never served a day in uniform. It took all sorts, but – come on.

And then it hit him. He'd have realised immediately – at least he hoped he would – if his mind hadn't been on other things, but Michael Anderson was married to a woman that he knew. A woman called Olive.

Blimey, Olive. Missing? His stomach tightened, his mouth suddenly dry. He found himself hoping Detective Sergeant Thomas was as good as she was made out to be.

Lexy lived in a second-floor flat in a nice part of town. Huddled in a padded jacket, beanie cap and thick ski gloves, she was waiting on the pavement when Garry pulled up. A tall, thin woman who looked even younger than her years, she smelled of toothpaste, curry spices and alcohol when she climbed into the car. Before pulling away, he leaned over and opened the glove compartment to reveal the bag of Everton Mints he always carried.

'Help yourself,' he offered, as they joined the flow of traffic. The snow was settling properly by this time, even beginning to crunch beneath his tyres.

For a second, then another, she didn't reply. Then, 'Thanks,' she said, taking a sweet and tucking the wrapper into her jacket pocket. Most coppers, especially CID, would have dropped it into the footwell, knowing the vehicle would be cleaned by someone other than its driver.

She leaned back against the seat, closed her eyes and gave a deep sigh. Garry remembered that she wasn't known for light-hearted chat or banter. *Only talks to you when she wants you to do something*, a young PC had complained once.

'Don't suppose you've any caffeine?' she asked, as he headed south.

Her voice spoke more of English public schools than it did the

Wales of her birth; another reason why she wasn't overly popular. Northerners tended to distrust the posh.

'There's a McDonald's on the way,' he told her. 'Might have closed early, though. People will be wanting to get home.'

It was 0040 hours, twenty minutes before one o'clock in the morning.

'Not Olive Anderson by all accounts,' Lexy replied, her eyes closed again. 'Her husband's supposedly the sexiest man in parliament. According to *Daily Mail* readers, that is.'

'What do we know?' Garry had been given no real details by the duty sergeant. 'About the wife, not the husband.'

'She vanished from a hotel in Hexham, which strictly makes it Northumbria's case – if there is a case, and she hasn't just had one too many and lost her phone.'

The McDonald's, as suspected, was closed; Lexy swore under her breath.

'Been anywhere nice?' Garry asked, as he turned out of the empty car park.

She looked surprised for a moment, then, 'Just a takeaway.'

They passed a pub, that must have a late licence for the party season, because lights and punters were spilling out onto the pavement. The huddle of bodies suggested confrontation brewing. Two blokes faced each other down, surrounded by a scatter of scantily clad women. Garry slowed the vehicle, steering a little closer to the kerb, and cruised past. In his rear-view mirror, he watched the group break apart.

'Nicely done.' Lexy had been watching the same scene. 'Thanks for driving,' she went on. 'I'm not sure my car would have made it out of town.'

'What do you drive?'

'Mazda MX5 convertible. Completely impractical, but I love it.' She put a hand over her mouth to hide a belch. Garry was tempted to wind the window down an inch or two.

'Have another mint,' he said, instead.

'Thanks.' She reached out and helped herself. 'And to answer your question, yes, I probably am marginally over the drink-drive limit, but as I'm not officially on duty, I think you can put the judgement on hold. Control called me because there is, literally, no one else. The whole blessed team is dealing with the Tricks op tonight. It was me or just send uniform, and in case you didn't pick up on this, our caller is the local member of parliament.'

'I didn't say a word, Sergeant.'

'Your eyes spoke volumes. Not to mention the number of times you've sniffed since I got in the car. And you offered me a mint before I'd closed the fricking door.'

'Sorry,' he said, after a moment. 'Late nights can turn me into a bit of a Charlie.'

She didn't smile, but her face softened. 'No worries. And call me Lexy.'

No, he wasn't going to do that. Lexy wasn't even a name.

'Is it short for something?' he asked.

'Alexandra. I hate that. Don't even think about calling me that.'

Pity. He quite liked Alexandra.

'Shit, it's really coming down, isn't it?' Lexy wiped the condensation from the side window and peered out at the snow.

'First winter in the north?'

Out of the corner of his eye, he could see her nodding her head. 'I'm from Pembrokeshire,' she said. 'Snow is something of an event there.'

'Is anyone making the connection with tonight's operation?' Garry asked as they joined the A171 that would take them east. Michael Anderson and his family lived a couple of miles outside the market town of Guisborough, on the northern edge of the North York Moors National Park.

Lexy looked his way. 'Why should they?'

Instead of answering, he asked, 'How much do you know about the Tricks family?'

'Only what I've read. Family of dock workers who began supplementing their wages with smuggling. Moved on to drug trafficking, illegal immigration, receiving stolen goods, especially gold, and people trafficking. Rumoured to dispose of their enemies by taking them out into the North Sea and dumping them overboard.'

'Sounds about right. Also, like most organised crime gangs, they're not above a bit of vigilante activity.' He changed gear to overtake a car hugging the verge and said, 'There are rumours we've turned a blind eye in the past because when a family like the Trickses keep an eye on a neighbourhood, it keeps crime down and reduces the need for community policing.'

She was staring directly at him now. 'What's that got to do with Michael and Olive Anderson?'

'Michael Anderson isn't popular with the Tricks family,' Garry replied. 'He's made bringing down organised crime one of his things.'

'And his wife vanishes the same night we launch our op.'

'It's worth considering. Hold on tight.'

Almost too late, Garry had seen the half-concealed sign. Braking hard, he swung left onto a single-track lane that led to the Anderson home. For a little over a mile, he drove past fields that grew crops in the summer, and others that grazed livestock when the weather was better. On the third bend, Garry caught a glimpse of lights and then, finally, they came within sight of the house, its front elevation gleaming a soft gold.

'Blimey,' Lexy said.

Home Farm was a large, stone-built manor in the Elizabethan style.

'I'm guessing he's a Tory,' Lexy said.

'You'd be wrong. And this place belongs to his first wife's mother. Anderson married well.'

'His first wife?'

'Died a few years ago. Nice lady.'

Eloise Anderson, nee Warner, had been gorgeous, with the sort of beauty that could make a man tongue-tied and weak at the knees. Garry had helped her extricate a high-heeled shoe from a grate once and she'd been embarrassed, flustered and grateful all at the same time. He'd caught notes of jasmine, spruce, even chocolate cosmos in her perfume.

An Audi Q3 sport utility vehicle was parked at the front of the house. It had been Garry's dream car, one he'd dismissed as too pricey for a traffic copper, even one with a bit in the bank. He wouldn't have picked that colour himself. Tango red in metallic paint was nice but a bit showy. For a Labour politician who wanted to be noticed, though? Pretty much perfect.

There were footprints in the snow around the front door, the tracks of an adult male who'd stood at the porch more than once that evening.

'Do you know him?' Lexy asked.

Garry switched off the engine and logged the end of the journey. 'Done protection duty a few times. Seems a decent bloke.'

'Sexiest man in parliament, huh?' Lexy seemed strangely reluctant to leave the car. Then she pulled off her hat to reveal a mass of short, very clean, blonde hair. Pulling down the passenger mirror, she ran the fingers of both hands through it.

'Have another mint,' he told her as he climbed down, deliberately taking a detour to bring himself closer to the Audi. It gleamed like a dark ruby in the light from the house, and the tracks in the snow showed the distinctive chevron of the all-season tyre. Sensible bloke, Garry decided, although he always switched to winter tyres himself in the colder months.

From somewhere nearby came the soft lowing and rich earthy smells of barn-kept animals, then the front door of the house opened, light flooded the porch, and Michael Anderson stepped out among his own footprints to greet them.

21

Sound came back first: the almost-musical zings and twangs of hot metal contracting, followed by a rush of curious wind whispering through the car, then the crackle of melting snow, and the steady chink, chink of droplets of water.

Sound, quickly followed by pain, so severe that it was impossible to pinpoint its origins. Olive lay still, hot and freezing cold at the same time, and waited for the pain to find its own focus. The lower part of one leg seemed to be burning and a massive weight was pressing on her chest. She was breathing – she knew that because of how much it hurt; every breath felt like a tiny dagger was being stabbed into her heart.

Keep breathing, stay conscious; don't let the world slip away.

She had no idea whose voice that was – her own or coming from outside the huge bubble of pain. Either way, it seemed sound advice.

Slowly, breath by painful breath, Olive became conscious again of her body. It was twisted, like that of a rag doll tossed carelessly into a box. Her neck was unnaturally squashed, pressed into a shape it had no business to be in.

Keep breathing, don't think about how much it hurts, just keep the breath coming in and out.

Disconnected memories flashed through the pain: snow appearing in the sky like pinpricks of light as she'd driven from Carlisle; dusk falling early; a sudden image of Hexham, its frosty streets and garish Christmas lights; a woman yelling about black ice; the world spinning out of control amid the thundering sound of a vehicle in free fall.

Into Olive's bewildered brain crept the knowledge that she wasn't alone. And something was tapping against the side of her face, something strangely warm.

A fresh sound: human, a moan of pain. Her own?

She opened her eyes and only at that moment learned that they'd been closed. For a second or two, she thought she'd been thrown free of the car. She was looking at snow, inches away, a wall of white pressing against the side window of the car. She could feel the cold of it radiating towards her.

The warm tapping against her face was wet. Something warm and wet was dripping on her cheek.

A clang, a groan and the car shifted again. Olive felt the world move beneath her and terror was the only possible response; then stillness, and the odd, metallic percussion once more.

The cry of an owl from somewhere close. She pictured it, peering down at the carnage, and knew, without articulating the thought, that an owl meant it was still night. She risked letting her eyes drift away from the snow and looked up.

She saw the stranger. In an instant, she remembered everything.

Olive's abductor was suspended directly above her, held in place by the seat belt. One hand, the colour of old wax, seemed to be reaching down for her, as though, even unconscious, she wasn't going to let Olive go. Her head was barely inches away. An open wound on the side of her head was bleeding and her blood was dripping onto Olive's face.

In the thin, cold light of the moon, against the dull white of the snow, the stranger's blood looked black as tar.

22

The sexiest man in parliament was a tall man in his mid-forties. His eyes and brows were dark, his hair beginning to show some grey, his mouth full and red. His face, that might otherwise be considered too beautiful for a bloke, was saved by a once broken nose and a faded scar on his chin.

'Thanks for coming out.' He ushered them inside a large, square room in which blackened oak beams stood out against whitewashed walls. 'Terrible night.'

It was Garry's first time in Anderson's home and he took it all in as the MP exchanged pleasantries with the detective sergeant. The huge, brick-lined fireplace was empty and a wrought-iron chandelier held unlit candles. On a large central table sat a bowl of roses. They'd been teamed with Dusty Miller, a silver-grey leaf that to Garry's mind didn't quite work with the salmon pink of the flowers. Myrtle would have been better, with long trails of green ivy stretching across the polished wood. And that fire needed to be lit, the room was crying out for soft light, for rugs on the stone floor, for warmth.

Anderson led them towards an open door at the far end of the hall and into a room beyond. A woman in her early seventies with perfectly styled, pale gold hair stood by the TV, a remote in one hand. She looked sufficiently like her late daughter for Garry to recognise her as Anderson's mother-in-law.

'Gwendoline Warner,' Anderson introduced them as they approached. 'My daughters' grandmother. And my daughters, who were told to go to bed an hour ago.'

Garry registered three large bottle-green sofas, the double set of French windows against one wall, the baby grand piano in the corner. The paintings on the walls were modern and looked both original and valuable. Two teenage girls were perched on sofa arms.

'We're worried about Olive,' the elder said. Neither looked anxious, and Garry reminded himself that Olive Anderson was not their mother.

'We might have important information,' the younger added.

'Anything you haven't shared already?' their father snapped.

'Bed,' the grandmother told them. 'We'll wake you if there's news.'

Sighing, the girls uncurled themselves and slouched from the room. They left the door open.

'Start at the beginning, please, Mr Anderson,' Lexy said, when they'd both been invited to sit, and Garry had taken out his notebook.

Anderson sat across from them on a facing sofa. Gwendoline Warner took a seat beside him.

'My wife is a senior oncology nurse,' Anderson began. He didn't have a discernible accent, but his voice, like that of most northerners, was pitched low. 'As well as her duties at Middlesbrough, she visits other hospitals in the area to monitor their procedures and suggest how they can improve. She carries out training, too, from time to time.'

Lexy had her eyes fixed on Anderson. She inclined her head to encourage him to continue.

'She was in Carlisle and Lancaster yesterday, due in Newcastle tomorrow. She'd booked a room at the county hotel in Hexham for the night.'

Garry made a note in his book. *Mrs A stayed in Hexam. Why?*

He wondered if he'd spelled Hexham correctly. It didn't look quite right. And Lexy might ask to see his notes. He added a H. Hexham? No, he still wasn't sure.

'I've been in Westminster all week,' Anderson went on. 'I called her from the car at nine thirty. She didn't answer. I tried again at ten and ten thirty and again when I got home about half eleven.

No answer any time. I tried the Find My Friends app and it couldn't find her. That's when I called the hotel reception and asked to be put through to her room. After keeping me on hold for a while, they told me she and her "partner"'– Anderson made air quotes around the word – 'checked out sometime earlier.' Jaw tense and eyes cold, he held his phone out. 'You can see the call record,' he said.

Garry wondered if Lexy was thinking the same thing he was. As she photographed the screen on Anderson's phone, he made another note.

'Do you often track your wife's movements?' Lexy asked.

Anderson's face flushed. 'We all have that app,' he said. 'I insist on it for the girls, so we have it too, even Gwen. It's useful, if you're meeting up somewhere, to find out where the other person is without constantly bothering them with phone calls.'

Garry wondered if Anderson knew how defensive he sounded.

'Do you have any idea where she might have gone?' Lexy asked, when she looked up from the phone. 'Or who she left with? Any friends in the Hexham area?'

'None that I know of. But we haven't been married long. There could be someone she hadn't got round to mentioning, I suppose. Look, maybe this is a waste of your time. I was just shocked, I suppose, when I heard she was gone. Or supposedly gone. I made a bit of a fuss with the hotel. Told them I'd be calling the police as I was concerned for my wife's safety. That's when the chap I was talking to admitted there'd been a recent shift change and that no one still on duty had actually seen my wife leave. He asked me to leave a number and said he'd get back to me once he'd had chance to check she really had gone.'

'And then you called us?' Lexy said.

Anderson lowered his eyes. 'No, I didn't want to overreact. I was going to give it some time. But the hotel called Northumbria Police. They, in turn, called me to say they'd try to get someone out there, but a lot of the roads around Hexham were closing because of the snow. They did say, though, that my wife had definitely checked out around ten o'clock, that her car had gone too, and that she'd paid her bill, including a meal for two in the restaurant. They told me they had no reason to list Olive as a missing person at this time and to get in touch tomorrow if I still haven't heard from her.' He looked up at Lexy. 'Are you from Northumbria? If you can drive all the way down here, surely you can go to Hexham?'

'We're from Cleveland Police,' Lexy replied. 'Northumbria asked us to reach out to you as a courtesy.'

Garry made a note that Anderson, himself, had not contacted the police. And yet the tension in him was obvious. He was sweating, in spite of the night's chill, and was continually fidgeting, a mass of nervous energy. He looked like a man barely holding himself together.

Anderson's eyes went from Lexy to Garry, then back again, and something in them hardened.

'The Northumbria Police and the staff at the hotel think my wife is having an affair,' he said. 'From a look that came into your eyes a few minutes ago, I can see you think the same, Sergeant.'

Garry glanced down at his earlier note. One word: *afair?* Suspecting that his wife was playing away from home could explain the state Anderson was in.

'We've been married six months,' Anderson went on. 'We're happy. I don't believe my wife is cheating on me. I think something's happened to her.'

So why hadn't he called the police? Something here wasn't adding up.

Gwendoline began to twist a gold bracelet around one wrist.

'Mr Anderson,' Lexy asked, 'have you or your wife received any particular threats in the last few weeks?'

Anderson frowned. 'MPs get abuse all the time. My Twitter feed is a cesspit; I don't look at it most of the time.'

'I understand that, but anything that stood out, or caused you any particular concern?'

'My constituency agent goes through it. She'd have let me know if anything seemed out of the ordinary.'

'What about Mrs Anderson?'

Anderson seemed to think for a moment. 'She's had her share. Less so since she set her accounts to private. As I repeatedly told her to do.'

'But before then?' Lexy asked.

Anderson's eyes shifted to the left. 'There was some stuff that upset her a few months ago. She didn't tell me about it for a while. Probably because she'd ignored my advice to change her settings.'

'There was that incident with the car in the lane,' Gwendoline said. 'Back in August, wasn't it? Maybe we should have taken that more seriously.'

Garry and Lexy waited.

'You'll find it on file,' Anderson told them. 'Olive thought someone was following her. She couldn't get a number though and only a very vague description. We told the police, but there was no follow-up.'

Garry made a note to check when he got back to the station.

'Did she leave any of her devices behind?' Lexy asked. 'We can have someone go through them, see if there's anything of concern.'

Anderson looked around the room and seemed on the point of standing up. 'Her personal laptop should still be here. She uses an official one when she's working. I can see if it's upstairs.'

'She usually takes it with her,' Gwendoline said, quickly.

Anderson looked uncertain. 'It's worth checking,' he said. 'She keeps it in the bedside cabinet. I'll go—'

Gwendoline jumped up. 'I'll get it.' She strode briskly from the room.

Lexy got to her feet. 'Mr Anderson, I'm going to call the hotel when I get back to the station,' she told the MP. 'The chances are they'll tell us more than they were prepared to tell you. We can get a description of the person she supposedly left with and maybe an idea of your wife's state of mind at the time. We can run her registration number through the system to see if we can get an idea of where she might be headed. And we can call her phone. Even if it's switched off, she'll probably check it. If she sees a police number flash up, she may be more inclined to start answering. Also, if you give us contact numbers for her family members and close friends, we can start making enquiries with them. Perhaps her boss at work too?'

Anderson remained in his seat, as though trying to prolong the interview. 'Will you go up there?'

'If we feel it's merited, and if it's possible in the current conditions. To be honest, though, if Mrs Anderson wasn't your wife, we probably wouldn't be taking any further action. She's not vulnerable, and there's nothing to suggest at this stage that she left the hotel unwillingly.'

Anderson took in a deep breath and let it out slowly.

He's catching up, Garry thought. He's reached the same page as the rest of us and knows his wife's cheating on him. And it's going to break him.

He surprised himself by speaking up. 'It could still be a crossed wire, sir. A town-centre hotel at this time of year will be packed. The receptionist could have got your wife mixed up with another lady. Try not to worry too much.'

Anderson looked as though he'd like to believe it.

Gwendoline came back with a laptop under her arm that she handed to Lexy. 'I'll show you out,' she said. 'Michael, pour yourself a drink. One for me too – heaven knows we need one after the last two hours.'

Anderson got up with what looked like an effort. 'I'm going to Hexham,' he said.

'Not a good idea, sir,' Garry said. 'The roads are bad. Better stay here where we can get hold of you quickly.'

Anderson looked about to argue.

'You have surgery in the morning,' his mother-in-law reminded him. 'Evelyn called earlier. Every appointment taken, starting at eight.'

'Do you have a photograph of Mrs Anderson?' Garry asked.

It took a second or two for the question to sink in, then Anderson gave a vague nod. 'In my study. I'll get the other stuff too. I'll catch you on the way out.'

Gwendoline waited until the door had closed on the MP before turning to Lexy. 'Sergeant, I hope we can rely on your discretion.'

Lexy waited for the older woman to go on. She didn't.

'I'm sorry, Mrs Warner, what do you mean?'

'My son-in-law is a high-profile member of parliament. He's a shadow minister, his party are riding high in the polls and people are talking about him as a future leader. This could be very damaging for him.'

Lexy nodded sympathetically. 'Once we launch an official missing persons enquiry, that will be in the public domain,' she said. 'Nothing we can do about that, I'm afraid. But, at this stage, there's nothing other than Mr Anderson's understandable worry to suggest any foul play.'

The older woman glanced at the door. 'Exactly.' When she spoke again, she'd lowered her voice. 'And don't believe that nonsense about them being happy. He's besotted with her, but she . . .' She broke off.

'She what?' Lexy asked.

'Let's just say I'm not sure she really knew what she was letting herself in for when she married an MP,' Gwendoline replied. 'I think she got carried away with the glamour, not realising MPs work long hours, a long way from home. I don't think she knew what she was taking on with the girls, either, although heaven knows I do all the work.'

'Do you have any reason to suspect an affair?' Garry asked.

The woman's eyes fell. 'Not as such. But there's something, I don't know, something very distant about her. I'd describe her as a cold woman, but never when Michael is around. She's very different when he's not here. And she's out a lot when Michael is working away. She works shifts and spends time away. She definitely has the opportunity.'

'Hexham's not that far from here,' Garry voiced something that had been on his mind for a while, had been waiting for Lexy to mention. 'Neither is Newcastle, where Mrs Anderson is due in the morning. Why didn't she come home for the night?'

The corners of Gwendoline's mouth turned down. 'Very good question. And not the first time she's stayed away unnecessarily.'

'Anyone in particular spring to mind?' Lexy asked.

A dismissive shrug. 'Someone at the hospital, I imagine. Or one of the hospitals she visits. Let's face it, it could be anyone.'

She led them back into the entrance hall. Snowflakes had drifted in through the open front door, settling on the flagged stone floor. Michael Anderson was standing outside, staring out at the darkness as though, if he looked long and hard enough, his wife might appear.

23

Olive was thirsty. The snow on the car window, some of it melting in the heat from her breath, was inches away. She felt her tongue creeping out towards the glass. Everything would feel better if she could only reach that snow. The car radio had fallen silent and she had no idea how much time had passed.

She was so very cold too. Her breathing was shallow, rapid, and she felt exhausted. More than anything, she wanted to sleep, and she knew it would be the worst thing she could do.

Stay awake, keep breathing.

Did she risk trying to move? Her fingers were stiff with cold. Her left arm was trapped, but she could move her right. Her right foot flexed and bent, rotated first one way and then the other. The left foot – no! Pain shot through her whole body.

Don't pass out. Don't vomit. Keep breathing.

And then a fresh danger. Her lungs that hurt with every breath were filling with a bitter cocktail of noxious smells: burned rubber, urine, petrol. That last was the worst. Fuel was leaking from the car, and a ruptured fuel tank meant fire. She had to turn off the ignition.

Slowly, she turned her head, lifting her eyes until they reached the woman suspended above. The steady drip, drip of blood had stopped.

Dead women didn't bleed.

24

'What do you think?' Garry asked.

They were back on the road to Middlesbrough and Lexy had been staring at her phone for over five minutes; she spoke without looking up. 'I think he's learning his marriage isn't as perfect as he believed and wishing he hadn't made such a fuss that Northumbria put the missing persons wheels in motion.'

It was pretty much what Garry himself thought. Except, the second Michael Anderson had handed over the photograph of Olive – a professionally taken portrait shot that he'd pulled from a silver frame – a wave of what he could only describe as déjà vu had swept over Garry. It was as though . . .

'I also think Olive Anderson is out of her tiny mind,' Lexy said, breaking his train of thought.

'He lives up to the hype then?'

'Oh, more than. He's smoking hot. I don't know though, there's something about him that would warn me off, even if he were single and remotely in my league.'

'What's that then?' Garry asked, surprised at finding himself drawn into what was essentially girls' talk.

Lexy seemed for a moment to be checking Garry out, rather than thinking about Michael Anderson. She let her eyes linger on his, then drift down towards his feet. Then she said, 'He seems too much, somehow. Too much to handle. Like a fabulous-looking meal that sets your mouth watering, but you just know will turn your stomach before you've finished half of it.'

She'd put into words how Garry had felt about Anderson's first wife, too beautiful to be real. A woman to be admired, not loved.

'I was at school with Olive,' he said after a moment.

Lexy cocked her head onto one side. 'Why didn't you say?'

'Didn't seem relevant. I didn't know her well. Same year, different form.'

'What was she like?'

He thought for a moment. 'Popular. Attractive. Not in the first wife's league, mind you. Sporty. Was always up in assembly for winning stuff. I thought she joined the army. Must have got that wrong.'

'Not necessarily. She could have been Medical Corps. Michael Anderson served in the Yorkshire Regiment. Did a tour of Afghanistan. Maybe they met in the forces.'

'Will you do all that stuff you said?' Garry asked. 'Phoning the hotel, checking ANPR?'

Again, he couldn't help the feeling this had all happened before.

Lexy pushed her phone back into her pocket. 'Can't not do it now. Boxes have to be ticked. I'll request the cyber team have a look at her laptop. If she's up to anything, she'll have left a trace. If you can be spared, it would be good to have someone drive to the hospital and have a word with her colleagues.'

'I can do that,' Garry agreed. He'd also have time to do a background check on Olive. It would throw up any previous incidents, if there were any and he wasn't barking up the wrong tree.

Lexy said, 'I'll be amazed if we do end up launching an MPE in the morning, though.'

'You think Anderson will have second thoughts?'

'I'm sure he will. After a night to sleep on it, he'll come to the same conclusion as the rest of us. Mrs A is out on her jollies and may or may not be planning to come back. Either way, she'll be in touch. Trust me, Garry, once we've ticked our boxes, no one will be looking for Olive Anderson.'

25

Olive had drifted away again – for how long she had no way of knowing, but at some point, the car had shifted once more. Her weight now seemed to be on her upper shoulders rather than her neck and when she opened her eyes, she could see the windscreen, still miraculously intact.

She had no idea how long it had been since the crash.

The smell of petrol seemed stronger and she knew, somehow, that that wasn't good, but her brain couldn't make the connection between petrol and danger. There was something she needed to do, but . . .

She was in less pain now and that had to be a good thing, didn't it? On the other hand, the freezing damp of the night seemed to be seeping through her coat and into her bones. Beyond the windscreen, snow was still falling. The flakes, large and round against the black sky, were melting on contact with the glass.

Her thirst had grown worse.

Beyond the car, darkness still cloaked the world. At this time of year, this far north, dawn wouldn't come until close to nine o'clock in the morning. She could have been here for hours already.

She could still think, though, and that had to be a good sign, because while her brain was still working, her body couldn't be too far gone. When she started to give up, when she allowed herself to drift into sleep, then she would be slipping beyond the point of no return.

But she had slept, hadn't she? It was so hard to remember. She'd slept and she'd woken, so how could sleep be bad? Especially when she was so very, very tired.

The snow landing on the black windscreen was beautiful in its way. The flakes weren't melting quite so quickly now but merging to form bigger, more intricate patterns. They were coating the glass, enclosing her in a white cocoon.

Olive allowed her eyes to close, just for a moment. And slipped effortlessly back in time, to the same car, different night.

This time, the sky was barely dark and it was the evening of her birthday, five months previously.

She'd sat in her car outside the kitchen door of Home Farm, watching the wind blow flurries of white petals against the windscreen. There'd been a storm earlier, heavy rain and wind, and it had played havoc with Gwen's rose garden. Most of the early blooms had been lost. Even now, late in the evening, it wasn't completely spent. The petals were beautiful, perfect shallow cups. They looked like the first snowfall of the year.

Snow in July? Even in the north-east that was unheard of.

She opened the side window of the car and sat for a while longer, listening to the sounds of the night – a fox barking, the high-pitched chattering of a robin, the crackle of silver birch leaves. Then, reluctantly, she climbed out. Leaving the cards, gifts and the jaunty birthday balloon on the back seat, she slipped in through the rear door of the house. It was a little after nine. With luck, the girls would have gone to bed and it would only be Gwen she'd have to face. Alone, each of the three was easier; together, they gave one another a mean sort of courage.

The kitchen was empty of humans and Gwen's old spaniel, Molly, who didn't share the general antipathy towards Olive, seemed pleased to see her. Pausing for a moment to pet the dog, Olive opened the fridge. Several Tupperware dishes of leftovers sat on the top shelf, each carefully labelled: *Gwen's lunch, Amelia's supper, To Be Frozen.*

Olive had lived at Home Farm a month. It had taken a week to realise that food would never be cooked for her. Most days, she brought a salad or a ready-meal home; that day, because of all the

birthday stuff, she'd forgotten. She'd also forgotten what it felt like
to come home from work and relax.

And yet it had made perfect sense, when she and Michael had
discussed living arrangements, for her to join the others in what had
become the family home. He'd impressed upon her how much the
girls loved the farm, the benefit of the twenty-four-hour childcare
they had in Gwen. Shamelessly appealing to her better nature, he'd
dropped hints that his daughters were already struggling with the
idea of someone replacing their mum; to drag them from a much-
loved home would feel too cruel.

Olive had gone along with it all because marrying Michael, at any
price, had seemed the only thing important. After only a month,
though, she knew that Michael had considered mainly himself in
the arrangements, the girls a little, and her not at all.

She carried her uniform through to the room off the kitchen
that served as a laundry and dropped the tunic and trousers into her
own basket, checking there was enough for a load. She'd put it on
before she went up. Her ironing was heaped in another basket. The
housekeeper who came in to help Gwen three days a week didn't
do Olive's laundry and only ever cleaned the rooms she and Michael
shared when he was due home.

Gwen paid the housekeeper, not Michael. It hadn't been something Olive had felt she could challenge.

She checked her phone again. Nothing from her husband. Was
it possible he didn't even know today was her birthday? A year ago,
they'd barely started dating, and she hadn't mentioned it. Her birthday was something they hadn't yet had a chance to celebrate. But
to marry a woman and not make a point of learning her birthday?
That suggested a very self-absorbed man, didn't it?

Gwen and the girls knew.

'Somebody's birthday?' Amelia had enquired that morning, in the
tone she might have used if someone had farted. She had glanced
briefly at the three handwritten envelopes on the kitchen table
before turning her back to root through her bag.

'Mine.' Olive had hated herself for feeling embarrassed. Their

brand-new stepmother had a birthday, neither they nor their grandmother had remembered, and she was the one feeling uncomfortable.

'You should have mentioned it.' Gwen didn't turn round from the
dishwasher. 'Many happy returns.'

'They from Dad?' Jess, the younger of Michael's two daughters,
was frowning at the cellophane-wrapped flowers that had arrived
with the postman. Two pink roses, two orange gerberas, some spray
carnations and greenery.

'No, my parents.'

'Thought not. Dad sends really nice flowers. Do you remember
the ones he used to send Mum, Melia?'

Her big sister had looked up. 'Always white roses on her birthday,
one for each year, and he joked that he'd started a savings account
for when she got older because they cost a bomb and it would bank-
rupt him by the time she got to eighty.'

Tears sprang into Jess's eyes. Silently, her older sister went to put
her arms around her and the two of them held each other.

How is this my fault? Olive had found herself thinking.

Their grandmother had pushed the dishwasher door closed and
turned to face the room.

'This was always going to be difficult, girls. Come on, let's get you
both to school.' She had barely glanced at Olive as the three of them
left the kitchen. Neither of the girls had said goodbye. 'Perhaps keep
them in your room,' she'd said, nodding down at the flowers. 'For
the girls' sake.'

It was possible, Olive supposed now, that Gwen and the girls had
relented during the day, bought a card or two, and that she'd find
them pushed beneath her bedroom door. In the meantime, she had
to decide whether or not she was hungry. Not really, but . . .

She would batch-cook, she decided, as she carried a slice of bread
to the toaster. On her days off, she would freeze individual meals for
herself, and she'd even label them *Olive's Meals*, because that seemed
to be the way the household worked.

Shit, she was not going to cry, not on her birthday.

Headlights shone through the window as a vehicle arrived in the yard outside; it would be Gwen, back from an evening WI meeting. Olive dabbed at her eyes.

She could hear the TV in the other room and knew she'd have to poke her head round the door, say hi, make an effort at conversation, because if she didn't, if she crept up to her room without speaking, it would give them more ammunition against her.

'She sneaks in without a word, doesn't come and say hello to us, just goes straight up to her room. To be honest, Michael, the girls find it a bit unnerving.'

It was so very easy, when you were the outsider, to find yourself in the wrong.

Behind Olive, the door was pulled open and the sweet smell of the July night leapt into the room. Molly dived out from under the table and Olive turned to face the enemy.

Her husband stood in the doorway.

'Hi there, birthday girl.' The top button of his shirt was loose and his lower jaw showed a full day's worth of beard growth. He'd never looked more handsome.

'What are you doing here?' As Olive's pulse picked up, her stomach churned.

He was carrying roses. Pink ones, but that was OK, pink ones were much prettier than white, and she couldn't count them in a hurry, but there seemed to be a lot. Maybe not thirty-six, but what did that matter, it wasn't as though she cared a jot about flowers. By this time, she was in his arms, breathing in the smell of him, feeling his lips on the top of her head.

'Sneaked out early,' he said. 'Got to drive back in the morning. I couldn't miss your first birthday as a married woman, could I?'

She lifted her head, knowing he wanted to kiss her, and damn it, if only he'd warned her, she could have been home earlier. She could have showered, cleaned her teeth, and she had no idea when she'd last washed her hair. Why did men think surprises were so wonderful?

'Is that Dad?'

'Dad, what are you doing here?'

The girls, barefoot and in pyjamas, hair trailing behind them, ran into the room. Michael's arms fell away from Olive and reached for his daughters, who threw themselves on him.

'Presents!' Jess had squeezed out of the hug and had her eyes on a pink gift bag that Olive hadn't even noticed until now. The child bent to peer inside. 'What did you bring us?'

'It's not for you, monkey.' Michael ruffled his youngest's hair. 'It's for your mother.'

The temperature in the room fell.

Michael reddened. 'Slip of the tongue, I'm sorry. But it is Olive's birthday.' He made a point of scanning the room. 'Don't we normally keep birthday stuff in the kitchen?'

'Olive preferred to take her cards and flowers upstairs.' Gwen had appeared too, was standing in the kitchen doorway, an unusually nervous expression on her face. 'I expect you'll see them when you go up. I wish you'd warned me, Michael. Have you had dinner?'

'Dad, I got 83 per cent in my chemistry test.' Jess was pulling at his arm. 'And I'm in the netball team for the game against Harrogate next week.'

'Julia Connor's going to pony camp in Wales in August.' Amelia wasn't going to be outdone. 'Gran said I had to ask you.'

Michael raised his voice. 'Girls, what did you get Olive for her birthday?'

'Mike,' Olive began.

He held up a hand to shush her. It was a habit he had, one she didn't particularly like.

'We didn't know,' Amelia said, her eyes on the floor.

'Yes, you did. I told you all last week.' He let his eyes drift up, from his daughters, to Gwen, almost as sullen-faced as her granddaughters but better able to brazen it out.

'Really, Michael, so much goes on around here, it's hardly surprising it slipped my mind,' she said. 'But we did have a little celebration with Olive this morning, before she left for work. We had quite a conversation about flowers.'

Michael looked at Olive for confirmation.

'It's fine, really.' She smiled at him. 'Gwen's right; the girls have had a very busy week.'

'It's not fine,' Michael said.

Bursting into noisy tears, Jess ran from the room. A second later, after a glare in Olive's direction, Amelia followed.

'They need time,' Gwen said. 'We all do.' She turned. 'I'll talk to them.'

'Michael should go,' Olive said, surprised at her own daring. 'This is between the three of them.' She glanced at her husband. 'I need a shower anyway. See you in a few minutes?'

When Michael was asleep (he always fell asleep quickly after sex), Olive remembered the pink roses. They'd wilt if left overnight and she knew how much that would please Gwen and the girls. The house was silent and dark as she made her way downstairs. The flowers were still on the kitchen table.

It would have been the easiest thing in the world for Gwen to put them in water, even to half fill the sink and prop them in it. A small gesture of apology.

No Olive branches for this Olive.

And why was the kitchen so cold suddenly? It was the middle of summer, and yet an icy wind seemed to be blowing through the house. She shivered and, for a moment, the kitchen grew dark.

Then there was a vase in her hand and she was unwrapping the fat, fragrant blooms – twenty-four, not thirty-six. Leaving them in the centre of the kitchen table – she was damned if these, too, were to be banished to save the girls' feelings – she walked silently back upstairs.

In the bedroom, she stood at the foot of the bed, staring down at her sleeping husband.

26

A little after three o'clock in the morning, Garry got back to Middlesbrough police station to find that Lexy had gone home. She'd left a scribbled note for him in the keeping of the desk sergeant.

Anderson and his mother-in-law telling truth about Olive's 'stalker'. Incident reported and on file. Also, spoke to hotel's night security guard. Staff member who checked Olive in and out gone home, waiter at dinner also gone. Room booked in name of Mr and Mrs Anderson. Odd that, given she was there alone? Can't do much more tonight. Will pick up tomorrow. Call if hospital visit uncovered anything.

   BTW, I hear the Tricks op went well!!! Look forward to hearing all about it.

He should have known, of course. It was only a matter of time before every member of Cleveland Police, down to the office cleaners and the canteen staff, knew how badly he'd messed up. On the other hand, he was touched that Lexy had written an actual note, rather than texting him. He tucked it into his pocket.

This really had been one of the worst nights he could remember, and his sense of something going badly wrong had been growing by the hour.

His trip to the hospital had uncovered nothing, but, on the drive back, Garry had found himself remembering the first time Olive had spoken to him. He'd been taking part in an inter-schools' cross-country event, had been a decent enough runner in his day, a sport strongly encouraged by his family. *A copper has to be able to run.* He'd been towards the front of the boys' field, had overtaken most of the girls who'd started ahead, and came across a wide, water-filled ditch. He'd watched a boy from a Newcastle school leap across, landing in ankle-deep mud and then saw a girl in his own school's colours – Olive – on the far side looking down into the water. Her left shoe had been sucked clean off her foot and was stuck beneath the water surface, barely visible. There was no way she'd be able to finish the race without it. As he'd hesitated, another boy approached, took an almighty leap, and sped off on the other side.

Gritting his teeth, Garry had jumped into the freezing water and waded forwards. He'd reached down, retrieved Olive's shoe, and scrambled out beside her.

'I can't believe you did that.' She had dropped to the grass to re-place it. 'Thanks so much.'

Unable to think of a single thing to say, he'd turned and run off. He didn't win the race, had never really expected to, but finished in the top ten, which was decent enough. Olive won the girls' race, though, and, afterwards, she'd never passed him in the corridor without smiling.

He'd forgotten, until that moment, that for the remainder of their time in school he'd had a massive secret crush on the girl now married to Michael Anderson. At the same time, it struck him that his first interaction, with both of Anderson's wives, had been footwear-related.

Already, in the station car park, he'd tried Olive's mobile number. *Come on, Olive, pick up. Let's fix this before it's out of all our hands.* She hadn't answered, and he'd come inside with an inexplicable sadness in his heart.

Now, at Lexy's desk, he accessed the paperwork the detective had left behind. She'd recommended contacting Michael Anderson again in the morning to check how he wanted to proceed. If he insisted on having his wife listed as missing, the usual protocols would kick in. Family and friends would be contacted, financial enquiries insti-gated; they'd look at her telephone history, her internet and social media usage. Olive's laptop had already been signed into evidence. They'd check Anderson's too.

While the tech people were working their magic on Olive's various devices and accounts, corresponding physical searches would take place. Anywhere Olive might have gone would be investigated. Normally, if thought necessary, police dogs, helicopters and specialist search teams would be deployed.

The bad weather, set to continue in the coming days, could make that close to impossible. Olive really had picked the worst time of year to go missing.

27

She'd been dreaming, Olive realised. The night of her birthday. A warm night, when the remnants of a summer storm had blown petals against windows, when the man she'd married had lain close, his skin hot against her own, his breathing heavy and slow in her ear.

Dreaming meant sleep. At the back of her mind, Olive knew that sleep was dangerous; but so very sweet, transporting her from a world of ice-cold pain into one of warmth and safety.

So much nicer to stay here, in the soft darkness, listening to her husband's low-pitched sleep sounds. A sigh, a cough, an odd, high-pitched purring, then a series of repetitive grunts.

Olive felt sweat breaking out on her forehead.

This wasn't Michael. This was something else. A living creature was close: snuffling, exploring the unfamiliar smells of the crashed car and the broken humans. The smell of blood had lured it through the darkness. It had come cautiously, because creatures of the night were timid, but had probably been watching her for some time.

Deer, fox, badger? How soon before it knew she couldn't move?

Her heart was thumping against her chest; she hardly dared breathe.

She heard it brush against the side of the car, the snap of a twig, a grunt, and always the constant snuffling as its nose crept along the ground, tracking the scent, looking for a way in. She knew she had to stay awake, get ready to bang against the car's framework, even sound the horn if she could reach it, but she really was so very tired, and again, the night was gathering around her, the world slipping away.

*

Michael turning over in his sleep roused Olive. She had no idea how long she'd been standing at the foot of the bed, lost in thought, but as she made her way towards the window, she caught a glimpse of the clock on her husband's bedside table. It was no longer her birthday.

The moon had risen, casting an eerie, silvery glow over the room. Curtains were never drawn when Michael was home – he hated the claustrophobic feeling they gave him – and as the house was overlooked by nothing other than miles of countryside, Olive had never demurred.

Her robe was hanging, phantom-like, on the back of the door, her bag on the chair just inside the room. On her way out, she had to step round the birthday gift bag. Earlier, she'd caught a glimpse of a Mappin & Webb box inside. Earrings would be nice, she supposed, maybe a necklace. She knew no one would ask to see it, whatever it was.

On the ground floor, she made tea and carried it into her husband's study, the one room in the house, other than her bedroom, where Gwen and the girls rarely came. Curling up in an armchair, she found her iPad, opened Facebook and flicked through the birthday messages. Cheery good wishes from her sister, an aunt, an old school friend, a couple of mates from uni and a few work colleagues; also, several of Michael's constituents and members of the local party whom she'd felt obliged to add as friends. She scrolled down, liking and thanking, adding the odd polite comment. MPs' wives had to be so well behaved.

She was on the point of closing the site down when another comment appeared at the bottom of the birthday thread.

I see you, Olive.

That was it. Nothing else.

Without thinking, Olive looked up. The study window was a black, blank square in the wall.

I see you, Olive.

The comment had been posted by a man called Howard Wayne.

The name meant nothing, nor did Olive recognise his profile pic. She opened his page and knew, within seconds, that it was fake. The picture was professionally taken, a good-looking, youngish man with a sailor's cap drawn down over one eye. His background picture was a shot of a marina. The real giveaways, though, were the number of friends – just seven, including a couple of minor celebrity types who friended anyone – and the limited history. Howard Wayne had posted only ten times, all within the last few weeks, giving away nothing of the person behind them. No status updates, no interactions with friends. Howard Wayne was a ghost.

She'd accepted his friend request, as she'd done so many others since her engagement to Michael had been announced; she'd probably seen the nautical theme of his profile and assumed it was someone from the yacht club.

She deleted the strange comment and went to block him, just as a tiny red numeral 1 flashed into her message box. Nervously, she opened Messenger. A new thread. From Howard Wayne.

Still here, Olive.

He was typing again, she could see the three little dots – what were they called, the ellipsis? – flickering in the bottom left-hand corner of the screen. Another message flashed up.

You're never going to be enough for him. He's always going to want more.

Without thinking, she typed out a reply.

Who are you?

She shouldn't have done that. Never feed the troll.

He was typing again.

Who do you want me to be?

This was stupid. Michael would tear her off a strip if he found out. How often had he nagged her to set her accounts to private?

A fifth message landed.

You and I have a lot to talk about. Why don't you step outside? Or shall I come to the window?

The iPad fell to the rug as Olive leapt to her feet. Rushing to the window, she pulled the curtains closed and left the room to check the doors. The front was locked and bolted, as were the French windows in the drawing room. Only when she saw that the kitchen door, too, was secure did she relax.

A thumping sound made her jump, but it was only Molly, beneath the table, wagging her tail.

Or shall I come to the window?

There couldn't be anyone outside. The house was a mile from the road and vehicles approaching were always heard. He was messing with her.

She screenshotted the message exchange before unfriending and blocking Howard Wayne. Then she poured her undrunk tea away and attached her iPad to one of the charging stations. Unusually, there was one free.

Another message flashed in, from a different 'friend' this time. Feeling sick, she opened it.

Can't get rid of me that easily, Olive.

Not giving him a chance to send her anything else, she screenshotted, then unfriended and blocked again. Tomorrow, she'd go through her entire list of friends, deleting any she wasn't completely sure of.

On the upstairs landing, Olive caught sight of a light shining weakly from beneath one of the bedroom doors. Amelia had either fallen asleep with her light on or was still awake.

Only one mobile had been on charge in the kitchen. The girls were supposed to leave their devices downstairs while they slept. It was a house rule, one Michael and Gwen enforced rigidly. Was Amelia on her phone right now?

Was she on Facebook?

Olive crept to her stepdaughter's door and pressed her face against it. Nothing. Slowly, she turned the knob, wincing as it creaked. Going into her stepdaughters' rooms while they slept would be ammunition they'd grab with both hands.

She's creepy, Dad. She watches us while we're asleep.

That might strike a chord with Michael; the number of times he'd almost woken to find her at the foot of the bed.

'Amelia, are you awake?'

The room was in darkness now and there was no sign of the phone on the bedside table.

Amelia herself was invisible beneath the covers, nothing more than a bump on the bed. She could easily be hiding her phone right now.

It wasn't something Olive could investigate. Opening the bedroom door was one thing, pulling back covers from a sleeping child another.

'Do you have your phone with you, Amelia?'

No response.

'Are you on Facebook right now?'

No response, and the corridor was getting very cold, as though an icy draught was blowing through the house. Olive softly closed the door and went back to her own room.

28

As Garry's shift ended, signs of a new day were limping towards the start line: lights in shops, a kerb-crawling refuse vehicle, the tailgates of delivery vans bouncing down onto fresh snow. This far north, though, the sun wouldn't appear for hours and even then might struggle to penetrate the snow clouds. Meanwhile, the sky remained black as a slag heap, and somewhere in the lingering darkness, the first girl who'd made Garry feel good about himself might be in trouble.

Earlier that morning, he'd received the results of the ANPR search. The system had found a shot of Olive's car on the main road through Hexham, then a second crossing the river on the A6079. The woman in the passenger seat, obviously Olive, was looking away from the driver and seemed to be sitting very upright. She didn't look like a woman on a romantic adventure. Her companion, on the other hand, was harder to make out. He could see dark hair, a tall figure, nothing else.

Two major roads led away from Hexham. The A69, running east to west, and the A68, north to south. Neither had picked up Olive's car. Wherever she'd gone, she'd travelled on minor roads.

He'd remembered something else about Olive, as he'd been waiting for his shift to end. The second time the two of them had spoken at school, around a year after the cross-country race. He'd found a note in his locker, slipped in through the gap between door and metal frame.

Want to walk me home tonight? We can discuss the prom? 3.45 at West Gate. Linda Moore.

Garry had slipped the note into his pocket, feeling a bit like he did on the start line of a big race. This was major. Linda Moore wasn't the best-looking girl in his form, but she had natural blonde hair, big blue eyes and even bigger . . . well, it wasn't a word he liked using – but he knew exactly what the other guys meant when they huddled together and sniggered about what they'd like to do with her.

He sauntered to the West Gate when school finished. No sign of Linda, but he knew the girls often hung around in the toilets after school. Leaning against the gate pillar, he checked his watch before brushing his fingers over his jacket pocket, as though to check the note was still there, that he hadn't imagined it.

A group of lads across the street caught his eye. None were looking his way, but there was something about them that didn't feel right. They weren't talking or messing about the way boys released from school usually did. And there was a group at the bus stop, girls and boys, an odd quietness seemed to be hanging over them too.

Was it his imagination, or were there a few too many people hanging around the West Gate? And they were all too quiet. No, not quiet, alert. Waiting for something.

And then he heard a snigger behind him.

'All right, Garry.'

Not Linda herself but three of her friends, all with identical, mean smiles on their faces. That's when he knew. Linda wasn't coming, probably hadn't even written the note, and the entire year was hanging around to see him look a fool.

Then a hand grabbed his arm and squeezed it. Hope and joy surging, he turned his head to see . . .

Olive.

'Sorry I'm late.' She tugged at his arm, forcing him to start moving, to walk alongside her. 'Some twat took my coat.'

As Garry stared down, wondering what on earth was going on, Olive smiled up at him. She was way, way prettier than Linda Moore, anyone could see that.

'You know she's not coming,' she whispered.

'I figured.'

'Dickheads. Smile at me. They're still watching.'

And so the two of them walked away, leaving the school gate behind, and still Olive clung to his arm. One of the school buses passed and several heads on the back seat turned round to look at the two of them, arm in arm, grinning at each other. Olive's smile didn't look fake at all, and, funnily enough, his didn't feel it either. A sudden thought struck him and he spoke without thinking.

'So, do you want to go to the prom?'

She pulled a face. 'God, no. Thanks, but my parents would never agree. Girls get pregnant at the prom, Garry.'

'Right.'

'Really not my thing, anyway. And this is me.'

They'd reached a junction in the road. Olive's journey home took her a different way. She let go his arm and gave him a cheery wave with her fingertips.

'I'd say we're even now, wouldn't you?'

Garry sighed and turned on his engine. He wasn't going home yet.

Keeping his speed down, he joined the A66, saying a silent prayer that the main roads would be clear enough to get to Hexham. His own car, a six-year-old Subaru four-wheel-drive estate, wasn't as handy in heavy weather as the police Range Rovers but decent enough on his weekend foraging trips, even coping with a bit of off-road work.

As it turned out, he made good progress. The snow kept his speed down, but traffic was light. He might even have made it in record time, but halfway up the A68 he was forced to pull over to help a middle-aged couple who'd been stranded in their car all night.

He'd wanted to drive past, but the bloke had looked so pitiful, up to his calves in snow, in a stupidly inadequate coat. The car had left the road, probably when the markings had become invisible under snow, and hit a ditch.

'We thought no one was coming.' Garry could hear the woman's teeth chattering as she climbed into the back seat. Garry turned the car heater up.

'We kept the engine on as long as we could,' her husband explained. 'The petrol ran out two hours ago.'

Inwardly, Garry shook his head at folk who were stupid enough to venture out in snow without warm clothes, blankets and hot drinks. Not to mention enough fuel in the tank.

'I had visions of us stuck for days,' the woman said, as Garry dropped them off in Hexham. 'There's more snow forecast. We could've starved.'

'Died of exposure first,' her husband added, cheerfully.

'Not for a few more hours,' Garry told them. 'Get yourselves inside and stay warm.'

The sky was noticeably paler as he set off again: a soggy grey, like old porridge. He wasted another ten minutes pulling over to a roadside van serving breakfast and arrived at the county hotel a few minutes before eight o'clock. The night security guard hadn't yet left for the day.

Garry introduced himself, produced his warrant card, and explained that while he was off duty now, and not here officially, he'd been in the area and thought it might be worth popping in.

'I went to the lady's home last night to interview the family,' he explained. No need to mention he'd only been the driver. 'We'll be up to our eyes in it today, what with the snow and it being Christmas and all. I thought I might get ahead.'

The guard, a man called Alan who hadn't arrived until midnight, was happy enough to talk.

'It all went quiet about four,' he explained as he ushered Garry into a small office behind the hotel's reception. 'Once I'd cleaned up the worst of the vomit and turfed a drunk bloke out of the ladies' toilets, I had a chance to check footage from earlier.' He pressed play on the office computer. 'This is the car you're interested in. Audi Q3, Sportback, nice motor. I didn't see Mrs Anderson myself, she was gone before I arrived, but I checked the register. All guests have to give their car's registration numbers, like.'

The footage showed a silver car, its bodywork covered in snow. The image gave no indication of who might be in the car. The time worked, though. A little after ten o'clock. This was Olive and her mysterious companion leaving the hotel.

'So, then I checked out the earlier footage,' Alan explained. 'And I found the same car arriving. Three minutes past seven o'clock. What is it you guys say, nineteen oh three hours?'

'On her own,' Garry mumbled. The picture was better from this angle and the woman at the wheel looked a lot like Olive. The passenger seat was empty.

'MP's wife, is that right? That bloke down Middlesbrough way?'

'I'm afraid we're not allowed to discuss details,' Garry muttered. 'National security. Keep it to yourself for now, won't you?'

'Aye, I can do that. I found some pictures of her checking out as well.'

Excitement surged inside Garry. 'Can you show me?'

A few more seconds passed, and then Garry watched footage taken from behind the hotel reception during the previous night's festivities. At five minutes past ten, Olive approached the front desk and stood waiting, still as a statue. Her eyes, huge and dark in an unsmiling face, darted here and there. Then the receptionist moved in front of her, effectively blocking the camera's view, and after several minutes, Olive turned and left the hotel.

'On her own, wouldn't you say?' the security guard said. 'Although the booking was for a double room, double occupancy.'

Garry wasn't sure. Another figure, whom the camera had only caught a glimpse of, had turned along with Olive and appeared to be leaving at the same time. Taller than Olive, he thought, wearing a heavy tweed coat. The mysterious companion?

Garry used his own phone to get a shot of the image. 'Can you make sure this footage is saved?'

'Aye, I can do that. Do you want to see her room?'

Garry did; he also knew it could be a step too far. 'I can't,' he said. 'It's a potential crime scene. No one should be going in there until CSIs have had chance to sweep it. You'll make sure it isn't cleaned, won't you?'

'Can't see how it's a crime scene myself,' Alan said. 'She left happily enough from what I could see.'

Garry remembered Olive's wide, staring eyes, her clenched jaw. 'You think so?'

Outside again, he took a walk around the car park, finding the spot where Olive had parked, the tracks of her car long since covered by snow. He found the window of room seven, but the curtains were drawn and he wouldn't have been able to see inside even if it had been on the ground floor. Opposite, some fifty metres across the car park, was a three-storey building. As he watched, a blind folded itself away to reveal a woman in the room beyond. Garry waved, then walked towards the door.

Ten minutes later, he was out in the street again. He could do no more here. What he knew was that Olive and the mystery companion hadn't arrived together. They'd met at the hotel – whether by accident or design, he had yet to learn. So how had the other person arrived? There were no unclaimed cars in the car park. That meant on foot, or possibly via a local taxi. The taxi firm he could check. Given enough time, he could look at CCTV around town, local transport links, shops and so on. The tweed coat was distinctive enough. Given time, he'd find some trace. He wouldn't have that time, though. Someone else would be following Olive's trail.

As he climbed back into his vehicle to drive home, Garry found himself wishing it was his case after all.

29

Half-awake again, Olive was trying to assess herself for spinal cord injuries, knowing they were common after serious road traffic accidents. The pain in her neck and shoulders, her odd, twisted position and her impaired breathing were bad signs. On the plus side, she badly needed to pee, so hadn't lost bladder control, and she could feel and move her fingers and toes.

The golden rule was to wait for emergency care. Specialist equipment existed for retrieving and transporting patients with possible spinal trauma. Trying to move now could be her worst mistake on what had already been a disastrous night.

On the other hand, being immobile for any length of time, practically upside down, was putting too great a stress on her body. And if she was bleeding internally, she might have hours, at best.

So, this was her choice: risk paralysis or probable death; spend the rest of her life a shamed cripple, the byword on everyone's tongue – *This is what happens to sexually promiscuous women;* or slip quietly away.

A new sound broke through the night. A car engine. Another vehicle on the road, that might see the broken fence, the skid marks in the snow. If only she weren't so tired. If only she could reach out and sound the horn. The sound of the engine grew louder. If only . . .

Olive lost consciousness again.

She hadn't mentioned the Facebook trolling at first, even when it spread to Twitter and Instagram. It was something politicians dealt with, and so their wives learned to deal with it too. And yet, no matter how many people she blocked, a new offender seemed to appear every other week. Constantly, Olive found herself tagged in old photographs of Michael and Eloise, the latter always impossibly glamorous, at some constituency function or other. Occasionally, pictures of Olive and Michael's first wife would appear side by side, with viewers invited to compare the two. The photographs were always unflattering of Olive, the opposite of Eloise, and there never seemed to be a shortage of lowlifes only too happy to find fresh ways to insult her.

When the hashtag SecondWifeSecondBest appeared, even gained some traction, she did what Michael had been nagging her to do for months: she set her accounts to private. She even told him why, skimming over the volume and being vague about the content of the abuse. She couldn't rid herself of the suspicion that it stemmed from closer to home than Michael would ever accept. The girls, like most teenagers, were constantly on their devices and more than once she'd caught them looking at her maliciously from over the top of their phones.

Two teenage girls, though, could not follow her home after a night shift, trailing her car like an inexperienced police tail, all the way to the farm track that led to the house. The first time it happened, unnerved though she was, Olive had put it down to coincidence: a lost driver who'd been clinging to the tail lights of another vehicle in the hope of eventually finding the right road.

The second time, she'd been less generous, had driven too fast, trying to shake the vehicle off. The pattern repeated itself: the car pulling back seconds before Olive turned into Home Farm.

The third time, she'd taken her courage in both hands and pulled over round the first bend in the track. Leaving the car, she'd jogged back towards the road, thankful that she was wearing dark clothes. She had no desire to be seen. All she wanted was to get the registration number, make and model of the car, maybe even a photograph, something to ensure the police took her seriously when she reported it.

A few metres shy of the road, she stopped. The headlights of the car that had been following her had been switched off. At first, Olive wasn't even sure it was still there. The hedge in late summer was thick with foliage and she could see nothing through it.

Phone in hand, she leaned out far enough to get a view back up the road. The car was less than a hundred metres away.

The second she raised her phone, the car's headlights shone out, half blinding her; at the same time, the engine fired up and the car shot towards her.

Olive ran, sprinting back up the lane towards her own car, hearing the engine behind and the crunch of tyres on the rough track that told her the car was following. She reached her own vehicle and leapt inside, only then realising the pursuing car had stopped. It was parked at the end of the lane, headlights on full beam, engine revving.

Olive reached for her phone. The police would come; for the wife of a sitting member of parliament they'd come immediately.

The sound of the other's car's engine changed. It was moving. Olive's hand shot to the ignition key. The other car was metres away, it would be on her in seconds. Her own engine roared to life.

The other car was reversing. In the rear-view mirror, Olive watched it back onto the main road. She twisted round in her seat to make sure, just in time to see it speed away.

In real time, the car that Olive had heard passed by fewer than a hundred metres away. Falling snow had already softened their skid tracks and the driver, intent on the road, didn't even notice the broken fence.

Silence settled once more on the night, and the temperature continued to fall.

30

Garry was not entirely surprised, when he pulled into the drive of the house he owned in the Hemlington area of Middlesbrough, to find Mrs Tyler, his next-door neighbour, still in dressing gown and slippers, on her front doorstep. She knew his shift patterns better than he did and would have expected him home hours ago.

'It's a foot deep.' She was pointing a bony finger at the path that led down the centre of her front garden. 'I'll break my neck if I try to get out.'

'Three inches, Mrs T,' he told her, locking the car. 'I've just come off nights. I'll get to it later. I need some kip right now.'

'There'll be no grit left,' she argued, looking towards the road corner, where a square wooden box held a mixture of sand and grit for residents' use in bad weather. 'Them at number eighteen have been at it already. They've been stockpiling it round t'back. Some-one should do something.'

That someone being him, no doubt. In Mrs Tyler's mind, police officers were never off duty. If she spotted something wrong in the neighbourhood, it was always Garry she called. It didn't matter how many times he reminded her that the numbers he'd pinned to the board in her kitchen were the correct ones for any given situation, she called him.

'Later, Mrs T.' He closed the door and fastened the bolt, as though it might prove any sort of barrier against a determined old lady. If he was lucky, the snow would keep her indoors for most of the day.

There was still the phone, though.

Knowing he really needed to sleep, he pulled the phone lead out of its socket beneath the hall table. He did the same with the phone in the bedroom and turned off his mobile. Then he pulled off his travelling-to-work-in-winter clothes, folded them neatly, all apart from underpants and socks, which went into the linen basket in the bathroom, and put them away in the drawer he kept for clothes currently in use. Naked and shivering, he found his pyjamas from under the pillow, pulled back the duvet and climbed between freezing sheets.

He'd forgotten his hot-water bottle; he never forgot his hot-water bottle; too late, he wasn't getting up again now. On a whim, he leaned out of bed and pulled the window blind up a few inches. Outside, the snow was falling again. He watched the flakes, tiny at first, but getting bigger and denser, and thought about Olive, who might be watching that same snowstorm somewhere.

The doorbell woke him. As his eyes opened, as he dragged himself back up to consciousness, he had a feeling it had been ringing for some time. There had been a dream, he and Olive had been racing, or at least trying to, through thick snow. Both of them barefoot, she'd been explaining to him that no one scaled the brook without leaving their shoes behind. The crowd that should have been cheering them across the finishing line were all pressing buzzers. The noise had been deafening.

He glanced at the clock. Noon. Seriously, Mrs Tyler?

Garry got up, not even bothering to put on a dressing gown. Let her know she'd dragged a hard-working public servant out of bed barely two hours after he'd got into it. He could see her outline through the glass of the front door and at least the daft old bat had thought to put a hat and coat on. He released the chain and pulled open the door.

'Now, look, Mrs T—'

It was Lexy.

Lexy. Looking a whole lot better than the last time he'd seen her. Her make-up was fresh, her eyes bright and shining, and the pink beret on her head really suited her. A matching scarf was wrapped around her throat. Her cheeks were the same colour, and her lips. She was even wearing earrings like tiny, pink pearls. As Garry felt his own mouth stretching into an unfamiliar shape, two things happened: first, he remembered that he was wearing pyjamas that didn't have a terribly secure fly, and second, she started yelling.

'What the hell were you thinking?'

His smile faltered. 'I'm not on duty,' he managed.

'Exactly. You're not on duty. What the hell were you thinking of going to Hexham?'

Her eyes, he saw, were a bright sapphire blue. How had he not noticed that last night? And, bloody hell, it was cold with the front door open. He remembered the insecure fly and felt a draught in a place that didn't usually respond well to low temperatures.

He said, 'What are you doing here?'

'Ripping you a new one. Are you going to let me in or not?'

Not, was the first thought that sprang into his head, but some kids building a snowman on the pavement opposite were watching with interest, as, he realised with dismay, was Mrs Tyler.

'Everything all right, Garry?' she called over. Fully dressed, she was wearing yellow wellingtons. She still hadn't ventured onto her path, though. 'It's still coming down,' she added, making it sound as though the weather were his fault.

'Come in.' Turning his back on Lexy, Garry glanced down to make sure his credentials weren't on show. He didn't think so, but hard to be sure. He pushed open the door of his living room. 'Wait in here. I'll get dressed. You do know I'm not on duty?'

'I know that. Question is, do you?'

In his bedroom, Garry found himself flustered. He wasn't sure he had clothes suitable for an unexpected weekend caller. Then he remembered it wasn't the weekend anyway and this wouldn't be a social call. Lexy was working. He decided to be practical and found the corduroy trousers he wore for winter foraging, a brushed cotton plaid shirt and a thick sweater. As he was straightening the covers on the bed, he heard her shouting again.

'For God's sake, Garry, we're not going to a ball. I haven't got all day.'

Her voice was coming from the kitchen. He pulled on slippers and joined her.

'Do you have any real coffee?' she asked. 'That's gorgeous, by the way. Where'd you get it?'

Moving at a speed he found bewildering, Lexy was filling the kettle, switching it on, taking milk from the fridge. She nodded out of the kitchen window to the lean-to area where he kept his tools. She'd seen the arrangement, a free-style he'd put together in a long, low, pewter trough: some russet leaves, silvered grasses and black twigs, hellebores in bud and a few late white roses from the allotment. The making of it, temporarily at least, because they would go over faster than everything else, were the pale, bulbous fungi he'd found in the park. He'd left the arrangement outside because it would last longer in the chill.

'My mum volunteers at the church hall,' he said, using a white lie he'd found convincing enough in the past, except when talking to his mum. 'She often brings flowers home after events are done.'

Lexy raised her eyebrows, and he remembered the cluster of red berries in the bright silver vase in the living room. He'd teamed them with dark ivy and a single white rose. She would have seen that too.

'She gets hay fever,' he added lamely. 'She can't have them at home.'

Lexy gave him a long, curious look that he couldn't interpret and said, 'Nice PJs by the way.'

The pyjamas, flannel and very warm, had been a Christmas present from his parents a couple of years ago. They featured cats in Christmas hats, pulling crackers. He felt a blush starting to glow in his cheeks.

'I've had exactly two hours' sleep,' he complained.

'Shouldn't have gone to Hexham then, should you?'

Fair enough, he probably shouldn't have gone to Hexham. Lexy was right to be annoyed. It still didn't explain why she was here.

'You couldn't have phoned?' he said, wondering how much stick he was going to take down the station when everyone knew about his pyjamas.

'I tried. Repeatedly.'

Darn it, he'd unplugged his phones. Turning his back, he found his mobile from where he'd left it on charge and switched it back on. Sure enough, several missed calls from Lexy.

The kettle boiled. Lexy pulled open a cupboard door at random and took out two mugs. Stepping to one side, she found his jar of Nescafé, tutted when she saw it was decaf, and plucked a spoon from the drawer.

'Have you been here before?' Garry asked.

'My grandad lives in a place exactly like this,' she said. 'Old people are very predictable in their habits.'

Did she mean him? He wasn't that much older than she was. Five years, six at a stretch.

'My grandad did live here,' he was surprised to find himself saying. 'He left it to me when he died.'

Pulling a face that suggested she wasn't surprised, she added milk to their coffees.

'How did you know I went to Hexham?' he asked, as she handed him his mug. She'd made it too strong, but he'd learned to pick his fights. She'd been right about the sugar though; he'd weaned himself off it a couple of years ago.

'I'm a detective,' she said. 'You realise you could have messed up the investigation completely? Another one?'

That wasn't fair. A destroyed memorial teddy was hardly going to compromise the Tricks op.

'Does that mean there is one?' he asked. 'Have you launched a missing persons?'

Lexy was still clearly annoyed. 'No. Michael Anderson called the boss first thing. Wants to hold off making it official for now while he talks to Olive's friends and family. Looks like he spent the night wrestling with the conflicting demands of his love for his wife and his need to protect his career and reputation and decided the wife could look after herself. On the other hand, she hasn't arrived at the hospital in Newcastle, even though she was due an hour ago and they've heard nothing from her. I don't know about you, Garry, but I'm not happy about that.' She pulled a bar stool out from beneath the counter where Garry ate breakfast and said, 'So, what did you learn in Hexham?'

Garry found the picture on his phone of Olive and a possible companion in reception.

'Whatever's going on, I'm not convinced she's having an affair,' he began. 'I got chatting to a woman who lives in a flat directly opposite the hotel. Bit of a curtain-twitcher. She saw Olive Anderson at the window of room seven at around seven thirty, then a few minutes later crossing the courtyard to go to dinner.'

'Alone?'

'Yep. Then, not five minutes after that, she saw a light come on in room seven again. A dim light, a torch or bedside light, but she could see someone moving around inside. And Olive had left the curtains partly open. Whoever it was stayed there another five minutes, closed the curtains properly, and then the lights went out again.'

'Could have been Olive herself,' Lexy said. 'She forgot something.'

'No, because she didn't see Olive return to her room. She did, though, see someone leave the annexe and head towards the dining room.'

'Male or female?'

'She wasn't sure. Someone tall in trousers, so could be either.'

Lexy said nothing but held her hand out for Garry's phone again. She found the picture of Olive checking out and her eyes narrowed.

'We know the two of them didn't arrive in Hexham together, but if they'd arranged to meet at the hotel, why would Olive go down to dinner alone?' Garry asked. 'And how did this person get into her room?'

'She could have left it unlocked.' Lexy thought for a moment. 'And she went ahead to the dining room to make sure they had a table.'

Garry opened his mouth to say it was possible, he supposed, but his mobile began to ring.

'It's Alan,' he said. 'The night security guard at the hotel. He said he'd get back to me if anything came up.'

Lexy gave a sharp intake of breath, then, 'Put him on speaker,' she said.

'That you, Gazza?' The man sounded as though he were yelling down the phone. 'So, like, I was having a chat with one of the cleaners before I clocked off. Michele, from Corbridge way, worked here since the glue factory closed in '95.'

Lexy's eyebrows rose again.

'Any road, she were here about ten days ago and she took a call. There were no one behind reception, like, the girl had gone to the loo or something, and Michele answered the phone. It were Mr Anderson's secretary, phoning about his wife's reservation.'

Lexy climbed down from her stool and leaned closer to the phone.

'Alan, this is Detective Sergeant Lexy Thomas. You and I spoke last night. I'm here with Gazza getting a debrief. Did Michele recall what the secretary said?'

'Aye, because it were unusual, like. She said her boss would particularly like Mrs Anderson to be given room seven, because they'd stayed in it before, and it had nice memories for them, and that he was going to join his wife as a surprise. And that he was planning to have flowers delivered to the room too, because it was an anniversary. She said there'd be a nice tip in it for Michele if she could make the arrangements. Well, Michele spoke to reception and they agreed to put Mrs Anderson in room seven and share the tip and now they're both a bit annoyed, like, because no tip's been left.'

Lexy looked up at Garry; she really did have very blue eyes.

'Alan, this is very helpful, thank you,' she said into the phone. 'We'll take it from here.' She hung up, then looked at Garry again. 'I was wrong,' she said.

'How exactly?'

'You were right to go to Hexham. What are you up to the rest of the morning?'

'I was planning to sleep,' he said.

Her face twisted, with what could have been an apology, but he wouldn't put money on it. 'Well, I'm planning to go and see what Mr Anderson says about this latest development.' She looked at him, expectantly.

He said, 'I thought you'd been stood down.'

'No, I've been asked to keep a watching brief while events unfold. I doubt my car will make it to Guisborough. I barely got here without tail-ending a taxi.'

She wanted him to drive her.

'Nice-looking Subaru in the driveway,' she said. 'Bet that's handy in the snow.'

He made her wait for a second, then, 'It does all right.'

Her hand raised in a fist, as though she were about to punch him on the arm, then thought better of it. 'Oh, come on, Gazza,' she said. 'You know you want to come with me. You can fill me in on the way with everything else you learned on your moonlight.'

Of course, he wanted to go with her; he just didn't like being bounced in it.

'Call me Gazza again and I'll abandon you on the North York Moors,' he said. 'I'll get my coat.'

31

Olive opened her eyes again. Snow still covered the car's windscreen, but the light behind it was different. While she'd been unconscious, dawn had broken. Somewhere close by, water was dripping in a rhythmical, almost musical, sound of melting snow. Knowing she'd made it through the night gave her a tiny burst of hope. She'd be missed. People would be looking for her.

The fragile bubble burst with the sinking feeling that no one would have the first clue which direction she and her abductor had driven in or how far they'd travelled. Their tracks could have been covered already by fresh snowfall. Worse, they'd crashed among trees. She remembered tall, dark columns against the white landscape as the car had plunged over the embankment. A tree canopy would shield the car from view. Her car, a pale silver, might be invisible from the air.

She tried to find some sense of urgency, something that would force her into action, however painful. And couldn't. She was too tired.

Darkness claimed her again.

The car following Olive home was the last straw. She would tell Michael, together they'd talk to the police, and if a search of her social media accounts threw up anything he'd find difficult to deal with, well that was tough.

Knowing it would be an easier conversation to have away from home, she'd waited until parliament resumed after the summer, had even taken time off work to travel to London and stay overnight in the flat he used during the week. Her train had been delayed, though, and it had been coming up for seven in the evening before she arrived at the small flat, a short Tube ride from Westminster.

Music was playing as she let herself in and she could smell food.

'Hey, babe,' Michael called. 'We're in here.'

The flat had just one reception room, from the window of which the slick, black gleam of the river could be seen in the distance. The lights were low, Adele singing softly, and the table under the window laid for three. Olive had barely time to recognise the woman striding towards her before she was grasped by a stocky, muscular body that smelled of the ocean.

'Carla, what are you doing here?'

Carla, a sergeant in Michael's old regiment, who'd served with them in Afghanistan, was wearing her usual skintight jeans, high-heeled boots and a silk shirt. Her chestnut-brown hair had grown longer since Olive had last seen her and was loose around her shoulders. Her skin, normally weather-beaten – Carla ran extreme marathons – was unusually pink, but the heating in the flat had been cranked higher than felt necessary. It wasn't exactly cold outside.

Carla wasn't unattractive, but her features were heavy, her mouth a little too wide, her jaw square. In the time they'd been together, Olive couldn't remember Michael ever mentioning her before.

The hug lasted longer than felt entirely comfortable – Carla and Olive had never been close – the other woman only stepping back and releasing Olive when Michael made a point of clearing his throat. 'You look amazing,' Carla said, gazing appreciatively at Olive. 'Doesn't she, Michael?'

'Always,' he agreed.

Only then did Olive's husband get up from his armchair by the fire to greet her. He'd been watching the two women as though they were doing something curious, something he'd never seen before, but then, almost as though he'd forgotten Carla was in the room, he walked right up to Olive, lifted her chin and kissed her.

The kiss, like Carla's embrace, went on for far too long, and besides, Olive could practically hear Carla breathing, she was standing so close to them. She pulled back, feeling Michael resist for a second before letting her go.

They'd eaten, a perfectly decent curry that Michael had made – Olive hadn't even known he could cook – and she'd tried not to be annoyed that her plans to have a proper heart-to-heart had been sabotaged; nor could she help the suspicion it had been deliberate. The wine had helped, and her glass seemed to be filled with increasing regularity, by Carla as often as Michael, as though the two of them were the hosts and she, Olive, the guest. When the second bottle had emptied, it was Carla who'd got up to find another.

Olive drank, and then drank some more, and forgot her annoyance. Carla was surprisingly good company: funny, verging on outrageous at times. As they finished the cheese, she unfastened two buttons of her silk blouse, revealing the edging of a red lace bra.

'Woah!' Carla used a napkin to fan her face. 'I'm sweltering. So there we are, up by the perimeter fence, it's black as the ace of spades, one of those really dark Afghan nights when there's no moon, no stars, nothing, so we thought we were pretty safe, and the captain is going down on me, and I'm just at the point of no return, and I might be getting a bit noisy, but, fuck me, there's no one within a hundred yards to hear us, and then we're both lit up like a fucking Christmas tree. Suddenly, bright as day.'

Olive glanced at Michael to find him looking at her rather than Carla. His eyes had a glazed look, almost as though he'd taken something more than alcohol, but that was impossible; Michael didn't do drugs.

'There's an Apache directly above us, on its way back from a surveillance mission. They thought we were a couple of hostiles trying to sneak into the base.' Carla was in full flow now. 'So, they had the searchlight trained on us and half a squad of blokes on board who thought their birthdays had come early.'

'I'm surprised you didn't hear it.' It wasn't the first outlandish sex story Carla had told that evening and Olive was getting a bit sceptical. Carla, she suspected, had quite the imagination. She also thought most of the stories had been directed at her, rather than Michael, as though trying to get a rise out of her. 'Apache helicopters aren't exactly quiet.'

Carla gave her a long, sly look. 'What can I say? Neither am I.'

'What happened to the captain?' Michael asked. 'Found himself in the shit, I imagine.'

'She,' Carla emphasised the pronoun, 'was sent home following disciplinary action. I had my knuckles rapped and became one of the most popular women on the base. Never had so much sex in my life.' Finally, she took her eyes away from Olive, but now she was directing that same challenging, provocative stare at Michael. 'Men do love the idea of a bit of girl-on-girl action.'

'Is that right?' Michael answered, his eyes locked on Carla's, and Olive had a sense of being on the verge of something that could quickly spiral out of control.

And then the telltale spinning of the room began. She'd lost count of how much wine she'd had. A whole bottle, maybe more? She needed some water. And wasn't it time Carla went home?

Olive stood, not really sure why: to turn down the heating, open a window, find Carla's coat? Oh right, water. She stumbled and slid back down into her chair; a giggle escaped before she could stop it.

'Do you have a preference?' Michael asked Carla.

'I do.' Carla turned back to face Olive and leaned across the table. Olive could smell her perfume, and her sweat. The flat really was very hot. Michael's eyes were flicking between the two women. 'I prefer both at once,' Carla finished.

'I think we all need some coffee.' Olive tried to get up; at least, she tried to try. Maybe she only thought about getting up.

Then a hand crept onto Olive's knee and she felt a surge of annoyance at Michael; he should be backing her up, recognising her discomfort and gently steering their guest towards the door. Not touching up his wife. And then she spotted both his hands on the table, cupping his wine glass, and the thigh being gently stroked was her left, closer to Carla than to her husband.

'What do you think, Olive?' The hand crept higher. 'Shall we try a kiss? See what you think?' And then she was moving, gliding up out of her seat, leaning over Olive. 'You really are quite beautiful,' she murmured, as she bent her head.

'Mike?' Leaning back, away from the other woman, Olive waited for her husband to say this had gone far enough.

He didn't. He shifted on his chair, as though uncomfortable, as though he had an erection. There was no help coming from him.

'No.' Olive pushed herself up. 'This is inappropriate. It's time for you to go, Carla. I'm calling you a cab.'

Without waiting for a response, Olive found her phone. She had the number of several London taxi firms saved and the first she tried promised to have a car round in ten minutes. Several MPs had flats in the block and the local firms were always punctual.

Ignoring the other two, she began clearing away, loading the dishwasher, carrying uneaten food to the fridge. She made her movements harsher, more deliberate, noisier than they needed to be, partly to disguise the fact that she was still a little drunk, but also so they wouldn't see her hands shaking. Out of the corner of her eye, she saw Carla exchanging glances with Michael, even having a whispered conversation. When the doorbell rang, she forced herself to say goodbye politely, but refused to go anywhere near the woman.

As the door closed behind their guest, Michael yawned. 'Bed, I think,' he announced. 'Don't be long, babe. You and Carla have rather got me worked up with your antics.'

Olive heard the sound of water running in the bathroom, the lavatory being flushed. She heard the beeping sounds as he set an alarm for the morning, then the bed springs settling. She stayed where she was, in a room that seemed to have lost all its heat, feeling weak and exhausted but wide awake at the same time.

She also really wanted sex right now, just not with Michael, damn it.

When she knew it was either sleep on the couch or go to bed, she went into the next room. A lamp was shining softly on her side of the bed and Michael was still awake, propped up against the pillow. She ignored him. He watched her undress.

Olive found a T-shirt and kept her knickers on, lying down on the very edge of the bed, her back to her husband, as far from him as she could get. She switched out the light, hoping he'd get the hint; at the same time, hoping he wouldn't.

She heard the sheets rustle, felt the mattress move beneath her, then Michael's hand on her shoulder pulled her to face him as he leaned over her in the darkness. She stiffened beneath him, even as sparks were flying in her stomach.

He slipped his hand into her pants. She squirmed away, not wanting him to know how wet she was, but his finger found her and she felt the soft tickle of a deep sigh in her ear. She closed her eyes. The darkness would help, it always did.

'Ever wondered what it would be like with a woman?' he asked as his finger moved inside her.

Olive's eyes opened. The London flat was never fully dark and she could see her husband's eyes gleaming, inches above hers. His finger stopped moving.

'Well, have you?' he repeated.

She moved her hand down to find his and pressed it into her groin, pushing rhythmically. He pulled back, forcing her to answer him.

'I suppose,' she said. 'Most women do at some point. When they're young, usually, not that sure about their sexuality.'

As though to reward her honesty, his finger began moving again. Another joined it, widening her folds, slipping inside her. Olive opened her thighs.

'Ever wanted to try?' he asked, shifting his weight so that he was directly above her.

'Not with Carla,' she said. 'What was that all about?'

'Nothing.' He bent his head to kiss her neck. 'Just messing about.'

Olive stiffened. 'It didn't feel like nothing. It felt like a test.'

He sighed, as though she was the one being unreasonable. 'Don't make a big deal out of it. You're enough for me, you know that, right?'

Olive murmured her assent and he carried on kissing her, his head moving lower as he slid down the bed. She opened her legs wide to allow him in and closed her eyes again.

So, it had begun.

32

'No, absolutely not. I didn't have anyone make calls to the hotel in Hexham and I never had any intention of joining Olive there. When did you say it was supposed to have happened?'

Not long back from his morning surgery, Anderson had horses to see to, and had asked if Garry could talk to him while he gave them their lunchtime feed. They'd set off towards a quadrangle of stables a short distance from the house.

'We don't have an exact day and time yet, sir,' Garry replied. 'We need to speak to the people at the hotel again.'

The wind was bitter, blowing snow into their faces, and even at midday, the sun couldn't penetrate the cloud cover. It was an exposed spot, where wind had blown snow across vast acres of open moorland. Drystone walls, even hedges and short, stubby trees, had all but vanished in places; in others, the dead vegetation stood upright like the pelt of an old animal. Dull brown sheep left filthy trails behind them.

It had been Lexy's idea to split up. 'I'll take the mother-in-law,' she'd said. 'I've a feeling she might talk if Anderson isn't in earshot. You speak to him.'

'You don't think you should do that?' Garry had been struck by an attack of nerves. 'You're the detective, not to mention the sergeant.'

'You've had detective training. And been freelancing already today. I think you can cope.'

Garry hadn't argued further, had even been touched by her confidence and by learning she'd been asking about him. Then he'd realised the make-up and smarter clothes might be for Anderson's benefit and felt himself deflating like a three-day-old party balloon. And, if she knew he'd been through detective training, she also knew he'd failed his exams. Twice.

Anderson stopped by the open door of a storeroom, stepped inside and handed a bucket containing small brown pellets out to Garry. Two more followed and then, carrying three buckets himself, Anderson led the way across the quad.

'As soon as you've got details of that phone call, let me know,' he said. 'Chances are, I can prove it wasn't from my people.'

Anderson might have had even less sleep than Garry. Deep shadows lined his eyes. He'd shaved, making an effort for his constituents at that morning's surgery, but his breath, when the two men got close, smelled of stale booze and stomach acid.

'Have you ever been to the hotel in question?' Garry asked, as Anderson opened a stable door, used his shoulder to push the waiting horse out of the way and released one of the buckets. He came out with an empty bucket.

'Kicks his water over several times a day,' he said, as he filled it at a nearby tap. 'Stroppy bugger. And no, I haven't. Neither had Olive before last night, as far as I'm aware.'

'DS Thomas tells me you were planning to talk to Mrs Anderson's friends and family this morning,' Garry said. 'Any luck?'

Anderson shook his head. 'I spoke to the three women she sees most often,' he said. 'All oncology nurses at Middlesbrough. And a couple more from her gym. None of them have heard from her.'

'Were they surprised?'

Anderson gave him a sharp look. 'How do you mean?'

'You call out of the blue, telling them your wife's gone missing. They would have been alarmed, surely?'

'I played it down as much as I could.'

'How?'

'What?'

'How do you play something like that down? I mean, I can't think of any way of saying, I don't know where my wife is, that wouldn't set alarm bells ringing.'

'You're a traffic constable, is that right?' Anderson said. 'Here as DS Thomas's driver? You'll forgive me if I say I'd prefer to be interrogated by a detective.'

'I did the training,' Garry muttered, as Anderson set off along the row of stables, leaving him behind. For several seconds, he was tempted to throw in the towel. Anderson was right, this wasn't his job, and there was a reason he'd twice failed his exams.

And then he pictured Lexy's face if he did.

'Big place you've got here,' Garry said, as he caught up. 'Must take some looking after.'

Anderson glared round for a second before showing the politician's ability to turn on the charm. 'Tell me about it,' he said. 'But it's Gwen's place, not mine. The Warners have farmed here for two centuries. We've three hundred head of cattle and five hundred of sheep, plus the arable land. Half these horses aren't ours, though, they're paid liveries. And Gwen runs the farm shop. Anything to make the land pay.'

Another stable, another bucket dropped off. Across the quad, Garry spotted a girl in her teens leading a blanket-covered brown horse towards an empty box. Then Anderson led him into another outbuilding, this time a hay store. It felt warmer in here, probably the insulating effect of so many bales of hay and straw stacked around the walls; an open loft, accessed by a ladder and covering nearly half the internal space, held more neatly stacked bales. As a boy, Garry had had an odd fantasy about sleeping in a hayloft. As he looked upwards, a beam of sunlight made a patch of hay gleam like gold.

'This is still a farming community,' Anderson was saying. 'Living here gives me credibility with a lot of constituents, especially the ones who used to vote for the Conservatives.'

'How does Mrs Anderson like it?' Garry followed the other man outside, to see that the brief flash of sunlight had vanished without trace. 'The second Mrs Anderson, I mean.'

Anderson gave him a sharp look.

'Eloise and I – that's my first wife – didn't live here. We had our own place in the village. The girls and I moved in after Eloise died.

I had to be away most of the week, and it seemed the best way to give the girls some stability.'

Garry reminded himself that politicians were experts in neatly avoiding questions they didn't like. He waited, knowing silence sometimes worked better than insistence.

Anderson sighed. 'When Olive and I got married, there was no question of her giving up work and the girls didn't want to leave. She and I agreed it was best for her to move in here.'

Garry said nothing.

'Maybe I should have insisted we have our own place,' Anderson went on. 'But the girls were pressuring me, Gwen didn't want us to move out and Olive seemed OK with it. I opted for the easy life. Maybe I'm paying the price now.'

He stopped at the last loose box and let the remaining bucket clang to the ground. The waiting horse bent to nuzzle the side of Anderson's head. He gave another heavy sigh and raised his hand in an absent-minded pat of the horse's neck. Tears filled his eyes.

Push him, Lexy had said in the car. The bloke's relationship with his wife is key to this.

Yet another reason why Garry had failed to make the grade: he wasn't ruthless enough.

'I was at school with Olive,' he surprised himself by saying. 'Nice girl. I liked her a lot.'

Anderson looked at him with renewed interest. 'Everyone likes Olive,' he said. 'She has a charm about her. Simply walking into a room, she lifts your spirits somehow.'

Yes, that was how it had been. A smile, a snatched hello – because apart from that incident by the West Gate of school, they'd never said much more to each other than that – and his day had been made.

'Do you think she was happy here?' Garry turned a half-circle, gesturing out to the stable buildings, the barns and sheds, the acres of land. 'It's a lot to deal with if you're not from this sort of back-ground. And living with the mother of your late wife? I'm sure she's a very nice lady, and your daughters are lovely girls, but Olive wasn't their mother. Or Mrs Warner's daughter.'

'You think I don't know that?' Anderson looked angry now. 'You think we didn't talk about it? I'm not a fool. But Olive had a busy job, she was out ten, twelve hours a day. When I was home, I made sure we had time together, quality time. She knew how much she meant to me. It wasn't ideal, but it was the best compromise.'

Anderson was angry with himself, Garry realised, not with the unassuming copper who'd come to question him.

'Come on,' Anderson said, as he set off again. 'It's freezing. Let's get some coffee on.'

The back door of the farmhouse was barely a hundred metres away. Through a window, Garry could see two heads of blonde hair.

Push, Lexy had said, you're not trying to make this guy your mate.

Garry said, 'Do you mind me asking how the two of you met?'

'She nursed my late wife,' Anderson replied. 'Eloise died in Middlesbrough General. Olive was amazing. I think I fell in love with her the night my wife died, and I know how strange that sounds.'

It didn't sound strange at all to Garry that someone should fall in love with Olive.

Abruptly, Anderson stopped walking. 'We've only been married six months,' he said.

Push him, Lexy had insisted. Damn it.

'And are you happy? Sorry to ask.'

Anderson turned so quickly, Garry felt a stab of fear.

'I was,' he said. 'Happier than I've ever been.'

33

Olive felt for her seat-belt fastener and a spasm of pain shot through her chest. Blanking it out as best she could, breathing through it when she couldn't, she tried again and this time made it. She heard it unclip, then the rustle of the webbing as it reeled itself in. She reached out towards the headrest of the driver's seat. With a solid grip on that, she could pull herself upright.

Now.

Bracing both feet in the footwell, she pulled herself away from the passenger door, even as her lungs felt like something was ripping them from the inside. The metal of the car groaned as though it might fall apart and the vehicle gave a sickening lurch. Olive's head banged against the dashboard. The world went dark.

Olive's head jerked up. She couldn't have fallen asleep, not standing up, her forehead pressed against the cold bathroom tiles, but for a moment there, she'd actually gone somewhere else in a sort of weird, half faint. Her forehead hurt, as though she'd banged it. Turning, she caught a glimpse in the mirror; her face was ashen, her eyes reddened. Around her, the bathroom was silent. The sound of the cistern had subsided.

She crossed the huge, ridiculously luxurious room – clawfoot bath, shower big enough for a party, the place even had a padded chaise longue for God's sake – and opened the door to the bedroom: another enormous space with a king-sized four-poster on a raised platform. She hadn't known places like this existed outside the movies. It was all ridiculously expensive, but, as Michael had argued, it was only for four days.

A four-day honeymoon. He'd been so apologetic, explaining how leaving the girls for any longer felt the wrong thing to do; they were building a family now, not spinning a cocoon around themselves to the exclusion of all else. He'd been pathetically grateful when she'd agreed without question.

Michael was on the stone balcony that overlooked the hotel's terrace and surrounding parkland. He watched her step out through the French windows to join him.

'OK?' His face was a picture of concern.

'Fine. Sorry about that.'

The second she sat beside him, he reached out and took her hand, giving it a little tug so that she was forced to make eye contact.

'Olive, are you—'

How many times could she tell him she was fine? 'Am I what?' It came out sharper than she'd intended.

He looked to be plucking up courage before, 'Are you pregnant?'

'God, no.' It came out without thinking. 'No,' she said, more slowly. 'I'm not pregnant. I told you, one of those prawns wasn't fresh.'

'And of all those plates they had to put it on the bride's.'

There had been nothing wrong with the prawns. The prawns, like everything else at the wedding, had been perfect. But throwing up four times in thirty-six hours would have anyone asking questions.

Michael sighed. 'I can't bear to think of you not . . .' He left the thought hanging.

'Not perfect?' she asked.

'Not perfectly happy,' he corrected. 'Not happy the way I am.'

Her new husband got up and leaned over her chair. Olive closed her eyes. The kiss went on for a long time, predictably going from tender to passionate. Olive found herself wishing she hadn't cleaned her teeth, hadn't repeatedly doused with mouthwash, because if Michael had tasted the vomit in her mouth, he might finally have some idea of what she was going through.

34

The kitchen wasn't a large room, certainly by the standards of some of the huge modern family kitchens Garry had been in, but it was spacious enough, with plenty of light; and warm, thanks to a shiny green Aga against one wall. The cupboards were wood, painted a colour somewhere between milk and cream, and the ceiling beams low enough for him to feel an urge to stoop. A brick-lined fireplace faced the Aga; a saddle sat over one stool.

On the wall immediately behind the door was a large cork notice-board. Garry took a seat at the table, close enough to see what the Andersons had pinned to it. Recipes, concert tickets, a train ticket linked to a senior citizen's railcard, a thin, stapled-together stack of A4 paper with the logo of Middlesbrough hospital along its top edge. Most of the space was taken up by a month-by-month calendar with family movements scribbled in most of the squares.

'You should,' Lexy said, when Gwen asked if Garry would like coffee. 'You need to know what real coffee tastes like.'

Garry smiled and thanked Gwen. The coffee she poured was rich and strong and he could almost feel his heartbeat picking up in response.

'I must get to the shop,' Gwen said. 'I'll leave the three of you to talk.'

As Gwen left the room, Lexy said, 'I'm new in the area, but I believe you've made a bit of a stand with regard to a local organised crime gang, sir.'

Anderson's eyes narrowed. 'The Tricks family? They're one of the biggest problems we face in the area. Half the youngsters in prison or on drugs are as a result of the Tricks family's drug-smuggling activities. We've had young Eastern European people, men and women, working as slaves in Middlesbrough thanks to them. And that's before you get started on the whole vigilante business. So, yes, I've spoken out against organised crime. You could say, it's my thing.'

Garry felt something brushing against his leg; he bent, to see a young black spaniel gazing up at him curiously.

'On the other hand, I'm not sure I've achieved much. My late wife, Eloise, was involved in a money-laundering prosecution that could have seen several of them go down. The trial collapsed when vital evidence mysteriously vanished.'

Garry said, 'The late Mrs Anderson was a criminal barrister, is that right, sir?'

Anderson nodded. 'She kept her maiden name, though. Eloise Warner.'

Lexy said, 'Have you received any threats that you could, perhaps, link to them?'

Anderson's body tensed. 'You think this is something to do with the Tricks gang?'

'We've no reason to think that at this stage,' Lexy replied quickly. 'But we do have to consider all possibilities.'

Anderson got to his feet. 'If it was the Tricks family, I'd have heard something, wouldn't I? A ransom demand, some idea of what they wanted?'

He walked to the window and stood looking out, towards the outbuildings he and Garry had recently been in and out of: the stables, tack room, hayloft.

'We've no reason to believe the Tricks family are involved,' Lexy repeated.

'The footage we've got of Mrs Anderson leaving the hotel doesn't appear to be an abduction,' Garry added, remembering all the while that Olive had looked far from happy.

Without Anderson's eyes on him, he leaned closer to the cork board and glanced over it. There was no reference to Olive that he could see on the calendar, but the A4 stack was a printout of her hospital schedule.

'But we are concerned that she didn't show up at work this morning,' Lexy said. 'From what I understand, that isn't like your wife at all.'

Still, Anderson stared out of the window. 'No,' he said. 'It isn't.'

'How long before you make this public?' Anderson asked as he led them back towards the front door. 'I need to brief my constituency office, and my team in London. I should probably call the leader of the opposition's office as well.'

To one side of the door stood a slender hall table, its surface barely visible beneath rows of silver-framed photographs. From visiting houses such as this one, Garry had learned that posh people kept family photographs on tables; if they were rich enough, on grand pianos. Never, like in his own parents' house, on the walls.

'I need to prepare the girls too,' Anderson went on. 'They're used to media attention, but nothing like what this will unleash.'

Several of the pictures featured a sailing boat, sometimes with white sails, other times a huge green and purple sail at the front. In most of them, Anderson was at the helm, the women of the family gathered around him in the cockpit, checking ropes, looking up at the sails. There were family wedding photographs too, even one in which Olive stood front and centre in an ivory lace dress. Her bouquet was simple, but expensive, if those were gardenias he could see.

'There's no hard and fast rule,' Lexy replied. 'It all depends on the circumstances, the wishes of the relatives, the vulnerability of the person involved. I'd say by Monday morning at the latest, if we haven't heard from Mrs Anderson, the chief will issue a formal missing persons enquiry. Sooner, if circumstances change.'

They paused on the threshold. 'I don't know what to do for the best,' Anderson said. 'If Olive has left me, a media circus won't do any of us any good, least of all her. On the other hand, if the Tricks family are involved . . .'

He didn't finish.

'I'll be in touch again the minute we know anything,' Lexy assured him. 'Garry, you ready?'

Garry dragged his gaze away from the photograph he'd spotted at the very back, obscured by several others. Taken in a hot, dry country, it featured a group of soldiers, all in heavy combat uniform. Michael Anderson stood in the middle of the group.

Garry moved swiftly away from the table. He and Lexy said their goodbyes, reiterated their promises to keep Anderson informed and climbed back into Garry's car.

'So, Olive Anderson does not get on with the women of her new husband's family,' Lexy said, as Garry drove away from the farmhouse. 'The girls hate her because she replaced their mother, and because their dad's nuts about her, and Gwen hates her because she's a constant reminder of the daughter she lost.'

'She said all that?'

'It's called reading between the lines. According to Gwen, it's all Olive's fault. Olive makes no effort with the girls, works late, spends her free time at the gym or out somewhere, monopolises Michael when he's home. And she picks fights, tries to get Michael on her side. Someone's been trolling her on Facebook. Gwen dismisses it as the usual stuff aimed at politicians and their families, but Olive was convinced it was the girls because there were a lot of unflattering comparisons between Olive and her predecessor. Gwen's take is that any reasonable person could measure Olive up against Eloise and find Olive lacking.'

'That's a lot of reading between the lines.'

'No, most of that she did tell me. She also told me that Olive is sneaky. More than once, Gwen caught her in the attic, although none of her own stuff was up there, and she spent a lot of time in Michael's study, but only when he wasn't in the house.'

'What was she looking for?' Garry asked.

'Exactly what Gwen wanted to know. She also thinks Olive's run away. She never really loved Michael, only married him because of his position, and has been unhappy from the beginning. She jumps at any excuse to be away, even booking hotel rooms when she's an easy drive from home.'

'Hexham,' Garry said.

'Exactly. She warned me she'll be advising her son to play down the disappearance as it will be very bad for his public image. She was, not so subtly, trying to suggest I drop my enquiry for the next forty-eight hours.'

'Sounds like she made her feelings very clear.'

'Oh, she did. Not to be confused with being truthful. Or telling me the whole truth.'

'How do you mean?'

'There's definitely something she's not saying. A bit more pressure might drag it out of her.'

As long as she didn't ask him to do it.

'I believe him, though,' Lexy added. 'He's gutted.'

Garry was disappointed, he realised, that Lexy, who he'd considered bright up until now – annoying, but bright – should have fallen for a handsome face.

'He's a liar,' he replied.

When she turned his way, he noticed her lipstick had gone, probably left behind on one of the family's coffee mugs. She said, 'How do you mean?'

'Anderson left the army seven years ago, right?'

'If you say so.'

'He did. I checked online last night. He told me he'd met Olive when she nursed his first wife in Middlesbrough General two years ago. Spun me a very touching yarn. Only it isn't true. I've just seen a photograph taken during his army days. Afghanistan, I shouldn't wonder. Olive was in the picture. He's known her for years.'

35

The bang on the head wasn't serious. Olive didn't lose consciousness for very long at all, maybe only a few seconds. She crouched in the footwell, waiting for the nausea caused by the fresh pain to subside. As her breathing became easier, pins and needles kicked in.

When she dared risk lifting her head, she saw that the angle of the car had changed again. Instead of the passenger door being the lowest point, in contact with the ground, it now looked as though the entire vehicle was balancing on the car's front left bumper. That should not be possible; unless that corner of the car had rolled into a ditch.

The groaning of metal continued. Olive waited, holding her breath, for the car to shift again.

And then something new was happening, even as she watched. The snow that had collected overnight against the fractured passenger window was falling away. It crumbled at first, almost like sand trickling out of an hourglass, then gathered momentum as gravity kicked in and bigger and bigger lumps of compressed snow broke off. Fragments of window glass fell too.

After hours of being enclosed in a tiny white cell, she could see into the outside world again. Light flooded the car. Olive could see blood on her hands and on the window surround. Were she to look up and back – which she really didn't want to do – she would see a corpse hanging above her.

What she could see, arguably, was even worse. It wasn't snow-covered ground a few feet below the empty window frame, nor was it rocky ground or the cushioning of undergrowth. What she could see was a void.

A noise, unnaturally loud in the quiet, startled her and it was several seconds before she realised what was happening. The snow from the roof of the car and the windscreen was falling too. The new angle the car had found for itself was making everything shift. She watched more snow appear in the square left by the window and then fall far below her. The windscreen cleared, leaving a blurry smear of white across the glass and through it she could make out the thick black limbs of trees.

This was impossible. The car could not have landed in a tree.

Taking her nerve in hand, Olive reached out and pushed the last remnants of clinging snow and fractured glass away from the window. Finally, she could see clearly; finally, she understood.

The ground was some thirty feet below.

The car had rolled to the edge of a gully, formed thousands of years ago by one of the smaller rivers that fed the Tyne. A cluster of spindly trees, little more than hedgerow plantings, were all that were stopping her car from plummeting over the edge.

PART TWO

The suspicious death of Eloise Warner

36

'Olive? Are you OK?'

Startled, Olive dragged her eyes from the living skeleton in the hospital bed. 'Sorry,' she said. 'I was miles away.'

'I'll say.' Stella sounded waspish, but she often did. 'Do you need a hand?'

'No, I've got this. Thanks, Stel.'

As Stella moved on to the next patient, a lady with dementia and stage-four liver cancer, drawing screens around the bed, Olive breathed a sigh of relief. Her heart was beating ridiculously fast, but that, at least, wouldn't be visible on the outside.

The skeleton on the bed stirred; a frown flickered across her face before she relaxed once more into a heavily drugged sleep.

Eloise Warner.

The bed notes told Olive that the patient was a forty-two-year-old female in the end stages of terminal ovarian cancer, prescribed palliative care. The only reason she wasn't in the adjacent hospice was a lack of available beds. She'd remain on the oncology ward, although there was nothing they could do other than keep her comfortable, until space became available.

Eloise. Such a lovely name. She'd been a lovely woman before cancer had sucked everything essentially human from her: tall and slender, with curly, strawberry-blonde hair and a perfect, heart-shaped face. A highly-thought-of criminal barrister, Eloise Warner was married to the local MP, with two daughters as good-looking as their parents. She'd had the perfect life. A short life, as it turned out.

Olive was still shaking. Eloise Warner. Utterly helpless. Entirely dependent now. Upon her.

What an extraordinary twist of fate.

'Olive, are you done? I need a hand.'

Olive joined Stella at the next bed and, as gently as they could, because the old lady was in some discomfort, they pulled away the sodden pants and changed the damp sheet. She whimpered, pitifully, when the cold wipes touched her skin.

'Shame.' Stella jerked her head towards Eloise's supine body. 'Mind you, gorgeous husband.' Even Stella had the grace to lower her voice. 'Be on the market soon.'

Olive made a *what the fuck* face. Stella, a decent enough nurse, could be appallingly indiscreet. Stella shrugged, glancing down at the elderly woman before mouthing *Away with the fairies* at Olive.

'Got a couple of kids too,' Stella went on. 'No one should have to die at Christmas. Especially not a young mum.'

Back at the nurses' station, in the brief lull between the medicine round and lunch arriving, Olive relented. 'I served with Michael Anderson,' she told Stella. 'In Afghanistan.'

She had a clear view of Eloise's bed, directly under the window. The woman didn't appear to have moved in over an hour.

Stella looked interested. 'Oh, well, you're in then. Head start on the rest of us.'

Stella had been married, happily as far as Olive knew, for over twenty years.

Olive said, 'I doubt he'll even remember me.'

She and Michael Anderson had rarely crossed paths out in Helmand and everything she knew about him back then had been by reputation.

Stella asked, 'What was he like?'

Olive thought for a moment. 'Good officer. Well thought of. Led from the front, but never reckless. Had a good instinct for what was happening on the ground.'

'Faithful to his wife?' Stella had an unseemly shine in her eyes.

'Far as I know. There weren't many women on the base, and those few weren't in his league.'

'I expect he'll be in later. If you want to, you know, touch up your lipstick.'

'You're a disgrace to the profession.'

'Hey, I'm only thinking of you. It's been – what – six months since Mark?'

'Nine,' Olive corrected.

She'd kept the story simple when she'd arrived on the oncology ward. She and her long-term boyfriend, Mark, had recently split. It had been a tough break, and if after-work socialising didn't really work for her right now, well, that was why. She'd discouraged questions, kept herself to herself and her colleagues at arm's length. For the most part, it had worked. People had accepted that Olive was something of a loner and that was exactly what she wanted. Above all, she didn't want anyone getting too interested in her former boyfriend.

Because Mark was entirely fictitious.

Towards the end of the afternoon, Eloise's family arrived, her two daughters first. Both looked tall for their ages, which, thanks to an internet search during her break, Olive knew to be ten and twelve, and both had perfect skin and curly fair hair. The younger was perhaps a little more like their mother, the older favouring their father. Both wore the uniform of a local private school.

'I'll get you some more chairs.' Olive made herself smile at the two girls. Visiting their sick mother over the coming weeks would take a lot out of Eloise's daughters, especially if she stayed on the ward for any amount of time. Eloise needed to be in the hospice, where she'd have her own room and where the family could grieve privately. The hospice had a family lounge in which visitors could make hot drinks and simple meals, watch TV or read for a while and rest. Few people understood, until they went through it themselves, how exhausting it could be to attend upon the dying.

'Your mum's been asleep most of the afternoon,' she told the girls when she returned, at the same time bracing for the sort of questions that came so often from children. *When can Mummy come home? Is she getting any better?* None came. These two knew their mother was dying.

'Sorry about that,' said a voice Olive knew and she turned to see a tall man in an impeccably cut suit slipping a mobile phone into his jacket pocket. 'How is she?'

Michael Anderson was several years older than when Olive had last seen him, but, if anything, had got better looking. Longer hair suited him and he made the most of it, slicking it back from his forehead to flop around one ear. He had a touch of grey at his temples and flecks of red in his close-trimmed beard. She remembered the once-broken nose, but not the soft grey eyes.

As Olive stepped out of the way, the younger girl took hold of her mother's hand. 'Mum, it's Jess. We've come to see you. Are you awake, Mum?'

Anderson was looking at Olive, not his wife. 'We know each other, don't we?'

Nothing to be gained by denying it.

'Olive Charles.' She gave him a half-smile, enough to show sympathy, not so much as to appear insensitive. It was easier with him, she found, than with the girls. 'Afghanistan,' she went on. 'Camp Viking. I'm very sorry about your wife's illness.'

As Anderson held her gaze, Olive saw Stella drawing closer. And the nurses' station had suddenly got a whole lot busier.

'Thank you,' he said. 'When did you leave the army?'

'Dad, Mum's trying to talk to you.'

Sure enough, Eloise's eyes were open and one emaciated, yellow-skinned hand was reaching up towards her husband. Turning his attention to his wife, Anderson took her hand and smiled.

'Let me know if you need anything.' Olive walked back to the nurses' station, taking in an arch stare from Stella as she did so.

The family's visit lasted a little under thirty minutes and during that time, Olive saw Michael Anderson's eyes flick her way more than once.

'Oh, I'd say he remembers you,' Stella muttered in her ear.

37

'You think Anderson is lying when he says he didn't have his secretary phone the hotel?' Lexy asked, as they reached the outskirts of town.

While Garry had spent much of the journey from Guisborough checking weather reports and racking his brain in futile attempts to figure out where Olive might be, Lexy had been on the phone, checking in with the station, and asking the hotel to compile a list of previous occupants of room seven. The crime scene investigators – CSIs – would be there that afternoon, she'd told Garry in between calls. Annoyingly, both the waiter who'd served the couple in the restaurant, and the receptionist who'd checked them out, weren't due back on duty until Tuesday of the following week. A couple themselves, they'd gone away for the weekend and so far the hotel hadn't been able to contact them. They'd learned nothing further about Olive's companion.

The companion was key to it, he knew. Find the companion and they found Olive. Meanwhile, Lexy had asked him a question: Did he think Anderson was lying?

'I wouldn't rule it out,' Garry said. There was something about Anderson that didn't add up.

'But why ten days before her stay? And why that elaborate charade about sending flowers? Why would he need her to be in a particular room?'

Questions he couldn't answer. 'Anderson got cagey when I asked him about his conversations with Olive's friends,' he said instead.

'I didn't even get onto her family. How do we know what they're saying to him? You should call them yourself.'

She nodded. 'I will. Wait, pull over! Emergency.'

Garry's reactions behind the wheel were lightning fast. In less than a second, he'd checked his mirrors, indicated, and braked to a halt. A spray of dirty snow fountained up and covered a cockapoo that had been stepping gingerly through the slush on the pavement. He held up a hand in silent apology to its owner.

'Won't be a sec.' Lexy opened the passenger door and jumped out.

'What's going on?' The street looked entirely normal: shoppers treading carefully, shops with their garish Christmas lights, a festive jingle playing somewhere close by. Mystified, he watched Lexy cross the pavement and disappear inside a Domino's.

'Well, I have to come in,' she argued, fifteen minutes later, when he pulled up on his drive. 'You wouldn't let me eat in the car and it'll be cold by the time I drive to my place. Come on, Garry, I'm starving. I got a large one.'

He was starving too. The bacon bap on the road to Hexham felt like a long time ago.

Sighing, he climbed out and opened the front door. Lexy followed him in, and for the next five minutes they didn't talk. She ate like she did everything else, at full speed. The box was barely open before she dived in, grabbing a slice and cramming half of it into her mouth. Garry found plates, knives and forks and tore off two squares of kitchen roll to act as napkins. He filled two glasses of water from the tap and, finally, joined her.

Lexy used the plate but ate with her fingers. Hating messy eaters, Garry braced himself for the usual feelings of revulsion. Still waiting, he helped himself to a slice. The pizza was sweet, greasy, slightly sickly, and every bit as delicious as she'd promised.

'Are you expected back at work?' he asked, when he thought he had a chance of getting an answer. Lexy had wolfed down two slices and was pouring water down her throat.

'Yep.' She wiped her mouth on the back of her hand. 'But I've a feeling I'm going to be diverted onto another job. So, I need a favour.'

'Another one?'

As a knock sounded on the front door, Lexy pulled a quizzical face. 'Your next-door neighbour's very anxious to have her path cleared,' she said. 'We had quite a chat while we were waiting for you to get out of bed.'

If only, thought Garry. If only it was Mrs Tyler on the front step. Wondering briefly what the chances were of smuggling Lexy out the back, he went to answer the door.

'Hi, Mum.' He bent to kiss his mother's cheek. 'You shouldn't have come out in this snow. I could have brought everything round this evening.'

'I had a few errands.' His mum brushed past him towards the kitchen. 'I wanted to get them done before it starts again. Hello, who's this?'

'I'm Lexy.' The sergeant grinned. 'Garry and I are working a case together. Would you like some pizza?'

'And will you be on duty over Christmas, love?' Janet Mizon was saying, when Garry came back into the kitchen from his brief trip out back. 'Or will you get home to see your folks?'

His mum had declined pizza, but that sounded like the kettle coming to the boil. He stood in the doorway, holding a box of earth-encrusted vegetables.

'Duty, I'm afraid, Mrs M,' Lexy replied. 'I probably won't have to go in, but they need someone from CID on call. I'm the newbie, so it falls to me.'

Garry kept hold of the box, hopefully signalling he was ready to carry it out to the car. He wanted his mum safely on her way home; the last thing he needed was to be worrying about another woman he cared about. Janet, though, gave him a brief smile and turned her attention back to Lexy.

'But that's the worst of all worlds, isn't it? You'll have to come round to us.'

Oh, good grief.

'I can't do that.' Lexy shot an amused look at Garry. 'You want your family around at Christmas, not a perfect stranger.'

'Rubbish, you're a friend of Garry's. We hardly ever get to meet his girl— his friends. He's always been close. We can put you up in the spare room so you don't have to worry about having a drink.'

'Mum, the last thing Lexy needs is to spend her precious day off with a crowd of noisy strangers,' Garry objected. 'And I'm not sure you can fit another chair round the table, to be honest.'

His mum tossed her head. 'Brian's lot aren't coming this year. It's you, me and your dad. And Lexy, now.' She beamed at the younger woman. 'Brian's Garry's uncle. He comes every other year with his wife, two kids and their partners. They're with his wife's family this year.'

'Small mercies,' Garry muttered, striding to the sink. He'd spotted an Asda label on one of the beetroots. He turned on the cold tap and held the beet under the running water.

'Garry doesn't get on with his cousins,' Janet was explaining behind his back. 'Not his fault. They resent him, have done since he was a kid. He was his grandad's favourite. And he got all the money when the old chap died.' Getting up, she joined Garry at the sink, and peered into the box. 'What have we got then?'

The label was caught in the drain, thankfully unrecognisable.

'I didn't realise you were an heiress, Garry,' Lexy said. 'You're suddenly much more attractive.'

He could ignore that; with his back turned, she wouldn't see him glowing red. His bloody mum missed nothing, though. She threw back her head and cackled, a noise he'd never heard coming out of her mouth before and hoped he never would again.

'She's a laugh, isn't she?' His mum had actually nudged him in the ribs. 'Those parsnips look nice. How are the sprouts coming along?' She looked back over her shoulder. 'Is there anything you don't like, love?'

'I'll eat anything that stays still long enough,' Lexy replied.

'Sprouts will be fine next week,' Garry said, loudly. 'I'll drop them round on Christmas Eve.'

'Haven't bought veg for ten years,' Janet told Lexy proudly. 'Not since Garry inherited his grandad's allotment.'

'Land as well as money. It gets better,' Lexy said.

'Not rich, just comfortable,' Janet said. 'I wouldn't want you getting the wrong idea. The old chap left Garry this bungalow, his allotment and a little nest egg. You could do worse, you know.'

Jiminy Cricket, his mum had actually winked at his sergeant.

'Already worked that out,' Lexy said, winking back at her.

'Mum, there's snow forecast any time now,' he said. 'You need to get moving. I'll carry this to the car. Say goodbye to Lexy.'

'Lovely to meet you, love.' Janet beamed at the sergeant as she pulled her coat back on. 'I'll make Garry give me your number so I can be in touch about Christmas. Now, you two won't work all weekend, will you? Have a bit of time off.' She turned back at the kitchen door. 'And if you can do something about his clothes, I'll be forever grateful. I've been nagging him for years.'

'Drive safe, Mum,' Garry said, opening the front door. 'Text me when you're home.'

'Bye, Dumbo, love you.' She stretched up for a kiss and then set off carefully down the path.

Back in the kitchen, Lexy was folding the empty pizza box to make it small enough to fit in the bin. She'd carried the dirty plates and his cutlery to the sink and thrown the napkins away. 'Be grateful arranged marriages aren't a thing in our culture,' she said.

Garry realised, with a sinking heart, that he'd be on the receiving end of jokes about his forthcoming marriage to Lexy for the next six months. Probably until she got herself a local boyfriend and the ribbing no longer felt appropriate. The thought made him sadder than he'd have expected. He was probably just worried about Olive.

'Sorry about that,' he said, annoyed to find himself apologising. Lexy had totally encouraged his mum.

'Why don't you introduce your girlfriends to your parents?' she asked.

He gave her a look. 'You need to ask?'

'She wouldn't be like that if she was used to meeting women here. It was the novelty that made her overexcited.'

'You don't need to come for Christmas,' he said. 'I'll have a word with her.'

For a second, Lexy's face fell. Then, 'Come on then, show me your wardrobe.'

'My what?'

'Your wardrobe. I promised your mum I'd sort your clothes out.'

The kitchen door was already open, but Garry took a hold of the handle all the same. 'Goodbye, Detective Sergeant Thomas, take care on your way back to the station and do let me know if there's anything else I can do to help. I'm back on duty Monday afternoon.'

Monday afternoon? Jeepers, anything could have happened to Olive by then.

For a moment, he thought Lexy would argue, but then she fastened up her coat, collected her bag and pulled on gloves and that cute pink hat, pausing only on the threshold.

'Why does your mum call you Dumbo?'

'I was a plump kid,' he replied. 'She called me her baby elephant.'

'Bit cruel.'

'What can I say? We do tough love in the north-east. Mind how you go, Sergeant.'

Closing the front door, Garry felt breathless, like he'd run the sort of race he hadn't taken part in for years. He was probably more tired that he realised.

In his bedroom, the blinds were still down. He stripped off his clothes without bothering to fold them and slipped, naked, into bed. After several seconds, he realised he'd never sleep.

His phone rang. It was Lexy.

'That favour you said you'd do . . .' she began.

For a second, he was tempted to argue, just so she knew he wasn't a pushover, and decided it wasn't worth the effort.

'I need you to get onto the hotel in Hexham and ask about keys. Was only one given out to room seven? And did Olive make a reservation in the restaurant and, if so, for how many?'

'Why can't you do it?' He might be a pushover, but no need to make it obvious.

'Because there were umpteen arrests last night in connection with the Tricks op and the team only have a few more hours to complete the interviews. Between the two of us, it's not going that well. None of the bullion's been found yet and in spite of your best efforts that necklace is still missing.'

One day he'd hear the end of that. One day before he died.

'So, anyway, they've got me involved and I've prep work to do. Can you help me out, Garry?'

He faked a heavy sigh. 'Leave it with me. Sleep's overrated anyway.'

She was gone.

He got up, shivering in the sudden chill, dressed quickly and got back into his car.

38

Eloise was hobbling her way across the ward when Olive returned from the sluice room. She hadn't bothered with slippers or a dressing gown and her nightdress – ankle-length flannel, chosen for comfort not style – hung loose on her thin, rigid frame. She walked as though stepping on gravel, each step painful, but she was still walking, still insisting on getting out of bed and making her own way to the toilet.

Olive watched her slow, shaky progress across the floor.

The MP's wife hadn't eaten much in the twenty-four hours or so that she'd been on the ward, but her fluid intake had been satisfactory. She slept much of the time and struggled to maintain a conversation for more than a few minutes, but she still watched TV, especially the news, and made an effort to engage when her family visited. In Olive's view, she was some weeks, possibly as much as a month, from death.

One could never know for sure, though.

Two metres from the bed, Eloise swayed, her eyes losing focus.

Olive was by her side in seconds. 'Steady on, Ms Warner.' Her arm wrapped around the other woman's waist. 'I've got you. Take it easy now.'

While her words were the same she'd have used for any patient, and the arm supporting the sick woman offered the same combination of strength and gentleness, Olive was conscious of a coolness inside. This was the only patient on the ward whom she addressed formally. Ms Warner, not Eloise.

She lowered the patient onto her bed and carefully lifted her feet. Eloise winced as her legs were drawn up.

'Sorry.' Olive drew bedcovers over the stick-thin legs. 'We can always bring you a bedpan, it's really no trouble.'

'You're very kind,' Eloise gasped, her breathlessness the result of pain as much as exertion. The tumour would be pressing on her internal organs, her nervous system, even her bones. She was on a strict regimen of pain management, but break-through pain was a constant battle in final-stage cancer. 'I wasn't going to the toilet, though,' she went on. 'I was coming to find you, or one of the nurses.'

Olive refrained from pointing out that there was a call button by each patient's bed.

'There was a woman in here a minute ago,' Eloise went on. 'You may have passed her in the corridor.'

Olive had a vague recollection of a tall woman whisking past as she'd pushed open the ward door with her hip. She'd barely caught more than a glimpse.

'I don't want to see her again,' Eloise gasped. 'Can you make sure she doesn't come in again? I can ask my husband to organise security if it's needed.'

'Not a journalist, surely?' Olive asked. Earlier that day, photographers and even a TV crew had been spotted hanging around the hospital's main entrance in the hope of catching a picture of the grief-stricken possible future prime minister. An official complaint had only resulted in them moving to the car park. Coming up to the ward though?

Eloise was shaking her head. 'Not a journalist,' she muttered.

'Any visitor upsetting you will be asked to leave immediately,' Olive said. 'If you give me her name, I'll make sure the other staff know not to admit her.'

Eloise's eyes dropped. 'She didn't give a name. She was one of Michael's constituents, I think. A disgruntled one. There are always a few. She wanted me to argue her case with Michael. I can't. I don't have the energy.'

'Of course not. Look, try to get some rest now. I'll make sure all the staff know to be vigilant about people approaching your bed. We might be able to get the door locked temporarily as well. I'll make enquiries.'

'Thank you.' Eloise looked exhausted. 'And could you put that away, please?'

Olive followed the other woman's line of sight towards a photograph of the Anderson family on a yacht. In sailing gear, all four were gathered around the huge, leather-covered wheel. The youngest daughter appeared to be steering, her father directly behind her, his hands guiding the girl's smaller ones. He was clean-shaven, his hair blowing across his brow, male-model handsome. Olive felt her chest tightening.

'The photograph?' she clarified.

Eloise nodded her head, slowly, as though even her neck hurt. 'In the drawer. Put it away, please. I'll get the girls to bring me another one.'

'It's a lovely picture,' Olive said, taking in the smiling children, the mother's bright curls flying in the wind. 'You all look so happy.'

'We're a politician's family,' Eloise replied bitterly. 'We have spin down to an art form.'

Still, Olive was slow to put the picture away. 'Is that Hartlepool marina?' she asked, although the marina in the photograph's background was impossible to make out from the shot.

Another painful pause and then, 'Yes, do you know it?'

'No, I've never sailed. But I had a friend who went there a few times.'

She waited, to see if Eloise would ask about the friend, who he or she was, what boat they sailed on, but the other woman's eyes had closed. Her breathing, though, hadn't changed. She was still awake.

Interesting.

39

Dusk was falling as Garry pulled up outside the Tricks mansion. He left his car a decent distance down the road from the police tape that still surrounded the property. With a bit of luck, he might not even be noticed.

No one would approve of him coming here, but as long as he stayed away from the crime scene itself, he wasn't actually breaking any laws. What he really didn't want to do was bump into any member of the Tricks family. According to Lexy, though, who'd phoned him again in the car on the way over, they weren't due to be released for another couple of hours.

The front door to the house stood open and a groom could be seen at the entrance to the stable block. Lexy had told him that the search was ongoing, but no one really expected to find anything now. Somehow, Howie Tricks had got wind of the police raid and moved the booty.

The second he reached the grass verge where he'd caught Tina the night before, Garry knew his plan wasn't going to work. A couple more inches of snow had fallen in the last twenty-four hours and he could barely make out the spot where the two of them had struggled. The chances of finding any fragments of bone – the ash would be long gone – were close to zero.

He walked down the lane all the same, shining his torch onto the snow. Even a few pieces, packaged in a nice box with a floral wrap, might have helped Tina feel better.

'You after something, mate?'

Garry turned to see a man not four metres away wearing an

oversized flying jacket and heavy-duty boots. In the fading light, his tan looked a sickly shade of yellow, but his movements were as sharp as they'd been the previous night. Howie Tricks, who would have very good lawyers, had been released already.

Garry was conscious of his chest tightening. 'I was here last night. I thought I might have dropped something.' It was his prepared lie. How could he have known he'd have to deliver it to the man himself?

Tricks didn't ask him what he'd lost.

'I hear Michael Anderson's wife has gone missing?' he said, as he took a step closer. 'She been found yet?'

Garry forced himself to look the other man directly in the eyes. 'I'm not on duty today, sir, I'm afraid. Not really up to speed. Sorry to have bothered you.'

He turned towards his car before Tricks could make the connection with the gormless officer who'd destroyed his wife's memory bear. He saw movement in the corner of his eye a second before a hand touched his arm.

'You were by the door, weren't you?'

Garry took a step back to get out of arm's reach. He was the bigger man by several inches and about twenty pounds heavier, but he'd never learned to fight dirty. He'd have been very wary of this man, even without everything he knew about him. Howie Tricks was dangerous.

A dangerous man who knew that Olive was missing.

'That's right, sir,' he said. 'I was part of the tactical team.'

'Thought so. I never forget eyes.'

Garry remembered something else then, something that might have kept him well away from the place if he'd thought of it before. The Tricks gang was known for blinding people they made enemies of, when they didn't kill them outright. They blinded them by strapping them down and dripping acid into their eyes.

Coming here had been stupid.

'I'll leave you in peace, sir. Have a good evening.'

A sigh of relief escaped Garry as he closed and locked the car door. A second caught in his throat when he saw Tricks raise his mobile phone and direct it towards him. He'd taken a picture of Garry's car.

As Garry drove away, he could see the other man in the rear-view mirror, still watching him.

40

Eloise's solicitor arrived during the afternoon when the boiled-meat smell of hospital lunch hung in the air and when most of the patients on the ward were asleep or scrolling lethargically through their phones or tablets. Several of the nurses were on break, and those who weren't had been called away to other tasks. Olive was attending to Eloise's near neighbour, the dementia patient. The bed opposite was empty and the only other occupant of the four-bed bay had been taken downstairs for tests.

'Hello,' a voice called. 'Anybody here?'

Olive poked her head out from the surround of privacy curtains to see a man with a shock of white hair. He wore a good suit, was of middling height and younger than his hair suggested.

'May I help you?' she said.

'Ms Warner,' he replied. 'I'm her solicitor.'

'I'm here, Peter,' Eloise called from behind the curtain in her shaky, sexless voice.

Without further acknowledgement of Olive, the solicitor crossed to Eloise's bed and greeted her.

Olive waited a beat, then another, before easing her way round the curtains until she could see Eloise's bed.

The solicitor was sitting in Eloise's armchair, which strictly wasn't allowed, for reasons of infection control, but Olive decided to let it go. He had a slim briefcase open on his lap. Eloise had raised her bed so that she was a little more upright. Both looked at Olive.

'I'll give you some privacy.' Olive reached up to draw the curtain along the bottom of Eloise's bed, the one that would effectively close in the patient and her visitor. 'Is there anything I can get you, Ms Warner? Do you need your bed raising any further?'

'I think we're fine, thank you.' The solicitor's attention was on his paperwork.

'Right you are,' Olive said cheerily. 'I'll be at the nurses' station if you need me.'

She slipped quietly within Mrs Reynolds' curtains and waited, knowing that people could be stupid, even those with the brains to know better. So often they assumed the impossible: that curtains were soundproof.

'OK, so I think I've done everything you asked,' the solicitor was saying. 'Can I run through it with you?'

Eloise must have indicated her assent because he went on quickly.

'All your personal assets, and your share of the joint assets, including the value of the property you currently own with your husband, will pass equally to your daughters when they reach the age of twenty-one. Your husband has the right to remain in the marital home for his lifetime, but should he sell it, your half of the proceeds will become part of your estate.'

Another pause; a scraping of chair legs over the tiled floor.

'I'm sure you understand, Eloise, but I wanted to be clear. In effect, you're leaving your husband nothing.'

'I understand,' Eloise croaked.

'Right then. Moving on to guardianship. It's customary for the surviving parent, assuming he or she is in good health, to assume full guardianship of any minors.'

'No.' Eloise's voice seemed to have gained in strength.

The solicitor cleared his throat. 'So, this document, which appoints your mother as joint trustee of the girls' funds, also makes her a legal guardian. It means she will have a say in the day-to-day care of the girls, in decisions about their education and health, and in how their assets are invested. Should anything happen to your husband, barring any further arrangements he makes, she will become sole guardian.'

'Yes,' Eloise replied. 'That's what I want.'

'This is going to come as a shock to Michael, you know that?'

A pause, then, 'Michael should think himself lucky he's only disinherited.'

It was hard to be sure – Eloise's voice had been changed by pain and illness – but the woman sounded furious.

The solicitor's sigh was audible in the next cubicle. 'Eloise, is there anything . . .? I don't want to pry, but—'

'Nothing you can do, Peter. But thank you.'

When the solicitor spoke again, he'd lowered his voice, as though conscious that he might be overheard. Olive pretended to be looking in the bedside cupboard.

He said, 'I still have your unsigned divorce papers on file back at the office.'

'Shred them.'

'I will. But, Eloise, when you . . . without you, I'm senior partner. I have to think about the firm. This is not simply about you and Michael having marital difficulties. If he's done anything that could throw the firm into disrepute, then—'

Silence for several seconds, then, 'Don't fret, Peter. I'll take my secrets to the grave. Sooner than any of us bargained for.'

The solicitor asked, 'Was he unfaithful?'

Eloise gave a short, bitter laugh; or she could have been coughing, it was hard to tell.

'An affair I could have coped with. An affair would have been . . . nothing.'

There was a muffled, choking sound.

'Oh Lord, hold on,' the solicitor said. 'I've got a handkerchief somewhere.'

From beyond the curtain came the rattle of a trolley. Olive's time was up. Silently cursing the interruption, she stepped out from the curtains and moved out of earshot.

41

'Aye, I remember you. Captain of the boys' cross-country team.' The man in the doorway had a strong north-eastern accent. 'Barry, isn't it?'

The house was a typical 1920s semi-detached in one of the nicer parts of Darlington. Two bay windows dominated the front, and the small garden had been paved to create a parking spot for a four-year-old Nissan Micra. A modest porch kept the snow at bay, a fact for which Garry was grateful. It had been coming down a lot faster since he'd left home.

'Garry,' he corrected.

George Charles, Olive's dad, was a slight, thin man in his late sixties. His grey hair was short and spiky and his eyes, deep-set and almond-shaped, were Olive's eyes.

'Off duty, is it?' His face took on a guarded look, one Garry had seen before on those to whom he was about to give very bad news.

'There's no news, I'm afraid,' he said quickly. 'But we've no reason to believe Olive's come to any harm at this stage. I popped round because . . .'

What was he doing here exactly? After getting back from the Trickses property and making Lexy's phone calls to the hotel, he'd been too keyed up to sleep. Short of heading up to Hexham to start a one-man search in ever-worsening weather, visiting Olive's parents had been the only thing he could think of.

'Because Olive and I go way back,' he said. 'And I knew you'd be worried. I thought maybe I could help answer any questions about police procedures and so on.'

'I appreciate that, lad. Come on in.'

The hallway that Olive's dad led Garry along was dimly lit, apart from a tiny spotlight on one wall that illuminated a hanging crucifix. Garry thought he recognised the wood as mahogany. The Christ figure and the Latin word INRI had been wrought in a silver-coloured metal. He should know the meaning of INRI.

The door ahead opened into a cluttered sitting room. The furniture seemed oversized and no visible surface had been left free of ornamentation. Garry quickly counted two standing lamps and three table lamps, four occasional tables and over a dozen pictures on the walls. The curtains were heavy and elaborate with drapes and swirls and tiebacks. One glass-fronted cabinet was crammed with royal memorabilia: commemorative plates, mugs, porcelain figures, china bells, even framed photographs.

A small, elderly dog jumped up, gasping out a hoarse bark. A corgi.

'Steady on, Duke,' George Charles muttered. 'Mother, this is Garry. Used to run with our Olive back at school. He's in the police now. Come to let us know the latest.'

'Completely unofficial,' Garry said, as Olive's mother got up. Behind her, on two cupboards that stood either side of the fire, were several family photographs. He spotted one of Olive in army uniform, and another of her sister in graduation robes. There was even one of the cross-country team and he thought he could see himself in the back row. The largest and best framed was a group shot taken at Olive's wedding.

Another crucifix stood in the centre of the mantlepiece.

'I'm here as an old friend of Olive's,' he repeated. 'Anything I can do to help.'

For the first fifteen minutes, after tea and angel cake had been served, Garry fielded the older couple's questions.

'One theory we're working to,' he explained, 'is that Olive has gone to stay with a friend, possibly because she and her husband have had a disagreement. He's insisting they haven't, and we understand he might not want strangers prying into his affairs, but it's important for us to know. I wondered if you had any reason to believe Olive was less than happy recently?'

The two shared identical looks: puzzled, defensive.

'Olive's never been happier,' her mother said, glancing back towards the wedding photograph. 'She and Michael are devoted to each other.'

'Yes, I could see that.' Garry suppressed a sigh. 'But the situation can't be easy. Two teenage stepdaughters, living in a house owned by the late wife's mother?'

'Gwen's a brick,' George said, a little too quickly.

'Olive adores the girls,' Anne added.

'I'd like to talk to her close friends.' Garry tried a different tack. 'Can you put me in touch with any?'

The following pause lasted longer than felt natural; Garry took out his notebook to nudge them along.

'Who was that lass she shared a flat with for a while?' George was looking at his wife. 'Before she joined the army.'

'You're thinking of Emma.' Anne was frowning. 'I don't think she's been in touch with Emma for years. There was a girl called Mattie who we met a few times, but I haven't heard Olive mention her lately.'

Garry waited.

'She goes to a gym,' George offered. 'Not sure which one, though. Michael could probably help you out.'

'She works antisocial hours,' Anne said. 'All medics do. They socialise among themselves for that reason. You need to be talking to her work colleagues.'

'Makes sense.' Garry nodded, as though it made perfect sense; it didn't, it felt wrong, but he nodded all the same. 'Who was she closest to at work, would you say?'

'Well, there's a woman called Stella,' George offered.

'No, she doesn't get on with Stella,' Anne countered. 'Stella's too fond of putting her nose in other people's business.'

Garry waited a few more seconds.

'More tea?' Anne offered.

Garry tried a different approach. 'We've reason to believe Olive left the hotel last night in the company of someone else. Maybe a man. I'd like—'

'Impossible.' Anne was tight-lipped.

'We brought our girls up with a strong moral code.' George, too, had stiffened in his chair, as though his family's morality was intrinsically linked to his spinal cord. 'We don't hold with shenanigans.'

'It might have taken Olive a while to find the right man,' Anne added. 'And I won't deny we were getting worried – well, you do, don't you, when a woman is over thirty and never had a serious boyfriend – but she was saving herself for the right man. Like Lady Di.'

Anne's eyes went triumphantly to the central plate in her royal collection: a twelve-inch porcelain commemoration of the engagement of the Prince of Wales to Lady Diana Spencer. Garry refrained from pointing out how badly that particular act of self-sacrifice had turned out.

He got to his feet and pulled a card from his pocket. 'I won't take up any more of your time.' Handing the card to George, he added, 'Obviously, if you think of anything, anything at all.'

On the point of leaving the room, he looked again at the wedding photograph. Unlike the one he'd seen at the Anderson house, this was a group shot, taken from a height, looking down at what could be the entire wedding party standing in front of a stone building. He estimated forty to fifty people in the picture.

'May I?' he gestured to the picture and, at a nod of agreement from Anne, picked it up. George turned on the overhead light to give him a better look.

'Such a lovely day,' Anne said, smugly.

'Do you mind if I take a snap of this?' he asked Olive's parents. 'It could help us make sure we track down all of Olive's friends.'

'No problem, lad,' George agreed. 'Most were Michael's side, but anything that helps.'

Garry took the picture, capturing the original image as best he could, then thanked the couple and left the house.

*

When he got home, he uploaded the picture onto his desktop computer before enlarging it to the point where the detail became hazy. Olive and Michael stood in the centre. He spotted the two girls in cerise pink, reluctant bridesmaids if facial expressions were anything to judge by, and Gwen Warner in sombre navy blue. Olive's parents – Anne in a hat suitable for any royal wedding – a woman in a wheelchair and a couple of pushchairs. No parliamentary characters or local bigwigs that he recognised. This had been a wedding of family and close friends. Except for one thing.

Two things, to be precise. At the back of the group were a man and woman in their forties, flashily dressed, the woman sporting a bright pink dress and big hair.

Howie and Tina Tricks.

42

Saturday 8 December, two years previously

'I made you some tea,' Olive said.

Michael Anderson looked up at the sound of her voice. The skin around his eyes was reddened, the whites bloodshot. He looked like he'd been asleep; at the same time, as though he hadn't slept in days. His face softened, though, when he saw who'd approached.

'Didn't realise that was part of the service. Not in the NHS.'

'It isn't.' Olive leaned across him and put the mug – her own – on Eloise's bedside table. The patient seemed to be asleep. 'But I'm not busy for the next-half hour or so. Is there any news on the hospice?'

Anderson looked weary. 'We're second on the list after Mrs Reynolds, but—'

He didn't need to go on; a hospice bed would only become available when one of the current residents died and wishing for that seemed heartless.

'It's late,' Olive said, conscious of the blackness outside the windows. 'Have you just arrived from London?'

Anderson sighed. 'We're in Christmas recess now, thank God. I don't have to go back till January.' He glanced down at his wife. 'Maybe not even then. It's a weird sort of limbo, isn't it? Waiting. I guess you're used to it.'

'To a point. It's a very different experience for families. And for the patients themselves, of course.'

He lowered his voice still further, forcing Olive to step closer to catch what he was saying. 'You must have seen this before, many times. Any idea how long we have?'

An impossible question. 'Weeks, rather than days,' she said quietly. 'But not many.'

Anderson's eyes clenched tight, as though he'd absorbed all of Eloise's pain into himself.

'But no one can really say for sure,' Olive hurried on.

'Half of me wants it over now,' he said. 'This waiting, it's close to unbearable.'

'I know.'

Visibly pulling himself together, Anderson picked up the mug, almost smiling when he saw it properly. Three small arrows pointed upwards above text reading: *This is what an awesome soldier looks like.*

'Thank you,' he said, giving Olive a hesitant smile. 'Although I guess it wasn't meant for me. Not originally, anyway.'

'My parents gave it to me,' Olive replied. 'But maybe neither of us deserve it. We're not soldiers anymore.'

Anderson looked around, taking in the silent ward, the vacant nurses' station. 'Do you have a couple of minutes?' he said. 'I know I'm taking a bit of a liberty, but . . .'

Olive waited.

'I miss it,' he went on. 'I miss everything about it. Even the violence and the terror, even the mud and the heat and the stench of it. I even miss being away from home for months on end.'

'You miss the danger.' Olive pulled forward the extra chair she'd made sure had been by Eloise's bed all afternoon. 'I do too. And it's not something you can ever explain to those who've not experienced it for themselves.'

He smiled at her, a proper smile this time, showing even white teeth. 'Exactly.'

'Is that why you sail?' Olive asked.

'Sailing isn't dangerous,' he replied. 'Unless you're doing it wrong. Do you sail?'

'Never tried,' she replied. 'Although I'd like to. I ski, and rock climb. I have a mountain bike. I tried surfing a couple of times but couldn't get my balance. Stats tell me bull fighting is one of the most dangerous sports of all, but it doesn't happen a lot in the north-east.'

They were smiling at each other.

'And all the time I feel guilty,' she went on. 'Dicing with my own death while I spend every day caring for people who'd give anything to be sure of life. I hate myself for being so reckless, and I still can't stop.'

Anderson drank tea and cradled the mug in both hands. 'Were you there the night the camp was attacked?' he asked. 'It was April, I think, back in—'

'Late March,' she corrected. 'Zero three hundred hours when the refuelling station went up.'

A night Olive didn't think she'd ever forget. A dozen Taliban fighters, after months of careful planning, had invaded the allied forces' base in the early hours of the morning. Separating into three teams, one group had gone for the refuelling station, a second for the commander's private residence and a third for the aircraft hangar. Seven allied soldiers had been killed and another five injured before the attackers were all shot dead. Olive, who'd been on call at the time, had found herself taking cover from heavy fire and a rebounding bullet had nicked her shoulder. The injury had been minor, but, technically, she'd been shot.

'Sometimes,' Anderson said, 'I think I haven't felt properly alive since I came back from Afghanistan.'

'So why leave the army?'

He shrugged. 'I had two daughters who needed their dad. And it was a promise I'd made to Eloise, that my military career would have an end date. I had political ambitions too. How about you?'

'I fell in love.'

'Well, that sounds like the best reason of all.'

Olive was pretty sure he glanced down at her left hand.

'Not really. It didn't work out.' Olive made a show of looking around the ward, although it was still quiet. 'I have to get on,' she said, getting to her feet. 'Let me know if there's anything I can do, Mr Anderson.'

'Michael,' he said. 'Thank you, Olive. You've helped more than you know.'

43

That evening, Garry made his Christmas wreathes: one for his own front door, another for that of his parents'. Normally, he liked to have them in place a good two weeks before the big day, but the berries on the hedgerow ivy had been slow to turn black this year.

He began with moss, gathered over several foraging weekends from tree stumps and old fences, wrapping it around the wire frames; then he attached the huge, hessian bows. Greenery came next, a mixture of spruce, myrtle, white snow berries and juniper and finally the accents: preserved apple slices, fir cones, bundles of cinnamon sticks and dried limes. Last year, his wreathes had been riotous, full of colour; these were more subtle, classier. He told his mum he got them from a florist in Durham, one too far away for her to pop in to and thank.

When he was done, he put the wreath intended for his parents out back where it would stay cool. In the morning, he'd take it round, hang it, and vanish before his mum had a chance to bend his ear about Lexy. It would be weeks, months even, before she let up. *How's Lexy, Garry? Seen much of Lexy lately? Two of you been working together again?*

He opened his front door to find a white ledge in the door frame where the snowfall had blown. Tiny flakes were still floating around in the night air and the sky seemed too close to the earth. The bad weather wasn't done, not by a long shot.

Barely pausing to admire the effect of the wreath, he closed the door on the freezing night and, back inside, switched on the computer in his small spare bedroom. Opening Google Maps, he typed Hexham into the search bar and enlarged the area around it.

Olive's car had been spotted crossing the Tyne on the way out of Hexham, heading towards the A69, the main east–west route. It hadn't been picked up on any of the A69's cameras, though, meaning it couldn't have stayed on the main road for long. On minor roads, at night, in those conditions, it was unlikely they'd been planning to go far. Instinct told him that Olive was still somewhere in the Hexham area.

He could find a list of all pubs with rooms and rental properties within, say, a fifty-mile radius of the Hexham hotel and phone every one. But that wouldn't help at all if the person she left with had a house in the area.

His landline was ringing. Sighing, because he knew it would be his mum again, unable to resist a bit of digging on the subject of Lexy, he answered it.

'It's me,' Lexy said, as Garry knew, deep down, he'd been hoping it would be. 'Get any sleep?'

For a second, he hadn't a clue what she was talking about; a lot had happened in the last few hours. 'Yes, thanks,' he lied. 'Anything new?'

'Not really.' She sounded tired. 'I've been interviewing all day. Did you get a chance to ring the hotel?'

'They provide one key per room,' Garry told her. 'And that was given to Olive when she checked in. Only she signed in, but there was a note on the booking that her husband would be making a surprise visit – arranged by the woman claiming to be his secretary, remember? – so the chances are no one questioned her arriving alone. Significantly, she made a reservation in the dining room for one. She might have ended up dining with someone else, but she didn't initially expect to.'

'Interesting.'

'I thought so. But not nearly as interesting as something else I learned this evening.'

'Keep talking.'

'Howie and Tina Tricks were at Olive and Michael's wedding six months ago.'

Lexy listened in silence as Garry filled her in: that Howie knew about, and was interested in, the disappearance of Olive Anderson and that in spite of a very public enmity between Anderson the MP and the Tricks family, Tina and Howie had been at the couple's wedding.

He went on to tell her about the internet search he'd done since getting home.

'Anderson was pretty vocal on the subject of organised crime in general and the Tricks gang in particular from his running for parliament six years ago to roughly three years later when suddenly his focus switched. He started talking in vague terms, about how it's a nationwide problem. Now, he talks about foreign gangs moving here and taking the problem to a whole new level. Basically, three years ago, he backed off on the Trickses. And his wife's money-laundering case collapsed at roughly the same time.'

Lexy thought for a second, then said, 'And they become such good friends that Howie and Tina attend the wedding? Garry, are you sure?'

He looked again at the picture. 'I wouldn't bet my mum's life on it, but, yeah, I'm reasonably sure. I'll send it over.'

Lexy said, 'I need to think this through. Have you told anyone else?'

'Not yet.'

'Don't. I'm going to Anderson's constituency office in the morning. Ten o'clock in Guisborough. Want to come?'

'You mean you need a driver.'

A second of silence on the line, then, 'Actually, I can ask someone on duty to drive me.' She almost sounded hurt. 'I thought you cared about finding Olive alive and well.'

'I'll pick you up at nine thirty,' he told her. A few more seconds of silence and then, 'Thanks,' he said.

'No worries.' She put the phone down.

Before he went to bed that night, Garry took the wreath off his front door. He'd given more than enough of himself away to Lexy already. Only as he was drifting off to sleep did he realise that that must mean he was hoping she'd come round again.

44

'Are you married, Olive?' Eloise asked, as Olive gently shampooed her hair. The woman's once plentiful blonde curls had thinned and paled to a dull silver. It was fine, brittle hair now, but even people in the last weeks of their life appreciated a clean head.

'No.' Olive was grateful that from her seat at the rear of the bathtub, Eloise couldn't see her face.

'Ever got close?'

Cradling Eloise's head in one hand, Olive rinsed away the soapsuds.

'You think I'm impertinent, don't you?' Eloise went on when Olive didn't answer. 'But when you have as little time left as I do, social niceties tend not to be quite so important.'

Olive poured again, then squeezed the excess water out of Eloise's hair. The water was cooling and cancer patients got cold very quickly. She wrapped a towel around her patient's head before laying it gently back against the bathtub.

'Surely you've had other patients say the same thing.' Eloise was unusually talkative this evening.

'They don't put it quite so well, but yes, I suppose I have,' Olive replied. 'The truth is, I'd have liked to have got married, once.'

As she spoke, she felt the familiar heaviness creep into her limbs, the twisting in her stomach, the ache in her chest.

'What happened? It's no good, you know, I'm not going to waste my time being polite. If I want to know something, I ask.'

'Well, I can understand that. The truth is, I'm not sure what happened. I may never know. It didn't work out.'

'How long ago?'

'A little over a year.'

Eloise made a soft whistling sound. 'You'll find someone else,' she said. 'I mean, look at you. You're gorgeous.'

Olive closed her eyes. More than a year and it still hurt so much. 'Thank you. But I don't think so. Lightning only strikes once.'

'He must have been very special.'

Olive allowed herself a soft laugh. 'No,' she said, after a moment. 'Exceptional. This water's getting quite cool now. Maybe we should get you out.'

'Another couple of minutes. This might be my last bath.'

'I really don't think so.'

Eloise had been on the ward three days and Olive still thought she had a couple of weeks left in her. The end signs hadn't kicked in yet.

Gently wafting the water, Eloise said, 'I'm sorry it didn't work out, but at least you had something special. I guess we all have to be grateful for the good things we have. Even if they don't last.'

'That's true. And you have a lovely family,' Olive said. 'They must be a great comfort.'

'I have two beautiful girls, certainly.'

Interesting choice of words. 'And your husband? He seems quite something.'

'As you say, exceptional.' Eloise gave a deep sigh. 'I adored Michael,' she went on. 'For a long time. But I was never enough for him.'

Olive waited a moment and then said, 'I'm sure that's not the case.'

'Now you're being polite. He struggled when he left the army. More than most. There was something about the lifestyle he needed.' Her voice lowered, almost to a whisper, and she said, 'Or maybe I'm fooling myself with that one.'

'Do you mean he missed the danger?' Olive suggested, remembering her own conversation with Michael on the subject. 'The adrenaline rush of not knowing whether you'll be alive when the sun goes down?'

'Of course, you knew him, didn't you? In Afghanistan?'

'Not really. Our paths never crossed. He wasn't injured, thank goodness.'

Eloise was silent for a moment and then, 'Do you miss it too?'

Olive smiled. 'People say I'm an adrenaline junky, so maybe.'

Eloise said, 'With Michael, it's almost as though he needs to take risks. The more dangerous, the better. And to hell with the consequences. No matter who he hurts, no matter who gets dragged along with it. You'd do well to remember that.'

Olive could feel her body tensing. 'I'm not sure I'm following.'

For a moment, Eloise didn't reply, then, 'I hear you've arranged for the ward doors to be locked while I'm in here, and that all visitors have to be checked at the nurses' station. Thank you.'

'You're welcome. There haven't been any more problems, have there?'

'No, but politicians often make dangerous friends. I've learned to be on my guard.'

Telling herself to be careful, that Eloise must not suspect this was anything more than harmless chatting, Olive said, 'Mr Anderson mentioned his love of dangerous sports. I can see how that would be worrying.'

Eloise gave a soft, mean laugh. 'You sound like you're fishing, Olive. All that glisters is not gold, you know. And you're right, this water is cold. I need to get out now.'

45

'It's all about the ears, Dumbo.' Lexy put a hand on his arm. 'Look at the ears.' Then she slapped him.

Garry woke with a start. Coming off night shifts always disorientated him and, for a few moments, he had no idea what time it was. All he knew was the dream he'd that second fallen out of had been important.

Closing his eyes, trying to sink back into it, he went over as much as he could remember. He'd been walking down a long corridor, looking at posters on a wall. Posters featuring Olive.

They'd been missing persons posters, the old-fashioned kind that at one time were plastered around community noticeboards, shops, schools, post offices. The digital age had largely made them redundant.

Each image of Olive had been slightly different. It was a Spot the Difference game, the sort found in newspapers, magazines, children's puzzle books. He'd always been good at Spot the Difference; almost as good as he was at Where's Wally. I mean, it was obvious where the geeky boy in the red and white stripes was – he stood out a mile.

'Stripes on her shirt go a different way,' he'd said to Lexy, who'd appeared by his side in the way of dreams. As they'd moved on to the next image, he'd said, 'Different earrings in this one.'

They'd moved on. 'Buttons,' he'd said, and then, 'Hairslide.'

'I don't know how you do it,' Lexy had muttered, in an admiring voice, but, at the same time, sounding disturbingly like his mum. Then, 'It's all about the ears, Dumbo. Look at the ears.'

He'd looked and watched as Olive's ears had grown huge and wrinkled, become drooping grey elephant ears.

Holy Moly, Guacamole, that had been one weird dream.

Properly awake, Garry rolled over to check his phone. No messages had come in overnight and it was a little after seven in the morning. Olive had been missing for nearly thirty hours.

He sat up, mulling over what little he and Lexy had learned since the midnight call-out. In spite of expecting to stay at the Hexham hotel alone, Olive had dined and left with a companion, about whom they still knew nothing. The hotel claimed Michael Anderson had been planning to surprise his wife by joining her; he denied having made any such arrangements. Olive's car hadn't been traced beyond its initial journey out of Hexham, so either she and her companion hadn't travelled far, or they'd stuck to minor roads, probably heading north. According to Gwen, she hadn't been happy in her new marriage. Most worrying of all, she'd reported being followed home in the late summer, had been concerned enough to report it to the police. And a dangerous local gangster had her in his sights.

Garry raised the bedroom blind and looked out to see more snow had fallen. He kept the lawn in his back garden to a minimum: a – normally – green trail that curved from the house towards the rear fence, narrowing as it went, winding its way around a wrought-iron bench before vanishing behind a laurel bush. Most of the garden was given over to shrubs, small trees and swaying grasses, all valuable for providing framework, texture, movement and contrast, all heavy and drooping now with glistening white crystals.

Behind the fence was a local park, densely wooded, giving the impression that the garden went on forever. Normally, Garry spent the first few minutes of each day looking out, at changes wrought by the weather or the seasons, at tracks in the soil, and the first bursts of colour. Always, the sight of his small, perfect garden and the park beyond both grounded and calmed him.

That morning, the sky was a soft pink, and a robin hopped along a dogwood branch, its coppery chest matching the bare stalks of the shrub. It was precious colour in a monochrome world, but somehow the garden wasn't working its usual magic. Garry tried to imagine how he'd feel if someone he loved had been missing for nearly thirty hours in these conditions and found he couldn't. His imagination was letting him down again.

Or maybe he just didn't love anyone enough.

46

Monday 10 December, two years previously

Olive was making her way back to the ward when she met Eloise and Michael in the corridor. Eloise sat in a hospital wheelchair like a living scarecrow, wearing a padded coat and with a rug over her legs.

'This has the look of a trip,' Olive said, as she stepped back to let the couple pass.

'I'm taking Elly to the garden,' Michael replied. 'We're going to watch the snow.'

'Nice idea,' Olive replied, although she thought it very ill-advised. The temperatures outside were close to freezing. 'Maybe don't stay too long, though. It's very cold.'

'Ten minutes max,' Michael promised.

Eloise kept her eyes on her lap, not bothering to even acknowledge Olive.

'Actually, I'm glad we bumped into you,' Michael went on. 'We've a favour to ask.'

Eloise sighed.

'How can I help?' Olive asked.

Michael glanced down at the figure in the chair. 'I've set up a trust fund for my wife,' he explained. 'A lot of people, especially in the House, were asking if she had a favourite charity and whether they could donate, so I made it official. It's had a bit of news coverage too, so the public have got involved. We haven't decided what we're supporting yet, but it will almost certainly be something to do with the hospital here.'

'That's a lovely idea,' Olive agreed.

'And we wondered if you'd be one of the trustees?'

'Me?'

He gave her that great smile, the one that would see him in Number 10 one of these days. 'Who better than Eloise's nurse? You know us, you know the hospital and what it needs. It won't involve much work. And nothing immediately.'

'Nothing till I'm dead,' Eloise added. 'Shall we go before I'm due my next round of meds, Mike?'

'Think about it?' he asked Olive, looking back over his shoulder as he wheeled his wife away.

She gave a small nod of her head.

When they were out of sight, she followed, making sure the lift had swallowed them before running downstairs to the ground floor.

The hospital had one small, square garden, an enclosed courtyard surrounded by four sides of offices and wards. Mainly used as a place for visitors and patients to smoke, it had several bench seats, a rain shelter and some rather spindly shrubs. It would almost certainly be empty on such a grim day.

Knowing the exact location of the shelter the Andersons would need because of the snow, Olive made for a small room directly behind it that housed a photocopier and stationery store. The light in the courtyard outside was a dull creamy-yellow and the air thick with falling snowflakes, but the snowfall had softened and plumped the shrubs, turning them into intricate white sculptures. She had time to crank the window an inch before she heard the door to the hospital open, followed by the crunch of wheels over snow.

Olive stepped back, away from the window. She heard the wheels come to a halt, then a heavy sigh from Michael as he sat down beside his wife.

Eloise spoke first. 'I've warned her about you.'

'Who?'

'Florence Nightingale.'

'I take it you mean Olive.'

'I'd tell you to watch yourself if I cared enough. She's not the angel she pretends to be. There's something in her eyes. I've learned to spot it over the years.'

Michael's sigh was audible. 'Elly, is this really the time?'

'Oh, I think I get to choose how I spend my time now, don't you?'

Olive leaned her face against the cold outside wall, as though to get closer to the conversation she needed to hear.

'I've always loved you, you should know that,' Michael said. 'You always came first, you and the girls.'

When Eloise spoke again, she sounded angry, and with a volume and strength Olive had rarely heard in someone so ill. 'God help me, if you ever hurt them, I swear I'll come back. I'll come for your soul, Michael, if you so much as—'

'For heaven's sake, you know I won't.'

'I don't, that's the point. I know you won't mean to, won't want to, but you might not be able to help yourself. You never wanted to hurt me, and you still—'

'Really?' Now Anderson was annoyed. 'You hated it that much? Because there are things I remember—'

'Don't you dare.' Eloise put a surprising amount of energy into snapping at her husband. 'I died, inside, every time. Each time you made me do it, I wanted to kill you, and kill myself, and sometimes the only reason I didn't was because I knew what it would do to the girls. I would not have believed the things I'd do to keep my family together.'

'Neither would I.' Michael's voice was flat, accusing, furious.

Silence.

Then Eloise came back at him. 'That was your fault.'

'No, I'm not taking the blame for that. It wasn't—'

'I don't want to hear it. I'm serious, Michael, if you carry on, I'll start screaming.'

'OK, OK.' A heavy, exhausted sigh, then the rustle of someone getting to their feet. 'I think we're done here. Let's get you back inside.'

47

Garry picked Lexy up at nine thirty for the short drive to Guisborough. She was wearing the same outdoor clothes as the previous day but had exchanged her business suit for jeans and a thick pink sweater.

'Olive's not been hurt,' she said, as she climbed into the passenger seat. 'I finished the check late yesterday. No one remotely matching her description has been admitted to any of the hospitals in the area. And her vehicle is not listed in any reports of RTAs.'

'Good to know.'

And then she fell silent, gazing out of the window so that her head was turned away from him, occasionally checking her phone. Garry drove on, telling himself he wasn't bothered. If anything, he was grateful to have a few moments of peace. He'd never liked people, men or women, who never stopped talking. He told himself versions of the same thing for fifteen long minutes and then his resolve broke.

'Are you annoyed I went back to the Trickses property yesterday? And to see Olive's parents?'

Lexy seemed surprised. 'Would you care?' she asked him.

Yes, he would. 'Not especially,' he said.

'I had you down as a maverick yesterday morning,' she replied. 'But for what it's worth, no, I'm not annoyed. It has thrown up more questions than answers, though.'

Garry waited for her to spell out what those questions were, wondering whether they'd be the same ones as on his mind, or if she'd been able to see things he couldn't. He'd have to expect so. She was the hot-shot detective and he the traffic cop.

Maverick traffic cop, mind.

'So, what do you normally do at weekends?' Lexy said. 'When you're not moonlighting as a detective?'

The change of topic was a relief; his brain had been starting to hurt. 'Usual stuff,' he said. 'Food shopping. Laundry. Chores. Work on the allotment.'

He had a moment of wishing he could tell her about something more interesting: manoeuvres with the territorial army, a spot of skydiving, volunteering at the local homeless shelter.

'Really?' Lexy was giving him a knowing look but was on the brink of smiling again and he decided he much preferred her smiling. Even if she made fun of him most of the time.

'What's that supposed to mean?' he said. 'You don't believe I have an allotment?'

An allotment? He was thirty-five and his main weekend hobby was working on his allotment.

And that was definitely a smile playing at the corners of her mouth. 'My grandad has an allotment,' she told him. 'So, I know for a fact that home-grown vegetables are never as perfect as that lot you palmed off on your mum yesterday. Not a slug, not a maggot, not a wormhole to be seen.'

I'm a detective. Well, she had warned him.

'Maybe I'm a better kitchen gardener than your grandad,' he said.

She smiled properly this time. 'Maybe.'

Cheese and crackers, he might actually have to come clean with this girl.

'Is she really missing?' the constituency agent, whose name was Evelyn, said, when she'd served weak coffee and opened a packet of cheap biscuits.

The party chairman, a short man in late middle age who'd introduced himself as Richard Potts, had added a nip of something from a hip flask to his own, offering it round the group. All had declined, but as Garry tasted his coffee, he almost wished he'd accepted. Lexy, he noticed, took one sip and put her mug down.

Evelyn continued, 'Because we've seen nothing on the news, have we, Richard? And we're going to need a briefing. You've no idea of the calls we get when something happens.'

'At this stage, we haven't launched a missing persons enquiry and don't plan to until Monday morning, unless something new comes up,' Lexy told them. 'But with someone as high profile as Mrs Anderson, we need to be prepared.'

'Do you know if Michael managed to contact that friend he was trying to track down?' Evelyn asked.

Lexy glanced at Garry. 'Sorry, what friend would this be?'

'Michael was here yesterday for Friday morning surgery as normal,' Evelyn explained. 'He was anxious to find an address on file, someone Olive knew of old, he said, who might have some idea what had happened to her. I offered to look for him, but he insisted on going through the files himself.'

'Do you remember the name of this friend?' Lexy asked.

'No, that's my point. He didn't mention a name. If he had, I'd have been able to look myself.'

'Thank you.' Lexy spoke slowly, as though thinking hard. 'We'll double-check that with him. Meanwhile, do either of you have any other information that might be relevant?'

'How do you mean?' Potts asked.

'Was Mrs Anderson worried about anything, to your knowledge? Had she received any threats? Did Mr Anderson ever mention that he was concerned about his wife?'

Agent and chairman looked at each other with identical expressions: vague, puzzled, wary.

Lexy fixed a polite smile on her face. 'Is it possible that relations between the Andersons were less than happy?'

Evelyn pursed her lips. 'You're asking us to gossip?'

Potts, Garry noticed, had a gleam in his eyes; he, at least, was enjoying the drama.

'I'm asking you to co-operate in what could become a

serious investigation,' Lexy countered. 'No one has heard from Olive Anderson in thirty-six hours.'

Garry got to his feet. The walls of the office were lined with photographs. It had been a photograph that had proven useful at the Andersons' house, and again at Olive's parents' home.

'How well do you know Olive?' Lexy tried. 'She and Mr Anderson have been married, what, six months? Has she spent much time here?'

'She's a nice lass,' Potts offered. 'We don't see as much of her as we did the first Mrs A. She's always pleasant, though, when she accompanies Michael out and about.'

Most of the photographs showed constituency activities: formal dinners, ribbon cuttings, school visits. Eloise appeared in several, the girls in one or two, Olive not at all.

The yacht appeared in these photographs too, again with Anderson at the helm. In one shot, the crew all wore red rosettes.

'Mr Anderson's mother-in-law, Mrs Warner, thinks Olive may have been unhappy enough to have left her husband. Does that feel likely to you?'

Garry glanced back to see Evelyn shake her head. 'I wouldn't have thought things had got to that stage. They'd only been married months. I'll tell you what I do know. Olive was getting some abuse on social media, mainly Facebook. People suggesting she'd never live up to Eloise.'

'Must have been upsetting for her.'

'Upsetting for Michael too. The thing is, Olive suspected the girls were behind it. Now, I'm not saying it was them, or that the grandmother would have encouraged them, but I doubt any of them took it as seriously as they should, if you know what I'm saying.'

'Yes, I think I do. Tell me something, do local businesses and wealthy local people make financial contributions to the party?'

'A few,' Potts answered. 'Not as many as donate to the Tories, of course. Most of our funding comes from party members and the unions.'

'So, if it's not that big a number, you'd know who they are?'

'Of course,' Evelyn said. 'And it's all publicly available information. The Labour Party has nothing to hide.'

Garry had a feeling he knew where Lexy was going with this, and that it wasn't something the party would want made public.

'What about the Tricks family or any of their associated businesses?' Lexy asked. 'Might they appear on this list?'

Both agent and chairman wore identical expressions of shock.

'You must be out of your mind,' Potts said. 'Michael can't associate with that lot. It would be political suicide.'

48

'Here's our favourite nurse,' Michael said, as Olive approached to check Eloise's vitals.

The patient did not echo her husband's smile. If anything, her eyes grew cold.

Michael seemed oblivious to his wife's discomfort. 'Did you know she was commended for her role in the Taliban attack on Camp Viking? She risked her own life to pull an injured man to safety. And was shot in the process.'

Michael hadn't known that the last time he and Olive had spoken or he'd have mentioned it; he'd been checking up on her.

'Much less cool than you make it sound.' Olive wrapped the blood-pressure monitor around Eloise's upper arm, avoiding eye contact with Michael as she did so.

'Why didn't the girls come?' Eloise asked. 'They don't have any-thing on Tuesdays. They could have come.'

'Last-minute thing at school.' Michael turned his attention to his wife. 'They break up tomorrow. You'll see them soon.'

Olive wouldn't bet on it. Children, however much they loved their parents, pulled away from imminent death. Faced with seeing their mother growing weaker, in greater pain, each time they visited, they'd inevitably choose not to see her; they'd start the process of grieving before death had actually occurred. She'd seen it before.

'Are you working over Christmas?' Michael was talking to Olive again.

'I won't be here for Christmas,' Eloise countered. 'The hospice will have space before then.'

'Let's hope so.' Olive recorded Eloise's blood-pressure reading. 'Although we'll be very sorry to see you go.'

'Yes, I'm sure you will,' Eloise replied, and her tone belied her words.

The moment of silence stretched; Michael scrolled through his phone.

'Almost done.' Olive kept her eyes down as she checked oxygen levels and then her patient's pulse. She would, actually, be very sorry to see Eloise go in the next few days. She wasn't done with her yet.

'Father Simon's planning to see you this week.' Michael's voice sounded unnaturally cheerful. He looked up at Olive. 'Do you think my wife can be moved briefly to a private room, so that she can talk to our priest properly?'

'I don't want him to come,' Eloise said. 'Tell him not to come.'

Michael allowed his surprise to register. 'He's been asking about you.'

Eloise shook her head. 'There's really no point.'

Michael reached out and gently stroked his wife's hand. 'It might make you feel better.'

Eloise didn't look at her husband. 'It won't.'

'Elly, I'm not talking about giving you the last rites. He only wants to see how you're doing.'

Her head flicked to the side to face her husband. 'Tell him I'm dying. That nobody can do a goddamned thing about it. And that while I might be answering to God a whole lot sooner than you will, your turn will come around. Maybe you should talk to him. Maybe it's time he heard your confession.'

Michael stood up. At the look on his face, Olive took a step back. The man was furious.

'Whatever you say, Eloise,' he said. 'I'll tell the priest you've got this.'

49

'Is this you, sir?' Still in the constituency office, Garry paused by a photograph of Michael Anderson and Richard Potts shaking hands in front of a country house. Both wore red rosettes.

Potts twisted round in his seat. 'It is. Shortly after I was elected chairman of the party.'

'Your house?'

Potts gave a short laugh. 'I know what you're thinking. Truth is, I'm a Turncoat Tory. I was a conservative for thirty years, then Michael came along. He convinced me. I joined the Labour Party and gave him my support.'

The office phone rang at that moment and Evelyn moved to answer it. Lexy stood and thanked Potts for his time. He indicated that he would show them out.

'No pictures of Olive?' Garry questioned as the other two drew close.

Potts made a show of giving the gallery the once-over. 'Can't say I've noticed. Evelyn looks after the office. I take your point, though.' He stopped in front of a photo of a line of men on the street, each sporting red rosettes. In the centre was a very pretty, dark-haired woman. For a second, Garry had thought it was Olive, before realising it was just a woman who looked a little similar. Same colour hair, right sort of age, both slim. Not as tall as Olive, though.

Potts said, 'This was taken back before the last election.'

'Who's the girl in the centre?' Garry asked. Her face was rounder, whereas Olive had an oval face. And this girl's eyes were bigger.

Potts pulled out a pair of reading glasses. 'One of the activists,

I think. You know, the people who knock on doors in the run-up to elections.' He shook his head, as though trying to dislodge a hidden thought. 'Hasn't been around for a while. Evelyn would probably know more.'

'She looks like Olive,' Garry pointed out.

'Aye, well they say men stick to type,' Potts replied. 'I'll show you out, officers.'

'What do you mean, sir?' Lexy practically pounced.

'Come again?' The man was feigning innocence now.

'You said, men stick to type. If there's anything that could be relevant, I need to know.'

They'd moved into the hallway and Potts made a point of checking the interior door was closed. 'You didn't hear this from me, right?'

'Go on, sir.' Lexy was making no promises.

'And it's only gossip, right? I can't verify it.'

'Understood.'

'There were rumours about that girl,' he pointed a tobacco-stained finger back in the direction of the photograph. 'That she and Michael were seeing each other. There's talk her partner showed up at the office one day, creating merry hell.' He shook his head. 'This was before my time, mind, and if you ask Evelyn, she'll clam up tighter than a crab's arse. She won't hear a word against Michael; thinks the sun shines out of him.'

'Please tell us what you've heard,' Lexy ordered.

'Well, apparently the girl left, nobody ever said why, and then her husband, boyfriend, whatever, turned up demanding to know where she was, and accusing Michael of being far too close and having spirited her away somewhere. All very embarrassing and uncomfortable from what I understand.'

'Was Mr Anderson in the office at the time?' Garry asked.

Potts couldn't hide his glee. 'No, but Eloise was.'

They were in the open doorway now and Potts gave an exaggerated shudder.

'Excuse my language, love, but they do say once a shagger always a shagger. Maybe Michael hasn't left old habits behind. And MPs spend a lot of time away from home. You ask me, young Mrs A could be getting her own back.'

'We're just going to show up?' Garry asked, as he and Lexy approached the Anderson house for the third time in thirty-six hours.

'Let's see how they do when they haven't had time to plan their stories.'

Garry had barely parked before Lexy jumped out and strode up to the front door.

More slowly, Garry followed. 'Far be it from me, but—'

Her head shot round to face him. 'What?' she said.

'I know you're a great believer in pushing witnesses, but what is it, exactly, you're going to push on?'

'I'm going to ask him if he's been unfaithful,' Lexy replied. 'To either of his wives.' She reached out and rang the doorbell.

'Can I wait in the car?'

'And I'm going to ask him why he lied about when he and Olive met. And I'm definitely going to ask why Mr and Mrs Tricks were at his wedding when he and the Trickses are supposed to be sworn enemies.'

Garry could hear footsteps approaching from inside the house; he was ashamed at the relief he felt when he realised they weren't those of a man.

'I'm afraid Michael is out,' Gwen told them when she'd opened the door. 'He's gone to pick the girls up from hockey.'

'We'd like a word with you if we could, please,' Lexy replied.

Gwen looked as though she might refuse, but after a few seconds turned and led the way inside.

'When did Michael and Olive meet?' Lexy asked, as they followed Gwen along the hallway. In the kitchen, Molly the spaniel greeted Garry like an old friend.

'She nursed Eloise, I thought you knew that.' Gwen didn't sit, neither did she invite the two of them to do so.

'There's a photograph in the hallway of Mr Anderson and Olive in the army,' Garry said. 'And we know he left the forces before your daughter became ill.'

Gwen's face looked like stone. 'That's impossible.'

Lexy said, 'Does Garry have your permission to fetch it?'

Garry's heart was beating uncomfortably fast. Lexy, on the other hand, was bright-eyed and her cheeks were a becoming shade of pink. She almost looked like she was enjoying herself.

'I'll go.' Gwen set off back towards the door. 'Show me the one you mean.'

Heart sinking, feeling sure he'd made a stupid mistake, Garry followed Gwen into the hall and indicated the photograph.

The older woman picked it up and peered. 'I need my glasses.'

She led the way back into the kitchen. A few seconds later, glasses on her nose, she carried the silver frame to the window.

'There must be two dozen soldiers in this picture,' she said. 'All in full combat uniform, all with helmets. They've got that camouflage paint on their faces. And I think they're all men.'

'May I?' Garry asked.

The photograph was handed over.

'There.' He let his finger hover over the figure he'd spotted the previous day. 'She's in full kit, her hair's tied back, and she's a few years younger, but I'm pretty sure that's Olive.'

The picture was snatched back.

'You're right,' Gwen said, after a few moments. 'That is Olive. I can't believe I didn't see that.'

'Garry's unusually observant,' Lexy said. 'And he and Olive were at school together.'

'I can't understand why neither of them told me.'

Still holding the photograph, Gwen sat down at the kitchen table. Lexy looked at Garry and discreetly put a finger to her lips.

'These pictures all came boxed up from the family's old place,' Gwen said, after several long seconds. 'I was the one who put them out around the house. Michael couldn't bear to look at them in the early days. I put ones with my daughter at the front. I wanted the girls to see their mother every day. I don't think I've ever looked at this one properly before.'

The older woman's voice was shaking.

'This must be very difficult for you,' Lexy said.

'No, actually, you've made it easier.' Gwen put down the photograph and looked up at Lexy and Garry. 'Eloise wasn't happy in her last year,' she told them. 'She wouldn't tell me what was bothering her, so I suspected it was something to do with Michael. She was always very loyal, would never say anything against him.'

'Did she suspect him of seeing someone else?'

The older woman's mouth tightened. 'Olive, you mean? I'm not sure she'd even met Olive before she went into hospital. But she could have had more general suspicions. Or it could have been as simple as the two of them not getting along as well as they once did. They met when they were very young.'

Garry heard the sound of a car pulling up outside.

Gwen said, 'She said something to me, in the last months, when we were still trying to come to terms with the fact that she wasn't going to get better. I've never forgotten it.'

'What was that?' Lexy asked.

'That she thought perhaps her illness might be rather convenient for Michael.'

'Did you ask what she meant?'

'Of course. But Eloise had a way of closing down conversations.'

Gwen had heard the car outside too; her head went up like a rabbit that had caught a dangerous scent. Pushing back her chair, she strode to the window, looked out for a second and then turned quickly.

'The day before Eloise died, she told me she wanted to speak to me privately. I'd got into the habit of taking the girls in to see her every day. She asked me to come alone the next day, but when I did, there was a lot going on around the ward. Doctors in and out of her room. We didn't get a chance. I said I'd come back as soon as I could, but she died that night.'

She took a deep breath. 'I had no idea it would be the last time I'd talk to my daughter. I thought – we all thought – she had weeks left. I never even got a chance to say goodbye.'

From outside came the sound of car doors being slammed, of high-pitched voices.

As Garry noticed glassy tears in Gwen's eyes, Lexy said, 'Do you have any idea what she wanted to tell you?'

'At the time, I didn't. Now, I'm wondering if she knew about Olive and Michael. I guess we'll never know. But I wouldn't put money on the marriage having continued if she'd lived.'

'And yet Michael lives in your house,' Lexy pointed out. 'Will you challenge him? Now you know about him and Olive being in the army together?'

Gwen closed her eyes. 'What would be the point? My daughter's dead. The girls are all I have left. If I fall out with Michael, he'll take them away. Olive, if she ever comes back, will be more than happy to move out. I'll lose them.'

50

Wednesday 12 December, two years previously

'I'm frightened, Mum,'

A rustle of bedclothes, as though the older woman had reached out for the younger. Then a rattle – maybe something dropped – that almost drowned out what was said next. Olive picked up the listening device and held it closer to her ear.

Olive was at home, in the flat she rented in central Middlesbrough, and her shift had finished an hour ago. The conversation had taken place earlier that afternoon, between Eloise, now in her seventh day on the oncology ward, and her mother, an older, stiffer version of the daughter, who'd fallen into the habit of visiting most afternoons, sometimes with the girls.

The listening device had arrived two days ago; it was astonishing what you could buy on Amazon these days. It had been the easiest thing in the world for Olive to slip it onto the underside of Eloise's bed, retrieving it when she thought there might have been a conversation worth listening to. Even if it was discovered, and Olive was pretty certain it wouldn't be, anyone could have left it there. Nothing could link it to Olive.

Soon, Eloise would move to the hospice, be beyond Olive's reach. She couldn't risk missing any of her conversations.

'I know,' Gwen, Eloise's mother, replied. 'We all are. But you're being so brave. We're all so proud of you.'

'No, not of dying. I am, of course I am, but I don't mean that.'

'What then? Leaving the girls? They'll miss you terribly, but I'll be there for them, so will Michael. They'll want for nothing. And we'll never let you be forgotten.'

Several seconds of silence followed, and Olive pictured Eloise taking her time, gathering the strength to go on.

'I've made you their guardian,' she said eventually. 'Peter brought the papers in a few days ago. They're signed and witnessed. It's official.'

'Me? What about Michael?'

'He is too. There's no way around that. But I've given you a say. I've given you authority. And you're one of their trustees.'

'Gosh.'

A longer silence this time. Then, 'Has anyone come to the house, Mum? In the last few days? A woman, asking for Michael?'

'What sort of woman?'

'A constituent. An angry one. Blaming him for something he promised to do and didn't. You know the type. She came here last week.'

'She did what?' Gwen sounded outraged. 'Does Michael know?'

'No, I didn't tell him. And the hospital have upped their security. I'm fine. But I don't want her coming to the house, causing trouble, upsetting the girls. Promise me you won't talk to anyone who just shows up.'

Another pause, then, 'Elly, is there something you're not telling me.'

'You need to be careful of Michael.'

'What on earth do you mean?'

'I'm not sure you can trust him. He won't deliberately hurt the girls, but he'll always put himself first. I need you to remember that. And he knows some bad people.'

'Elly, now I'm frightened.'

'Good. You should be. You should be frightened of Michael.'

51

'I haven't lied to you. I haven't lied to anyone. What are you talking about?'

In the few moments he'd been back in the house, Anderson's mood had gone from frightened to furious. Garry, who'd seen more fights break out between angry men than he cared to remember, moved to put himself between Anderson and Lexy.

'Dad, what's going on?' The older girl, Amelia, already sent from the kitchen once, had reappeared. Her younger sister could be seen hovering close behind.

'Amelia, go into the other room, I won't tell you again. Take your sister and close the door.'

Nervously, the girls did as they were told.

'You told Garry that you and Mrs Olive Anderson met when she nursed your late wife,' Lexy insisted. 'We know that can't be true. There is a photograph here' – Lexy broke off to indicate the picture now lying face up on the kitchen table – 'that clearly shows the two of you together in your army days. You served with the same regiment.'

'You never told me that,' Gwen said. 'Why would you not tell me that?'

Anderson picked up the photograph. 'Where the hell did this come from?'

Gwen was alarmed too – Garry could see her hands shaking – but she didn't back down. 'From your old house. Did Eloise know you and Olive were . . . acquainted?'

'I haven't seen this in years,' Anderson said.

'Is that Olive in the picture, sir?' Garry asked.

Anderson allowed his head to fall and rise as he kept his eyes fixed on the photograph. 'She wasn't in my regiment, she was in the Medical Corps. She worked with us for a while in Helmand. I barely knew her.'

'Nevertheless, you told me you and Olive met when she nursed your wife,' Garry said. 'That was misleading.'

'I think you're misremembering, constable,' Anderson replied. 'I told you that's when we got to know each other. I remembered her from the army days, of course, but she'd been nothing more than an acquaintance then.'

Garry was pretty certain that hadn't been what Anderson had said.

'Unless you have a recording of the conversation,' Anderson went on. 'In which case maybe I did mislead you.'

He let the comment hang in the air.

'Do you?' he asked when Garry didn't respond.

'I don't,' Garry admitted.

'And, as I pointed out yesterday, you're not a trained detective, so it's hardly surprising if mistakes were made.' He turned to Lexy. 'I'd prefer to be interviewed properly in future, DS Thomas.'

In someone's pocket, a phone alert sounded.

'I assure you PC Mizon has acted properly at all times,' Lexy snapped back. 'And his considerable powers of observation led to a misunderstanding being cleared up.'

Anderson pulled a phone from his coat pocket. 'You're not in uniform, PC Mizon. Are you even on duty?'

'Were Howie and Tina Tricks at your wedding, sir?' Garry asked.

Anderson stared at him. 'What?'

'I was with Olive's parents last night. They had a wedding picture that seemed to include most of the guests. A couple at the back looked a lot like Howie and Tina Tricks. I saw them both two nights ago, you see. I even apprehended Tina when she tried to run away, so their appearance is fresh in my memory.'

'We can have the photograph properly examined,' Lexy added. 'If Garry is right, forensics will confirm it.'

'That won't be necessary,' Anderson replied through what looked like clenched teeth. 'Howie and Tina Tricks were not invited to my wedding. They both happened to be staying at the hotel that day. Or, at least, that's what they claimed. Personally, I don't believe it was coincidence, I think they booked in there to intimidate me. I didn't realise they'd gatecrashed that group photograph until we saw the pictures. Well, I wouldn't, would I? I was at the front of the group.'

'Can anyone confirm this?' Lexy asked. 'Anyone else at the wedding who realised what was going on?'

Anderson gave a heavy sigh. 'Abuse, intimidation and threats are daily occurrences for members of parliament,' he said. 'Tricks could have been telling the truth. I wasn't about to ruin my wedding making a fuss.'

'I can confirm they weren't on the official list,' Gwen added.

Anderson's phone alert sounded again and he held it out towards them.

'Sky News,' he said. 'They've left a voicemail.'

'Can you play it please, sir,' Lexy asked.

Taut-faced, Anderson pressed play.

'Mr Anderson, this is Jenny Hughes from Sky News. We've had a report that your wife, Olive, has gone missing and that there's currently a police investigation into her disappearance. Can you give me a call back, please?'

'Great.' Anderson looked furious. 'I'll be asking questions about how news I specifically asked to be kept confidential has been leaked.'

'This isn't good, Michael,' Gwen said.

He spun round to face her. 'Oh, you think?'

'More likely one of Mrs Anderson's friends, or her family,' Garry said, surprising himself. 'They'll be worried about her, understandably. Which reminds me, sir. We spoke to your agent a short while ago, who said you'd been looking for an address yesterday morning. One of Olive's friends. She said you were very anxious to find it, but that you wouldn't let her help. Can we have that person's name, please?'

Anderson had gone very still. 'I don't know what you're talking about,' he said. 'I think you've got the wrong end of the stick. Again.'

'No, I was there too,' Lexy jumped in. 'As was Mr Potts. Your agent definitely said you'd been looking for an address of one of Olive's old friends. Did you find it, and can we have it please?'

Anderson shook his head. 'Then it's Evelyn who got her wires crossed. I needed several addresses yesterday morning. All people who've raised queries with me that I need to get back to. I was probably talking about Olive's friends at the time and she got mixed up. To be honest, I'm not sure she's really up to the job anymore. And now, I have things to do, not least of which is decide how I deal with Sky News. Gwen, as you let them in, perhaps you can show the officers out?' He turned and left the room.

Silently, Gwen led the way to the front door. On the threshold, she spoke again, so quietly that Garry almost didn't catch what she said.

'He's frightened,' she commented. 'He gets aggressive when he feels things are slipping out of his control. I've seen it before, when Eloise was dying.'

'Perfectly understandable,' Lexy said, in soothing tones.

'And someone pranged his nice new motor,' Garry added, his eyes fixed on the damage to the rear left bumper of Anderson's Audi. The paintwork had been scraped through to the metal beneath. Shame.

52

Thursday 13 December, two years previously

It was Eloise's last night on the ward. A bed had become free in the hospice, and she was due to be moved the following day. Spotting Michael through the window of the private room his wife had been moved to, Olive made a mug of tea.

'I missed you,' she said, hovering in the doorway. 'You slipped in while I was at the other end of the ward.'

'I'm going to miss you,' he replied.

Olive glanced over towards the nurses' station – Stella always watched her closely when Michael was on the ward – then entered the room, closing the door behind her.

'It'll be easier in the hospice,' she said, as Michael took the tea. 'They're better geared up for the care your wife needs now. And for you and the girls.'

'But you won't be there.'

Olive glanced nervously at Eloise, but to all appearances she was asleep. In the reflected glass of the outside window, she spotted Stella in the corridor. Michael, too, saw the other nurse. They both waited until she was out of sight.

'Does she talk to you much?' Michael asked.

'From time to time,' Olive replied. 'There's a sweet spot between the effect of the meds starting to wear off and the pain kicking in again. She can get quite chatty then.'

'What does she talk about?' he asked, and it could have been her imagination, but there seemed to be an edge to his voice.

'The girls mainly,' Olive said truthfully. 'And you, from time to time.' She held his gaze steadily, but if there was anything behind his eyes, she couldn't see it.

And that sense she had of time running out had grown stronger. Even if Eloise had days left, she was moving on tomorrow, away from Olive.

'You must have lots of friends,' Olive said, changing tack. 'But if you ever need someone to talk to . . .'

She paused. Another two colleagues had appeared directly outside. Both could see into the room, but unless they, too, had installed listening devices, they'd have no idea what was being said.

'If you're offering, I'll say yes,' Michael replied.

'I'm offering,' Olive told him in a low voice. 'I know what it's like to lose someone.'

'I think I knew that already,' he told her. 'It's in your eyes.'

Olive felt something catch in her throat. 'It's really that obvious?'

'You look sad. It's the first thing I noticed about you. Well, almost the first.'

Michael took a deep breath then and, when he let it out, he seemed to deflate, as though more than air was seeping out.

'I want it to be over with now,' he said. 'And I know exactly how that sounds, but—'

'It's a very common feeling in the end stages,' Olive told him.

He met her eyes, sharply, almost eagerly. 'And is that where we are? The end?'

Silently, she let her head rise and fall. Eloise had several days left, in her opinion, but Olive's own time with the Andersons was running out. For her, it probably was the end.

Michael dug into his jacket and pulled out a business card, scribbling a number on it. Olive took it, knowing that Michael giving her his number would be halfway around the hospital before the evening was out.

'How will I contact you?' he asked.

Olive glanced down at the card. Apart from the scribbled mobile number, it contained details of his constituency office. 'I'll email you,' she said. 'When . . . things happen – a short note of sympathy. Then, if you still want to . . .'

'Thank you,' he said.

'I need to get back.' Olive stepped backwards towards the door. 'Good luck, Michael. I'll be thinking of you. Of all of you.'

She glanced back as she left the room. Michael was watching her. He didn't see that his wife's eyes were wide open.

53

At the end of the single-track road, Garry jumped down to open the huge metal gates. Lexy, who'd probably expected to be taken to his house to eat lunch, was unusually silent. Back in the car, he pulled forward and put the handbrake on again. The gates had to be closed at all times; it was a council rule.

'I'll get it.' Lexy put the steaming parcels in the footwell before getting out. Seconds later, gates closed, she was back. 'You've brought me to your grandad's allotment.'

'I can see why you're on the fast track.' Garry stopped after another hundred metres. 'We walk from here.'

Even heavy snowfall couldn't disguise the cluttered disorder around them: old wood collected for bonfires, huge plastic vats to hold rainwater or compost, thick black polythene, torn green netting, bamboo wigwams. Empty plant pots and hoses like dead snakes poked through the snow as Garry led Lexy down the pristine white path. Theirs were the first footprints to mar it; today even the hardiest of allotment gardeners had stayed away. Many of the beds they passed were empty for winter, but a few crops of Brussel sprouts, winter cabbages and onions could be seen among the dead stems and shrivelled fruit bushes.

Lexy clutched the fish and chips to her chest as a makeshift hot-water bottle and Garry had a stab of misgiving. He'd brought a girl he liked – jeepers, when had that happened? – to an allotment on what had to be the coldest day of the year.

They reached the indiscernible edge of Garry's patch and he steered Lexy towards the shed, feeling a moment of ridiculous pride that the winter clematis had never looked better. The shed was a mass of creamy white flowers, speckled with purple, and with lime green centres. Lexy might freeze to death, but she'd do so against a backdrop fit for a fairy queen.

'Give me a minute,' he said, fumbling for his keys.

In the shed, he found a spade and quickly wiped the snow off the adjacent bench. He put a sheet of polythene over it to keep out the damp and, when Lexy sat down, spread a blanket over her knees. She gave him a look – one that said she wasn't quite sure about the winter picnic plan – but when he sat down beside her, she moved closer so they could share the blanket.

'Can't see any veg,' she said, as the delicious aroma of fried food wrapped around them like a warm, salt-and-vinegar hug. Her fingers – she'd removed her gloves to eat – were bright pink with cold. He was starting to associate the colour pink with Lexy, he realised, and found himself envisaging flowers that would make up a bouquet for her. Roses, of course, something like Pink Martini or Alnwick, but some fat peonies too and blush-edged ranunculus for contrast. Camellias would be perfect in the right season or dahlias later in the year. He'd use myrtle for the greenery.

'There isn't any,' he admitted. 'This is my cutting garden. Not much to see right now, but you can probably make out the hellebores down the bottom. They're the flat white flowers with yellow stamens. People call them Christmas roses. The small yellow ones are winter aconites and there's a bed of heather just out of sight.' He pointed. 'Over there are my cyclamens and the snowdrops should be coming through soon. It's mainly shrubs that flower in winter – you know, Daphne, Mahonia, quince – and those I grow in the garden back home.'

Lexy carried on eating.

'Everything grows in raised beds,' he went on, 'so I can make sure the soil conditions are always perfect. And I mix them up, spring bulbs and autumn-flowering dahlias, so that no bed has to work too hard at any one time.'

He spotted a late bloom in his rose bed.

'Greenhouse behind the shed,' he continued. 'That's for the stuff that won't grow too well in this country – gardenias, orchids, and suchlike.'

'You're a florist,' Lexy announced. 'I knew you'd done those arrangements you have at home. I found your tools when I was looking for cutlery. You have a drawer full of tape, wires, secateurs.'

'And you knew those for florist tools? You are good.'

'I had a Saturday job in a flower shop when I was fifteen. I lasted three weeks. They sacked me after I fell on a bucket of roses that cost two quid a pop. They all broke.'

Garry winced. 'I'd have sacked you as well.'

'So, what is it? Secret second job? Retirement plan? All-consuming hobby?'

'I think it's a dream.' As he said the words, Garry was abruptly re-minded of his dream of early that morning. 'Speaking of dreams—'

'No, hang on a minute. You can't throw that at me. Traffic cop who dreams of being a florist. Why? I mean, flowers are nice, but they're hardly the stuff that makes the world go round. What we do, *what you do*, is important.'

Garry knew that was true; in his heart, though, he simply couldn't feel it.

'Flowers aren't nice, Lexy, they're perfect,' he found himself saying. 'Florists take simple, perfect beauty and they build it into so much more. There's a structure to flowers. An order. They do what they're told, for the most part. Flowers don't swear at you, or spit, or puke over you. They don't knock you to the ground and kick you in the kidneys when you're down. They don't pull the same crap over and over again so that you despair of ever making the world even a slightly better place. All they do is look perfect for a few days and then move on to make way for the next.'

Garry couldn't remember the last time he'd used so many words in one go.

Lexy was silent for several seconds. Then, 'Why don't you change careers?'

'Have you met my mum?'

She didn't reply.

'I come from a long line of police officers.' He sighed. 'My great-great-grandad hunted Jack the Ripper, he's actually mentioned in the original police reports. Folk in CID still talk about my dad. My second cousin's a detective with the Met. She's been involved in more high-profile cases that you can shake a stick at. My grandad wouldn't have left me this allotment, never mind the house and cash, if he'd thought I'd be a florist. My dad would think I'd shamed him.'

Lexy was silent for a moment. Then, 'You're a very weird bloke, Garry Mizon.'

'Tell me something I don't know.'

'I like you, though.'

He'd known that too, on some level, but he didn't tell her so.

54

Friday 14 December, two years earlier.

Three o'clock in the morning; the graveyard shift. The patients were all asleep, some moaning or muttering to themselves, but oblivious to what was going on around them. Two of the nurses were on break, which meant they'd be napping in the staffroom.

Soft conversation at the nurses' station and the regular low-pitched sounds from dozens of instruments provided a gentle hum of ambient sound. Lights were turned to their dimmest setting. Muffled footsteps, the creaking of trolley wheels. A telephone rang, its shrill notes cutting through the air; it was answered quickly.

On her way back from the staff bathroom, Olive happened to glance towards Eloise's room. Blinds on both windows and doors were drawn, making it impossible to see inside. They hadn't been earlier. During Michael's visit, the blinds had been up. Someone had drawn them and that wasn't customary procedure at night.

Gently, soundlessly, she turned the door handle and pushed. The room beyond was lit only by the few instruments currently switched on. Eloise wasn't hooked up to any monitors. There was nothing they could do for her anymore but manage her pain and that medication was administered by a simple canula taped to the back of her left hand.

Eloise's slight form was barely distinguishable on the bed, but Olive knew instantly that something wasn't as it should be. There was a stillness in the room, an emptiness. Something essential was missing.

'Eloise?' Her voice barely broke the silence and Olive realised that she was shaking. And that her heartbeat had picked up. She could feel it, thumping against her chest. Her right hand reached for the light switch, but something held her back. In the gloom, she took two steps closer to the bed. If the patient was breathing, she was doing so silently.

A weak beam of light had forced its way through the window blinds, but Olive herself was in its way. Until she took one more step closer to the bed, she was unable to see Eloise's face. She took that step. And learned that Eloise had stopped breathing some time ago.

The dead woman's mouth had gaped open. Her eyes were open too, staring at something beyond the room's ceiling.

Olive took hold of her patient's left wrist and felt for the pulse, although she knew it was unnecessary. The limb was cold, the skin oddly moist. She'd been dead an hour at least, maybe longer.

It was 0310 hours, and it would be Olive's job to verify death.

Glancing round at the door and internal window, although she knew she was shielded from view, she walked quickly round the bed and bent to retrieve the listening device from its underside. It would be some time before she could check exactly how much of the conversation that she and Eloise had had earlier was on record.

For now, she had a job to do.

55

'I don't like Anderson,' Garry said, as he was getting to the end of his fish and chips.

Lexy, who'd eaten as much as he, gave a soft laugh. 'Really? I'd never have guessed.'

'How about it was him who met Olive in Hexham? There was time for him to get there, leave with her, do . . . whatever it was he did – and get back to Home Farm before anyone questioned his movements.'

'Really?' Lexy huddled closer. 'In this weather?'

'Yes, really. I could have done it. Maybe he could too.'

'Why would he want to hurt his wife six months after he married her?'

'Eloise wanted to tell her mother something important. She died before she had a chance. What if she told Olive instead?'

Lexy paused before replying, giving the impression, at least, that she was thinking about it. Then, 'Even if she did, Olive married him, eighteen months later. Why would she do that if she knew he was a villain?'

Garry had his answer ready. 'OK, what if she later learned something she shouldn't? Gwen said she was sly, remember? That she caught her sneaking around the house more than once, hanging around in his office, maybe trying to access his computer. What if she found out the same thing Eloise knew? He'd have to get rid of her too.'

'Sorry, what? You're saying he bumped off Eloise as well? Garry, she had terminal cancer.'

'I wasn't, but now I'm wondering. Eloise died before she was expected to. Only a matter of weeks, maybe even days, but still. What if there was something she needed to get off her chest? Maybe something to do with the Tricks family. And what if Anderson couldn't risk that happening? Eighteen months later, Olive finds out the same thing.'

'I'm hearing a lot of what ifs.'

Garry started fidgeting, on the point of getting up. 'We need to find out if he was with Eloise when she died. We need to get back to the hospital.'

'Whoa there, tiger. You're about to accuse our local MP of double murder. I'm not sure I can have your back on that one.'

'How could Howie Tricks know that Michael Anderson's wife has gone missing?'

Lexy sighed. 'Howie will have contacts at the station, you know that. These people have a way of finding stuff out.'

Garry had eaten enough. He wrapped the few remaining chips and got up to carry them to the compost heap, pushing them down deep to discourage foxes. Lexy was right. He was putting two and two together and making a ridiculous number.

On the way back, he took a detour around the rose bed and leaned in to pick the solitary bloom he'd spotted earlier. It was a Gabriel Oak, a ruffled mass of carmine petals, a deeper pink than he'd have chosen for Lexy, but its scent was glorious. He walked back to the shed, twirling the rose in his fingers, wondering if he'd have the nerve to give it to her. He tucked it into his breast pocket and felt a fool.

'What will happen now?' he asked, as she got to her feet and they took the blanket and polythene back into the shed. 'Now that Sky have got hold of the story?'

'No option but to launch the missing persons.' If Lexy noticed the rose in his pocket, she didn't comment. 'Every station will be informed, all the social media accounts activated. Given the Andersons' profile, it will probably make the news.'

'Searches?' Garry locked the shed and they set off back towards the car.

Lexy gave a small shake of her head. 'Where do we start? They won't call the helicopter out in this weather, not unless they're pretty sure they know where she is and can recover her. Drones will be useless until we have an idea where to look. Same with foot searches and dogs. Unless we get some intel we can act on, there really is nothing the force at large can achieve that you and I haven't been doing already.'

Garry strode ahead as they approached the car, beeping it open and holding the passenger door for Lexy. He pulled the rose from his jacket pocket, relieved to see it had come to no harm. 'Last of the year,' he said, holding it out. 'Be a shame to let the frost get it.'

For an uncomfortable second, he thought she might turn it down, but then her lips twitched at the corners. 'Thank you,' she said, looking up directly into his eyes, as though waiting for him to—

'Dreams,' he announced. Leaving her abruptly, he strode round to the driver door. 'I had one last night,' he went on, when they were both in the vehicle.

As they left the allotments, he filled her in with his poster dream.

'I slapped you?' she said, when he'd finished.

'It's what woke me up. But it's what you said before you slapped me that could be important.'

'*It's all about the ears, Dumbo?* I'm not seeing it. This is something to do with Olive's ears?'

'Not Olive's ears, mine.'

Lexy thought for a second. 'Nope. Still struggling.'

'My family don't call me Dumbo because I was a fat kid.'

'I knew that.'

'Please don't interrupt. They called me Dumbo because I was known as the family elephant. I never forgot a thing. I'm serious, not a thing. I can tell you which of my cousins got a Spider-Man car for Christmas and who got a Barbie doll and I can name the year.'

She nodded. 'Makes sense,' she muttered.

He had no idea what that meant but didn't want to get distracted. 'Ever since I heard Olive was missing, I've had the oddest déjà-vu-type feeling. As though I'm remembering something. As though it's happened before.'

Her eyes narrowed. 'You think Olive's gone missing before?'

'Probably not as simple as that, but we should check. I think last night's dream was my subconscious nudging me that this is important. If I can work out what it is I'm supposed to remember, it will help.'

'I didn't have you down as a touchy-feely type.'

The main road was unsurprisingly quiet; even a little after midday, a dull sort of twilight had crept across the world. It was the sort of day when businesses closed early, and all but the hardiest types cancelled any plans they might have to go out.

'Best driver on the force, good at spotting trouble, often before it starts, easily distracted and likes to focus on one job at a time, crap at paperwork and useless in an exam room. Occasionally trips over his own feet. That's what they told me I'd get. Instead, it's all interpreting dreams and floral arrangements.'

She was making fun of him again.

'What are we doing now?' he asked.

'We're going back to the station to face the music.'

'There's music?'

'Oh yeah. Anderson was well pissed off with us and he won't take it lying down. Brace yourself, Garry, and keep your mouth shut. The fan's about to start spinning.'

56

Friday 14 December, two years previously

Olive was still preparing Eloise's body when Michael arrived. Normally, she found 'last offices' soothing; not this time.

'Thank you,' he said, from the doorway of the room. He wore jeans and a thick, sage-green sweater with a half zip. It was the first time since Afghanistan that Olive had seen him not wearing a suit.

Insisting on doing everything herself, Olive had been combing Eloise's hair, painstakingly slowly, because the last thing she wanted was to start ripping it out in clumps. She lowered her patient's head gently, grateful that the least pleasant job, the cleaning of leaking bodily fluids, had already taken place. She'd even sprayed air freshener around the room.

'Come in,' she said. 'I'm not quite finished, but you may as well come in and help. Unless you'd prefer to wait in the visitors' room. I can have someone bring you a hot drink.'

Michael stepped into the room, his eyes on his wife's face. 'When did it happen?' he asked.

She'd told him this already on the telephone, but the shock of bereavement often played havoc with memory.

'Between midnight and 0200 hours, we think. She was last checked a few minutes after midnight and was still with us then. The doctor thinks it was a sudden cardiac arrest. We weren't expecting it, certainly not today, but it's not uncommon at this stage.'

Michael's eyes closed and he seemed to sway on his feet. Olive was by his side in seconds, wrapping an arm around his waist.

'You need to sit down,' she told him, as she pushed him towards the bedside chair. 'This is a lot to take in. You shouldn't have come alone.'

'Gwen wanted to come, but we couldn't leave the girls. We didn't want to wake them, either. They don't know yet.'

Leaving him briefly, Olive darted to the door of the room and signalled to the nurse she knew would be looking their way. She made the drinking sign and pointed into the room before going back inside.

'I know it's a shock,' she said. 'But, in time, you might come to think it was better this way. She's been saved a lot of pain.'

'I should have been here,' he said. 'She shouldn't have had to go alone. Why is her mouth like that?'

'It's very common.' Olive went back to the other side of the bed where the trolley was stationed. 'The muscles in the jaw stop working after death, so the mouth falls open. I've put an extra pillow under her head to minimise it, but the undertakers will soon sort it out. They'll have her looking beautiful in no time. Perhaps wait until she's in the chapel of rest before the girls see her?'

Michael had taken hold of his wife's hand. 'She was beautiful. She was probably the most beautiful woman I ever saw. I thought losing her looks would be the hardest thing for her to deal with, but she hardly seemed to care. All her thoughts were for the girls, and me.'

'I have some jewellery for you.' Olive reached over the bed with a small plastic bag in her hand. Inside were Eloise's wristwatch, a simple gold necklace and two pairs of earrings. 'What do you want to do with her wedding ring? We always recommend that it's removed as soon as possible, but it's up to you.'

In response, he raised Eloise's hand and twisted the plain gold band off her finger. 'I put it on,' he said. 'Right that I should take it off.'

Olive held the bag open and the ring was dropped inside. 'Slip it into your pocket,' she said, marvelling at how malleable the freshly bereaved were. 'You don't want it lost.'

'She barely spoke to me earlier,' Michael said. 'She was asleep for practically the whole visit. It feels like such a waste.'

Eloise hadn't been asleep though; she'd heard Michael and Olive exchange telephone numbers, arrange to meet up when the wife was out of the picture.

'I didn't say goodbye.'

'The chances are she slipped away in her sleep,' Olive said, although she knew it hadn't been the case; Eloise's eyes had been wide open when she'd been found. The bedclothes had been ruffled too, as though she'd tried to move. 'It wouldn't have made any difference. Not to her, anyway.'

'Did she say anything after I left? Did she wake up at all?'

Eloise had indeed woken after her husband went home; Eloise had had quite a lot to say.

'She woke briefly,' Olive replied. 'She was telling me about the sailing you used to do together. Something about a spin-, a spinny-something.'

'Spinnaker?' Michael's eyes had narrowed. He looked tense. 'Why would she mention the spinnaker?'

Olive shook her head. 'I don't even know what a spinnaker is.'

Michael's voice hardened, as though she'd offended him. 'Seems an odd thing to talk about. Anything else?'

'No, not really.'

He got to his feet. 'Will there be a post-mortem?'

'No. The doctor signed the paperwork. As I said, this sort of sudden death isn't uncommon when patients are as ill as your wife was.'

A noise in the corridor startled them both. The door opened and two hospital orderlies appeared, pushing a trolley between them.

'You need to say goodbye for now,' Olive told Michael. 'You can see her later, when she's ready.'

The body was moved quickly and efficiently and then the door of the room closed once more. Michael leaned against the rail at the foot of the bed. His head dropped, so that his chin almost rested on his chest.

'It's over then,' he said. 'Really over.'

Olive moved closer to stand by his side. She felt the skin of her right hand brush against his left and then, a second later, his hand clasped around hers. He squeezed, once, and then let her go.

57

'Well, it's out there,' the deputy chief constable said, after the piece had aired on the early-evening news. The nation had been informed that Olive Anderson, wife of the sitting MP for Middlesbrough South and East Cleveland, had been missing for nearly forty-eight hours. Neither the Anderson family nor Olive's parents had appeared; instead, a statement pleading for news of Olive had been read by the reporter.

'We'll hear from her in an hour,' one of the DIs yawned. 'It's one thing to publicly humiliate her husband, another to risk charges for wasting police time.'

'We'd better bloody hope so,' the deputy chief replied. 'In the meantime, PC Mizon, a word in your shell-like.'

'Sir.' As Garry approached the boss, he was aware of movement around him. Most officers in the skeleton staff went back to their desks. One or two watched with undisguised glee.

'Remind me of the job we pay you to do, PC Mizon.'

'Sir,' Lexy stepped forward.

'You'll get your turn, DS Thomas. In the meantime, I'm dealing with a complaint against PC Mizon here, for inappropriate and aggressive treatment of the family member of a potential victim. An important one, at that. On top of that, the Tricks family have made their complaint official.'

'Sir, that's unfair. The Anderson part anyway. I was with Garry most of the time we were with the family and he did nothing untoward. In fact, thanks to him—'

'One more word, Thomas, and you'll be on report. Now, Mizon, are you on duty right now?'

'No, sir.'

'Then I suggest you get yourself home, do whatever it is you do at weekends, put the Olive Anderson case out of your head and keep your fingers crossed Michael Anderson doesn't make his complaint formal as well. And if you could stop behaving like a complete twat, that would be a bonus.'

'Sir, I think Michael Anderson could be involved in Olive's disappearance,' Garry said. 'I think he's a liar and I think he's hiding something.'

'Remind me how many times you failed your detective exams, Mizon.'

Garry took a deep breath, at the same time registering surprise that he was still maintaining eye contact with the chief.

'I'm waiting, Mizon.'

What the heck, everyone knew anyway.

'Twice, sir. Nevertheless . . .'

The deputy chief took a step closer. Garry told himself he was not backing down. Not faced with someone three inches shorter than he was.

The chief said, 'Was any part of my instruction to go home and stay home unclear?'

'No, sir.'

'Then why are you still here?'

Knowing he was out of time, Garry turned. Avoiding eye contact with everyone, he left the room.

'Garry!' Lexy caught up with him in the car park. 'Where are you going?'

'Home,' he replied. 'As instructed.'

'It's all bullshit,' she said. 'You did nothing wrong. Nothing at all.'

He shrugged. 'Like you said, I'm a maverick.'

Damn it, he quite liked the idea: Garry Mizon – maverick.

'You're not going home, are you?' Lexy took a step back to look at him properly and suspicion seeped into her eyes.

'Course I am,' he lied.

'Seriously, you have to. Let me handle it now. I shouldn't have got you involved at all, I feel terrible. I'll keep you informed the minute anything happens, I promise. But you have to go home and keep your head down.'

'Roger that, Sarge.' He gave her a tiny mock salute.

She took another step backwards, still glaring at him. 'I'm going to phone you in an hour. On your landline. You'd better answer.'

'Looking forward to it.' He swung into the driver's seat and started the engine. As he drove out of the car park, he could see Lexy watching him from the station's rear entrance. He turned left, in the opposite direction to home, reflecting that he might actually find himself fired before the day was out.

Well, darn it. He didn't like the job anyway.

'Is there any news?' the nurse, Stella Cook, asked Garry as the two of them found a vacant table in the hospital cafeteria.

Stella, who'd been about to go on a break when Garry arrived at the nurses' station, had agreed to go for a coffee with him.

'We've all been worried,' she went on, 'since we heard from Newcastle that she didn't show up yesterday.'

'Nothing as yet,' Garry told Stella, who didn't look particularly worried. 'I understand she was Eloise Warner's chief nurse when she was on the ward. This would be around two years ago now.'

Stella pulled a face. 'We don't have chief nurses as such. Let's just say the family, or some members of it, had their favourites.'

'Are you suggesting Michael Anderson had a soft spot for Olive? I'm not digging the dirt here, but Olive's relationship with her husband could be important.'

The woman nodded. 'There was an obvious chemistry from the start. Some might say Olive had her eye on a man who was soon to be a very eligible widower and did her best to get in with him.'

Garry thought carefully before he spoke again; trying to defend Olive wouldn't be helpful right now.

'That would suggest she was pretty calculating? Going after a bloke while his wife was terminally ill with cancer?'

'Aye, well, she's an odd one. Good-looking girl like that, never had a boyfriend. Lot of nice lads asked her out, to my knowledge – doctors, senior nurses, managers. Not interested. And then Michael Anderson comes along and suddenly she's wearing more make-up, always has clean hair, making him tea, which I never saw her do for anyone else, hanging around the nurses' station and Eloise's bay when he was in.'

'You think she was doing the running?' Garry told himself this wasn't idle gossip, it was his job to find out what happened to Olive. And then remembered it wasn't actually his job at all. He glanced at his watch. Another thirty minutes or so until Lexy phoned him at home.

'Oh, I think he met her halfway. I know he gave her his number.'

'You saw that?'

Stella nodded. 'Right under his wife's nose. The very night she died.' She glanced at her watch.

'Can we fast-forward a bit,' Garry asked. 'How did Olive seem the last couple of months? Anything bothering her that you noticed? Anything that made you think the marriage wasn't working out as she'd hoped?'

Stella finished her coffee and picked up her bag. 'To be honest, love, I'm not sure I ever saw Olive happy. And that's my time up. Thanks for the coffee.' She got up.

'One more thing.' Garry stood too, knowing he barely had time to get home before Lexy rang. He wondered if she had plans for her Saturday night and whether – No, that was daft. She'd kept the rose though, using a mug as a makeshift vase and finding a spot for it on her desk. 'The night Eloise died, were you working?'

Stella gave a brief nod. 'I was, I told you.'

'You did, sorry. Can you remember anything else about that night? What time Mr Anderson arrived, when he left?'

Stella frowned. 'It was late, after normal visiting hours. I'd say he came in about half eight, stayed maybe an hour. Olive took him a cup of tea, as usual, and he gave her his number.'

'And how did Eloise seem after he'd gone?'

'Much the same. Tired. I helped her go to the bathroom shortly after he went. I'm pretty sure she went to sleep after that. Died a few hours later.'

So, Eloise had been alive when Anderson left; another daft theory debunked.

'I'm not trying to cause trouble or anything,' Stella said, her eyes darting around the room. 'This is probably nothing,' she went on. 'And I would never have mentioned it otherwise.'

Garry was suddenly very conscious of the time; he didn't want to miss Lexy's phone call. 'Anything you can tell me.'

Stella was looking over at the serving counter. 'You should have a word with Rick,' she said. 'He was working nights when Eloise died. He saw something.'

'What?'

She stepped away. 'You should ask him. Better it comes from him.'

58

After Michael Anderson left the ward for the second time that night, another hour went by before Olive could check the listening device that had spent the last few days beneath his late wife's bed. She locked herself in a stall in the staff bathroom and switched it on.

She had nearly thirty minutes of recordings to get through and wouldn't have long before someone came looking for her. She raced through, fast-forwarding and stopping frequently. When she got to the end, she couldn't move. The battery had run out at the worst possible time. The recording was useless. Absolutely fucking useless.

Only the certain knowledge that she'd never, in a million years, be able to explain it stopped her smashing every hard surface in the bathroom to pieces.

Anderson was wrong. It wasn't over. She was only getting started.

59

Rick couldn't leave the counter, but the café wasn't busy. At nearly eight o'clock on a Saturday evening, with the weather as it was, few people who didn't have to were inclined to hang around a hospital.

'Stella said you noticed something on the night of Thursday the thirteenth, Friday the fourteenth of December two years ago,' Garry began. 'The night Eloise Warner, wife of our local MP, died.'

Rick's face tightened. 'It were a while back, like.' He picked up a cloth and made a show of wiping down the counter.

'It's important. So, did you see anything?'

'Who wants to know?'

Garry stifled a sigh; he'd already introduced himself as an off-duty police officer.

'For now, only me,' he said. 'But I can get on the phone and have one of my colleagues come in. They might prefer to talk to you down at the station. It can get busy on a Saturday night, especially this close to Christmas. You could be there a while.'

Rick started talking. Ten minutes later, Garry was in the hospital's security office.

'Night of the thirteenth, fourteenth of December,' he said. 'Ground-floor café and the main entrance, please. Footage between the hours of 2100 and 0400.'

The security guard took a while to find the file, but eventually the two men were watching grainy black-and-white footage. The café, on the night Eloise died, was as empty and forlorn as it had been minutes earlier. An elderly woman sat at a far table. Two nurses approached the counter, bought hot drinks and carried them away. Rick, the attendant, examined his fingernails and scrolled through his phone.

'Café closes at ten,' the guard said.

'I know. The man I'm looking for left his wife's ward at around half past nine in the evening,' Garry said. 'Rick in the café says he served him that night.'

'Here we go. This your man?'

It was indeed his man. At 2136 hours, Michael Anderson approached the serving counter. After a few exchanged words with Rick, he took his drink and found a table close to the café entrance. He sat, without moving, for some time.

'I can fast-forward,' the guard offered, suiting action to words.

'Hold it,' Garry ordered, as Anderson jerked to his feet. Rick, the server, had approached. The two men were talking, then Anderson turned to leave. Rick followed him out, pulling down the barriers that closed the café off until the following day. 'Twenty-two hundred hours on the dot,' Garry muttered. 'So, does he leave the hospital?'

'Let's see.'

Minutes passed while the guard found a different set of files, and then the two of them were looking at footage of the hospital's main reception area. They watched, fast-forwarding occasionally, until nearly eleven o'clock in the evening. Michael Anderson was not seen leaving the hospital.

'He came back around four,' Garry said. 'See if you can find him.'

More time passed, and then the two men saw Michael Anderson stride quickly into the hospital through the main entrance.

'Must have gone home,' the guard said. 'He'd changed.'

Garry nodded. He too had spotted the casual clothes Anderson was wearing on his second visit. 'Are there other ways he could have left the building?'

'Several.' The guard got to his feet and stepped sideways to face a schematic plan of the hospital building. 'There's a door in C wing that leads directly out to the western car park. He could have gone that way. Plus several doors that visitors aren't allowed to use, but there's not a lot to stop them.'

'Can we check?'

The guard looked regretful. 'Can't be done. We've got a policy on CCTV, ruddy thing's pages long. I'm probably breaking all sorts of rules by talking to you. Basically, only footage from the main entrance and the bigger public areas like the café is kept for more than a year. If your MP friend went out another way, the record will have been wiped months ago.'

Garry took a breath. 'What about if he went back to the ward?'

'Same thing. And wards don't have CCTV anyway. Some of the main corridors do, but not the wards themselves.'

'Right, thanks for your time.' It was ten minutes before Lexy was due to call him.

'I assume someone's checked her locker?' the guard said.

'Come again?'

'Staff lockers. We all have one. Utility staff like me on this floor. Nursing staff one floor up.'

Garry couldn't remember anyone mentioning Olive's locker. He said, 'I know I'm stating the obvious, but lockers are locked, right?'

The guard nodded. 'Owners have keys, and a spare set kept in case of loss.'

'And those spare keys are . . .'

The guard turned and nodded at a flat wall cupboard.

'And is there a policy on handing out keys to all and sundry?'

'Naturally. But nothing to stop me opening a locker, especially when accompanied by an officer of the law.'

'Lead the way.'

Olive's locker held a black gym bag with a decorative key ring attached to the handle. No keys, just the key ring. Knowing he was pushing his luck, but unable to resist, Garry took out his handkerchief and wrapped it around his right hand before inching open the zip. He could hear the security guard breathing over his shoulder. The insides smelled of laundry waiting to be washed and a chemically produced floral. He saw black fabric, the heel of a training shoe, a cosmetics bag. He closed the zip.

'I can't take this,' he told the security officer. 'I'll get someone to collect it and sign it into evidence. Can you make sure no one but an on-duty police officer looks into this locker until then?'

'No problem,' the guard told him. 'I'll keep the key with me.'

Garry glanced at his watch. Short of teleporting home, he was going to miss Lexy's call, but she'd be pleased about the gym bag, wouldn't she? On a whim, he took a photograph of the bag and then a close-up of the key ring.

Now to see how fast he could drive home.

60

The snow was coming down again. Olive could see it falling into the void below. At first, she'd wondered if it was just wind blowing snow off the car and the surrounding branches, but it had been falling too thickly and too consistently for some time now for there to be any doubt.

She was so cold, so very cold, slipping in and out of sleep and sometimes struggling to tell when she was awake and when dreaming. The nurse she'd been once knew she was in the early stages of hypothermia. Early stages, if she was lucky. Even so, she didn't think she'd survive much longer in the car.

Some time ago – she was struggling to keep an exact track – she'd found paracetamol and a packet of mint humbugs in the glove compartment. Annoyed with herself for not thinking of it before, she'd swallowed four paracetamol, washing them down with snow, and crammed a handful of sweets into her mouth. When they'd dissolved, she'd eaten more until the packet was gone. Minutes later, the sugar and the painkillers had started working their magic. Since then, she'd managed to keep the worst of the pain at bay, although the sweets had long gone.

She knew she couldn't survive another night; if she was going to act, it had to be now.

61

Before leaving the hospital car park, Garry found the number for Olive's parents.

'Sorry to bother you again,' he said, when Olive's dad, George, had answered and Garry had explained that nothing new had come up so far, but that his colleagues were confident Olive would be in touch once she knew people were concerned. 'But something's been niggling me.'

He explained his odd feeling of déjà vu about Olive being missing.

'I've a pretty good memory,' he finished, when he'd heard nothing from George for several seconds, except, perhaps, silent disapproval. 'Is there anything that could explain that? Did Olive go missing previously? Maybe for a few hours? Maybe at school?'

It hadn't been at school. He'd have known and remembered if Olive had gone missing back then.

'No, lad.'

'Nothing at all?'

'Our Olive's never been in trouble. She's a good girl, our Olive. Never anything untoward.'

'Got it. Thank you for your time, Mr C.'

He was talking into thin air; Olive's dad had put the phone down. OK, now that was bothering him as well. Why did he get the feeling that George Charles was on the verge of defensive when he talked about his daughter? A bit too keen to tell the world she was a good girl? In the meantime, he still had no way of knowing, or proving, what time Anderson had left the hospital on the night Eloise had died.

As he reached his bungalow, he realised he might have a way; Eloise's mother might tell him. Without even leaving the car, he dialled the number, knowing he'd be in a whole heap of smelly stuff if Anderson answered.

'Home Farm,' said the unmistakeable voice of Gwen.

'I heard you'd been taken off the investigation,' she replied, in frosty tones, when Garry told her who was calling.

'I was never on it, Mrs Warner. I'm a traffic officer. But I was friends with Olive at school.' OK, that was a stretch. 'I liked her. I liked your daughter too. I met her a few times. Very nice lady. She got her heel stuck in a grate once. I happened to be there. I don't suppose—'

A soft laugh. 'She told me about that.'

He held his breath.

'What can I do for you?' she said after a moment.

This was where he took a big risk. 'I've been talking to the hospital about the night your daughter died,' he said. 'And I can't pin down the time Mr Anderson left. I know he was at the hospital till at least ten. Can you help at all?'

'That's a very odd question.'

'I appreciate that.'

Seconds ticked by.

'I can't help, I'm afraid. I tried to wait up for Michael that night. I wanted to know how Eloise had been. I was exhausted, though. I went to bed before he got home. The next thing I remember, he was waking me up, telling me she was dead. That was just after three o'clock in the morning.'

'I'm very sorry to be bringing back sad memories. Can you re-member what time you went to bed?'

'Ten? Ten thirty? I couldn't say. And you're not bringing back sad memories. They never went away.'

Garry took a deep breath. 'Mrs Warner . . .'

He heard movement down the line, as though Gwen, or someone else, had opened a door.

'Was a post-mortem carried out on your daughter?'

A moment of silence, then, 'I can't talk now.' Her voice had dropped to a whisper. 'Michael's on his way out. I'll call you back.'

She was gone.

As Garry opened his front door, the house felt unusually cold. He switched on the gas fire in the front room and knew he should cook himself something to eat. Something that wasn't fish and chips or pizza. He wasn't sure he could be bothered.

The light on his answer machine hadn't turned on; Lexy hadn't phoned.

62

The car hadn't moved for some time. Olive knew that if she could reach the back seat, she could access the boot where the bags were stored. If she could get to her bag, she'd have a phone, more clothes, drugs that could hold the pain back for long enough to get to safety. She could also find the stranger's laptop and hurl it into the void.

Heart thumping, sweating in spite of the cold, she began moving, easing her way up through the interior of the car.

It was painstakingly slow, and her mind kept drifting, as though the effects of cold, shock and pain were eating away at her brain. After a while, she found herself crouching on the back of the passenger seat. She wasn't entirely sure how long she'd been inching her way up the vehicle, but the switch that would open the rear side window was almost within reach and if the car's electrics hadn't given up, it should still work. If the window opened, if the tree branches held, she could climb out.

Being able to reach her bag would be a bonus, but the key thing had to be to get out of the car.

Her left ankle couldn't hold her weight, not even for a second, and breathing still hurt – she thought several ribs were cracked – but she kept going, onto the armrest between driver and passenger seat, into the rear footwell. Every movement careful, always aware of how fragile the branches holding her up must be.

Inches away from the rear door, she risked stretching up. The car groaned and dropped, like an airplane in turbulence. Even as her stomach plummeted, she reached for the handgrip above the rear window. A wrench of pain pulled at her chest, but she caught it and kept hold.

The car held. She was so close.

Clutching the grip in one hand, she pressed the window button with the other. The window grumbled against the hold the ice had on it, but moved – an inch, two inches, three. Snowflakes touched Olive's face and a rush of cold air blew through the car. She pressed again and the window opened. There was a branch, less than a foot above the open window, that looked strong enough to hold her weight. Gingerly, she stretched up. Her fingers brushed it, got ready to curl around it.

A hand grasped her injured left ankle, sending another shock wave of pain through her body. Olive looked down. Blue eyes met hers.

Not dead. The stranger was alive. And now the car was shifting again, snow was sliding off its roof, its angle tilting. Olive stared down into the car interior, knowing the terror in the stranger's face was an exact mirror of her own.

63

Garry spent his first half-hour home cooking proper food – salmon with vegetables – that he forced down because he knew it was the sensible thing to do. He kept the TV news on, turning up the volume when he left the room, but there were no updates on the Olive Anderson case. Nothing on the force's Twitter feed either. And no messages.

By six o'clock, he was sitting at his kitchen counter, scrolling through his phone, wondering how he was going to get through the rest of the evening.

Lexy would probably be home by now; there'd have been no need for her to stay at work unless something big had come up. So, either there'd been a development that was being kept from the public – and him – for now, or she did have plans for her Saturday evening.

Something significant enough to be kept quiet could only mean that Olive had been found – neither safe nor well – and he certainly didn't want that. On the other hand, the thought of Lexy in a noisy pre-Christmas pub, pink-cheeked from the heat and the alcohol, smiling up at one of the DIs: no, that didn't fill him with any joy either. He honestly wasn't sure which he'd prefer; and what did that say about him?

For several minutes, he toyed with the idea of phoning Lexy – he did have the gym bag to tell her about – before deciding he'd already made a big enough fool of himself that day. He'd barely known her two days and yet Lexy knew more about him than anyone outside his own family; more than any of them, to be honest, and he was not about to give her additional ammunition to make him look stupid around the station. The ribbing he was going to get. A closet florist. It would be years, if ever, before he heard the end of it.

He'd give her till seven, then phone his report of finding the gym bag into the station.

He'd genuinely thought she'd call, though.

Enough. He was not spending the entire evening obsessing over his phone like a teenage girl. He got up, leaving it on the counter, and left the room. He'd have a bath, watch a bit of TV, then get an early night and try to catch up on lost sleep. There was honestly nothing more he could do right now.

His mobile was ringing. Garry banged his hip on the door frame as he raced back into the kitchen. Lexy. He caught his breath and told himself to let it go to messages. No need to make it blindingly obvious he had no life to speak of. He held off for four rings.

'All right,' he said, in a passable attempt to sound casual, wishing he'd thought to have some music playing, something low-key, soft, something that might suggest he wasn't alone.

'Garry, I'm really sorry about this, honestly I am, but I've got no one else to call.'

She was actually crying, he could hear the suppressed sob in her voice.

'What's happened? Where are you?'

The line crackled and cut off for a second; wherever she was, reception wasn't brilliant.

'Lexy. Talk to me.'

Another crackle, then: 'You're going to be so pissed off with me. After balling you out for irresponsible behaviour as well.'

'Where are you?'

She sniffed. 'I'm in a ditch.'

A beat.

'Come again.'

'I thought I'd make it. It's all main roads, and they've been gritted. But the Hartlepool road was blocked, so I went up the A19 and then turned east. I thought, what's the worst that can happen, I've been watching you drive in the snow all day. It didn't look that hard.'

She'd taken that stupid car of hers out in this weather. 'Where? Where did you turn east?'

'At a village called Enwick? Ewick? God, I can't remember.'

She was on the Elwick road. 'Are you hurt?'

'No. Just freezing. I've been stuck here an hour. I called the AA, but they're dealing with loads of trapped vehicles and they're not sure when they can get to me. And I didn't crash so much as slide. There was a skid. I've never been in a skid before. And then I lost control. There was no steerage.'

Always drive into a skid. Everyone knew it, so few managed it. It was so totally counter-intuitive.

He said, 'Do you know exactly where you are?'

'I passed a farm a few minutes before the skid. On the left-hand side. I didn't catch the name.'

OK, right. Middlesbrough to Hartlepool took thirty minutes in good conditions. These were not good conditions. It could take an hour or more to find her, even if he made it that far – of course, he'd make it, he was the best driver on the force – and she didn't sound in a good way.

Did people actually say that about him? Best driver on the force?

Focus. First up, tow ropes, torches, shovel, snow socks, first-aid kit – all in the boot of his car where they'd been since early November. Second, fuel, water and washer fluid – topped up several times a week in winter, no need to worry about that. Third, hot drink, hot-water bottle, sugary snack, warm blankets, fresh clothes – he could have them ready in five minutes. Ten minutes at the outset and he'd be good to go. In the kitchen, he switched on the kettle and found a flask.

'Garry, you still there?'

'Where the Dickens were you going?'

'Hartlepool marina.'

He poured a quarter pint of milk into a jug and shoved it into the microwave. 'Why?'

'Better if I tell you in person. You will come, won't you?'

He checked his watch and gave her an ETA. 'Stay in the car, Lexy. Keep your engine running.'

64

The car slid. A branch broke. Metal screamed and so did the two women. Olive saw the branch she'd been reaching for slipping away into the night. She braced herself for a few seconds of free fall followed by excruciating pain and then . . .

The car stopped moving. Miraculously, something – the flimsiest of branches maybe – was holding it up.

'Don't move.' She glared into the stranger's cold blue eyes. 'Don't move a muscle.'

Those eyes were no longer terrified, but dull with pain. They looked like eyes on the brink of drifting away into sleep, or something much more permanent. The grip on Olive's leg loosened. A sudden shake would free her. Olive braced herself for the pain and got ready to pull herself free.

'Maddy?' the stranger said, her eyes desperate and pleading, still gazing into Olive's own. 'How is this possible?'

And with five simple words, everything changed.

PART THREE

The strange disappearance of Maddy Black

65

July, three years previously

Olive was on the point of leaving the club when she spotted the girl on the dance floor. Looking back, she thought it was the outfit she noticed first, because even in the Strawberry Palace, the trendiest gay club in the north-east, it stood out as being a bit . . . out there. Like, if the Royal Ballet staged a zombie version of *Swan Lake*, then, yeah, that was the kind of tutu the dancers would wear. The net skirt, in shades of grey and dull purple, hung in tattered layers from a skintight bodice, while a huge silver bow sat on the girl's right hip and matching gloves stretched up over her elbows. She wore black lace tights and platform boots that must have two dozen buckles on each leg, from ankle to inches above the knee.

Were a fairy to take up lead singing in a grunge band, that was how she'd look.

So, probably the outfit, but it might have been the girl's face, because Olive had never seen a face that beautiful. Heart-shaped, with a tiny, pointed chin and perfect nose, eyes that threatened to swallow you whole and brows that made your fingertips itch to stroke them. It was a face to gawp at, to spend the rest of your life comparing to others in the vain hope one might come close to measuring up.

It could even have been the hair Olive noticed, long and thick, almost to the girl's waist, shining black in the club's artificial lights and seeming to dance with sparkles.

What it couldn't have been, because after several minutes of watching her leap and twirl and grind on the dance floor – she still couldn't quite believe she was seeing it – was that the girl was watching her. Olive. Watching and smiling at her as though they shared the naughtiest, most delicious of secrets. Knowing she was making a fool of herself but simply unable to stop, Olive turned round to learn who was really enjoying the attention.

No one she could see.

She turned back to catch the glee on the dark fairy's face. She saw the left hand raised, two fingers pointing into the fairy's eyes and then her forefinger directed at Olive. *Watching you.* Watching Olive.

She almost ran.

Then the girl was heading her way, weaving in and out of the dancers, ignoring the glances from both sexes that darted at her like missiles. Olive clutched her drink so hard, she thought the glass might break. The girl stopped, directly in front of Olive. Without the platform shoes, she'd be tiny. She didn't speak, simply looked up, smiling, waiting for something.

Hi.' Olive cleared her throat and tried again. 'Hi, I'm—'

The girl held a hand directly in front of Olive's face. 'Stop you right there.' She didn't even have to shout to be heard above the music; her voice was light and clear, with a trace of the north-east. 'Tell me three things about yourself that will stop me walking away.'

'Excuse me?' Olive couldn't help a glance round. Was this a prank? Was she going to end up on YouTube, trying to proposition someone in a gay nightclub? She'd known coming here was risky, but practically no one knew her in Newcastle and, sometimes, the need to be among her own people was just—

'You're cute, stranger, but I haven't got all night. Three things, starting now, or I'm moving on.'

'I was shot,' Olive said. 'In Helmand. Trying to save a squaddie's life. I still carry the scar on my right shoulder.'

The fairy pursed her lips and cocked her head. 'OK,' she drawled, 'better start than most. Give me another.'

Christ, what to say. Talk about putting her on the spot.

'I spent yesterday morning persuading a PTSD patient who'd locked herself in the men's bathroom that I wasn't an assassin from North Korea on special orders from Kim Jong-un.'

It was half true, half fantasy. She'd spent half an hour talking the woman out of the bathroom, a further half-hour cleaning shit off the walls. The woman at one point had accused Olive of trying to kill her. North Korea hadn't been mentioned.

'I'm listening,' grunge fairy said.

'I was born in the circus,' Olive said in desperation. 'My dad flew the high trapeze and my mum was a clown.'

The fairy held out her hand. 'I'm Maddy.'

The fairy's hand felt warm and small in Olive's. She held on, reluctant to let the weird, wonderful creature walk away.

'Olive,' she replied.

The fairy – Maddy – did a double take. 'For real? You're called Olive? I never met an Olive before. You could have led with that.'

'Well, in fairness, I tried.'

The hand was tugged gently away, but the smile widened. 'So, Olive, do you want to get out of here?'

66

Snow was falling again when Garry left Middlesbrough, but the road was gritted and had been well travelled earlier in the day. Even Lexy in her ridiculously unsuitable car had made it along the A19. The difficulty would arise further north when quieter roads made both snowdrifts and abandoned vehicles more likely. It was coming up for 1900 hours when he'd passed Stockton-on-Tees and then Billingham to find the Hartlepool road still closed.

A stab of fear poked at him as he climbed out of the driver's seat. The temperature had dropped further as he'd driven, the snowfall was getting heavier by the minute, and he couldn't help the nagging feeling that he was being dangerously distracted. Olive was the one in trouble, somehow he knew it for a fact, and she'd been missing nearly forty-eight hours. He should be looking for her, not digging his sergeant out of a snowdrift.

Darn it, Lexy, I thought you had more sense.

'Lorry jackknifed by Greatham.' The traffic officer on duty had his shoulders hunched over and his gloved hands tucked into his armpits. 'We've got eight vehicles stuck and no way of getting them off before daylight.'

'What's the A19 north like?' Garry asked.

'Clear for now. Wouldn't go that way unless you have to though, Gazza.'

The bloke was right. There was no way he should be out on a night like this. Lexy was a grown woman, she'd got herself into this mess and no one would blame him if he left her to it. What was the worst that could happen to her?

'Looks like I have to,' he said. 'Have a good one, mate.'

Garry walked back to his car, thinking that if his colleague knew he was planning to leave the A19 and take the Elwick road he'd lose his reputation as one of the most reliable drivers on the force. Mind you, that bridge could have been burned already. He was Garry the maverick now.

In spite of everything, he was on the brink of smiling as he climbed back into the driver's seat. He was Garry the chancer, Garry the unpredictable, and if worst came to worst, he could leave the road, cut open a gate or two, and get to Lexy over the fields. He found some music – his go-to playlist when he was a touch more nervous behind the wheel than he wanted to admit – and turned it up loud. The dramatic finale from Rossini's *William Tell* overture rang out – ta da da, ta da da, ta da da ta ta – familiar the world over as the theme tune from *The Lone Ranger*. He started the engine.

Hi-Yo, Silver!

67

July, three years previously

To Olive's surprise and relief, Maddy had no plans to rush quickly to one of their homes. The thought of sex with this enchanting stranger was close to terrifying; she wouldn't know where to begin. Instead, they walked through the dark city, Olive following Maddy's lead, in more ways than one. They took Maddy's suggested route; they stopped for food at the kebab van that Maddy claimed was her favourite and it seemed a given that Olive would pay; they talked about subjects that Maddy deemed acceptable. Nothing dull or factual, she didn't want to know where Olive worked or lived or what car she drove. She wanted to know what she thought, how she felt, what mattered.

'This is beautiful,' Olive said, when they stopped at a point high above the old castle keep. 'It's like the city's made of gold.' She'd walked through Newcastle many times but never really looked at it before. The keep stood on a bank of rock, all that was left of the once-great castle from which the city got its name. In the near distance, gold lights gleamed out from beneath railway arches, spreading their glow over the surrounding streets.

'I know.' Maddy pressed closer. The night was chilly and she was only wearing a thin leather jacket over her dress. 'The circus thing was a lie, wasn't it?'

'Afraid so,' Olive replied. 'Does that mean we have to go back to the club?'

'Nah, I give you a pass for having a quick imagination. So, are you married, Olive? Involved?'

It was the first personal question she'd allowed.

'I'm not,' Olive replied. 'Relationships are tricky. I have very old-fashioned Catholic parents.'

'Do you live with them?'

'No, but they're a constant presence. How about you? Are you married?'

She hated how important the answer had become.

'Not in my heart of hearts.' Maddy let the sentence hang in the air, torturously vague.

'What does that mean?' Olive felt herself pushing against resistance and ignored the warning bells. Maddy had asked first, damn it.

'It's better if I know,' she said, when Maddy still hadn't answered. 'I'm not really into one-night stands. And I don't handle rejection well. Or abandonment. Did I mention I'm trained in armed combat? You should have asked me for four things.'

'That's another lie. You're a nurse. Tell me what turns you on.'

'I've been in the army for nearly eleven years. Medical Corps. I could take you out in three moves. And please – we've only just met.'

Maddy was smiling again. 'I don't mean in bed. All in good time. I mean in life. What are you passionate about?'

Olive took a step back. 'Why do I get the feeling I'm being interviewed for a job?'

'Say vacant position and you'd be close.'

Olive felt her heartbeat picking up. 'So, are you with someone?' Why did she keep pushing that? Why couldn't she be cool?

'The position of keeper of my heart is currently vacant. So, come on, your passions.'

You, thought Olive. *It would be so easy to become passionate about you.*

68

Garry's phone rang when he'd travelled a mile up the A19. He turned down the music – *Pirates of the Caribbean* – and almost greeted Lexy, he was so sure she'd be calling. He saw the caller ID just in time.

'Mrs Warner.' He killed the track. 'Thanks for getting back to me.'

'Michael's out.' Her voice was pitched low. 'I don't know how long he'll be, so we have to make this quick. He's told me not to talk to you again, under any circumstances.'

Something tightened in Garry's chest; this was not what he needed right now. 'Mrs Warner, are you and the girls in danger?'

'No. Nothing like that. No, I'm sure we're not. You were asking about a post-mortem. Would you mind telling me why?'

No, that was one cat that had to stay firmly in its bag; but how to get what he needed without saying more than he had to?

'To be honest, Mrs Warner, I'm probably heading down another blind alley. But until we have something concrete to go on, we have to follow every lead, even if most of them go nowhere. I'm sorry to upset you, but . . .'

She was quiet for several seconds. Garry could hear the wind whistling around the stable buildings, the snort of a horse, the clatter of metal shoes on concrete. Even with Anderson not in the house, Gwen had chosen to go outside to call him.

'There was no post-mortem, although it was talked about at the time,' Gwen said. 'They aren't routinely carried out on terminally ill patients who die in hospital, but there was a question mark in Eloise's case, given that she passed earlier than expected.'

Garry asked, 'Who made the decision?'

'Michael. In fairness, he talked to me about it. He questioned what the point would be and said it would be better for the girls if we could get the funeral out of the way before Christmas. It never occurred to me to argue.'

'No, of course not.'

'I should have. I should have paid more attention to what my daughter was trying to tell me before she died.'

Garry waited. The wind howled, a clanging, the sound of Gwen's breathing.

Losing patience, he said, 'Mrs Warner, you said Eloise had something to tell you the last time you saw her. Do you have any idea what that was?'

'I thought I didn't, but you asking about that dreadful couple at the wedding brought it back to me. That man came here, one time, to Home Farm, spent some time with Michael in his study.'

OK, this was huge. 'Can you remember when?'

'Shortly after Eloise was diagnosed, so I'd say two and a half years ago. My daughter had changed that year. I thought for a long time it was her illness, but it started even before we knew there was anything wrong. So now I'm wondering if it was something else, completely unconnected. Something was eating at her. She wasn't the same woman, and now I'm wondering if it wasn't only the cancer.'

Garry took a deep breath; he was so out of his depth with this.

'I know I'm not making much sense,' Gwen went on, 'but the day that man came to the house—'

'You mean Howie Tricks?' Garry clarified.

'Exactly. She didn't go anywhere near him, but we watched him leave and she said something that, well, it made my blood run cold at the time.'

'Something about Tricks?'

'No, about Michael. She said he was the sort of person who created chaos around himself, that he couldn't help it, but that sooner or later, he dragged everyone around him into it.'

So, Michael Anderson was involved with the Tricks family somehow; the anti-organised crime stance that everyone made so much of had been an act. How could that not be related to Olive's disappearance?

'There's something else,' Gwen went on. 'I'm not sure if it's relevant or not, but Michael was out much of last night. He said he was going to drive around people who knew Olive, see if any of them had heard from her. He told me this morning that he'd got back about eleven, that it had all been hopeless, but one of the girls, Jessica, told me she heard him coming back and that it was after two in the morning. Well, where would he have been at that time? And in that weather?'

Very good questions. And Anderson was out again now.

'Mrs Warner, you need to leave this to us now. Don't try to ask your son-in-law anything else. Don't rock the boat in any way. Do I have your word on that?'

'I suppose. What will happen now?'

If only he knew.

He thanked Gwen Warner, finished the call and took a deep breath. Then he turned the music up and carried on driving.

It took nearly an hour to reach Lexy, mainly because a few metres past Elwick Garry lost concentration for a second and hit a bank of snow. By the time he'd dug himself out and put the snow socks on the car's tyres, he'd warmed up nicely. From there, it was less than five hundred metres to where Lexy was stuck.

If he hadn't been looking for an abandoned car, though, he might have missed it altogether. Even the bright red paintwork of Lexy's Mazda was almost completely covered by snow when he found it, making the car indistinguishable from the undulating land between road edge and hedgerow. When he was sure he'd spotted it, he sounded his horn and flashed his headlights. A second later, the driver door of Lexy's car opened and, far too slowly, she climbed out.

As Garry drew level, Lexy barely seemed to notice that she was up to her knees in snow. She stared towards him like a deer caught in headlights. Garry pulled up and jumped out. Lexy took a step towards him and stumbled.

Blistering popsicles, why did no one, even smart people like Lexy, dress for bad weather? Her coat was ridiculously inadequate and those thin leather gloves would be soaked on first contact with snow. She wasn't even wearing proper boots, just some daft, fashion ones. He reached her, wrapped an arm around her waist and half lifted her towards the car. She was shaking like an abandoned puppy.

'Frost got your tongue?' Garry pulled open the passenger door and pushed Lexy in. As the theme from *Mission Impossible* began, he found what he needed from the back seat. The first blanket went over Lexy's knees, the second around her shoulders and he pulled a fleece hat over her damp hair. She let him do everything, neither thanking him nor objecting. Her eyes weren't quite focused.

This wasn't good.

More concerned than he wanted to admit, Garry pulled off her boots and socks – soaked – and replaced them with a pair of his own thick woollen socks. Her skin felt cold and clammy at the same time.

'Inside your coat.' He held out the hot-water bottle. When she didn't move to take it, he unzipped her jacket, tucked the bottle against her chest and zipped her up again. He pulled off her wet gloves and draped them over the heater outlets to dry off. Then he found the flask and poured out half its contents. This could actually be more serious than he'd expected.

'Lexy, look at me.' He touched her under the chin, forcing her to make eye contact. 'I want to know your name, rank and shoulder number. And, for good measure, the name of the prime minister and what eight times six makes.'

Her blue eyes met his; not a whole lot behind them that he could see.

'Lexy, I'm serious. I'm going to start shouting in a minute.'

She gave herself a little shake. 'Lexy Thomas,' she managed. 'Detective sergeant, 3079, that twat with the stupid hairstyle and fuck knows, I'm shit at maths. Thank you, Garry.'

OK, not too far gone.

'Drink this.' He wrapped her cold fingers around the cup. 'Sip it slowly. Eat a Kit Kat. The seat's heated and the car heater's on.

Don't fiddle with it. You can't warm up too fast. I'm going to have a look at your car.'

Ten minutes later, he was back in his own vehicle. Lexy had emptied her cup and there was a Kit Kat wrapper on the dashboard. Good signs.

'Right, your shout, DS Thomas.'

Lexy glanced his way, but whether annoyed, embarrassed or plain frozen, he couldn't interpret the look she was giving him.

'I can probably pull you out of that ditch and tow you back to Middlesbrough, although I'm not sure you're fit to be behind a wheel right now, even under tow. A wiser course would be for me to drive you right back and get you tucked up in bed.'

He shouldn't have said that – it was the sort of inappropriate comment that could get him on report.

He hurried on quickly, 'Or we can carry on to Hartlepool to do whatever it was you thought you were doing when you set out. First, though, you have to convince me you're not in the early stages of hypothermia.'

'I'm fine.' She sounded exhausted. 'Hartlepool marina please. But I need my bag. It's on the passenger seat. And what's this I'm drinking? It tastes like coffee and hot chocolate. Did you get confused?'

'It's both. Mocha. All the rage in the trendy coffee bars, but I make my own. Coffee perks you up and chocolate gives you a sugar rush. And your bag's on my back seat. I rescued it.'

She held the cup towards him. 'Can I have some more?'

Smiling to himself, he leaned across and poured the rest of the drink from the flask. Then he cranked up the music again – *Raiders of the Lost Ark* – and released the handbrake.

'Have another Kit Kat,' he told her.

The snow seemed to be lessening as they travelled on, but Garry knew it was only the warming effect of the ocean. Snow rarely hung around on the coast. Back inland it could be as bad as ever and there was no guarantee the two of them would make it back to Middlesbrough tonight.

A night in the car wouldn't be good. Lexy needed dry clothes, a warm bath and bed.

'I phoned a doctor I know from uni,' she said, when a faint yellow glow in the sky meant they were nearing the town. 'I wanted to know how he'd murder a terminally ill patient on an oncology ward.'

'I hope he told you he wouldn't.'

As they reached the edge of town, Garry pulled up one of his numerous mental maps to check the route. He could head directly east for a mile or so and the road would take him to the marina. In traditional coastal towns, all roads led to the sea.

'Actually, the amount of thought he'd already given the matter was a bit worrying,' Lexy said. 'I was thinking pillow over the face, given Eloise was in a side ward, but he said that would result in bloodshot marks in the eyes. Morphine overdose isn't possible either because it's very carefully controlled. How my doctor mate would do it, he said, would be to smuggle in a small amount of something nasty and inject it into the patient using the canula in her hand.'

'Anderson's movements between the hours of 2200 hours the night Eloise died and 0400 hours the next day can't be accounted for.' Quickly, Garry summarised what he'd learned at the hospital.

'Nothing we can prove, though,' Lexy replied. 'He only has to claim he left through the west car park and that's that. Garry, seriously – what are we listening to?'

They'd reached the outskirts of Hartlepool and, on the track, the *Star Wars* theme.

'My difficult-driving soundtrack. Ever done an eight-hour night shift behind the wheel in the middle of winter? No? Then don't judge.'

At a fork in the road, Garry thought for a moment. Either route could be blocked, but going left gave him a better chance of weaving through the numerous side streets. While he was thinking, he filled Lexy in with his earlier conversation with Gwen.

'Michael Anderson is secretly friendly with the bloke who, in public at least, is his number-one enemy,' he finished, as he pulled out of the junction. 'His first wife knows about it and isn't happy. His second vanishes the night we raid the Tricks property. How can that be coincidence?'

Less used to inclement weather than their inland counterparts, the residents of Hartlepool had chosen to stay indoors. Two or three inches of snow lay on the ground, but no abandoned vehicles blocked their way. As the minutes ticked by, the neon yellow of the street lights around them fell away, to be replaced by a wall of solid darkness ahead. They were nearing the ocean.

'It's messy,' Lexy agreed, after a minute or two. 'But there's no way an MP, no matter how high profile, could stop a police raid from taking place, whether his wife had been kidnapped or not. Howie would know this. So, what would be the point?'

Garry slowed down to make a sharp turn.

'To lose one wife, Mr Anderson, could be regarded as misfortune; to lose two looks like carelessness,' he said, as he took the ungritted road towards the waterfront. 'Where've I got that from?'

'Dunno,' Lexy replied. 'Go to the lock. We're meeting someone there.'

Hartlepool marina was a large, enclosed stretch of water on the eastern edge of town. Two sea walls slunk their way into the waves like great, grey snakes, holding back the worst of the North Sea swell. A further, smaller, pair provided additional shelter. To access the marina itself, boats passed through a lock, controlled by the harbour master. Within was berthing for several hundred boats. Residential apartments lined one edge, restaurants, shops and take-aways another. Even in bad weather, the place looked busy.

When Garry had driven as far as he could go in a non-amphibious vehicle, he pulled into a parking spot on a narrow spit of land be-tween the sea edge and the calmer waters of the marina. Spray hit the windscreen as a gust shook the car.

The waterside buildings gleamed a warm copper in the harbour lights. Five storeys high, they were mock-Georgian, stone-built, with multiple balconies. Yacht masts, gleaming in the same light, soared into the black sky like golden wands. Across the water stood a Premier Inn. The sight of it made Garry feel uncomfortable and he didn't want to ask himself why. He turned to Lexy, relieved to see she looked a little more like herself. Not completely, but enough.

She said, 'And it's three. Not two, three.'

At that moment, a gull swooped low, close enough almost to touch the car's windscreen. Lexy gave an audible squeal.

Garry said, 'Come again?'

'I was at my desk earlier, keeping my head down, because the deputy chief stayed way past his bedtime, and I was thinking about what you said.'

Lexy waited, as though for Garry to fill in the gap. He couldn't. He'd said a lot of things.

'About your feeling of déjà vu over Olive being missing,' she prompted.

'I was wrong,' Garry admitted. 'I phoned her parents. She's never been AWOL before.'

'You were right. I did some googling. It was a bit like trying to find the right combination from a set of random numbers and it took ages. I searched for Olive Anderson missing, Olive Charles missing, Eloise Warner missing, Eloise Anderson missing. In the end, probably by accident, I typed in Michael Anderson missing and bingo.'

'What?'

'I need my stuff.'

From her bag on the back seat, Lexy pulled out a laptop. Firing it up, she angled a screenshot towards Garry so the two of them could read it together. A missing persons notice.

Beneath the red MISSING letters appeared a photograph of a young woman with curly dark hair who looked naggingly familiar. Her name was Madeleine Black and she was an artist from Whitley Bay on the north side of Newcastle, last seen on the first of November three years earlier. Her clothes struck Garry as being on the eccentric side: a dark red sweater with matching cape encircling her shoulders. Crystal beads hung from the cape. Her earrings were giant chunks of rainbow-coloured glass. The whole effect was a bit punk, maybe hippyish, not quite either of those.

What was he not seeing?

And then he saw it. 'Jiminy Cricket,' he said.

'Knew it wouldn't take you long.'

He'd seen that woman's picture before, on the wall of Michael Anderson's Guisborough constituency office. She'd been standing next to Anderson, part of a team of people out campaigning for the local Labour candidate.

'She's known as Maddy,' Lexy said. 'And she's still missing.'

69

August, three years previously

'I don't think I've ever been to Whitley Bay before,' Olive said, as Maddy unlocked an internal door in the bland, concrete building and leaned in to switch on the lights.

It was four weeks to the day since they'd met and Olive couldn't remember a previous time when her every thought, from waking to sinking back into wonderful, erotically charged dreams, hadn't been entirely consumed by one being. Maddy.

'I grew up nearby.' Maddy led the way into a high-ceilinged space about the size of a suburban, two-car garage. 'My grandparents brought me a lot when I was a kid.'

Maddy's studio smelled of paint, spirits and fire and also, a little, of Maddy herself. Not the perfume she was wearing that day, but one Olive remembered from a previous encounter. The studio held an echo of Maddy, a Maddy from a day gone by. There were lots of Maddys, Olive had learned over the past four weeks, and she wanted them all.

Afraid, as she so often was these days, of her own longing, she said, 'Is that why you moved here? Childhood memories?'

Maddy's voice flattened. 'Sam's house is in Whitley. We can see the sea from the upstairs bedroom.'

Olive turned away, ostensibly to look around, in reality to avoid what she knew would be an uncomfortable exchange. Maddy never wanted to talk about Sam.

The studio was cluttered but with an order of sorts beneath the surface disarray. A counter ran round three walls, with shelves beneath containing an abundance of multi-sized, multicoloured boxes;

a third wall held metal shelving systems, and a central table was laden with drawing instruments. In one corner stood a kiln, and finished pieces of decorative glass hung in the window and around the walls. Maddy painted here too. Olive could see a folded easel, several stacked canvases, tubs of brushes and of paint.

There were times when Olive felt cheated. Maddy had made a point of finding out, the night they'd met, that Olive was single, as though sharing her would be a deal-breaker. And yet Olive was expected to share Maddy with a stranger known only as Sam; never to meet her friends or family, never to be taken to her home, not even allowed to call or text, but always to wait for Maddy to contact her, for Maddy to have time for her.

A workspace on the counter seemed to have been only recently abandoned. A stool lay beside it, while cutting and drawing tools hadn't been put away. A paperweight held a rough pencil sketch and a photograph had been sellotaped to the window directly above it. Olive thought she could see men in uniform. Curious to see the last project Maddy had been working on, she moved a little closer.

Every time the two of them said goodbye – and they had so little time together – she was determined to press Maddy the next time, to ask how long this would go on, whether she was ever going to be anything but an illicit affair. For her part, she'd even decided she was ready, finally, to tell her parents the truth; to come out as a gay woman.

Inevitably, by the time Olive heard from Maddy again, she'd reached the stage of being prepared to do anything to keep this wonderful woman in her life.

'There's a garden shed at the cottage,' Maddy went on, surprising Olive. She'd never before talked about her home. 'I think Sam hoped I'd work there, but the light isn't good enough. And I can't be distracted. I need to be alone when I work.' She beamed at Olive. 'Like Garbo.'

'And yet, I'm here.'

Maddy approached Olive in that strange, almost dance-like strut she used when the two of them were alone. 'That's different,' she said, stopping a tantalising foot away. 'You're here to work.'

'So, let's do it.' Olive resisted, with difficulty, the temptation to step forward and kiss her.

Smiling, Maddy handed over a stiff, canvas apron and safety goggles before pushing Olive towards the central table. 'Something I made earlier,' she said. 'This is the rough sketch.'

Taped to the tabletop was a crayon drawing of trees on rough ground. A figure in blue leaned against the trunk in the foreground. It was crude, almost childish.

Maddy gave Olive an arch look. 'I don't need anything more than this. The picture's in my head. And here's the first stage.'

She unwrapped a piece of glass that was about twenty inches long by a little less high, not quite square, most of its surface covered with greens: the deep, dull colour of a dirty emerald, the subdued tones of desiccated leaves. Patches of soft blue gleamed through in places. It didn't look like anything much.

'Trust me, I have a plan,' Maddy said. 'This is an underpainting. Basically, the idea, drawn on a piece of glass in broad strokes, the colours created by glass powder, then fired. I always have a plan.'

'Do you have a plan for us?' Olive asked, even as a voice inside her head was screaming, *No, don't do it, don't rock the boat.*

Maddy folded the cotton wrapping and put it to one side. 'I wish it was that simple,' she replied after several seconds. 'Artists don't make a lot of money. Neither do nurses.'

'You don't want to believe everything you hear,' Olive said. 'I do OK. And I have two bedrooms. I've got space.'

She was not going to let money, or lack of it, keep them apart.

Maddy's perfect brows bounced. 'A month and you're asking me to move in with you? What about when you go away again? Being an army wife is a lot to ask. Especially a lesbian army wife.'

Olive sighed. 'I'm asking if I'm ever going to be more than an affair.'

'You've never been an affair.' Maddy's face was totally serious now. 'I love you.' She gave a nervous laugh. 'You do know that, right?'

Olive stepped close, grabbing hold of Maddy and hugging her, pressing her face against the other woman's hair. In a little while she'd be happy, for now she was shaking with relief. For several seconds, the two of them didn't move. Maddy was wearing one of her loose, flower-printed dresses and she never wore a bra. Sometimes she didn't wear pants and Olive still felt a sharp tingle in her groin remembering the first time she'd discovered that. As though reading her thoughts, Maddy stiffened and pulled back.

'We didn't come here for that. Not to fight either. We're making art.' She pushed Olive back round to face the rectangle of glass. 'Can you tell what it is yet?'

'Landscape?' Olive ventured. 'Orchard?'

'Close. So now we add trees.' Maddy crossed the room, returning with another sheet of glass, something between brown and grey. 'This is going to be tricky because the trees I have in mind are ancient and twisted. I'll start you off.'

Taking a felt pen, Maddy began drawing crooked vertical lines on the brown glass, all tapering as they neared the top.

'Now you try.'

Butterflies dancing – she'd always been rubbish at art – Olive began drawing the line of a tree.

'Curve it a bit,' Maddy urged. 'Make it a really bent old specimen. Now, a few thicker branches and we can cut them all out.'

The cutting took a long time. After half an hour, Maddy's phone rang. She glanced at the screen, then left the room, telling Olive to carry on without her.

Glad of a break – the cutting was quite intense – Olive left the work table, not towards the door, because that would be eavesdropping, but back to the photograph she'd spotted earlier.

'Sorry about that.' Maddy was back. 'Are you done?'

'Was that Sam?'

Maddy's face tightened. 'No, actually.' Her eyes darted past Olive. 'Someone else.'

Olive said, 'Does Sam know about me?'

'God, no.' Maddy frowned. 'Olive, I'm serious. You don't want to mess with Sam.'

'Are you scared?' It wasn't the first time the thought had occurred to Olive.

'No, not really.' Maddy sighed. 'I want to be with you, OK? And I will be. Soon.' She gave herself a little shake. 'Now we build the picture. Come on, this is the fun bit.'

Maddy loved her, the two of them would be together one day. It was more than she'd ever got before. Was it enough?

Maddy took Olive's hand, guiding it towards a long shard of glass. 'Think about perspective, the thicker, taller trees at the front.'

It had to be enough; walking away from Maddy was unthinkable.

Together, the two women placed the brown glass trees on the piece of coloured glass until it did begin to resemble an orchard.

'I think I have a way out,' Maddy said, when they were nearly done. 'Can you give me some time?'

The woman was a constant puzzle. But wasn't that what made her so exciting?

'Can't I help?' Olive said.

'No, I don't want you involved. Now we add the frits to give contour.' Maddy leaned across the table to reach some plastic tubs. Each contained miniscule pieces of broken glass – brown, beige, cream, dull pink, crocodile green.

'This is going to be a sombre piece,' Olive reflected.

'We're dealing with an arid landscape,' Maddy snapped. 'It's not a cherry orchard.'

'What then?' Olive asked, as she scattered the glass fragments.

'Patience. And now the bright green,' Maddy told her. 'In the trees.'

Olive dotted gleaming green speckles among the duller green foliage.

'Few more,' Maddy urged. 'We need to see these. Now about a dozen black ones.'

Olive did what she was told.

'And that's it,' Maddy said. 'All we can do for now.'

Olive's back was aching. She arched it, rubbing her knuckles into it the way she did after a long shift.

'That picture,' she said, her eyes going back to the photograph. 'Is that Helmand?'

'Probably.' Maddy's eyes were on the worktop as she cleared away equipment. 'I'm doing a piece for one of the men. Chap called Anderson. An MP actually.'

Olive wandered over to the photograph of men in army uniform. Michael Anderson stood in the middle, the tallest, best-looking of the group – if that was your sort of thing. 'I know him,' she said. 'I was in Afghanistan at the same time. I'd forgotten he lived in the north-east.'

When she turned back, Maddy's attention was entirely on the tabletop, clearing away the tubs and tools and leftover shards of glass.

'What are you making for him?' Olive asked. 'Can I see it?'

'Haven't started it.' Maddy didn't look up.

Olive waited for several seconds. Then, 'Have I said something wrong?'

Maddy paused what she was doing. Which wasn't anything, Olive realised. She'd simply been moving things around on the tabletop.

'What is it?' she asked.

'Nothing. Ignore me. We have to fire your piece now.' Maddy moved over to the kiln and pressed a switch. 'And then we've one last layer to add.'

'What's in the next layer?'

'We'll use a black enamel,' Maddy said over her shoulder. 'To really pick out some of the detail on the trees, and on the figure in the foreground, and maybe some gold for a real colour pop.'

'There is no figure in the foreground.'

'We do her last.' Joining her again, Maddy let her finger hover over the glass, a little off-centre, where the principal tree sprang from the ground. 'She's going to be leaning against this, maybe sleeping, maybe thinking, we won't be sure. She'll be wearing blue to echo the sky, and to give a real burst of colour in the foreground.'

She stared up at Olive, as though challenging her.

Deliberately, Olive glanced down at herself. 'I'm wearing blue,' she pointed out.

'Of course, you are.' Maddy stepped closer. 'This is an olive grove. Olive in the olive grove.'

Olive felt tears springing into her eyes. 'I want you to be in it too.'

Maddy's arms wrapped around Olive's waist. 'I will be. I'm always with you, even when you can't see me.'

70

'Garry,' Lexy said. 'What is that horrible noise?'

At night, the marina was beautiful; the sound it made, especially in high wind, was not. Even with the engine running and the windows closed, the relentless clanging that flew to them on the wind and wrapped itself around the car was discordant and unnerving. After the heavy silence of the snow-filled landscapes, the metallic cacophony was almost painful on the ears and it didn't help that every few seconds a gust rocked the car.

'That would be the wind in the rigging,' Garry replied. 'This place can hold up to 500 boats, most of them yachts. Want me to put the music back on?'

'Definitely not. What's rigging?'

'Exactly, I'm not sure. Vaguely and generally, it's all the ropes and lines and things on sailing boats. They clang against the masts in high winds. It's eerie, especially at night.'

'You sail?'

'No, but I've been here before. And I asked the same question. So, go on, tell me about Maddy.'

'She was an artist and a political activist who lived at Whitley Bay a little way north of here.'

'Was?'

'If she's still alive, she'll be thirty-three. Officially, we don't know one way or the other. She went missing in November three years ago. Northumbria dealt with it, but I couldn't persuade anyone to send me over the full file this evening.'

'Don't tell me, they couldn't release it without proper authorisation and no one at the station was prepared to give you that without a better reason than that Michael Anderson was acquainted with the woman.'

'Exactly. I'm sure we can get hold of it first thing on Monday, but . . .'

She left the thought hanging; Olive might not have till first thing on Monday.

'On the plus side, I did find someone who was prepared to give me the salient points. Are you paying attention?'

'Undivided.'

'So, Maddy was last seen at her workshop in Whitley Bay on . . .' Lexy glanced down. 'November the first. She gave no indication to the other people in the building that she was going away or might not be around for a while. She was officially reported missing by her wife, Samantha Elliott, ten days later.'

'Ten days? And these two were married?'

'I know. Partly explained by the fact that Elliott was working away on a construction site in Scotland for a week. Even so, she'd been home for three whole days before she went to the police and she didn't report it immediately because Maddy had gone missing before. It was kind of her thing. Elliott had been hoping she'd come back of her own accord.'

'What had she taken with her?'

'Good question. Passport, some other key documents, a week's worth of clothes and what little money she had. The two of them pooled their money and Maddy had no access to the accounts. Elliott controlled it.'

'Sounds like that's not all she controlled.'

'Exactly. And Northumbria were pretty keen on her for a while. Neighbours talked about the two of them having very vocal arguments, of hearing stuff being broken.'

'So, Elliott became a suspect?'

'She did. She was taken in and questioned several times, but nothing came of it. Maddy seemed to have vanished while Elliott was in Scotland with some cast-iron alibis. She stayed on the missing list, but after several weeks, the hunt was scaled back. By the year end, no active police action was being taken.'

Garry nodded. It was standard procedure. Not every missing person was found.

'And her connection to Michael Anderson is that she campaigned for him? Did Northumbria talk to his office?'

'They did. But not being near an election, there was no need for her to be in touch with the party particularly. They couldn't help.'

'They say men stick to type,' Garry commented. 'That's what the party chairman said. Hinting that Anderson and Maddy were friendlier than they should have been.'

Lexy made a *there you have it* gesture with both hands. 'And that's the Anderson connection.'

'Except that Maddy was gay,' Garry pointed out. 'Possibly bi.'

'Indeed,' Lexy agreed.

'So, three women whom Anderson was close to have potentially come to a sticky end.'

Lexy gave a short, humourless laugh. 'I'd have said were well and truly fucked over, but I'll go with your version.'

'So why are we here? Don't tell me the chap you spoke to has agreed to meet us on a night like this. He must have less of a life than me.'

Why? Why had he said that?

Lexy gave him a look. 'Oh, I'd say yours could be looking up. But no, he wasn't about to go that far. He told me one more useful thing, though. There was an unconfirmed and very unreliable sighting of Maddy here at the marina, possibly after she was seen at the workshop. He almost didn't mention it, but I got the impression it was bugging him.'

'And Michael Anderson keeps a boat here. So, who's this witness?'

'Lock-keeper. Although I think that's an honorary title. The harbour master's office is staffed twenty-four seven, and they have responsibility for the lock. This is some little old guy who's been here for decades, a sort of a caretaker-come-handyman. He has a cottage next to the harbour office. And did I mention, he's an unreliable witness?'

'You said unreliable sighting.'

'Because he's an unreliable witness. Bit simple, by all accounts. And a bit too fond of the hard stuff. Apparently, he's expected to go in the water any time now and no one will miss him.'

'So why is he employed? Marinas are dangerous.'

'I think he might own it.'

'What? The marina?'

She shivered. 'I don't know. It's complicated. Let's talk to him and get it over with.'

Garry felt a wave of misgiving. 'Lexy, are you sure you're up to this? There's not as much snow here and the temperature's higher, but that's a very strong wind out there.'

'I'm fine.' She opened the car door. 'Come on, Gazza.'

In spite of her bravado, Lexy seemed taken aback by the force of the wind and didn't object to Garry taking her arm and steering her round the edge of the water.

'What the hell's that?' She stopped in her tracks.

'That would be the Hartlepool monkey,' Garry explained, as they drew nearer to the bronze statue of the huge, mournful ape.

She pressed a little closer to him as they stopped.

'A French ship was wrecked off the coast here in the early 1800s. The only creature to survive was a monkey. Don't ask me why French sailors had a monkey on board. It made it to land, only to be seized by the locals, who'd never seen a monkey before, or a Frenchman for that matter. They hanged it as an enemy of state.'

'Seriously? I mean, northern men are really that thick?'

Garry found himself fighting the temptation to wrap an arm around her waist. 'We go to school now. Things have improved a bit.'

She turned and took his arm this time. 'Just to warn you, I was strongly advised not to bother coming out here. We may have made a wasted journey.'

'Oh, I'm having the time of my life,' Garry said, as they walked on. It wasn't, he realised, entirely untrue. Setting aside his increasing fears for Olive, spending time with Lexy – well, there wasn't anything else he'd rather be doing right now.

The lockman's cottage was a misnomer. It was a sizeable house, genuine Georgian if Garry was any judge. Both ground and upper floor had three windows, mullioned, with rotting wood, looking out east, north-east and south-east, to maximise views of the sea. Its existence probably hindered valuable redevelopment at a prime spot in the marina, but it would almost certainly be listed. Short, stubby wings stuck out on either side of the main building. The roofs were slate, with several pieces missing; one ornate chimney had crumpled. A narrow strip of well-tended garden held driftwood, lobster pots and large shells. An ornate wellington boot, planted with sea thrift, had fallen over. As Lexy banged on the anchor-shaped door knock, Garry bent to set it upright. The wellington was rubber, a woman's size, blue and with a fantastic design of fairies and pixies. Around the rim hung a ring of crystal beads. The colours were faded, and the rim frayed, as though it had spent some time in the water. He stood up as the front door opened, a full three minutes after Lexy had knocked.

The man on the threshold was six foot two at Garry's best estimate, possibly taller, and must have weighed sixteen stone. His hair was a shock of white and he wore mustard trousers, a red cravat over a striped shirt and a tweed jacket that smelled of wet Labradors and second-hand shops.

'Richard Hamilton-Minor?' Lexy queried.

'Dick.' He looked the two of them up and down. 'Come in, both of you. Look sharp.'

The carpet of the dimly lit hall was threadbare, with a paisley pattern in yellow, green and purple; it reminded Garry of his grandmother's house. A heavy curtain fell into place behind the door when he closed it and to one side of the hall was a stand containing a dozen or more walking sticks carved from driftwood.

Hamilton-Minor led them towards the rear of the house; it was bigger even than it had looked on the outside.

'I don't heat the big rooms,' he barked back at them. 'Costs a bloody fortune.'

He took them into a small sitting room. Bookshelves lined one wall and more evidence of the man's beach-combing hobby lay scattered around in the form of shells, driftwood carvings and a huge orange crab, its spindly legs hanging over a small table. Above the generous, and very welcome, fire was a family coat of arms carved in wood: a knight's helmet above a shield, feathers, a fleur-de-lys, a thistle.

'Have a seat, if you can find one,' their host told them. 'I'll get the kettle on. You both look bloody frozen.'

Garry left Lexy to organise herself a chair; he'd already given it up for hopeless. Most of the available seats held small sleeping animals. At least, he had to hope they were asleep; the house didn't smell too good.

A photograph on a cabinet had caught his eye. It was a formal picture of a wedding, taken at the church door. At first sight, it looked entirely ordinary: pretty young bride, smartly dressed groom, couple of bridesmaids, a cluster of guests surrounding the happy couple. The flowers were decent, if unexciting. A perfectly ordinary wedding, except that the two guests to the immediate right of the bride were Queen Elizabeth II and her husband the Duke of Edinburgh.

'Sister's do.' Hamilton-Minor had returned with three mugs balanced on a tray. 'Late sixties. That's me, far right. Scrawny little bugger I was then.'

Garry couldn't help himself. 'The late Queen a good friend, was she, sir?'

'Hadn't seen her in years. The duke and Pa were close for a while. Served together, maybe. Could have been at school. The stuff one's expected to remember.' He balanced the tray on a small table.

'And your father is . . . if you don't mind me asking?'

'My asking, not me asking, don't they teach grammar anymore? Earl of Glenmoran. Only a Scottish title. Doesn't mean that much, not these days. I was the third son, so bugger all left when it got to me. Not that there was much for Bunter – he was the eldest – short of junk, old dogs and death duties. I joined the merchant navy. Means I'm handy around water. Sit down, won't you, I won't ask again. Come on, cats don't bite. The dog might.'

Garry picked up a fat ginger tom and made an encouraging gesture to Lexy. Eyes wide, she took the seat. Garry gave her the cat. She stiffened, but it settled on her lap almost immediately.

Body warmth, he mouthed at her; she glared back.

The only other free chair, apart from the one closest to the fire that was obviously Hamilton-Minor's own, was occupied by a West Highland terrier. It glared up at Garry. *Go on, I dare you.*

Hamilton-Minor was bending over something in the corner. Garry heard the sound of glasses being chinked.

'Something to take the chill off.' He turned, holding glasses out to Lexy and Garry. Cut glass, chipped and not too clean, but each with a generous measure of something.

Lexy had both hands wrapped around the coffee cup. 'No thank you, sir. I'm on duty and Garry's driving.'

Garry held out his hand. 'Thank you very much, sir. Just the ticket.'

Lexy was glaring. 'Garry,' she began.

'If I can drive fifteen miles in a blizzard and pull you out of a snowdrift, I'm sure I can make my way back to Middlesbrough with a small Scotch inside me. You should have one yourself, Sergeant. You still don't look too good.'

It wasn't a small Scotch, but what the Dickens. He sipped it. It was good.

'Scared of dogs?' their host asked with a glint in his eye.

'Been driving a lot today, sir. Need to stretch my back.'

Hamilton-Minor collapsed into his own seat. 'So what can I do for you officers?'

Moving carefully so as not to disturb the cat, Lexy opened her laptop and angled it towards their host so that he could see the picture of Maddy Black.

'I understand you saw this woman at the marina around the time she disappeared,' she began. 'It was in November, three years ago.'

'Pontoon C, roughly halfway down, heading away from shore,' the man replied. 'I was bringing in *Loose Lips* from a mooring up by the lifeboat station so she could go into dry dock for the winter. Barnacles on her underside needed a good scrape. Do you know boats are traditionally named after one's first sexual experience? Mine would have been the *Duchess's Cobbler*, but I never had a boat of my own. What would yours be, young woman?'

'Can't remember that far back, sir. Can you give me a date?'

Hamilton-Minor drained his glass and put his hands on the chair arm as though to rise. 'Two hours after high tide. I know that because I had to juggle the time I could pick her up with getting through the lock. I wouldn't normally move a boat in those conditions. Nasty winds. Springs as well. Fair ripping along. Three knots at least. No choice, though. Had to be done or she'd have missed her slot in the boatyard.'

'A date, sir?' Lexy looked as though she hadn't understood a word.

'Before Christmas, but not that close because we hadn't put the tinsel up in the harbour office. Top-up?'

'Not for us, thank you, sir,' Lexy said, with a sideways glare at Garry.

'Springs means a spring tide, doesn't it, sir?' Garry queried. 'Happens twice a month, during the full and new moon?'

Hamilton-Minor slapped his glass down. 'Good man. It was the full moon. Bang on. Risen early. I could see it in the sky above the buildings as I was making my way round B pontoon.'

'Are you sure about that?' Garry said.

'Course I'm bloody sure. You don't spend your life on boats and not know the bloody moon.'

'In which case, we could work out the date, couldn't we? Maybe even the time as well?'

'Smart lad. Pay attention to your boss, young woman. He'll teach you a thing or two.'

'Oh, he already has,' Lexy muttered.

'Won't be a tick.' The man staggered from the room.

Lexy said, 'Where's he gone?'

'I'm hoping to fetch an almanac,' Garry replied. 'That will tell us the times and dates of high tide during November three years ago. If we cross-reference to the time the moon rose, we'll have the exact date and time Maddy was seen at the marina.'

Lexy opened a new page on her laptop and began typing.

Hamilton-Minor was back with a doorstop of a book in his hands. He was looking down at an open page, his glass balanced precariously on its surface. 'Friday third of November,' he said. 'Two hours after high tide would make it ten minutes past three o'clock in the afternoon.'

'And the moon rose at half past two on that date,' Lexy confirmed, her eyes on the screen. 'Thank you, sir, that's very helpful.'

'Had you seen her before that day?' Garry asked.

'Oh, for sure. More than once. Two, maybe three times. Couldn't give you dates and times, though.'

'Any idea where she was going along that pontoon? How many boats were ahead of her?'

'Dozen or so. But I knew exactly where she was going. The MP's yacht. Bit of a pinko by all accounts, but a decent enough chap.'

Garry and Lexy exchanged glances.

Lexy asked, 'Did you see Mr Anderson that day?'

Hamilton-Minor shook his head. 'I didn't. But I was in the back room of the harbour office for much of it, sorting out the electrics.'

'So how did you know she was going to the Anderson yacht?'

'I'd seen her on it previously. Couple of times. And I saw her arriving by car one time with them.'

'With Mr Anderson?'

'No, his wife. The first one, I mean now. The one who died. Funny thing, she vanished round about the same time. I'm not sure I saw her again after that day. Anderson himself, and the kids, even an older woman, but not the first Mrs A. Mind you, she fell ill, didn't she? Or so they said.'

Garry really hoped Lexy was keeping track of all this. Maddy had been a regular visitor to the marina, apparently friendly with both Eloise and Michael. Eloise had vanished too? That made no sense.

Maddy had vanished in November three years ago; Eloise's illness didn't start for another six months or so. So why had Eloise stopped sailing?

Something had been bothering Eloise, though, according to her mother. From the start of the year. From Maddy's disappearance?

'She's not missing, though,' Hamilton-Minor said, while Garry was still trying to catch up. 'Least, not anymore. I've seen her a few times this year. She was here a couple of weeks ago.'

What?

Lexy said, 'She was?' with a bewildered look at Garry.

'Well, they're married now, aren't they? I'm sure I heard someone say as much.'

'Sir, Mr Anderson's current wife is called Olive. She and Maddy do look a bit alike, but I promise you, two different women.' Lexy tapped away on her keyboard and eventually produced the Missing notice of Olive. 'See,' she angled it towards Hamilton-Minor, 'different woman.'

Hamilton-Minor whistled through his teeth. 'I see it now,' he agreed. 'Mind you, I never saw either one close up, so understandable mistake. And she's missing too? Blimey, the bugger has form.'

Lexy said nothing, but Garry would have put money on knowing exactly what she was thinking. It was beginning to look exactly like Anderson had form.

'Oh lord!' Hamilton-Minor slapped a fat hand onto his own forehead. 'You're not the first people I've misled. There was someone else here asking about that lass. The first one, I mean now.'

'It's quite likely our colleagues in Northumbria came here to make some enquiries,' Lexy said. 'Maddy Black was the subject of a missing persons enquiry three years ago. If she'd been known to have connections with the marina, I'd expect them to have looked here.'

The lock-keeper frowned. 'This was last year. In fact, it was early October, because I was doing some work on the pontoon water taps. Took all the hoses off. Tripping hazard supposedly, health and safety gone mad if you ask me. Now all the boats have to carry their own hoses, and half of them forget half the time. Come to me to sort it out.'

Lexy looked puzzled. 'Right, so Northumbria Police were looking in October last year. I wonder—'

'She didn't say she was police,' Hamilton-Minor interrupted. 'I doubt it, to be honest. She didn't come across as being police.'

'A woman, sir?' Garry clarified. 'Did she give you a name?'

'No. Didn't show ID either, not like you two. Mind you, I didn't ask. I had my hands full and the weather was atrocious.' He stabbed a finger into the air. 'October it was. We'd had a gale, it was still blowing up a hoolie and I had a list of repairs as long as a donkey's todger.'

'A police officer would probably have identified herself as one,' Lexy said. 'Can you describe her at all, sir?'

'Young. Not a lass, but young. Be surprised if she'd seen her fortieth. Tall for a woman, short hair. Nice-looking. Not nice nature, though. Very short with me.'

'Anything else you can tell us, sir? Anything at all you can remember about the conversation?'

'Well, I told her I'd seen the girl she was looking for. I hadn't, I'd seen the other one – what did you say she was called – Olive? I told her I'd seen her visiting the boat with that MP chap. I'm not going to lie, when I saw the look on her face, I took a step back. Almost stepped off the bloody pontoon.'

'But you've definitely seen Mrs Olive Anderson at the marina recently?' Garry asked.

'Definitely. She comes with the family quite often, weekends mainly, not so much in the bad weather. The seas can get a bit rough round here. I've seen her on her own as well. She was here for an hour or so the other week.'

Garry felt a surge of excitement rising. Had anyone thought to check the boat for Olive?

Lexy said, 'Does she take the boat out by herself?'

'Not that I've seen. No, this last time, she was below in the cabin for a while. I was on D pontoon checking the power boxes. I saw her arrive and leave.' He straightened up in his chair. 'I'm glad you've sorted that out,' he said. 'I was going to offer her her wellington boot back. Would have been a bit of a shame, it makes a nice planter. Glad I didn't now. You've saved me making a Charlie of myself.'

Lexy said, 'Excuse me, sir? Wellington boot.'

'On the front doorstep,' Hamilton-Minor said. 'You'd have passed it on the way in. I found it on the foreshore shortly after I last saw her – the first one I'm talking about now, the one who vanished three years ago.'

Maddy. The boot by the front door, planted with sea thrift that would bloom purple in the spring, had belonged to Maddy.

'Buried in sand, but something was glinting at me so I dug it up,' Hamilton-Minor was still talking. 'I knew it was hers because I'd seen her wearing them and, well, it's not the sort of thing you see a lot of. I assumed she must have lost it in the mud at some point.'

Lexy got to her feet. 'Garry,' she said. 'I think it's time to have a look around Mr Anderson's boat.'

71

September, three years previously

The rain had been falling for hours when Olive arrived home in the pre-dawn darkness. It was only late September, but autumn in the north-east could be short and brutal, with winter chasing hard on its heels. On top of that, the cold-season rush of patients injuring themselves with greater frequency, catching more infectious diseases, falling prey to seasonal viruses, had already begun and the annual battle for beds was underway. It hadn't been the easiest of shifts. But her flat had enough food to last several days, she was up to date with laundry and had spent enough duty time with her parents the weekend just gone. Olive had nothing to do but sleep and chill until she had to return to work again. She found a parking spot, not too far from her block's entrance, and pulled over.

'Olive!'

The familiar voice, her favourite sound in the world, cut through the storm and Olive turned to see Maddy stumbling towards her on bare feet.

Oblivious to who might be watching – the street was deserted at that hour, but even so – Olive dropped her bag and rushed to Maddy's side. In the sickly yellow glow of a street light, she saw the swelling around her mouth and cheekbone, the bruising beginning to colour up Maddy's left eye, the cut across the bridge of her nose.

'Let's get you in the car,' she said. 'They'll see us quickly. One of the few perks of knowing everyone in A&E.'

'No.' Maddy pulled back. 'You do it. I want you to do it.'

Olive tilted Maddy's face up towards her own. 'You might need stitches. I can't do that here.'

'Course you can. You've got a needle, haven't you? I'm not going to hospital, Olive.'

Inside the flat, Olive cleaned the wound, gave Maddy a packet of frozen peas to hold against the swelling, and made her swallow paracetamol. She checked her temperature, vision and blood pressure – all normal – and went through the usual routine questions about medication. Only when she was confident the woman was in no danger did she strip off her wet clothes and tuck her up into her own bed. To all appearances exhausted, Maddy lay back and closed her eyes.

'Who did this?' Olive said, although she already knew the answer.

No response.

'I know you're not asleep. I can't let you sleep anyway, not with a possible head injury, so you may as well talk. Who did this, what happened, and why can't I take you to A&E? That cut will leave a scar if you don't get it stitched.'

Maddy's eyes stayed closed. 'Scars can be sexy. Yours is. You won't mind me with a scar.'

'Was it Sam?' Of course it was Sam.

'I fell,' Maddy said. 'In the studio. I landed on some glass.'

'Bullshit.'

Her eyes opened briefly. 'Olive, I'm exhausted. I've been waiting for you since midnight. Leave it, can't you?'

Midnight was over seven hours ago.

'Has this happened before?' Olive asked.

No response.

Olive felt rage building. 'You talk to me, Maddy, or you talk to the A&E doctors. And they're obliged to notify the police if they think a crime has been committed. I'm not. So, your choice.'

Maddy's eyes opened to reveal a glare. 'Bully.'

'I'm waiting.'

She sighed. 'Not really. Not for a long time.'

Olive had known, almost from the beginning, that Maddy was in a controlling, maybe even an abusive relationship. She should have done something before now.

'So, what happened?' Olive asked.

Another heavy sigh, and then Maddy's eyes dropped to the bed-cover. 'She thinks I'm seeing someone.'

Something gripped Olive's insides. 'Sam knows about me?'

A shake of the head. 'No, she thinks it's someone else.'

'Who?' Olive asked, the tightness in her gut turning solid and cold. Someone else? *There was someone else?*

Maddy glanced up, almost shyly, almost as though she was nervous of Olive now. 'Someone in the party. A mate, that's all. A bloke, can you believe it? She thinks I'm seeing a bloke.'

The party meant the local Labour Party. Politics, social justice, reform – just a few of the things Maddy was passionate about.

'Why would she think that?'

Maddy's appeasing look became a stare. 'Do you want her to come after you? Seriously?'

At that moment, it was exactly what Olive wanted. 'Oh, I think I can handle myself. Where is she right now?' She wasn't serious, not entirely. For one thing, Maddy shouldn't be left alone, but Olive was sure as hell Sam didn't frighten her.

Maddy caught hold of her hand and held on tight. 'No. You can't rock the boat. Not now. Please.'

'Leave her,' Olive said, knowing she was on the verge of begging. 'Leave her today. Don't go back. Stay here with me. I don't care who knows about us. The only thing that matters is you.'

'Soon. I promise. It'll be soon.'

72

The Andersons' yacht was a forty-foot Hanse named *Dora* and it lay, port side to, three berths from the end of C pontoon. As Lexy huddled close behind him, Garry opened the main hatch with the keys loaned by the harbour master – after a lot of persuasion, and only after Lexy had spelled out that they were looking for a vulnerable missing person who might, just might, be on one of the boats in his marina.

That same harbour master had insisted they wear life jackets even for the short walk along the pontoon and when Garry glanced back, he could see the glint of binoculars. The man in the office was watching their progress and Garry didn't mind. The pontoon, designed to rise and fall with the tide, was the very opposite of stable in strong winds. The wood beneath their feet was wet, strewn with seaweed and, should the two of them slip, he wasn't entirely confident he could get them both out of the water unaided. Hamilton-Minor, wisely, had returned to his house.

By the time they reached the boat, Garry was colder than he'd been all evening, which meant Lexy was too; and her core temperature hadn't been that stable to begin with.

'We can't stay here long,' Garry said, after the two of them had looked around the boat and found nothing to take them any further forward. The yacht had a white fibreglass outer shell with a cherry-wood interior, three tiny cabins and a central area with table, padded bench seats and a miniscule kitchen – galley, he supposed, he should call it. A last door revealed a toilet and he had a feeling that had a nautical name too, but already he was remembering that the last time he'd been on a boat he'd been seasick and he didn't like the way this one was bouncing.

Lexy leaned back against the chart table. Her face had paled and her hands, still gloveless, were shaking; her jaw was clenched from gritting her teeth to stop them chattering.

'It's too cold,' Garry went on, 'and you're looking ill again.'

A gust of wind tugged the boat against its lines; Garry could hear them scraping against the side of the pontoon.

'I'm fine,' Lexy insisted, before squeezing onto one of the bench seats. 'So, we've actually learned quite a lot tonight.'

'We have?' If what they'd learned so far made sense, he couldn't see it.

'Thanks to you being the touchy-feely type, we know that Anderson was linked to a woman who went missing previously.'

'Maddy,' Garry said, to show he was keeping up. 'A gay woman, possibly in an abusive relationship, whose wife, Samantha Elliott, was the initial suspect.'

'According to the local Labour Party chairman, Maddy and Anderson were closer than they should have been,' Lexy continued.

'And Maddy's partner, Samantha presumably, pitched up at the constituency office after she vanished, accusing Michael of spiriting her away.'

'I'd forgotten that, well done. And Eloise was there at the time. Best of all, we have a confirmed sighting of Maddy here at the marina on the third of November, two days after she was last seen at her studio. Lord Batshit told Northumbria, but because he couldn't pin it down to a date, and because he is, well, what he is, they didn't take him seriously. If you hadn't prompted him with your astronomical knowledge, we wouldn't be any further forward.'

Garry sat opposite Lexy and noticed that her face had taken on an odd, waxy colour.

'Ideal place for an illicit rendezvous.' Lexy's eyes went to the main cabin at the front of the boat. Bigger than the two at the stern, most of its floor space was taken up by a sizeable, triangular bed. 'Miles from Guisborough, few people around, especially at night and in winter. This could easily be Anderson's shag pad.' She shivered. 'That notwithstanding, it looks bloody tempting.'

There wouldn't be much room to manoeuvre, even in the big cabin; Garry would barely be able to stand upright in it and Anderson was as tall as he. And was that really important right now?

He said, 'You can bet your loose change the harbour master will have phoned Anderson already. We can justify looking round the boat; spending the night here, not so much.'

Making hot drinks was probably out too.

'And besides,' he went on. 'If Lord Batshit is right, Maddy came here with Michael and Eloise. She was a family friend.'

'But neither of them were seen that last day,' Lexy said. 'Maddy could have been here alone.'

'She wouldn't have got on the boat,' Garry reminded her. The harbour master had been very clear that spare keys were only given out with the express written permission of the owner and the loans were always recorded. The Anderson keys hadn't been loaned out at all that particular November.

'Even so, Maddy vanishes, Eloise stops sailing at the same time, and her mother reports her being troubled about something. Do you get the feeling something happened here?'

'Who do you think the other woman was? The one who came looking for Maddy last October? Could that have been Samantha, her wife?'

'If it was, she now believes, thanks to Lord Batshit, that her long-lost wife is still alive.'

'What a mess.'

Lexy didn't reply. She didn't look as though she disagreed.

Garry said, 'So why has Olive been coming here alone?'

'Me time?' Lexy suggested.

'Long way to come for that.'

'Looking for something?'

'Hiding something?' he countered.

'We're not getting anywhere fast, are we?'

'No,' he agreed. 'We're not.'

Lexy dropped her head down onto the tabletop with a clunk that must have hurt. For a second, Garry was afraid she'd fainted. He reached out, touched the side of her head.

'Lexy?' Her hair was incredibly soft.

She looked up. 'Do me a favour, Garry. Find out if this Samantha Elliott woman still lives in the same place in Whitley Bay. That can't be too far away.'

Garry wasn't sure he liked where this was going, but he said, 'No problem. What are you going to do?'

She eased herself down, out of sight, to curl up on the bench. 'I'm going to have a snooze. Wake me when you know.'

'Oh no, you're not.' He leaned over, grasped her under the arms and tugged. 'Come on, up you get. I'm getting you somewhere warm. This boat is bloody freezing. Come on, Lexy, I'm not joking.'

Coaxing her to her feet, Garry pushed her up the steps to the cockpit. While she slumped on one of the damp seats, he locked the boat. He wrapped an arm around her as they set off back along the pontoon. Only when they were back in his car, heater full on, did he speak again.

'I'm going to phone the Premier Inn and see if they have a couple of rooms. No, I'm going to request a twin because I don't think you should be on your own. You can't do anything else tonight.'

'Easy, tiger. We're going to Whitley Bay. Maddy and Olive are linked somehow.'

'Lexy, I know what hypothermia looks like and you're bloody close.'

'Wow.' She looked at him with her wide blue eyes.

'What?'

'I made you swear.'

It would be the easiest thing in the world right now, to lean forward and kiss her. And the very worst thing he could do.

'You never swear,' she said. 'That's another thing they told me about you.'

'Yeah, well, I do now.' He started the engine. 'Premier Inn. Some decent grub, a warm bed and I won't even offer to provide body warmth because, believe it or not, this is not my idea of a romantic date.'

He half expected her to argue, but he was done. Sergeant or not, he was off duty, had been warned off the investigation and this was his own car. Even Lexy couldn't make him drive any further tonight. She didn't argue though, and it took only five minutes to drive around the marina and find a spot in the Premier Inn's car park.

'I've got a bag in the boot,' he said. 'Give me a sec.' He strode round to the boot and opened it. 'Jeepers'.

'What?' Lexy had followed him.

Staring at the sports bag he'd filled with warm clothes, he said, 'You're going to kill me.'

'Doubt it, but what?'

'I found Olive's gym bag earlier tonight. In her hospital locker. I was going to tell you when you phoned, but then you didn't phone. Then you did and you'd got yourself into a proper fix and it slipped my mind.'

'Did you look inside?'

'Quick glance, that's all. I knew it had to be properly signed into evidence, so I left it where it was. Thing is though . . .'

'What?'

Garry pulled out his phone and found the picture he'd taken earlier. Olive's key chain. At the end of the chain dangled a piece of fused glass depicting an olive branch. It was a lovely piece, clearly not mass-produced.

'I think Maddy made this. Remember the glasswork on the wellington? She was a glass artist as well as a painter. I think she and Olive knew each other.'

'You're right, I am going to kill you. Slowly and painfully.'

'Sorry.'

'Are there fresh clothes in that bag of yours?'

Puzzled by the change of subject, he nodded. 'In case you were wet. Which you are. You can change when we're inside.'

'I'll change in the car,' she replied. 'We're going to Whitley Bay.'

73

October, three years previously

Olive came back from the shower to find Maddy standing in front of her chest of drawers. The top drawer, the one in which Olive kept her underwear, was a few inches open and Maddy had something in her hand.

'Tea,' Olive said, louder than was necessary, as Maddy stiffened and looked round. In one hand, she held a sheet of paper and Olive knew immediately what it was. She put her own mug down on the bedside table and wondered how she was going to handle this. She'd never thought of Maddy as a snoop, but the woman had never been alone in the flat before; their time together was so precious, there was no way Olive would willingly leave her alone.

Instead of apologising – Maddy never apologised – she held the letter up towards Olive. 'Was this something you were going to mention?'

Olive felt annoyance stealing over her. Maddy kept so much of her own life private, even secret, but Olive had to consult her about everything? She walked deliberately past her, putting the other mug on Maddy's side of the bed, before closing the underwear drawer. She'd have to open it again soon, to get dressed, but it seemed an important point to make. Maddy shouldn't be snooping around.

'Why didn't you tell me?' Maddy said.

'I did.' Olive kept her back to the other woman. 'I told you the night we met I wouldn't be in the army much longer.'

'You didn't say this soon. This is dated August.'

'Ten months from now is hardly soon.'

The letter Maddy had stumbled upon, that had been hurriedly

pushed out of sight the previous evening, was the army's official acceptance of Olive's resignation. Under the terms of her contract, she still had ten months to serve.

'Is this because of me?' Maddy demanded. 'Are you doing this for me?'

Olive's insides were clenching up now. 'Would that be a problem? You keep telling me we're going to be together, that I'm your future. How can we do that if I'm spending months away?'

Maddy opened her mouth, seemed to think better of it and instead pushed past Olive into the sitting room. Resisting the temptation to follow, Olive got dressed. Slowly. Ten minutes had passed before she went to find Maddy, who was immediately in front of the window, looking out at a rain-drenched Newcastle.

'What's this about?' Olive asked, as she handed over the neglected tea.

'I don't like the thought of you making sacrifices for me.'

'Why not? Isn't that what being in love is all about?'

Maddy reached out to wipe away condensation from the window pane. 'I'm not the woman you think I am, Olive.'

In the now clear glass, Olive could see Maddy's face. She said, 'What does that mean?'

Maddy gave a tiny shrug of her shoulders. 'I'm not worth any sort of sacrifice, never mind an important one.'

Wishing Maddy would look at her, Olive took her time before replying. 'Isn't that for me to decide?'

'It would be, if you had all the facts. You don't.'

'So fill me in.'

Maddy took a deep breath, as though bracing herself for something unpleasant. 'There are sides to me you won't like.'

'I can see that. I don't like the one I'm seeing now, sneaking around in my bedroom, then trying to gaslight me because I'm organising my life with the two of us in mind.'

'That's not what I'm doing.' Maddy's eyes were glinting; a tear threatening to overspill. Olive had seen the woman she loved in many moods, never this one.

'What then?'

Maddy shook her head and her bottom lip started to shake.

'Maddy, I've seen more women in abusive and controlling relationships than I can shake a stick at.' For the first time, Olive wondered if she might be on the verge of becoming one of them; Maddy certainly called all the shots. 'They all have their stories, they all have a reason not to leave, and they all find any number of excuses why they can't accept the help that's on offer. You're many things, Maddy, most of them amazing. I never thought of you as a cliché before.'

Maddy spun round to face her. 'Don't you dare! You have no idea what I'm going through so you and I can be together.' She poked a finger into Olive's chest, her repeated jabs sharp and painful. 'No. Fucking. Idea.'

Maddy took another deep breath, before she turned and fled the room. Less than a minute later, she'd left the flat.

A week went by before they met again; this time, Maddy insisting she and Olive meet in a local park, although the weather had been damp and cold for days. Convinced she was about to be dumped, Olive almost didn't go, and unexpected traffic meant she was running fifteen minutes late. To her surprise, Maddy was waiting, a diminutive figure on a bench beneath a sheltering oak tree, wearing a bright yellow raincoat and those ludicrous blue wellingtons she'd customised herself. Her head lifted when she saw Olive approach and she smiled. A sad smile.

My heart is about to be broken, thought Olive as she let herself be kissed, discreetly, on the cheek.

'I'm sorry,' Maddy whispered in her ear.

Course you are, Olive thought. *You're not a bad person. You're just . . . you.*

Maddy took hold of Olive's hands. Regardless of who might be watching, Olive let her. 'I want to make you a promise, Olive, and in return I need you to make me one. If you can't, I understand, but it's going to be a deal-breaker.'

Rain poured down. Olive felt it trickling past her collar and down her neck, could see droplets bouncing off Maddy's hood. She said, 'I'm not following.'

'Me first.' Maddy's hands were wet and cold. 'When we're together – properly together, I mean, not just seeing each other occasionally like we do now – I'll do everything I can to be the person you deserve. I'll try, so hard, to be what you believe me to be. I'll change, Olive. I'll be better.'

Olive couldn't keep track of the conflicting emotions flooding through her. Joy, because Maddy wasn't dumping her; bewilderment, because what on earth was she talking about, Maddy was easily the most wonderful human ever; beneath it all, a deep, inexplicable fear. She was about to learn something that could tip her world upside down.

'What am I promising?' she asked.

'That you'll forgive me,' Maddy replied.

74

The cottage at Whitley Bay lay nestled beneath an overhang of cliff a half-mile north of the edge of town. It had one neighbour, a twin dwelling, the two houses forming a short, stubby, weather-beaten terrace. The sea was out of sight behind a series of hedges as Garry pulled over, but he could hear the grumble of waves breaking on a long, flat shore and the scream of sea birds that had been woken by the storm. When he cranked the window a couple of inches, he could smell the pungent, rotting, muddy aroma of a river that drained at low tide and he had a moment – not the first – of wishing the two of them safely back in the Premier Inn.

Lexy's phone pinged, startling him. She'd called the station on the way over, requesting that Olive's gym bag be collected, searched and signed into evidence. She was expecting a call as soon as it was known what the bag contained.

She shook her head. 'My dad,' she said, as she declined the call. He knew practically nothing about Lexy, Garry realised, and yet in a short time she'd learned so much about him. The detective versus the traffic copper; it was never going to be a fair contest.

It was impossible to tell, in the dark, whether the cliff had a natural hollow or had been carved out at some point, for quarrying or surface mining. Either way, it curved round the two small houses like an overfed snake. The windows were small, with storm shutters, the front doors narrow, the roof low-pitched slate. The interiors would get very little natural light; it was not a place Garry would have expected an artist to live.

A Nissan Leaf was parked outside cottage number one. Samantha

Elliott's home, number two, showed no lights behind the windows and none of the curtains were drawn.

'I really thought we were going to find Olive here.' Lexy sounded dispirited. 'I thought we had it.'

'Doesn't look like Elliott's here either. You stay in the car. I'll have a look around.'

'Garry.' Lexy sounded weary. 'I'm your boss, not your elderly mother, and I don't need looking after.'

Without another word, she left the car. Garry followed and opened the boot to find his torch. Lexy had already turned on her phone light, but the weak beam didn't go very far.

'Sorry,' she said, when he caught up. 'I know I owe you big time. But you have to let me do my job.'

'Don't let my mum hear you call her elderly or you can wave goodbye to Christmas dinner.'

Lexy used the cast-iron knocker to announce their presence and the two of them listened hard. No sound other than the relentless breaking of waves a short distance away and the howling of wind around the clifftop.

Garry stepped back and looked the cottage up and down; he'd put money on it being empty.

'I'll have a look round the back,' he said. 'Unless you'd prefer to, Sarge.'

'Go ahead. I'll try next door.'

They separated, and Garry made his way round the side of the building. A sharp knocking sound made him jump, until he realised it would be Lexy, trying to alert the people in the adjacent cottage. Coming upon a tall garden fence with an unlocked gate, he wedged it open because it never hurt to have a good escape route. He wasn't an imaginative bloke, probably why he'd never made detective, but he knew he didn't like this place.

Once through the gate, he shone the torch around an outdoor space of around fifteen metres square. Someone had made an effort to plant tubs, but they'd chosen poorly. Terracotta cracked in the frost, and these hadn't been watered in months. A couple of wooden garden chairs and a small table lay close to the house, all gleaming with moss. In the bottom left corner of the garden was a shed, bigger than his own on the allotment.

The sound of voices drifted to him on the wind – Lexy talking to the neighbours – and knowing there was life close by gave him courage he hadn't known he needed until that moment. Something was drawing him to the shed. It was padlocked shut, but the catch was thin. He looked around, spotted a metal hand fork abandoned on the ground and used one of the tines to break the catch. Bracing himself, he pulled open the shed door.

Canvases in various sizes leaned against the wall space, while the floor was a messy array of old paint tins, buckets, glass jars. An artist's easel was folded in one corner. Garry took a step inside, feeling something brittle crunch beneath his feet. Shards of glass in multiple colours lay on the floor as though someone had thrown something down in temper and hadn't bothered clearing up. The space had a smell of old paint and turpentine.

Curious to see Maddy's work, Garry wandered to the closest stack of canvases and pulled one apart. A portrait of a man in seventeenth-century dress sitting on a high-backed wing chair staring wistfully at the painter. Beneath his chin, he cradled a violin, his left hand clenched around the strings. His robes were a rich deep blue and the feathered cap on his head bright gold. The background was dark, the light falling on the man's flesh and the gold of his cap in the style of the old masters.

A hand fell on Garry's shoulder and he let the painting clunk back against the wall.

'Woah!' Lexy took a step back. 'Jumpy much?'

'Sorry.' Garry's nerve endings were tingling. 'This place gives me the creeps.'

'It's not a nice suburban bungalow, that's for sure. Is that one of Maddy's?'

She studied the painting for several seconds as Garry held both it and the light.

'Not what I expected,' she said. 'Seems too traditional. A bit lame.'

'Look closer,' Garry told her.

She squatted down and peered. 'He's got tattoos,' she said after a moment. 'On his knuckles. Very modern-looking ones.'

It had been the tattoos Garry had noticed first. Simple, perfect line drawings: a flower, a ship, a palm tree, two crossed arrows.

'Look at the violin,' he told her, watching her face soften into a smile.

'Art is . . . What does it say?' Her finger reached out, not quite tracing the graffiti on the shiny wooden surface of the violin.

'Art is anything you can get away with,' Garry replied. 'Andy Warhol quote.'

Lexy led the way back outside. 'Young couple live next door,' she said. 'They think Elliott's away, but that's nothing unusual because it happens a lot. They can't tell me anything about Maddy because they moved in since she vanished. I showed them a picture of Olive, but they don't remember ever seeing her.'

At the rear wall of the house, Garry shone the torch into the larger of two windows and could see a range cooker, tiled worktops, a shelf holding saucepans.

'Gone but not forgotten.' Lexy nudged Garry's arm. He followed her line of sight and saw the row of fruit and vegetables hanging in the window where they'd catch what little light the rear garden saw. All perfect, all fashioned in glass.

'We need to get inside,' he said.

'Can't be done.'

Garry stepped sideways to the smaller window. 'Come and look at this, Sarge.' It was opaque glass, about five feet off the ground. 'Look at that paintwork. Does that look to you like the window might have been forced?'

'You think someone broke in?' Using her sleeve to shield her hand, Lexy tried to open the window. It didn't budge.

'It's been closed again from the inside,' Garry said. 'Which means whoever did it either left through the front door or is still in there. We need to get inside.'

Even he knew forced entry to a private dwelling was legally

permitted if there was genuine reason to believe someone inside was in danger.

'I already broke into the shed,' he admitted.

Lexy looked like she was thinking about it. 'How much damage will there be?'

'Better round the front,' he told her. 'Got any gloves with you?'

As he led the way, Garry pulled his wallet from his pocket and found his Tesco Clubcard. He'd already spotted that the cottage had both a deadlock and a Yale lock. If he was right, the deadlock wouldn't be engaged.

He was. It took him less than ten seconds to slide the card between door and frame to push back the lock mechanism.

As he opened the front door, he said, 'Our intruder tried to cover his or her tracks. Secured the bathroom window, then left via the front. Without the keys, though, he couldn't properly lock the front door.'

Lexy said, 'I don't know whether to be impressed or alarmed.'

'When you've attended as many burglaries as I have, you pick up a few tips.' Pulling on the disposable gloves Lexy handed him, he switched on the overhead light.

The front door opened directly into a sitting room. As wind rushed in behind them, a small cloud of ash rose from the empty hearth and hung in the air. Lexy closed the door. The cottage was chilly, as though the heating hadn't come on for some time.

The sitting room contained two armchairs, a small sofa, bookcase, TV, a few occasional tables and some lamps; nothing out of the ordinary and certainly no obvious signs of a break-in. No sense of a third person in the house. All the same, he told himself to stay on his guard.

'I'm going upstairs,' Lexy announced.

Garry opened his mouth and caught himself in time. She was his boss, not his mum. And, as he was learning, she got grouchy when she was tired.

'Watch yourself,' he couldn't help but say as she reached the bottom step. 'Don't turn your back on any cupboard doors.'

Conscious of Lexy's footsteps above, Garry checked the ground floor to find signs of Maddy everywhere. In the bathroom hung a picture of bathers in the style of a Monet painting, but they frolicked in the lily-strewn lake wearing modern goggles and wetsuits. Decorative glass panels hung in each window. Most of all, though, she smiled out at him from numerous photographs scattered around the sitting room. On the mantelpiece above the fireplace one in particular took pride of place: Maddy, on the beach, wearing the same blue wellington boots they'd seen at Hartlepool marina and standing next to a tall girl with short dark hair wearing an oversized tweed jacket.

Garry felt a moment of deep sadness for a woman he'd never met; the boot being pulled from the mud at Hartlepool probably meant Maddy was dead.

Then he saw what was staring him in the face.

'Garry, can you come up?' Lexy called.

He made his way up the narrow, low-ceilinged staircase. A hemp rope had been strewn against one wall to act as a handrail.

'In here.'

Lexy was in a compact home office, tidy apart from the waste bin that had been upturned, spilling its contents, mainly paper, over the carpet. On one wall was a large cork board covered in pinned papers, cards and photographs. Pictures of Maddy featured most of all.

'What's up, boss?' he asked.

A narrowing of her eyes showed she'd registered the dig. 'Learned a couple of things about our friend Ms Elliott.' She stepped aside to let him see the desk. 'Bit of an amateur spy.'

Stacked on the large ink blotter in front of the desktop computer were several books on forensic computer science, including one titled *Uncovering Your Device's Secrets*. Garry nudged one aside to see three words, handwritten, on the blotting paper beneath: *Judges, Logs, Proudest*.

'And there's this.' Lexy held up a sheet of paper covered in tiny type. 'Instructions for a covert video recording device. The box was in the bin. I can't find the device itself.'

Garry's foot caught against the upturned bin. 'Did you do that?' He nodded at the mess on the floor.

'No, I did not. That's how I found it. So, who was she spying on?'

'Got another question for you. Come back downstairs.'

In the living room, Garry led Lexy to the photograph of Maddy and a tall woman on the beach.

'Look at that coat,' he said, indicating the tweed jacket the other woman was wearing. 'Does that look to you like the coat worn by whoever followed Olive out of the hotel in Hexham?'

Lexy nodded slowly. 'That's definitely Samantha Elliott,' she said. 'There was a photograph of her and Maddy in the bedroom. Much more intimate than this one.'

'So, Olive left the hotel in Hexham with Elliott,' Garry said. 'Wherever she is now, Olive is with this woman.'

Now, what in the world would bring those two together?

75

November, three years previously

Olive had never known such pain. Each morning when she woke, it hit her anew, a fierce ache in her chest that seemed to get bigger and heavier as the day went on. It was pain that pulled her down, dulled her thoughts and robbed her strength. She was barely functioning at work, on the verge of being dangerous around sick patients, and all she wanted to do when she got home was drink wine and then sleep.

Maddy had gone. Maddy was ghosting her.

It made no sense. Their meeting in the park, when they'd exchanged promises in the rain, had felt spiritual, almost a marriage of sorts. Pushing down all her misgivings, Olive had promised to forgive Maddy – with no clue what she'd be forgiving her for – because she knew she'd forgive Maddy anything.

And one day, she vowed (but only to herself), she'd make Maddy tell her everything. Whatever she'd done, or been forced to do, or was about to do, she hated herself for it. Olive would forgive Maddy and help her heal.

But now she'd vanished.

Olive had been to the workshop twice to find it locked up and dark. The second time, she'd knocked on a few neighbouring units, but no one had seen Maddy for some time or knew how to contact her. One man, whose overalls were covered in fine sawdust, told her she was the second person in as many days to come looking for Maddy, the other a tall, dark-haired woman who'd barely been able to contain her fury.

'Are you Olive?' the man had asked, wiping dust from his spectacles.

Heart beating faster, Olive had replied that, yes, she was indeed called Olive. 'Why?' she'd asked when the man seemed at a loss as to how to continue.

He'd made an uncomfortable face. 'This other woman asked me about an Olive,' he'd admitted. 'Did I know you? Did I have any idea where you live? Did Maddy come here with any other women? I told her no, obviously, because I've never met you before and Maddy was always on her own, from what I saw.'

'Did she leave any contact details?' Olive had asked, nervously. The woman sounded like Sam, although Maddy had never really told her anything about the woman she'd married. Sam wasn't someone she could approach, but contact details might at least let her know where Maddy had lived.

'She didn't,' the man had replied. 'And, to be honest, I wouldn't hand them over if she had. I really didn't like the way she was asking about you.'

Three weeks went by. Olive called and texted Maddy repeatedly, although she wasn't supposed to, and each went unanswered. She'd suspected that Maddy used some sort of secret phone to contact her – what were they called, burner phones? – and now she'd thrown it away because it had served its purpose. To Maddy, Olive had been a fling after all, nothing more than a pleasant interlude.

And yet Sam was looking for her too; nothing made any sense.

Three long weeks. Olive lost first her appetite and then weight; it was all she could do to keep herself clean and properly dressed. Her colleagues noticed and her superior officer asked if there was anything she needed to talk about.

She stopped visiting her parents because she knew she wouldn't be able to hide the dreadful state she'd let herself get into. In her free time, she drove along the north-east coast searching for the cottage Maddy shared with Sam, but with so little to go on, and never any sign of Maddy's car, it was hopeless. She started combing art galleries, sales and exhibitions in the north, looking for places where Maddy might be exhibiting, and knew she'd turned into a stalker. She didn't care.

At the end of the third week, annoyed with herself for not having thought of it before, she tried a Google search and saw the Missing notice. Produced officially by the Northumbria Police, the online poster showed a recent picture, one Olive recognised immediately, because she remembered Maddy buying the dark red sweater with the dangly beads. She was described as an artist from Whitley Bay who'd last been seen on the first of November, days after she and Olive had been together.

Olive's first thought was relief: there was an explanation after all, followed by an emotion she knew to be joy. Maddy hadn't abandoned her, hadn't been lying to her, she loved her after all. Then, bitterly ashamed of her selfishness, she went to the police.

'Just a friend, you say?' The detective working on Maddy's case gave Olive a long, piercing look. 'And did she give you any clue at all that she was planning to leave, that she wasn't happy? Any problems she mentioned?'

Olive hesitated. She wanted to find Maddy, of course she did, it was the most important thing, but these were not ideal circumstances in which her own secret life could be revealed to the world.

'She told me she wanted to leave Sam, her wife, but that it was complicated. She wouldn't say too much, just that she needed money to get away. I offered to help, but she said it wouldn't be enough.'

'Would you say she was afraid of Sam?' The detective glanced down. 'Samantha Elliott, is that right?'

'Yes, that's it. I asked her that. She wouldn't really talk about it. She said she had a plan, that I had to be patient.'

Maddy had said a lot more than that, but Olive wasn't about to say anything that would land her in trouble, if and when she showed up.

She had to show up.

The detective's head bounced, as though it made sense, of sorts.

Olive said, 'Do you think Sam might have hurt her?'

The detective made a dismissive gesture. 'Nothing at this stage to suggest any harm has come to Miss Black. What we do know is that her car, that Miss Elliott paid the lease on, was left at Chester-le-Street railway station in the long-term car park. While Miss Elliott was in Scotland.'

Olive felt the fear shifting again. If Sam hadn't hurt Maddy, then who had? Maybe she wasn't hurt at all. Maybe she'd just . . . gone.

'What are you doing to find her?' she asked. 'Have you spoken to her family? Her other friends? Where does Sam think she's gone?'

'Of course. All that's routine. And Miss Black will stay on the missing list until she makes herself known to us again.'

Olive stared at him. 'That's it?'

The detective leaned back in his chair. 'As I say, we've no reason to believe any harm has come to Miss Black. If you and she are good friends, I'm sure she'll be in touch soon.'

'And what if she isn't?'

'Without evidence of a crime, there's not a lot we can do.' The detective got to his feet. 'Sometimes, Olive, people don't want to be found.'

Knowing her time was up, Olive picked up her bag and stood.

His hand on the door, the detective turned back. He said, 'Did Maddy ever talk to you about Michael Anderson?'

It took several seconds for Olive to place the name.

'The MP for Cleveland?' Curious, after seeing his picture in Maddy's studio, she'd done a brief Google search. 'Not really. I know he'd commissioned a glass piece from her. I don't know whether she finished it.'

'Maddy had some strong political leanings, according to Miss Elliott. She was one of the Labour Party activists in Cleveland.'

'That's true.'

'Miss Elliott seemed to think Maddy and Michael Anderson were close.' He paused. 'Maybe a bit too close?'

'Michael Anderson?' Olive shook her head. 'That's impossible. Maddy is gay. She'd never be involved with a man. Besides, she and . . .' On the verge of tears, she took a second. 'It's impossible,' she finished.

Impossible, and yet Sam had been so convinced she'd beaten Maddy up because of it.

The detective gave a kind smile that somehow made Olive feel worse. No, not kind, pitying.

'I probably shouldn't be telling you this, but Maddy's partner, Sam, did mention an Olive when we talked to her. Something she'd heard from a mutual friend. She had no details. I'm guessing that was you.'

That made it twice Olive had been given evidence that Sam was on her trail.

'It could have been,' she admitted. 'But I never met Sam. I don't want to cause any trouble. I just want to find Maddy.'

The detective gestured that Olive should precede him out. 'If you don't mind me saying so, Olive, four months isn't a lot of time to get to know someone,' he said. 'Maybe chalk this one down to experience?'

76

Still in the cottage that Samantha Elliott and Maddy had shared, Garry and Lexy sat either side of the empty fireplace.

Lexy spoke first. 'So, did Olive and Samantha know each other before Thursday? They must have done, or how did Samantha know where Olive would be?'

Garry was thinking back. 'Olive's schedule was pinned up in the kitchen at Home Farm,' he said. 'The rest of the family could see at a glance where she was.'

So, had a family member tipped Elliott off? Why did he keep coming back to Michael Anderson?

He stood up. 'I want another look at something.'

Garry ran upstairs, conscious of Lexy following. In the smaller of the two rooms, they stood in front of the noticeboard. One of the numerous photographs, one of the very few that didn't feature Maddy, had been taken in Hartlepool marina. A sailing yacht took up most of the frame.

'That's Anderson's boat,' he said. 'Why would Elliott have this?'

'Could have been Maddy's photograph,' Lexy replied. 'We know she went to the marina.'

Garry glanced around. 'So why is it still up in a room that smacks of investigation to me? And look at the water tap on the pontoon. No hose. The hoses were only taken out last October, according to Lord Batshit. I'd say this is Elliott's picture. And there's this.'

He pointed out a till receipt for a sailing jacket, dated several weeks before Maddy had disappeared three years earlier. Someone had written on it: *Whose credit card?*

'Samantha Elliott fits the description of the woman who went to the marina looking for Maddy,' Garry said.

'If it was her, she was told Maddy's still alive.' Lexy had been leafing through a bundle of papers pinned together on the board. 'Craft fairs,' she said. 'Dating back three years. And look at this. A list of gay clubs north of Birmingham. Samantha was looking hard for Maddy. It takes some level of intensity to keep looking for someone for three years.'

'Plus all the deep mining she did into someone's online history,' Garry added, his eyes sliding to the desk with its array of books on forensic computer science.

Lexy's phone started to ring as they reached the bottom of the stairs again. 'It's Ben,' she said, before flicking it to speakerphone.

Ben was the detective constable whom Lexy had asked to collect Olive's gym bag from the hospital. 'I'm sending you through some stuff, Lexy,' he said. 'Should get it any second.'

'Tell me what you found,' Lexy ordered.

'Well, mostly it was gym gear. T-shirt, trainers, socks, sports bra, that sort of thing. It was what we found in the inside pocket that was interesting.'

'Consider me interested.'

'First up, a picture of Olive and some other lass not wearing a lot. Next, a surveillance device for listening into private conversations. Not police standard, the sort you can buy fairly cheap off Amazon. Finally, two USB sticks.'

'What was she up to?' Lexy muttered, as Garry remembered the similar surveillance equipment they'd seen upstairs. Two amateur spies? Or working together?

Over the phone, Ben said, 'Coming over now. Three separate files. You should have them.'

'Signal's not great. Wait, here they come. Thanks, Ben. I'll be in touch.'

As Lexy ended her call and opened the first file, Garry joined her on the sofa and saw an image appear on the screen, a selfie, taken indoors. Olive and the woman he now recognised as Maddy were lying back with their heads on cushions. Their dark hair mingled, Olive's mascara had smudged, Maddy had a gleam of sweat on her temple. The shot stopped below the collarbone on both women, but neither seemed to be wearing anything, on their upper bodies at least. On Maddy's left shoulder was a small tattoo of a seashell. On Olive's right, a puckered scar.

'Well, I'd say Olive and Maddy knew each other,' Garry said.

'Any sign at school Olive swung both ways?' Lexy asked.

'At my strict Catholic secondary, not a chance. But stuff her parents said is making sense now. No boyfriends before Michael came along. Very keen to point out, more than once, that Olive's always been a good girl, never anything untoward. When I asked about friends, several females were mentioned, all of whom weren't around anymore.'

'But why marry Michael? And what weird triangle were she, Maddy and Samantha Elliott embroiled in?'

'Very good questions, boss.'

'I will slap you, you know. Let's see what else Ben sent me.'

She clicked on another file, this time the contents of one of the USB sticks. It was a video file and Lexy pressed play. They watched for several seconds.

'Jeepers,' Garry said.

Lexy said, 'Holy shit.'

'You're right,' agreed Garry. 'Holy shit.'

77

March, two years previously

'Well, it'll be nice to have you a bit closer.' Anne Charles hovered in the doorway between bedroom and sitting room, her tone managing to convey that the only thing to be said in favour of Olive's new flat was its proximity to the family home. 'We might actually see you from time to time. Especially now you're out.'

She made it sound like Olive had been released from prison.

Only weeks after meeting Maddy, Olive had submitted her notice to leave the army. The remarkable turn her life had taken since that night in Newcastle had been the push she'd needed to move on and plan a future. Hell, she'd thought at the time, she might even come out properly.

In the normal course of events, twelve months' notice was required, but Olive had been released early on the grounds of serious and prolonged depression.

She didn't look up from her unpacking. 'I've been in Newcastle for over a year, Mum. Hardly Afghanistan.'

A second's pause. 'Yes, well, it's not all about distance, is it? Where shall I put these daffs?'

Flower arranging – exactly what she needed right now.

'Do you actually have a vase?' Anne went on.

Olive took a moment to glance round at the overcrowded living room. More than a dozen boxes to be unpacked and her mother was still wearing her outdoor coat. 'Almost certainly,' she said. 'Probably at the bottom of one of these boxes.'

Anne sniffed. 'I thought they might brighten the place up a bit.'

A place that, half an hour ago, Olive's mother hadn't so much as seen. Was there ever a more passive-aggressive act than giving improving flowers?

'And you're in charge, at this hospital?' Olive's dad, at least, was attempting to help, and had unpacked most of the contents of a box marked *bedroom* onto the living-room carpet.

'I'm not the ward sister,' Olive explained. 'Although I do have equal rank, to borrow an army term. I'm more of a trauma specialist. I'll be working at all the north-eastern hospitals, hopefully sharing best practice.'

'Susan Robinson's eldest works at Middlesbrough, now I come to think of it.' Anne was still clutching the daffodils. 'Orthopaedics, I think she said. You'll remember Martin, Olive, couple of years older than you at school. He's single, too. We could have them round for lunch one Sunday now you're home. After church. You will be coming to church, won't you?'

'When I'm not working. Careful with that, Dad.' Olive jumped to her feet to take Maddy's glass picture from her father's shaky grasp. She'd wound bubble wrap around it until it was three times its own thickness, but even so. 'There should be a metal stand in that box. Can you have a look?'

Knowing it would only be minutes before one or other parent followed her, Olive carried the glass into her new bedroom. Hoping they wouldn't notice, she nudged the door shut with her foot and leaned back against the wall.

Deep breaths, it would pass. She couldn't cry in front of her parents.

Four months, and she still hadn't lost hope that Maddy would come back. Every time the phone rang, the first thought in her head – Maddy. An unexpected ring on the doorbell – Maddy? A text message from an unknown number – Maddy?

She unwrapped the olive grove picture and placed it carefully on the window ledge.

Where are you, Maddy? You said you'd always be with me.

'Righto.' Her dad was on his feet, surrounded by bedroom clutter, when she went back into the living room. 'That's another one done.

I think we need to get back if we're not going to be late for the Con Club, Mother.'

Olive's mum had found her way into the kitchen, daffodils in hand. 'Yes, well.' She looked around, as though a perfect, cut-glass vase might appear if she stood there long enough. 'If you're sure you can manage now, love. I'll leave these here.' She put the flowers down on the draining board.

'You might want to put this somewhere.' Coat on, hat in hand, Olive's dad held something out to her. 'Found it in the box. Computer widget of some sort. Might get lost if it's left lying around.'

He dropped a USB stick into Olive's hand.

That evening, when she'd finally unpacked the boxes and put most of her stuff away, when her computer was plugged in and working, Olive remembered the USB stick. If it was hers, she had no memory of it. Her dad had found it in a box of bedroom stuff: underwear, cosmetics, sports socks, and she had no idea why she'd have put a USB stick in her underwear drawer. Curious, with nothing much else to do, she plugged it in to her laptop. Seconds later, she knew she'd never seen it before. Maddy had left the stick in Olive's flat.

Her first thought after watching the contents of the file was that some things had finally started to make sense; her second, that she'd probably spend the rest of the night vomiting.

78

It was uncomfortable sitting so close to Lexy; Garry wished he could get up without making it obvious.

'Lexy,' he began, knowing he was about to state the obvious. 'This is porn.'

Not even lesbian porn, which might make some sense, given the selfie they'd just seen. Three people – two women and a bloke – had been involved in this particular home movie. The blonde, her back to the camera, sat astride a naked man, grinding into him. A second woman with long dark hair matched the blonde's position, only her thighs were either side of the man's face. The bloke's right hand curved around the blonde's ass, his left was holding the other woman, pushing them both, rhythmically, towards him.

'Shot on the Anderson boat.' Garry took in the tiny space, the odd, triangular shape of the room.

Lexy said, 'Could the brunette be Olive?'

'Really didn't know her that well.'

Almost as though she'd heard them, the brunette twisted round to face the blonde, giving a sly, split-second glance towards the camera. The blonde bent forward, and as the two women kissed, the man's face came into view. Still rocking his hips, he watched them.

'It's Maddy,' Garry said. 'Shell tattoo on left shoulder.'

'And that's Michael Anderson,' Lexy added. 'Do you think the blonde is Eloise?'

Garry said nothing.

'Come on, you met her. I didn't.'

Garry considered the woman's shape, her muscle tone and skin.

Not a teenager, but still young. The hair was the biggest clue: shoulder length, curly and, in the right light, probably the very distinct shade of strawberry-blonde he remembered.

'Could be. Probably.'

The video lasted three minutes and twenty-six seconds. By the time it finished, they had their answer. The three participants were Michael and Eloise Anderson and Maddy Black and the footage had been shot on the Andersons' yacht.

As Lexy switched it off, Garry got to his feet. 'I did not need to see what Anderson looks like when he's climaxing,' he said. 'Right, boss, we're done here. We drive back to Middlesbrough and on the way, you update the deputy chief. He can assign someone else to take over.'

'No!'

He was taken aback by the vehemence in Lexy's voice.

'I've only been here five months, Garry. Think what it will do to my reputation if it gets out that I had to be rescued from a snowdrift and then couldn't carry on with a live and critical investigation. And you know what they'll say even when we tell them what we've found. How can a three-year-old video of three consenting adults be relevant to Olive's disappearance two nights ago?'

'We've a very obvious connection in the positive sighting of Samantha Elliott, former partner of Maddy Black, leaving the hotel in Hexham with Olive,' Garry replied, knowing he was speaking slowly, as though to an idiot, and hoping she wouldn't yell at him again. 'We also know that Olive and Maddy knew each other. Possibly very well.'

Lexy was frowning, as though struggling to concentrate, but she was listening.

He said, 'So, the first thing we do – right now – is find out what car is registered to Samantha Elliott and we get it tracked down. Get Ben on the phone again. No, do it in the car. We need to leave.'

Lexy said, 'They left Hexham in Olive's car.'

'And if I were Samantha, I'd have my own vehicle somewhere close so that we could switch to it. If we trace the car, we find them.'

Lexy stayed where she was on the sofa. 'But there's so much I don't get. If Olive is gay, why marry Michael? And if Michael and Eloise were into kinky sex, why would he allow it to be videoed? He was in parliament for God's sake.'

'He didn't know it was happening. Neither did his wife. Maddy set up that recording, possibly using the surveillance equipment we saw upstairs.'

'How can you know that?'

Garry sighed. 'Of the three of them, Maddy was the only one conscious of the camera. She was the only one displaying herself, letting the camera see her at her best angle. She was sucking in her stomach, sticking up her boobs. The other two had no idea they were being filmed.'

Lexy didn't look convinced.

'Lexy, I've seen some home-made porn in my time, I know what I'm talking about. If you want to judge, fine, but do it in the car on the way back.'

Finally, she got to her feet. 'Why make the video at all? Blackmail?'

'Probably. And there's another question you should be asking.'

'There is?'

'What on earth was Olive doing with that USB stick?'

To Garry's surprise, Lexy sat down again. 'Hang on, Ben sent over three files. There's one more.'

79

The day of the Saltburn summer fair dawned cloudless and bright. It wasn't warm, but sunny enough for a woman wearing a baseball cap and sunglasses to pass unnoticed. Olive paid her entrance fee and made her way down a corridor filled with children's art towards the main hall.

Stalls selling everything from plants to preserves to pottery lined the big room, while fair-style games like Splat the Rat formed a central aisle. There must have been nearly two hundred people, which meant she would almost certainly not be seen or recognised.

There was a buzz in the room, the excitement of something about to happen. The member of parliament for Middlesbrough South and East Cleveland had taken to the stage, along with a small party of officials in dark suits and matronly dresses. The MP was the tallest of the group, the one who drew the eye, his physical presence apparent, even from the back of the hall. Olive reminded herself that she knew what he looked like when he was having sex.

A portly man in his fifties was hesitantly tapping the microphone, as though trying to wake it from a long slumber and a little afraid it might bite.

Anderson's wife, Eloise, whose online biography Olive knew by heart, was close to the stage, two skinny girls with fair hair by her side. She wore white jeans and high-heeled, strappy, red sandals, a striped shirt (red and white, of course) and a red box jacket. Her bouncy blonde hair was held back by a pair of designer sunglasses. She was unfairly slim for a woman who'd had two children, impossibly toned for one who worked full time.

It was unreasonable, of course, that Eloise had borne the brunt of her hatred since she'd discovered the video tape, but Olive knew in her heart that Maddy had been going through the motions when she'd had sex with Anderson. Maddy was not into men. Eloise, on the other hand? What woman wouldn't want Eloise?

Maddy on the tape had kissed Eloise on the lips, had stroked her hair, looked deep into her eyes and smiled her special Maddy smile; she'd done none of those things with Anderson. Maddy had liked Eloise, and Olive could cheerfully kill Eloise for it.

Worse than its contents, though, the video had been recorded in October, several weeks after Olive and Maddy had met. She'd known about Sam, of course, almost from the start, and had told herself she could deal with Sam, because Sam was on her way out. Sam, one day, would be history. But to learn that Maddy was involved with someone else, with two others, one of them a man, had come close to breaking Olive. Had she really known her at all?

I think I have a way out. Can you give me some time?

Was her connection to the Andersons, was the existence of that tape, Maddy's way out? Maddy must have made the tape herself. A high-profile MP, a family man at that, would never have let himself be filmed having unconventional sex. He hadn't known about the recording, which probably meant Eloise hadn't either.

Blackmail. It was the only possible answer. Maddy had been planning to blackmail the Andersons to get the money she needed to leave Sam. That and the sexual relationship that had made the blackmail possible were the dreadful deeds she'd needed forgiveness for. Maddy had been playing a very dangerous game. And something had gone wrong.

The police were here. Startled, feeling guilty in spite of having done nothing – yet – Olive stepped behind a tall man and took another, sidelong look at the uniformed police officer she'd spotted to one side of the stage. He was tall, with broad shoulders and short hair that, years ago, had been ginger. It had darkened since, and the once skinny frame had filled out, but Olive knew him instantly. Garry Mizon, the shy runner, who'd never had the courage to look her in the eyes but who'd once saved an important race for her. His eyes scanned the crowd, returning frequently to check on Anderson, on Eloise and the girls, taking his close-protection duties seriously. She hadn't known he'd joined the police. It made sense though; he'd always been so determined to do the right thing.

Should she do the right thing now?

So many times since she'd discovered the tape, Olive had been on the brink of taking it to the police, but her one further, tentative conversation with the detective in charge of Maddy's case had discouraged her. There had been zero developments, he'd told her, and absolutely no evidence of a crime committed. He'd made it clear he had many more important things to deal with.

The video, potentially explosive though it might be, wasn't evidence of a crime. It wasn't illegal for three consenting adults to have sex in a private space. Revealing it might ruin Anderson's new career as an elected member of parliament, but was that enough?

If they'd hurt Maddy, nothing would be enough.

And so Olive had held back, biding her time.

And now fate had thrown her old friend Garry in her way. Garry had liked her, he'd made that obvious, in his shy, unassuming way, and Olive had wished, more than once, that she could tell him it was hopeless, that she was never going to be attracted to him, or to anyone like him. Boys simply didn't do it for her.

Garry would listen to her. Garry would take her seriously.

Anderson's short speech came to an end, there was a burst of applause – more genuine than polite, the crowd had liked him – and he was leaving the stage. Olive watched him join his wife, receive her congratulatory peck on the cheek and then the local bigwigs were leading him out to the field at the rear of the building, where more stalls were set out. Garry followed and, after a moment, so did Olive. This was her chance. If she didn't talk to him today, it might be impossible to track him down again. Uniformed police officers didn't sit around behind desks waiting for calls from the public, and messages could go so easily astray. If she was going to do it, it had to be today.

Out in the sunlight, the officials had gone some way ahead, but the new first family of Middlesbrough South had become separated. Michael and the girls were heading for the arena where the dog show was about to begin, maybe he was the judge, and Eloise was heading back towards the hall, as though she'd forgotten something. Garry was hovering, his eyes going from husband to wife, as if unsure whom he should follow. And then Eloise stumbled, almost falling over. Her heel had caught in a grate on the edge of the playground.

In an instant, Garry was at her side, his arm around her shoulders. When she'd regained her balance, he helped her slip her foot out of the sandal. Eloise leaned against him, her bare foot held aloft, as he gently wiggled the sandal free. He slipped it back onto her foot in a display reminiscent of the iconic scene from Cinderella. As he got to his feet, he and Eloise exchanged a smile. She was thanking him, he acknowledging it modestly. He watched her walk away, a look on his face that was something close to adoration. His eyes skimmed over Olive and didn't linger for as much as a second.

Olive turned away too. Garry couldn't help her. She was on her own.

80

Lexy opened the remaining file. 'It's audio,' she said, turning up the volume.

From the laptop came a crackling and then a woman's voice, sounding broken, exhausted. 'I need to talk to you.'

A second woman replied. 'It's very late. And you must be tired. Can I give you something to help you sleep?'

'Olive, you have to listen to me. Michael likes you.'

'*Olive*,' Lexy mouthed as she and Garry made eye contact.

'No,' Olive on the recording said. 'He's grateful to the nurse who's taking care of his wife. We see it a lot here. We know it doesn't mean anything.'

Lexy stopped the recording. 'Is the other woman Eloise?' she asked Garry. 'Could this have been while she was in hospital?'

'Let me hear some more.'

Lexy pressed the go button.

'Trust me, it means something,' the woman who might or might not have been Eloise said. 'Once he gets going, he's relentless. He'll sweep you up. You won't be able to help it.'

Garry nodded; he'd recognised Eloise's voice.

Olive said, 'I can take care of myself.'

'You need to know what he's capable of. You need to know what you're dealing with.'

'Eloise, you're exhausting yourself. You have to take it easy.'

When she spoke again, Eloise sounded agitated. 'No, you need to listen.'

'OK.' Olive remained calm. 'I'll listen.'

The sound of footsteps and that of a door being closed, then metal scraping, as though someone – Olive – was drawing up a chair. Garry closed his eyes and pictured her, in nurse's uniform, her hair tied back, tired at the end of the day, sitting next to Eloise's bed and leaning in.

Silence. Then more movement in the hospital room and the sound of water being poured. Eloise coughed and cleared her throat.

'It started when he came out of the army,' she said. 'I think there must have been – let's say shenanigans before that – but nothing I knew about, until he left the forces.'

Olive on the recording said, 'What started, exactly?'

More coughing and then Eloise said, 'No, I'm OK, thanks.'

The sound of a glass landing on a hard surface.

'Michael wanted – no, he needed, it was like a compulsion – high-risk sex.'

Garry's eyes almost flickered open; he took a breath and kept them closed.

Several seconds went by before Olive spoke again. 'I'm not sure I understand.'

'I don't mean doing it without a condom. I'm talking seriously risky, multiple partners, indiscreet locations. It was like the greater the risk of being caught, the more he craved it.'

'I don't . . . Eloise, he's an MP. A public figure.'

Unable to resist any longer, Garry opened his eyes and looked at Lexy. She'd been watching him, but her face gave nothing away.

'Exactly,' Eloise said. 'He knew it would all be over for him if he was found out. That was the point.'

'And you knew about this?'

Eloise didn't reply.

'You were involved, weren't you?' Olive said.

'I didn't think I had a choice. At least he could rely on my discretion. And I was frightened of losing him. I think, as time went on, I came to hate him for what he put me through, but in the beginning, I did it for love. We tolerate so much for love, don't you think?'

A beat, then Olive said, 'Yes, we do.'

'It was only ever threesomes. Me, Michael and another woman. I refused to have anything to do with another man, and I don't think he was really into that anyway. We'd meet in hotel rooms, in our London flat, even his office in London.'

'That sounds reckless.'

'It was.'

Another pause, then, 'Who were these women? Strangers you picked up in bars?'

'No, that wouldn't have been nearly dangerous enough. These were women with as much to lose as us. Senior civil servants, always married, other members of parliament. You'd be surprised how well I know the current work and pensions secretary.'

'You're kidding me?'

'Do I look like I'm joking?'

'I'm sorry. It's just . . . well, it's a shock. And these women, they went along with it?'

'Not really.'

'What do you mean?'

'I think he coerced them to.'

'How?'

'I think they thought they were entering into a conventional affair. Still risky, of course, but nothing like what it eventually became. Michael could be so charming, and you've seen how good-looking he is. Not many women can resist him. And he had a knack of finding the ones who weren't happy, who were looking for something more. So, there'd be a passionate affair for a few weeks. I could always sense the excitement in him. He was like a kid the night before Christmas. And then one night, he'd invite her round to the flat and I'd be there. He'd get her drunk, or give her coke, whatever it took. Some didn't need any inducement at all. Others couldn't believe what they'd done when they sobered up. And it was never Michael who cleaned up the vomit.'

Eloise's voice on the tape was failing. She coughed, then came the sound of swallowing. After nearly a minute, she said, 'If the woman was into it, into me, into the sex, he'd quickly get bored and move on. It was the reluctant ones that kept him interested for months at a time. After they'd done it once, he could bully them into carrying on. It was as much about power as anything else.'

Another pause, and then Eloise said, 'I've shocked you. He doesn't look the type, does he?'

'No, he doesn't,' Olive replied. 'And I appreciate you wanting to warn me. Thank you. But, really, I think you've got it wrong. Michael hasn't eyes for anyone but you right now.'

Eloise's voice hardened. 'Allow me to know him better than you do. And if it was just sex, I wouldn't care. You're a grown woman, you look as though you can take care of yourself. But that isn't everything. Not the worst of it by a long shot.'

'It isn't?'

'I always knew it would go wrong one day. He'd walk into a honey trap or someone would set him up, or he'd target the wrong woman. And that's exactly what he did. The wrong woman.'

More sounds that could have been drinking; some gentle murmurs from Olive. Then she said, 'Who was the wrong woman?'

81

Silence. Garry and Lexy waited until the sound of the silence changed, going from a low-pitched humming of a running tape to dead air. Lexy fixed her attention on the laptop, pressing keys, the frown on her face deepening. After nearly a minute, she said, 'End of the file.'

'Did the tape run out?'

'Either that or the crucial bit has been deliberately cut off.' Lexy got to her feet and closed the laptop. 'The key thing is, if Eloise revealed a dark secret on her deathbed, Olive heard it.'

'We have to get going,' Garry said.

'We do,' she agreed.

The parking area at the front of Samantha Elliott's cottage was tight. In spite of his urge to be back on the road, Garry reversed slowly, his car alarm kicking in immediately. He glanced in the rear-view mirror. Nothing behind for at least four feet. He inched back. The alarm screamed.

'Won't be a sec,' he said, before getting out and striding to the back of the car.

Inches away was a low, dark-stone wall, almost invisible at night and too low to be seen from the mirror. He thought for a moment, then lifted the tailgate and found his torch again. A few seconds later, he called to Lexy to join him.

'I know who broke in here.' He shone the beam on the traces of paintwork, the gouges in the stone. 'Tango red metallic,' he went on. 'The colour of Anderson's shiny new Audi. I should have told you earlier, he was out on Friday night, from around seven till two in the morning. He told his family he was driving round Olive's friends. Looks like he wasn't. He came here.'

Lexi said, 'Which means he knows about Samantha.'

'Which means there's quite a lot he hasn't told us,' Garry replied.

'I'll get people out.' Lexy glanced back towards the cottage. 'That place needs to be properly searched. If we can tie that paint to Anderson's vehicle, we've got more evidence against him. And I'll make sure the boss knows Elliott is now a person of some interest. He can get someone out to Home Farm, see if anyone there admits to knowing her.'

'We may be running out of time,' Garry said, when they were back in the car. 'Gwen told me he'd gone out again, without telling anyone where he was going. And if he's been here, he might have found something Samantha left behind. He might know where they are.'

The results of the ANPR search into Samantha Elliott's car came in as Garry and Lexy were approaching the A1.

'That vehicle was spotted twice on the afternoon of the seventeenth of December,' they were told. 'First time at 1520 hours heading north-west on the A696 at Kirkharle.'

The seventeenth of December was the day Olive had disappeared from the Hexham hotel. Killing his speed – the weather had, predictably, worsened as they'd driven inland – Garry scrolled up through the car's navigation system. The A696 was the obvious road to take out of the Newcastle area if you were heading north, rather than due west. And 1520 hours wasn't much time before Samantha had met Olive in Hexham, which meant she probably hadn't driven much further than Kirkharle.

'Next and last sighting is on the A68, heading south, just short of the intersection with the A696. This was at 1618 hours.'

Garry pulled onto the A1.

'Nothing else?' Lexy asked.

'Nothing at all. That car's either parked up somewhere or it's been on minor roads with no cameras the last two days.'

Thanking the officer, Lexy ended the call. 'Does it help?' she asked Garry.

'Helps a lot.' Glancing back – nothing behind – he scrolled west on the satnav system and zoomed in. 'There's another camera on the A68 about seven miles south of the one that picked Elliott's car up, so we know she left the road before that point. For what it's worth, we already know neither camera caught Olive's car on Thursday night.'

As Lexy looked like she was struggling to keep up, Garry reminded himself that not everyone had his encyclopaedic knowledge of traffic cameras.

'Elliott made a point of finding out where the cameras are so she could avoid them,' he went on. 'She probably didn't think it was necessary earlier on Thursday evening because once she left the A68 she figured we'd have no chance of tracking her down.'

'She was right, wasn't she?'

'Not necessarily.' Garry checked all around before turning his attention back to the satnav. The A1 was quiet, and had been gritted, but very little of the tarmac surface could be seen through the snow now. 'There are two roads heading west off the A68 between those two cameras and they both lead to a village called Bellingham.' He tapped the screen. 'You'll see it if you zoom in. I reckon that's where Elliott was heading on Thursday, which means both women could well be there now. If we're going to follow them, I'll have to take the A69 and it's coming up soon. Your call.'

For a moment, Lexy said nothing, then asked, 'What if she went east?'

'Why?' The question made no sense to Garry. 'To go from the A696 to the A68 meant she was heading west. Why would she turn back and go east?'

Lexy said nothing.

'Think about it,' Garry urged. 'We know she and Olive went north from Hexham, but not on any of the A roads. Bellingham is north-west of Hexham.'

'I guess.'

'So, are we going home or to Bellingham?'

Still, she looked unsure. 'What do we do if we get there? Drive round all night in the hope we spot her car?'

'Look in my bag,' Garry said. 'Last night, I printed off a list of rental cottages and Airbnb places in the area. I meant to phone them all. It's possible they're both at one of those with a Bellingham post-code. If they made it that far.'

'What does that mean?'

'Nothing. It means nothing. It's the best plan we have. Am I going up there or not?'

Lexy nodded. In the nick of time, Garry turned off west.

'OK, so we're down to five possibles,' she said forty minutes later. 'A couple in Bellingham village centre, but I discounted those. If Olive's an unwilling travelling companion, Elliott won't want her within screaming distance.'

Garry simply nodded to show he understood. The snowfall was heavy again and the wipers were struggling to keep the windscreen clear. On top of that, the roads were worsening as they travelled north and the drive needed his full concentration.

Still, they'd made it to only four miles from Bellingham and in normal conditions they would cross the remaining distance in min-utes. These were not normal conditions. Snowdrifts on both sides of the road had turned it into a narrow white halfpipe, and even keeping to what he judged was the exact centre, his tyres lost pur-chase every couple of minutes. If he had to stop and dig himself out of drifts, it could take as much as another hour to get to Bellingham. If they made it at all.

The few rental cottages Lexy had managed to contact had told her they didn't hire out in the winter months. Several hadn't answered the phone and despite the very official-sounding messages she'd left, none had got back to her.

As Garry felt the car tyres slipping, he turned the wheel a frac-tion and they righted themselves. His heart was beating the way it normally only did when he was running, and he could feel sweat forming between his shoulder blades.

'There's also a couple of caravan parks,' Lexy said, as her hand slipped down to grasp the door handle – a sure sign of nervousness in a passenger. 'They must be possible, don't you think?'

The first of these was coming up on their right. With enough officers, the small village of Bellingham could be searched thoroughly in a few hours, but Garry doubted the local constabulary would send its staff out here for nothing more than his hunch.

He drove on past. Caravan parks were possible, but rental cottages more likely. Stick to plan A. They were on the outskirts of the village now and buried vehicles or equally hazardous obstacles had become a real threat. As they reached the first junction, they saw another vehicle approaching. When it swerved towards them and he narrowly avoided colliding with it, he knew he needed a break.

'I'm pulling over,' he said, spotting a P for parking sign a little way ahead. 'We can look at the list. Try to work out the most likely. A lot of these will be on single-track roads. We might not get up them, even in this.' He patted the dashboard. 'Even with me at the wheel.'

He cut a wide curve through the snow into the car park. The snow was even deeper than it had been on the road, but at least the chance of hitting something had lessened. Only one other vehicle was in the small space.

'OK, so most of them are on this map.' Lexy's laptop was balanced on her knee. 'I suggest we go to the nearest first. I mean, with no better—'

'Lexy,' he said.

'. . . information to go on, there's no point making it hard for ourselves. So, Waterfall Lodge. If you turn round, you can head left, then take the next left.'

'Lexy,' he said. 'There's no point. They didn't make it to the rental cottage.'

'What are you talking about?'

He nodded towards the only other car in the car park. A black Mitsubishi Warrior.

'Is that . . . ?' Lexy's eyes had opened wide as dinner plates.

'Yep.'

Samantha Elliott's car was parked not fifteen metres away from them.

'So . . .'

'If they'd made it to Bellingham, to whichever cottage Elliott rented, she'd have collected her car by now.'

Lexy looked mystified. 'I don't see.'

'She was covering her tracks, remember? On Thursday night, she'd have got a cab to pick her up from somewhere in the village and take her to Hexham, probably one with a dodgy record that wouldn't want anything to do with the police. She'd planned to get back to the cottage in Olive's car, but then collect her own so it wouldn't be out in the open too long. Which means the rental is probably the closest one to this point.'

'Waterfall Lodge. We can be there in seconds. We can probably walk.'

'They didn't make it. The car's still here.'

Lexy fell quiet and he let her catch up. 'So where are they?'

Garry started the engine again and turned the car.

'They left the road,' he said, as he pulled out of the car park. 'It's been playing on my mind since I rescued some folk early Friday morning on the way up to Hexham. Long story. Thursday was a bad night to be out. Plummeting temperatures and fresh snow on top of wet roads. Two days later, we've still got abandoned vehicles all over the north-east and, somewhere, Olive's car is one of them.'

'So, where are we going?'

'To find them. Eyes peeled, boss.'

'What are we looking for, exactly?' Lexy asked, as they left the village of Bellingham behind and entered the white-speckled darkness once more, this time heading south, along the road – assuming he was right – that Olive and Samantha must have been taking to reach the village. 'Tracks?'

'Long since covered,' Garry said.

Lexy was frowning. 'A crashed vehicle would have been spotted. We can't be the first people to drive this road since Thursday night.'

'We're not.' Garry had already seen evidence of that: several recent tyre tracks that hadn't yet been covered by fresh snowfall, plus older ones on the grass verges. 'So we probably won't see the car. That means we're looking for damage. Broken hedges most likely.'

When Bellingham was a half-mile behind them and even the lights at the edge of the village could no longer be seen, Lexy said, 'If they're still in the car, will they be alive?'

It was a question Garry had asked himself more than once.

'They won't be in a good way,' he said. 'Think of the state you were in. You'd only been waiting a couple of hours.'

Her voice dropped. 'They're dead, aren't they?'

Garry wished she wouldn't. If they were on the brink of finding two corpses, there was no point anticipating the horror. He knew from bitter experience it didn't help.

At a mile out of Bellingham, they'd seen nothing but snow, rapidly disappearing car tracks and a seemingly endless night landscape.

Garry said, 'If it was a bad crash, they could have been killed on impact. If they were able to leave the car, they could have made it to shelter. We won't know till we find it.'

By the time they were almost two miles out, Garry was starting to question the wisdom of driving much further. He'd cut his speed to 15 miles per hour, but it still felt recklessly fast. They were approaching a small stone bridge that crossed the upper reaches of the Tyne. It was steep and narrow, covered in a thick layer of snow. Garry put his foot down and reminded himself that, occasionally, good driving was about courage. The car reached the incline and the wheels struggled to maintain their grip.

'Garry, stop.'

Bad idea. If he braked now, they'd slide off in a direction he wouldn't be able to control. He carried on, only lifting his foot off the gas when they were on the other side and heading back down.

Lexy had twisted round in her seat. 'The fence was broken. On the right-hand side. I'm not kidding, Garry, I saw it.'

He eased off the accelerator, switched on his hazard lights and steered to the side of the road. He'd seen nothing, but a nervous pulse in his head was telling him that Lexy wasn't wrong.

Unsurprisingly, Lexy insisted on accompanying him. On foot, they re-crossed the bridge and sank knee-deep in snow as they left the road. Garry took Lexy's hand and she didn't object.

She was right. A whole section of fence had been obliterated. They found it, its outline still visible beneath a covering of snow, some five metres from where it had once stood.

'You OK?' he asked, and saw her nod out of the corner of his eye.

The land ahead, gleaming a pale, silver-grey in the moonlight, was sloping moorland. Garry caught glimpses of bilberry and broom peeking through the snow and knew they'd have to watch where they stepped. There'd be deeply embedded boulders that could easily turn an ankle, not to mention brambles, criss-crossing the land like snares.

A sparse copse of trees – Scots pine – lay ahead. There was no way a plummeting car could have travelled far through it.

There were no tyre tracks for them to follow. A few animal prints, the marks left behind by bird feet, but nothing to indicate they were on the right track. All they could do was follow the likely trajectory of a car that had skidded off the road.

Beyond the pines lay a line of shorter, denser trees. Willow meant the river was close. A plummeting car couldn't have crossed a river, even one as narrow as the Tyne at this point.

Garry ran his eyes along the treeline, taking in the drifted snow, the old, gnarled trunks, the curve of the landscape.

'I can see something,' he said.

The underside of the crashed car, only partially covered in snow, was about twenty metres away. The vehicle had almost upturned.

'Me too.' Lexy's voice was devoid of emotion. 'Is it Olive's car?'

'It's a silver Audi A3,' he replied. 'Yeah, I'd call it in.'

He walked ahead as Lexy called the station at Middlesbrough. Northumbria would attend, but the vanishing of Olive Anderson was a Cleveland case. It would be Garry and Lexy's senior officers who let Michael Anderson know that his wife's car had been found.

In a few more seconds, he'd know what else they'd be telling the MP.

Garry was ten metres away when he realised the full extent of the Audi's predicament. The Tyne had carved a gully over the years and old willow trees, once standing proudly along its bank, were clinging now to the gully's sides. One of them had halted the car's trajectory. A metre or two to either side and the car would have gone over the edge, to the almost certain death of the women inside.

They were probably dead anyway.

'Olive?' he called. 'Olive Anderson? Samantha Elliott? Can anyone hear me?'

A rustle of birds fleeing treetops; the whisper of snow falling from branches overhead; the distant bark of a fox. Nothing else.

None of the car's windows were visible yet; he'd have to get right up to it to see inside. He told himself he'd seen many victims of road traffic accidents in his time, that these two would be nothing he hadn't dealt with before. He wondered who would tell George and Anne Charles that their beloved daughter had died.

'Stay behind me, please,' he said to Lexy, as he heard her footsteps catching up. 'We don't know exactly what the land does here.'

He would, he decided. They deserved to hear it from a friend.

To his surprise, Lexy didn't argue; she'd probably never seen a dead body before. Garry felt a moment of regret that, for ever afterwards, she would associate the experience with him.

Five metres away. He was tall enough to see the right side-panel of the car now as it lay facing the night sky. He could see evidence of the brutal beating it had taken on its short, last journey from the road. His torch beam picked out a dark smear on the pale silver paintwork and he knew it to be blood.

Three metres. Two. He was almost close enough to touch the car, but the ground was falling away steeply and he didn't want to topple onto the vehicle. Grateful for his height, he shone the torch beam into the car's interior.

It was empty.

82

Two hours earlier

With a last painful heave, Olive pulled the stranger onto the stable ground at the gully's edge. The old willow tree, that had held the car in its grip for two long days, had proven strong enough to allow them to scramble to safety.

Their situation remained serious. They were still very cold, in deep snow, some way from the road, and both were injured. The other woman had taken a serious blow to her head and been unconscious for long hours. Internal damage, working its silent destruction on her brain was a distinct possibility. Olive herself had almost certainly broken several ribs – breathing still hurt like the devil – and her ankle could barely support her weight. She knew, too, that they were both well beyond the first stages of hypothermia. Shivering had long since stopped and the temptation to curl up in the snow and sleep was dangerously strong. On top of that, it had been dark for several hours; temperatures would be falling again.

The stranger was still panting with the effort of climbing from the car. 'I thought you were Maddy. When I saw you just now, I thought you were her.'

'I know,' Olive said. 'We did look a bit alike. People used to take us for sisters. You're Sam, aren't you? I should have guessed.'

Olive had never once asked to see a picture of the woman who shared Maddy's life, the woman Maddy had married; she'd never wanted to think of her as a real person. She waited for the hatred she'd felt for so long to wash over her, the way it did every time she thought about the woman. Sam Elliott had abused and coerced

312

Maddy, long before she'd blackmailed and abducted Olive herself, frightening and hurting her in the process.

It would be the easiest thing in the world now, to leave her here. Of the two of them, Sam was easily in the worse state; left alone, she wouldn't be able to move far from the car. No one would blame Olive for walking away.

Turning to grab Olive's hand, Sam looked into her eyes. 'Do you know where she is? All I want to do is find her. I'm sorry about what I did to you, but I know your husband knows where she is, I know he helped her get away from me, and I'm sure she had her reasons, but . . .'

In the other woman's face, Olive saw a reflection of the misery she'd felt herself for so long. Sam had loved Maddy too.

No. Sam had hurt Maddy, beaten her up when she suspected her of seeing someone else. Remembering Maddy's swollen, bleeding face, Olive's heart hardened. Nothing she'd ever done would be easier than walking away and leaving this bitch to die.

Except, she needed her. It was as simple as that.

'We have to get moving.' Struggling to her feet, she stretched a hand down to help Sam up. 'Can you make it to the road?'

In response, Sam sighed and seemed to sink into herself.

'Stand up.' Olive tugged on the other woman's arm, sending daggers of pain into her own chest. 'Sam, you have to get up. We'll die if we stay here.'

Sam didn't move. She didn't look capable of moving. Olive glanced back at the car. Both bags, with phones, were in the boot, and it might be possible to retrieve them. There might be some charge left.

Sam said, 'I only want to talk to her.'

It wasn't worth the risk. If Olive went back to the car, if she put any weight on it again, it could topple. And besides, her phone never lasted more than a few hours without charging.

'Get to your feet.' She nudged Sam with her foot. 'I know what happened to Maddy. I'll tell you when we're moving.'

The promise of information seemed to work, and Sam allowed herself to be pulled upright. Olive wrapped an arm around her waist and began the first difficult steps in what she thought was the direction of the road.

'It took me years to find you,' Sam gasped, when they'd travelled a few metres. 'Back when she vanished, a couple of her friends mentioned an Olive.' She broke off to catch her breath. The colour in her face was fading again to a sickly grey.

'Keep going,' Olive dragged her onwards.

'All they knew was you were a nurse,' Sam went on after a few seconds. 'I tried every hospital in the north-east, but none of them would tell me anything.'

Olive's uninjured foot sank into knee-deep snow, throwing both women off balance, and they tumbled over. Getting up again was harder the second time.

'When Michael Anderson married a woman called Olive, I knew it couldn't be coincidence,' Sam said, when they'd regained a slow but steady walking rhythm. 'I knew the two of you had to be working together. I knew you'd lead me to her.'

Above and ahead, Olive could see the fence that lined the road, the missing section her car had ploughed through. Not far now.

'He'll be looking for us,' Sam said. Olive was surprised she still had the energy to talk. Simply putting one foot in front of the other was all she could manage. Then she realised what the other woman had said.

'Who'll be looking for us?'

'Your husband. Anderson.'

Olive stopped moving. 'Why?'

'I sent him a text while you were checking out of the hotel. I attached a picture of you. He knows you left with me.'

Olive made herself resume walking, dragging Sam along with her. 'What did you say to him?'

'Something like, *Tell me what you did with my wife and I may let you have yours back.* What will he have done, do you think?'

'Keep moving.'

So, Michael had known, almost before she and Sam left the hotel. Nearly two days had passed. Had he done nothing?

The ground immediately below the road fell away steeply, and by the time the two women had clambered up it, both were close to exhaustion. Sam sank to her knees.

'Tell me,' she said. 'Please. All I want is to know she's OK.'

Olive crouched down beside her, knowing that part of her would take a twisted pleasure in what she was about to say. Sam deserved to feel pain.

'Maddy is dead.' No point sugar-coating it.

The woman recoiled. 'She can't be. The man at the marina, he said he'd seen her. I showed him her picture. He said he'd seen her on the Andersons' boat, only weeks ago.'

'That's impossible. If you mean the lock-keeper, he probably thought you were asking about me. She is dead. The Andersons killed her.'

83

The first vehicle to reach the scene was driven by a traffic officer from Northumbria who told them more cars and recovery vehicles were on their way, the incident taking priority over all other abandoned cars in the area. While the bloke went down to inspect the scene for himself, Garry took a walk, his eyes on the ground. Lexy, to his relief, was back in his car with the heater on.

The snowfall had slackened over the past hour, but the wind had picked up, blowing drifts across the open stretches of countryside. There were no obvious footprints that he could see, either at the roadside or anywhere near the crashed Audi. Samantha and Olive had left the car hours, maybe even days, ago. They could be anywhere.

Knowing he was probably clutching at straws, he opened an app on his phone, one he'd barely used before. He typed three words into the search bar: *Judges, Logs, Proudest.*

His phone was ringing. It was Ben, back at the station.

'Garry, I can't get hold of Lexy, can you pass on a message?'

Garry agreed that he could.

'We've had someone send that picture of Samantha Elliott to various of Michael Anderson's contacts. His constituency agent recognised her. Apparently, she came to the office a couple of times after her wife or girlfriend went missing. Seemed to think Anderson had something to do with it. She described her as rude, even aggressive, and she had to threaten her with the police to get her to leave.'

'Garry!'

Lexy was heading his way; thanking Ben, he hung up.

'We can't find Anderson,' she said, as she drew closer. 'He's not answering his phone and Gwen says she hasn't heard from him in hours.'

'You need to get back in the car.' As he filled her in with what Ben had said, he took her arm and walked her back up the road.

'Could they be lost?' Lexy was looking back down the moorland slope towards the wrecked vehicle. 'Got disorientated and gave up?'

'Possible,' Garry said, as he caught sight of flashing lights in the near distance; the recovery vehicles were close. 'You good to head out?' he asked as they reached the car.

'Where are we going?'

'Where we should have gone when you suggested it. Water-fall Lodge.'

84

Olive held Eloise's head cradled in one hand; in the other, she held a glass of water to the dying woman's lips. 'Take it easy,' she murmured, although she wanted nothing more than to scream. 'Take your time.'

Eloise indicated that she'd had enough and Olive let her head fall gently back to the pillow. She put the glass on the bedside cabinet and took her seat again. She made herself wait several seconds before asking, 'Who was the wrong woman?'

Eloise gave a soft, croaking laugh. 'God, if it had only been one. But trust Michael, he went for two wrong women, pretty much at the same time. The first was a woman called Tina Tricks.'

As Eloise took a moment to catch her breath, Olive frowned. This wasn't what she'd expected.

'You've probably never heard of her, although she's notorious in certain circles,' Eloise went on after several seconds. 'She's the wife of a local gangster. The very people Michael vowed to bring down when he was elected. I told you he couldn't resist danger.'

'So, this woman, Tina, she was involved in these ... these threesomes?'

'Not for long. Her husband found out. I wouldn't be surprised if he planned it all along, used his wife as a sort of honey trap.'

Another pause while Eloise grimaced in pain.

'The upshot was that Michael agreed to back off on local organised crime. And I had to drop a money-laundering case that was on the brink of trial. My professional reputation never recovered from that. Just one of many things I hope he rots in hell for.'

So, Michael Anderson was embroiled with gangsters. Olive could use that, she knew. But it wasn't enough. 'You said two wrong women?'

Eloise made eye contact briefly and said, 'Have you heard of Maddy Black?'

Olive's heart was beating fast now. 'I don't think so. Who was she?'

'She was an activist when Michael was running for election. She was young and very pretty. Dark-haired, dark eyes, curvy figure. Not like me at all, which made her perfect. Michael liked a contrast in bed, you see.'

Olive had a sudden flashback to Maddy in bed: her baby-soft skin, her energy and playfulness. She felt both hands gripping into fists.

'I told him it was stupid, that she was totally unsuitable,' Eloise went on. 'She had no social standing to speak of. She wasn't even happily married. I think she was looking for a way out.'

Yes, a way out; to be with Olive.

'But she agreed?' Olive asked.

'She had an agenda of her own, as we soon found out. She agreed. So, we met. A few times. And, well, I'm sure you can imagine.'

Olive swallowed down her fury. If she let her true feeling show now, Eloise would clam up. She said, 'Where did you meet?'

'The constituency office a couple of times. Mostly on the boat.'

'The one you keep at Hartlepool marina?'

Eloise gave an almost imperceptible nod of the head. 'That one. We'd all three take time off work and meet there. Sometimes we'd take the boat out and pick up a buoy somewhere, although Michael was never so keen on that. It was the risk of being seen that turned him on.'

'Actually, I think I'm remembering a Maddy Black,' Olive said slowly. 'At least I think that was the woman's name. Didn't she disappear a couple of years ago? She was never actually declared dead, though. Her body was never found.'

'She is dead,' Eloise said. 'He made sure of it.'

Olive's hands gripped into fists. 'What are you telling me?'

'She got too clingy, always wanting to know when she and Michael would be able to meet up again. She started calling him at his London office, and at home. She'd turn up at the house too. Michael told her it had to end and she wouldn't accept it. Imagine the worst, most painful break-up and then multiply it to the power of ten. That's what she was like. Then she turned nasty, threatening to go to the papers, demanding money from us. There didn't seem any way out.'

Olive felt her head swimming. Eloise made it sound as though Maddy had been obsessed with Anderson. How did that fit with how troubled she'd been in their last days together?

'And coming right after the business with Tina Tricks, I think Michael was pretty close to the edge.'

Olive told herself she could process all this later. For now, she had to let Eloise talk.

'So, what happened?'

'We asked her to join us on the boat one afternoon. We told her it would be to talk things through. I think Michael hinted he and I were planning to separate. He wanted to make sure she'd come. So, I picked her up at the railway station and drove her to the marina, where we met Michael. And then we went out.'

'Out?'

'Out of the harbour. Only the weather was shocking. Force-six winds, gusting seven, and very big seas. And that on top of a strong spring tide. There's no way we should have gone out, but Michael said we wanted to test our new storm spinnaker and Maddy wasn't experienced enough to question it.'

Silence.

Olive said, 'Was there an accident?'

'There was a very nasty spinnaker broach.'

'What's that?'

'We launched the spinnaker. That's the big colourful sail at the front of the boat. I was on the helm, Michael and Maddy had gone up to the bow deck to launch the sail. It went up, the wind caught it and we broached.'

'And that means?'

'The boat tipped. About ninety degrees, so that almost the entire starboard deck was under water. I managed to cling on to the helm, but both Michael and Maddy were flung sideways. Michael caught hold of the genoa shroud, but Maddy went over.'

Olive told herself she couldn't scream, not now. 'That's dreadful. But it was an accident.'

Eloise sighed. 'It was a carefully staged accident. Michael knew what would happen if he launched the spinnaker in those conditions.'

Olive told herself to keep going, ask the necessary questions. 'But he could have been killed himself. All of you could have been.'

'Not really. Because Michael and I were harnessed on, attached to the boat at all times. We might have broken some limbs, maybe even knocked ourselves out if we were really unlucky, but we were prepared for it. Maddy wasn't.'

She would only get one shot at this. Keep going. 'Why wasn't Maddy harnessed?'

'She thought she was. But when she and Michael moved up to the bow, he clipped her onto the wire guard rail. You never do that, they're not strong enough. It gave way the second she fell, as he knew it would. He staged her death.'

Olive took a deep breath and willed her voice to remain steady. 'Did you know he was going to do it?'

'He didn't tell me. Not in so many words, but I knew he was planning something.'

'She'd have been wearing a life jacket though?'

'She was. And we saw her, for a few seconds, once the boat righted itself and we managed to pull ourselves together. She drifted away very quickly of course, but she was still conscious. I heard her shouting.'

Olive tried to swallow. 'You could have saved her.'

'Probably. Not necessarily, because pulling people out of heavy seas isn't as easy as you might think. The point is, we didn't try. And there were no other boats around. We were a long way out by this time. She really didn't have a chance.'

'And you said nothing about it? You didn't report it?'

'No one knew she'd come out with us that day. Michael chose a time when the marina would be quiet. I'd picked her up, so her car wasn't there. There's no CCTV footage on the pontoon where our boat is kept. No one connected us with her disappearance.'

Olive got to her feet. 'Eloise, I'm going to call the police. You need to tell them what you've just told me.'

Eloise's eyes opened wide. 'The police? No, I'm not shopping him to the police. This was about warning you. Because I like you.'

Olive told herself to stay calm. She couldn't start shouting at a patient, no matter what the provocation. 'You have to talk to the police,' she said. 'He committed murder. You're a – what do they call it? – an accessory to murder. You can't die with that on your conscience.'

Eloise's voice hardened. 'What I can't do is deprive my daughters of both their parents. What I can't do is force them to grow up knowing their mum and dad were sexual deviants, because that's how the world will see it, and that they killed a woman to protect themselves.' She shook her head, and her eyes were implacable. 'Sorry, Olive, but you can't contact the police. If you do, I'll tell them you made it up. And then I'll complain to the hospital authorities that you've been flirting inappropriately with my husband while I've lay here dying. He'll back me up. He likes you, but self-preservation comes before everything with Michael.'

Olive took a step away. 'I think you're every bit as bad as he is.'

The woman actually scoffed. 'Yeah, well, I'm a little past caring what anyone thinks of me. You're right. I am tired. I'd like to sleep now.'

85

Garry was explaining to Lexy how the phone app what3words worked, and how the three, supposedly random words he'd seen written on Samantha Elliott's blotting pad: *Judges, Logs, Proudest,* led to Waterfall Lodge, when the deputy chief constable phoned.

'Mind your language,' she muttered to Garry.

'Well done, Lexy, bloody good work.' Their superior's voice seemed unnaturally loud over the speakerphone.

Garry swerved to avoid a drift and turned left onto the main road through the village. Christmas lights in rainbow colours danced on the blanket of white; in other circumstances, it might have looked cheerful.

'Garry's doing, sir,' Lexy replied. 'He figured out that Mrs Anderson and her companion must have driven to Bellingham. He spotted Samantha Elliott's car in the village and guessed they'd crashed. He knew the exact road they must have been travelling on.' She glanced across at Garry and winked. 'Mind you, I'm the one who saw the broken fence, so I don't want him getting all the credit.'

A second of silence, then the deputy chief coughed. 'Naturally, well done to you too, Garry. Don't suppose there's any update on the two women themselves, is there? That would be a good night's work. Might even make up for—'

'For being a complete twat, sir?' Garry asked and saw Lexy's eyes widen.

'Aye, well, we don't want to dwell too much on that. I mean, what kind of idiot keeps her mum's ashes in a teddy?' The sound of a laugh down the phone. 'The chief will be using it in his after-dinner speeches this time next year.'

Fair play, it was kind of funny.

'And I've some news that might cheer you up, Gazza, knowing your well-voiced suspicions of our honourable member of parliament.'

'What's that, sir?'

'Well, I read Detective Sergeant Thomas's report setting out your various reasons for suspecting Anderson of being involved in his wife's disappearance and I figured you had a point. So, I authorised a search of his property out at Guisborough. What is it called, Home Farm? No trace of Olive Anderson, but guess what we found tucked away at the back of the hayloft?'

As Lexy pulled a *haven't a clue* face, Garry remembered his one and only visit to the Home Farm hayloft, the warm gleam of sunshine on what he'd assumed was nothing but hay.

'Would it be several million pounds of gold bullion, sir?'

The deputy chief gave a soft laugh. 'Not as daft as you look, are you? So, we'll be asking a few questions of Mr Anderson when we catch up with him, along the lines of exactly what consideration induced him to accept and store stolen property.'

'Any sign of the necklace, sir?'

'Not so far, but we'll keep looking.'

He'd been right about Anderson; the knowledge would be some consolation in time, Garry knew. For now, they still had to find Olive.

'Sir, is there any chance of getting a helicopter out?' Lexy asked, letting him know she was on the same wavelength. 'Now we know roughly where the two women must be, an aerial search has to be the best way of finding them.'

'Working on it. And the dog unit should be up there in an hour or so. Bloody shite weather doesn't help. What are the two of you up to now? Are you heading back?'

'We thought we'd have a drive around the village, sir,' Lexy said quickly. 'You never know what we might spot.'

'Good thinking. Keep me posted. Oh, before I go, the cyber team got back to us. Seems no one told them to stand down the investigation on Friday and they gave it priority, seeing as how an honourable member was involved. You'll have to talk to them for the details, but they managed to dig up the abuse Olive Anderson was getting on social media. She'd deleted it, but as we know, nothing vanishes completely.'

'Does it tell us anything?' Lexy asked.

The boss was quiet for a moment. 'Happen it does. She was getting a lot of flack from someone who thought she didn't measure up to the first Mrs Anderson. Some quite nasty stuff. Not threatening as such, but not pleasant either.'

Garry spotted a relatively clear space at the side of the road and pulled over. He didn't want to arrive at Waterfall Lodge while the deputy chief was on the phone.

'Any idea who sent it?' Lexy asked. 'I know the social media companies aren't always quick to co-operate with police information requests.'

'They're not, and it would have taken some time normally, but this person wasn't all that sophisticated. She set up a few fake Facebook accounts but didn't think to use a different contact telephone number in each one. And the number she used was traceable.'

She? Garry mouthed, as Lexy said, 'Anyone we know?'

'Turns out it was Gwendoline Warner, Anderson's mother-in-law.'

Garry whistled under his breath.

'I called her myself about it,' the deputy chief went on. 'She came clean, said she'd been very hurt when Michael married again so quickly and had struggled to have Olive in the house where her daughter grew up. She insists she brought it all to a halt when she learned Olive suspected the girls of doing it.'

Lexy pulled a face at Garry.

'She seems to regret it now,' the deputy chief continued. 'Still going to be some difficult conversations in that household if Olive ever does come back.'

'Any evidence of online contact between Olive and Samantha Elliott, sir?' Garry asked.

'Glad you asked, Garry, because it looks like she was at it as well.

Elliott, I mean now. We think she was behind another set of fake accounts that were subtler but more threatening in nature. Stuff like . . . Hang on a minute.' There was the sound of shuffling papers, then, 'Here we are. *I see you, Olive*, sent late at night. *And shall I come to the window?*'

'And these came from Samantha?' Lexy asked.

'We think so. She was a bit more sophisticated than Gwendoline, but she used her own phone for the first set of posts – maybe she actually was outside the family home like she was claiming to be – and that we can trace without Facebook's involvement.'

'We really need to find Samantha and Olive,' Lexy said.

'We do that. Right, keep me posted,' the deputy chief said, before the line went dead.

'I was talking to you then,' Lexy said to Garry.

'I know.' He started the engine. They were minutes from Waterfall Lodge.

The car didn't move. The wheels spun, gaining no traction at all. Son of a gun, had he actually parked on ice? He increased the revs. Nothing. He tried reverse. The car jerked back. And tipped. Lexy gasped as the two of them fell back against their seats.

They, too, were stuck.

86

The sound was disorientating at first, like traffic, constant, fast-moving, and dangerously close. It took several minutes before Olive's overtired brain made the connection. Waterfall Lodge. It was water she could hear, a torrent of it, plunging from a great height.

The cottage was a mass of dark stone against the grey landscape, on the outskirts of the village of Bellingham. It wasn't large. At a guess, a couple of rooms downstairs, a couple more on the first floor.

Olive was exhausted, trembling with hunger and in pain; worse, she was dangerously cold. Even so, she was still the stronger of the two women.

The moon, not far off full, had risen, turning the endless moorland around them into a dirty-grey, formless landscape. There could have been mountains ahead, a vast, fertile valley, even a village or small town, and she could see none of it. It was as though the snow had become acid, leaching everything away, creating a vast, white void that would creep ever closer, until only she remained.

She was fading again, sinking into the detached, half-asleep, hallucinatory world that was hypothermia. She had to pull herself together, focus on what was close: the cottage they'd reached, the woman at her side, and what the hell she was going to do now. Pushing open the gate, she led the way into the snow-covered garden, half dragging Sam along with her.

It had been a long, difficult walk from the crash site to the cottage Sam had rented; there had been times when Olive hadn't been sure they'd make it, but the necessity of keeping moving had helped maintain both their body temperatures. And learning the shocking truth about Maddy had seemed to give Sam the will she needed to keep going. She'd even talked a little on the endless trudge through the snow, about how she'd spent the first few months after Maddy vanished trying to track her down, visiting craft fairs and glass artists all over the UK and continental Europe, checking out gay clubs and lesbian dating sites. After nearly a year of fruitless searching, she'd taught herself how to deep-search computers, unearthing photographs of Maddy and Olive together, along with the sex tape that Maddy had hidden a copy of in Olive's underwear drawer.

She and Sam staggered towards the front door. Beneath the white blanket that covered the garden, she could see the outline of children's play equipment and a wooden picnic table.

'Sam,' she said, as the other woman leaned on the cottage's front door to open it. 'When were you last here?'

Fresh footprints marred the otherwise pristine white garden path.

Sam didn't reply immediately. For some time now, her reactions had been dull, her speech slurred. 'Thursday,' she said at last. 'When I picked up the keys. Why?'

'Has there been any post?'

It was a stupid question. Someone – male judging by the size of their feet – had walked up to the cottage door in the last day or so and then continued round the back. Postmen didn't do that.

Sam went inside. Pushing her misgivings aside, Olive followed.

The cottage felt cold. A gust must have followed them in because Olive felt freezing air against her face, bringing a smell with it, one familiar and disturbing at the same time. She thought she should know that smell, that it was important to know it, and that if she stood still for a few seconds longer, breathing in deeply, then she would.

Ahead of her, Sam stumbled against the wall.

'We need to get the heat on.' Olive steered the other woman across a yellow-painted sitting room with cosy, padded sofas and a brightly coloured tapestry rug. Exposed oak beams criss-crossed the ceiling, creating an elaborate structure above their heads. A fire, ready to be lit, sat in the open hearth.

The odd smell had gone.

The sound of the waterfall seemed to have increased, as though the walls of the cottage were amplifying it. Olive felt a shudder wracking her body and somewhere, at the back of her mind, lurked the thought that it might not have been entirely caused by the cold. Sam had picked her torture chamber well: freezing, a deafening background noise, miles from anywhere, and the easiest thing in the world to string someone up around those exposed beams.

Enough. A lot had changed since Thursday night.

Getting warm was the first priority, then any rudimentary medical attention she could offer Sam. After that, food and – who knew what would happen then? This woman might seem harmless right now, but she'd abducted and blackmailed her, had been aggressive, unpredictable and physically violent.

She might be about to make a deal with the devil.

And then there was Michael to factor in. He knew she and Sam were together. Michael had had a two-day head start. He wouldn't have been idle.

Olive caught a hint of the smell again. There was smoke in it, which meant it must be coming down the chimney. It was unnerving all the same.

She glanced around. A pleasant enough room, tastefully decorated, with windows on two facing walls; the sort of room that would photograph well and appeal to middle-class families wanting a break in the national park.

An open-plan staircase led up from the living room. Olive saw three more doors. Behind one, only partly closed, she could make out the kitchen and she steered Sam into it. In different circumstances, it would have been a cheerful room, all pine wood and soft, sage-green paintwork. It was bitterly cold.

'Sam, where's the boiler?'

Sam looked as though she didn't know what a boiler was, but Olive spotted a radiator beneath the window. Warm. The heating was on, which meant the cold had to be down to her damp clothes. Spotting the kettle, she filled it and switched it on.

Sam had slipped onto one of the kitchen chairs, her head on the pine tabletop.

'Sam, you can't go to sleep, it's dangerous.'

Dangerous, but so tempting, especially when even walking around felt like wading through syrup.

In the living room, Olive found a couple of sofa throws that she draped around Sam. They wouldn't be enough. Dry clothes, a warm drink, paracetamol, if she could find any, and then – a plan? If only she could stop shaking.

A sudden sound cutting through the drone of the waterfall made her jump and, for a split second, she thought she saw movement in the corner of the window.

The window had a roller blind. Unable to help herself, Olive closed it, hoping that shutting out the vast empty darkness might make her feel less . . . afraid.

As the kettle came to the boil, she found tea, sugar and milk. When she'd made tea for both of them, she put the mug in front of Sam and wrapped her ice-cold hands around it.

'Drink,' she ordered. Sam really needed medical attention, but they had no car, even if Olive were fit to drive, and the chances of getting an ambulance out were slim. She'd seen no sign of a landline phone in the cottage and both of their mobiles had been left behind in the car.

Sam said, 'What are we going to do?'

So now they were 'we'.

'Do you have any clothes here?' Olive asked. 'We both need to change. Right now.'

No response.

'Sam, this is important. Do you have any clothes?'

'Upstairs. There's a bag.'

Not sure she could climb stairs, Olive swallowed some of the milk straight from the carton. It was painfully cold, but food of any sort would help. On the third step up, another scent crept into her nostrils: old leather, the smell of the tack room at Home Farm.

The cottage smelled of smoke and old leather, which shouldn't be strange at all, and yet . . .

The upper floor felt even chillier than the downstairs had, the sound of the waterfall louder. A small, square landing held three doors. Olive pushed the closest, felt for the light switch, and found herself in the master bedroom, overlooking the front of the house. Another door led to what she guessed would be the en suite. Sam's overnight bag sat on top of the double bed. Olive unzipped and upended it.

The bed looked so inviting.

Forcing herself to keep moving, she separated out a spare pair of jeans, T-shirt, sweater and underwear to take downstairs. She pulled off her own sodden clothes and pulled on a pair of thin, jogging bottoms and a long-sleeved T that she guessed Sam used as pyjamas. Dry clothes helped. Behind the door hung two thick towelling robes. Olive put one on, found a hand towel in the en suite and wrapped it around her neck.

On the way down, she caught yet another scent – black pepper – and her sense of unease increased. Faster than was wise, given how shaky she still was, she ran down the stairs and back to the kitchen. Sam had roused herself a little, had drunk half the tea and was cradling it against her chest like a hot-water bottle.

When Sam was dressed again, when fresh tea had been made, and when cheese, ham and bread were on the table, Olive sat. Sam had asked a good question. What were they going to do?

'What do we have against Michael?' she said. 'Do we have enough to go to the police?'

Sam stared at a torn-off piece of bread in her hand.

'Come on, Sam. You're the reason we're here right now. You forced my arm. What do we have?'

'I kidnapped you,' Sam replied, still unable to look her in the eyes. 'I blackmailed you.'

'Concentrate. What do we have on Michael?'

Calling him her husband felt like the last thing Olive could do right now.

'I found a video,' Sam said. 'On Maddy's hard drive. It took me ages, she hid it well, but I researched how to do it. She was having sex with Michael Anderson and his first wife. But—'

'I've got that too,' Olive interrupted. 'She hid a USB stick in my flat.'

Sam flinched. 'I found photographs of you and Maddy together,' she said. 'When you married Anderson, I felt sure you were involved.'

'I wasn't. I knew nothing about what happened to Maddy at first. Her disappearance nearly broke me.'

Sam's cold blue eyes narrowed. 'When did you know?'

Olive reminded herself that this woman had loved Maddy too, possibly too much, and that she'd only just learned of Maddy's death.

'For certain, only the night Eloise died,' Olive replied. 'So, I've known for two years. When I found that video, I knew her disappearance had to be something to do with the Andersons, but that was all. I knew it wasn't proof of anything.'

'She was my wife,' Sam said, and now there was an accusation in her eyes. 'She was cheating on me with you and with them. Was she using all of us?'

No, Olive would not let herself think that.

'Stay focused,' she said. 'We've got Eloise's confession. Only part of it recorded, and not the crucial part, but I'll go into a witness stand. I wrote down everything I could remember.'

Sam blinked at her. 'They'll ask why you married him.'

'I know. I won't look good, but that doesn't matter as long as they believe me.'

'Why did you?'

It was a very good question, one Olive wasn't sure she could properly answer, even now.

'I never planned to,' she said. 'At first, I didn't think I could let him touch me. I'd never been with a man before. But he really seemed to like me. I thought, by getting closer to him, by spending time with him, I could find something – anything – that I could take to the police.'

And, also, there'd been something in the sense of having her worst enemy in her power that had been strangely seductive. She'd married Michael Anderson to hurt him.

Sam said, 'I found some emails on Maddy's hard drive too.'

'What do they say?'

Sam shook her head. 'I don't think they'll help much. In one, she says half a million pounds will be enough for her to start the new life she's always dreamed of, but she was careful. She didn't put anything in writing that could be used against her. There was also a reference, in the last one, to a station car park. The one where Maddy's car was found.'

'These things will add up,' Olive said.

'And they're not emails to the Andersons – at least they don't appear to be. They're to a Gmail account that means nothing to me.'

'If it was one of the Andersons' accounts, the police can trace it back to them.'

'That's what I figured.' Sam lifted her mug and froze. 'What? What is it?'

Once again, Olive had seen movement in the glass of the window. Except the blind was closed. What she'd seen had been a reflection. Something behind her, in the house.

'Olive, what's wrong?'

Olive turned round slowly. 'Sam,' she said. 'Are you up to checking the house with me?'

Sam frowned. 'What do you mean? Check it for what?'

Olive said, 'I think there's someone here.'

Sam gave a half-smile. 'That's not possible.'

Olive felt fury creeping up on her again; this woman had no idea what they were dealing with. 'Michael knows where you live,' she said. 'Maddy's last address is still on file at his constituency office. I found it myself a couple of months ago. If you still live there, he could have been in your house. Did you leave anything behind to point the way here?'

Sam started to shake her head, slowly. 'I booked this place online,' she said. 'Unless he can access my computer.' Her eyes narrowed: she'd thought of something. 'There's no postcode here, so I looked up what3words. I may have written them on the desk blotter. But he'd have had to break in.'

Olive got slowly to her feet. 'The house is too cold,' she said. 'It smelled odd when we first came in. There were footprints outside in the snow. And I've seen something. Twice. Ground floor first. Did you bring any sort of weapon with you?'

She knew the answer even as she asked. There'd been no weapon in the bag upstairs.

A puzzled frown on her face, Sam pushed herself upright and crossed the room. She opened a drawer and pulled out a kitchen knife, its blade close to ten inches long. She handed a second one, slightly smaller, to Olive. The look on her face, though, suggested she wasn't taking it seriously. She didn't know Michael the way Olive knew him.

'I'll do downstairs, you do up,' Sam said. 'Come on, let's get it over with.'

Knife in hand, Olive climbed the stairs. The master bedroom was as she'd left it. Her clothes – jeans, shirt, underwear – still on the floor by the bed. Nowhere in the en suite that anyone could hide. The bedroom had a large double wardrobe built into the eaves. Stooping down, Olive checked beneath the bed. Nothing. Getting up, she reached out and pulled open the wardrobe doors. Empty, apart from spare pillows and blankets on a top shelf. Nothing else. She turned away, almost tripping over the pile of clothes on the floor.

Not as she'd left them; her sweater was missing.

'Sam,' she called, shocked at how weak her voice sounded. 'Be careful.'

No reply.

The door to the second bedroom was ajar. Olive was sure it had been closed when she'd last been up here. She pushed at it, nervously, as though frightened it might explode. Trembling, she felt for the light switch.

The room was icy cold. The window directly facing her was open. Its glass had been broken.

Two single beds, another built-in wardrobe, another en suite bathroom. By the time Olive had checked them all, the knife in her hand was slick with sweat and her headache was throbbing in time with the beating of her heart.

From downstairs came a crashing sound, as though Sam had fallen, or dropped something.

'You OK?' Olive called.

No reply.

The smell was back as Olive made her way down the stairs. Old leather, smoke and black pepper. Once already in the last few days, she'd smelled something incongruous, something that should have warned her that all was not as it should be. Twice, she'd ignored what her senses were telling her. She would pay for that now.

Her sweater was the first thing she noticed, draped over the back of one of the sofas; the second was the stock of a rifle that had been propped against the sofa back. It was a weapon she'd seen before in her husband's gun cupboard. A Remington 223.

Then she saw Sam.

She was standing on a wooden chair in the centre of the room. A rope, one Olive thought she recognised from the tack room at home, was strung around her neck in a noose, the other end tied around one of the low-hanging ceiling beams. As Olive opened her mouth to scream, a boot-clad foot kicked the chair from underneath Sam. She dropped.

'Hello, darling,' said Michael, as he stepped into view. 'I've been worried about you.'

87

Garry and Lexy continued on foot, making slow, tiring progress along the lane. After five minutes, his phone rang.

'Gwen Warner.' He held it up so Lexy could see the caller ID.

'Go on,' she said. 'She may have something useful.'

'Mrs Warner.' He could make out a building on the horizon, maybe a quarter-mile away. 'I've not got long, I'm afraid.'

'I imagine you've heard from your deputy chief constable, PC Mizon?'

She'd called him Garry last time they'd spoken.

'About the Facebook messaging? Not really important right now, Mrs Warner. Not while there's a chance we'll find Olive alive.'

'There's something else. One of your colleagues sent an image through. It's the woman you think Olive might have left the hotel with.'

She was talking about the picture of Samantha Elliott that Ben was circulating around Anderson's contacts.

'I never knew her name, but she came to the farm a couple of weeks ago,' Gwen continued. 'She came into the shop, asking about Olive. Claimed to be an old friend, but there was something about her that felt off.'

'What did Olive say when you told her?'

'I didn't.'

'Come again?'

'I didn't tell her. I'm not proud of it, but I guess I resented being used as a sort of secretarial service by the woman who'd taken my daughter's place. Besides, I told you, there was something not right about the woman.'

'OK, I'll make sure that's passed on. Thanks, Mrs Warner.'

'Wait, there's something else. She came into the kitchen. She asked if I could give her a glass of water and, well, I asked her in. There were people in the yard, it didn't seem like too much of a risk. Anyway, I caught her looking at the noticeboard, the one where we list all our memos and stuff.'

And Olive's schedule. So, that's how she'd known where Olive would be on Thursday night.

At his side, Lexy stumbled. She really wasn't dressed for trudging through snow in these temperatures. If anything happened to her now, it would be his fault.

'Thanks for that, Mrs Warner,' he said, taking hold of Lexy's arm and tucking it through his. She didn't argue, and they carried on towards Waterfall Lodge.

88

Sam wasn't dead, not yet anyway, her neck hadn't broken. Instead, she was choking, her eyes bulging, face reddening. Her hands clutched at the rope around her neck and her legs swung as though she was trying to walk.

'What the hell are you doing? Michael, get her down.'

Olive darted forward. If she could take Sam's weight, it would lessen the lethal choking hold the rope had around her neck. In the nick of time, she saw the cast-iron doorstop in Michael's hand. He raised his arm, as though ready to swing.

He said, 'Was it ever real?'

How long did Sam have? A minute? Two?

'Michael, she's going to die.'

How long did *she* have? This man had killed before. Olive glanced at the door. As though reading her thoughts, he stepped closer. She'd never make it out of the house, and even if she did, the house was a mile from the village.

'Was it, Olive? You and me, was it ever real?'

Sam was swinging, her frantic movements giving her propulsion.

'You were enough for me. The only woman who was. I could almost laugh.' He smiled, instead. 'I'd like to have seen you and Maddy together, though.'

Rage flooded through her. 'You killed Maddy.'

He gave a small start back. Not the reaction she expected. Not guilt, on his face, more puzzlement?

'Eloise told me everything, she told me how you staged the accident.'

Michael's eyes narrowed. 'Sounds like she spun you a line, Olive. My lovely late wife was entirely responsible for Maddy's accident. She unpicked the stitching on her harness so it would break when it came under pressure. She killed Maddy, not me.'

Olive stared at him, unable to take it in. Could it possibly be . . .

'And then she threw the boat keys overboard so there was no chance of getting Maddy back without the engine. The two of us barely made it back to the marina under sail, in that weather.'

'Liar.'

'Look who's talking.'

Sam's frantic movements had slowed. She was twitching now, the fight seeping out of her. Olive switched her attention to the dying woman.

'Cut her down, please. We can talk then.'

He didn't move.

'Michael, please. If what you've just told me is true, there's no need for this. We can sort this out.'

He shook his head. 'I'm still an accessory to murder, still going down for a long time. I'll make it quick, Olive. Believe it or not, I don't want you to suffer. I can't shoot you, I'm afraid.' He glanced back, as though to make sure the rifle was where he'd left it. 'The police would be able to trace the gun. So, I'll have to whack you over the head.' He glanced down at the doorstop in his hand. 'This thing weighs a ton. The first blow should knock you out, if you don't fight me.'

Knowing there was nothing behind her but the corner of the room, Olive backed away.

'I have to do it now, my love. I can't have the pathologist spotting that bitch died first. It's a murder suicide, you see. She killed you, then hung herself.'

Sam had fallen limp.

'Please don't.' Hating herself for begging, Olive knew she'd do anything to stay alive a few minutes longer. 'There's something I need to tell you.' There was nothing. She was clutching at straws.

He raised the heavy iron weapon. It was directly above her. Olive sank to the floor, huddled into the corner of the room, knowing it wouldn't help. When she heard the crash, she thought it must be the sound of her own brain exploding.

89

Garry kicked in the door of Waterfall Lodge. It wasn't the first time he'd broken down a door, but never with so much pent-up emotion behind the action. He caught it in his hand to stop it swinging back and a shadow dancing on the right-hand wall caught his eye: movement in the room to his left.

He didn't break stride.

He saw the woman hanging by the neck from a ceiling beam as he reached the door of the large, yellow sitting room. As he ran towards her, a whimpering sound and a rush of movement caught his attention and he glanced round to see Michael Anderson charging him, holding something that looked solid and very heavy.

Anderson's arm swung.

Garry jumped aside, avoiding being hit by a hair's width, and the break in momentum caught Anderson off balance. Garry grabbed him by the collar of his jacket with his left hand and swung with his right fist. It made a satisfying contact with Anderson's jaw and it hurt like the devil. Anderson stumbled and fell out of Garry's grasp. He hit the wall and went down.

'Oh my God.' Lexy rushed past Garry as he caught sight of Olive huddled in the corner. She looked up and made eye contact.

'You good?' he said, thinking his hand might be broken.

Olive didn't reply, but she was alive; the woman hanging from the rafters might not be. He turned to help Lexy.

The sergeant had upended a wooden chair and was standing on it. One arm was holding up the suspended woman – Samantha Elliott, he saw now – her other hand trying, and failing, to loosen the knotted rope around the other woman's neck. From his jacket pocket, Garry pulled out the knife he always carried – for foraging decorative branches he might stumble across – and handed it up. At the same time, he lifted the unconscious woman to take the weight off the rope.

'Garry, he's got a—'

Olive's voice. Before Garry could react, Samantha fell into his arms, almost sending him flying. Up on the chair, Lexy overbalanced and fell, landing inelegantly on one of the sofas. Glancing back, Garry saw that Michael Anderson was no longer slumped against the wall. Then a searing pain hit his chest. Suddenly, his body was on fire and all breath had fled from his lungs. He felt the weight of Samantha pulling him forwards and the two of them collapsed together. He stared at the intricately patterned rug and saw bright red liquid pooling beneath him. He'd been shot.

How was this possible? Just when he was on the brink of being happy.

90

It had taken several seconds for Olive to recognise the plain-clothes police officer who'd burst into the room. Garry. Her old friend Garry. A detective now, most likely, because he wasn't in uniform, but still tough as old boots, still coming to her rescue. She saw him hit Michael full in the face – were police officers supposed to do that? – and Michael fall out of sight.

A woman, tall with short blonde hair, was trying to help Sam, but it might be too late. She was no longer moving. Olive saw Garry kick the doorstop away from Michael and then turn to help the two women. Garry produced a knife. The blonde woman, standing on the chair now, began slicing through the rope. It took long seconds, but Garry had gathered Sam into his arms. The rope fell apart. Sam fell, so did the blonde woman.

And Michael got to his feet.

Olive watched her husband pick up the rifle and raise it to his shoulder. He was an excellent shot. He wouldn't miss, not at this range.

'Garry, he's got a—'

With Sam still in his arms, Garry stumbled. The gun went off. Garry jerked and fell forwards.

It hadn't been a clean shot. Olive had seen what guns did to living flesh. If Garry hadn't fallen at the critical moment, his chest might have burst apart.

Michael took a step closer to Garry and pointed the gun down towards the prone man. Olive realised that she was on her feet, the cast-iron doorstop in her hand. It really was very heavy. As Michael's finger twitched on the trigger, she swung the doorstop up and around, bringing it down hard against her husband's head.

91

Three months later

The fifteenth of March dawned bright and clear, albeit with a nip in the air and a dusting of frost on the ground. As he ate a solitary breakfast in his small, neat kitchen, Garry wondered if his injured shoulder might, finally, be up to some serious digging.

He hadn't been to the allotment since his visit with Lexy and he was surprised, maybe a bit miffed, that it had thrived without him. The narcissi were glorious: a great swathe of yellow and white running the full circumference of the patch. They weren't great for arrangements, but his mum did love her daffs. He'd gather her a car boot full before he left.

The hyacinths were good too. Breathing in their sweet, bluebell scent, he unlocked the shed and found the tools he'd need. He was turning over the ground beside the late hellebores when he spotted the tall woman in the pink coat heading his way down the allotment path.

Leaning on his spade, he watched her approach, glad that he hadn't yet broken into his flask of coffee. He made it from scratch now, even grinding beans himself. It gave him palpitations, but, somehow, he couldn't bring himself to go back to instant.

Lexy had come from work. That was a smart trouser suit she was wearing beneath her coat, and her shoes had heels. Her lipstick and fingernails matched her coat and he could see the blue of her eyes even from this distance. She was stunning. How had he not seen that before?

'If you can wield a spade in frozen ground, you can come back to work, slacker,' she called, when she was still several metres away.

'Back on Monday,' he replied, although he suspected she already knew that.

'So, what's new?' he asked when they were sitting on the bench. She hadn't remarked on the coffee. She was drinking it without complaint though, so he supposed that was progress.

'Anderson trial set for next February,' she said. 'You'll be needed, so don't book any skiing holidays.'

Michael Anderson had been charged with two counts of murder: of Madeleine Black and Eloise Warner, and a further three counts of attempted murder: of Olive Anderson, Samantha Elliott and Garry Mizon. On top of the charges for receiving stolen goods, of course.

'CPS still think the murder charges unlikely to stick?' Garry asked.

'We all do,' Lexy replied. 'The judge will throw them out. Apart from Olive's testimony – and she's not the most reliable witness – there's very little evidence against him with regard to Maddy. And we don't know for certain that Eloise was even murdered, let alone who was responsible.'

'He killed them both,' Garry said. 'You won't convince me otherwise.'

For a moment, he thought Lexy was about to take his hand, but she only tapped her fingers lightly against his knuckles for a second or two. It was something, though. Yeah, definitely something.

'Be grateful the three attempted charges are a slam dunk,' she said. 'And as one of the victims was an officer of the law – that's you by the way – he's going down for a good twenty years.'

As she spoke, Garry felt a familiar twinge in his right shoulder. He'd lost a lot of blood the night Anderson shot him, in spite of Lexy's attempts to stem the flow with every towel she'd found in Waterfall Lodge. Although police back-up had arrived quickly, it had taken nearly an hour for the ambulance to make it through the snow. As she'd confided to his parents, but only once he was out of danger, Lexy honestly hadn't thought he'd make it.

Of course, he'd made it. He was tougher than he looked and he looked hard as nails. That said, he'd spent three weeks in hospital and a further two torturous weeks at his parents' home while his mum fussed around him like a mother hen with only one chick left from a nestful. Even now she called round most days to make sure he was eating properly, that he was taking his pain relief, that he wasn't overdoing it. His last day of sick leave could not have come round sooner.

He asked, 'What will happen to his two daughters?'

'Their grandmother is still young enough to take care of them till they're adults,' Lexy said. 'They have money in trust from their mother's life insurance. They'll be OK.'

'Still tough.'

'Yeah. In other news, who do you think was accompanying Olive when she came in to make a statement last week?'

'I'm guessing not her parents.'

'Sam Elliott.'

'You're kidding.'

Lexy was smiling. 'Saw them pull into the car park together with my own eyes.'

Garry thought for a second, then said, 'Those two? Surely not?'

'There's nowt so queer as folk, Garry.'

'You've been in the north-east too long.'

Should he have said that? Did it sound as though he wanted her to leave?

While he was still thinking about it, she said, 'So, are you finally over your crush on Olive?'

He turned to face her. 'Who said I had a crush on Olive?'

She made a *come off it* face. 'I'm a detective.'

'Rub it in, why don't you.'

She laughed, then seemed to make a decision. 'Have you thought of being tested for dyslexia?'

It took him a moment to process. 'What?'

'I think you're dyslexic,' she went on. 'You've got classic symptoms. Your spelling's all over the place, you have poor self-esteem, and you like to focus on one job at a time. That's why you keep failing your exams. If you got a diagnosis, allowances could be made. If you want to try again, that is.'

Well, that was a thought.

'So, do you?'

He wasn't sure. 'I might take early retirement,' he said. 'Open that shop I've always thought about.'

Lexy leaned back on the bench and cradled her mug between both hands. 'Anything to do with flowers?'

The hyacinths really were spectacular. He could sell them at £2 a stem, maybe more. Next year, he'd try growing pink ones. 'Maybe,' he said.

'Have you told your mum?'

'Brought her here a week ago. She said she's known for years. She and Dad come out here from time to time to see what I've got growing. She says she knew I'd tell her when the time was right.'

'Oh Garry.' Lexy let her head drop against his shoulder for a second. When she lifted it, the place where her head had rested felt cold.

'Lexy,' he said. 'Do you fancy having a drink sometime? Just as friends, you know?'

As Garry held his breath, Lexy was silent and very still for a second. Then she said, 'No.'

Blimey. Even for her, that seemed brutal. 'No?' he repeated.

She seemed determined not to look at him now. 'I have enough friends, Garry. I'm not looking for another one.'

His heart was suddenly beating very fast. 'Lexy,' he said. 'Will you have dinner with me tonight? As a prelude to a possible romantic relationship?'

Still, Lexy didn't turn her head, but he saw the side of her face crease into a sudden grin. She said, 'I thought you'd never ask.'

92

Thirteen months later

It was a vile day, even for early spring in the north-east. March winds had lingered long after their time was up and April showers had come with a vengeance. The sea was a churning mass of iron-grey capped with dirty white froth. Gulls screamed angrily overhead and the river nearby stank of things long dead. The tide was high, but on its way out. It was a spring tide, so would go out fast and far. They'd planned it that way.

Sam was waiting by the water's edge, staring out at where the horizon would be, if it could be seen through the lowering clouds and relentless rain. She was dressed as she had been the night she and Olive had met.

The beach was pebbled, hard to walk on. Sam turned as Olive drew close and her eyes dropped to the wreath.

'Nice,' she said.

The wreath was way beyond nice, it was spectacular. Olive had asked for red roses, but Garry – he owned a florist shop now, who'd have believed it? – had persuaded her the effect of nothing but one colour of roses would be too harsh. He'd mixed in peach rosebuds and a tiny, daisy-like flower in the same shade, some red and orange tulips and dried orange slices. He'd even, with a stroke of genius, found some tiny glass strawberries and strewn them around the circle. It would float, he'd told her, until the oasis holding it together became sodden and then it would sink to the ocean floor. He hadn't let her pay for it.

Maddy would have adored it.

'So, what happened?' Sam asked, with the air of someone dreading the answer to her own question.

She was talking about Michael's sentencing. 'You haven't seen the news?'

'I can't,' Sam replied, shaking her head. 'I don't want to see him, not ever again.'

'Twenty-two years for three attempted murders,' Olive told her. 'He'll serve at least half that. Probably more. He got time for the stolen goods too, but that will run concurrently.'

'It's not enough,' Sam said.

As anticipated, the two murder charges hadn't got past the judge.

'I did think she might have drowned,' Sam said. 'When I learned she'd been sailing with the Andersons. But her body didn't wash up. I thought all bodies washed up.'

'No,' Olive replied, staring out at the iron-grey sea. 'It's all about the rate of decomposition. Putrefaction produces gases that swell the body like a balloon. So, it floats. But that happens best in warm, shallow water. Someone drowning in cold, deep water might never come to the surface. And Maddy died at the beginning of November.'

'You mean she was murdered at the beginning of November.' Sam sighed. 'Come on then, let's get this over with.'

Without asking, she took the wreath from Olive and hurled it out to sea. It went further than Olive would have been able to throw it, to be fair. For a minute or two, they thought the waves might bring it back in, but then the withdrawing tide caught hold and it began to slip away. To Olive, it felt like saying goodbye all over again. Not that she'd really had a chance the first time.

'You still planning to move abroad?' Sam asked.

She was. Somewhere no one had heard of Michael Anderson and his exploits, where Olive herself wasn't infamous, where a well-qualified nurse was rare enough to be welcomed, whatever her background.

'I may take some time off first,' she told Sam. 'A year, maybe more. I'm not sure I'm in the right frame of mind to care for others right now.'

'That must have been a good divorce pay-out?'

'In a way.'

Olive thought for a moment, then unzipped the top of her jacket and pulled the sweater away from her neck, allowing the other woman to see what was strung around her neck. Sam's eyes widened.

'It's called the Ring of Blood and Tears,' Olive said. 'I found it in the loft one day, when I was looking for stuff that might incriminate Michael. I hid it on the boat, wrapped up in a plastic bag in the bilges. I only just managed to retrieve it before the police got round to searching.'

'Ring of Blood and Tears,' Sam repeated. 'How appropriate.'

'I'll split it,' Olive offered. 'Once I've found a buyer.'

Sam gave a cold, bitter laugh. 'Thanks, but I'm good. Tell me, are your parents talking to you yet?'

It was Olive's turn to sigh. 'I'm not sure they'll ever come to terms with it. They genuinely believe homosexuality is a sin. You can't change the mindset of a lifetime.'

'Guess not.' Sam was silent for a few seconds as she looked out to sea. The wreath was a dot in the distance. 'So, where do you think she is?'

'Maddy? I think she doesn't exist anymore, not in the flesh anyway. She's become one with the sea.'

It was a nice thought, and better than the reality. Scavengers would have eaten Maddy's flesh very quickly, her bones subsequently scattered by the movements of the water. There had been times, the last few months, when Olive wished she knew less about biology.

Sam said, 'I should hate you.'

'Feel free. I hated you for a long time. Until I hated Michael more.'

'Fair enough. Tell me something – who do you believe? Michael or Eloise? Who really caused Maddy to go overboard that day?'

'I don't think it matters. I hold them both equally responsible.' Olive took a step closer to Sam. 'Are you going to be OK?'

Sam shook her head. 'Maddy didn't get justice. I'll never come to terms with that. The Andersons killed her and they got away with it.'

'Prison isn't a walk in the park, you know.'

'I know. And I know Eloise died, but it's not enough. Your evidence was discounted. She got away with it.'

Olive took a deep breath and said, 'No, she didn't.'

93

At two minutes past midnight, Olive pushed the soundless trolley into Eloise's room. No one saw her do it. The late medication round was over and several of the nurses had gone on break. Those still on duty were at the far side of the ward dealing with an elderly woman who'd tumbled out of bed.

She drew the window blind, locked the door, and pulled on disposable gloves.

Eloise lay supine, arms at her sides, perfectly still. For a moment, Olive thought she might be too late. She stepped closer and held her breath until she saw the faint rise and fall of the other woman's chest. Eloise was asleep.

The burning rage in Olive's head that had started when the dying woman had admitted to the heartless murder of Maddy had gone, and in its place was fury, glacier-cold and harder than diamonds. The monster on the bed actually felt better now, maybe close to being at peace. She'd confessed her sins and thought she could sink painlessly into oblivion sometime over the next few days with a clear conscience. Well, it wasn't going to happen. Olive was no priest and she sure as hell wasn't giving absolution.

The fact that the monster was dying anyway made no difference. This passing was not about to be eased. Quite the opposite.

Olive had thought everything through. If anyone questioned the locked room, she would say she'd needed to give the patient an intimate wash. She'd even brought in washing materials and soiled disposable pants retrieved from the sluice room, just in case.

Moving soundlessly around, she found the patient alarm and

moved it well out of Eloise's reach. There would be no summoning of help. She also checked the blind on the external window was closed tight. Then, she made her way round the bed, tucking the blankets and sheet beneath the mattress, as far as she could push them. When she'd finished, Eloise was as tightly pinned to her bed as if she'd been tied with rope. A fit, healthy person would be able to free herself in minutes; it was possible someone as weak as Eloise would fight her way out eventually, but it would take time.

Time she wouldn't have.

Back at the trolley, Olive lifted an upturned steel dish and took up the syringe beneath it. Filled with concentrated liquid potassium bought from a garden centre (it made a very good plant food), in someone as weak as Eloise it would cause acute abdominal pain more or less instantly and a severe, agonising heart attack quickly afterwards. She lifted Eloise's left hand in her own.

'Wake up, bitch.'

No response.

Olive leaned closer and slapped the other woman hard across the face. Eloise's eyes darted open.

'You're going to die tonight,' she told her patient. 'Very painfully. I only wish I could make it slowly too.'

Fixing the end of the syringe into the canula on Eloise's hand, Olive held the barrel between her first and second fingers and placed her thumb on the plunger flange.

'What . . . ?' Eloise's voice was little more than a croak. 'What are you doing?'

Then she pulled back with a strength that took Olive by surprise. In response, Olive tightened her grip on the other woman's wrist to the point where she knew she was inflicting pain.

'If they do a post-mortem, they'll be looking for who did this,' she went on. 'I'm going to make sure they find this very syringe, and the rest of the bottle of potassium, somewhere on your husband's person or property. He likes me, you said so yourself. He and I will be seeing a lot of each other in the coming months. Along with the recording I made of your confession earlier, it will be more than enough. He'll go to prison, and your daughters will be infamous. Maybe I can get their grandmother out of the picture too, see if I can get them sent off to a children's home.'

There was little chance of that, she knew. Olive wasn't even sure how she'd plant the syringe on Michael, but for now it didn't matter. This was about torturing Eloise.

'This is for Maddy,' Olive said, as she slowly depressed the plunger.

Acknowledgements

Heartfelt thanks to the usual team: Anne Marie, Rosie and Jessica; Sam, Sophie and Leodora; Lucy, Alex, Ellen and Paul. I couldn't do it without you.

Thanks also to Gareth, for some useful, if rather twisted ideas, and to Andrew, for keeping me company on my many trips to the north.

Credits

Sharon Bolton and Orion Fiction would like to thank everyone at Orion who worked on the publication of *The Fake Wife* in the UK.

Editorial
Sam Eades
Leodora Darlington
Sahil Javed

Copyeditors
Sophie Wilson
Francine Brody

Proofreader
Jade Craddock

Audio
Paul Stark
Jake Alderson

Contracts
Dan Herron
Ellie Bowker
Alyx Hurst

Editorial Management
Charlie Panayiotou
Jane Hughes
Bartley Shaw

Finance
Jasdip Nandra
Nick Gibson
Sue Baker

Marketing
Lucy Cameron

Production
Ruth Sharvell

Sales
Jen Wilson
Esther Waters
Victoria Laws
Toluwalope Ayo-Ajala
Rachael Hum
Ellie Kyrke-Smith
Sinead White
Georgina Cutler

Publicity
Ellen Turner

Operations
Jo Jacobs
Dan Stevens

If you enjoyed *The Fake Wife*, don't miss Sharon Bolton's Richard & Judy bestseller *The Split*

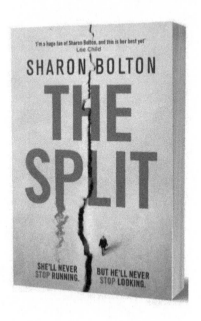

SHE'LL NEVER STOP RUNNING.
BUT HE'LL NEVER STOP LOOKING.

A year ago, Felicity Lloyd fled England to South Georgia, one of the most remote islands in the world, escaping her past and the man she once loved. Can she keep running her whole life?

Freddie Lloyd has served time for murder – and now he wants her back. Wherever she is, he won't stop until he finds her. Will he be able to track her to the ends of the earth?

TOGETHER THEY'LL FIND THEMSELVES TRAPPED ON THE ICE AND IN DANGER. WHO WILL SURVIVE?

Don't miss Sharon Bolton's gripping thriller about privilege, power and revenge, *The Pact*

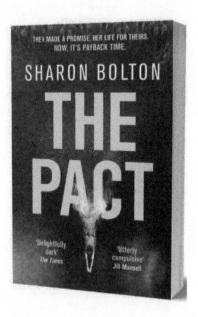

THEY MADE A PROMISE, HER LIFE FOR THEIRS.
NOW IT IS PAYBACK TIME.

A golden summer, and six talented teenagers are looking forward
to the brightest of futures – until a daredevil game goes
horribly wrong, leaving three strangers dead.

Eighteen-year-old Megan takes the blame for the crime, leaving her
friends to get on with their lives. In return, they each agree to a 'favour',
payable on her release from prison.

Twenty years later Megan is free.
It is payback time.
And her friends start disappearing, one by one . . .

Contents

Introduction

This second edition of *Scotland's Jews* includes an updated history of the Jews in Scotland and an account of the lively contemporary Jewish community. Amongst the new material in this edition are an overview of the demography of the Community, and an outline of Jewish concerns about health, employment and contemporary antisemitism. There is also a newly written overview of Jewish beliefs and practices, and an imaginative introduction to Jewish customs through an explanatory account of John K Clark's spectacular stained-glass windows, originally created for Queens Park Synagogue, and now housed in Giffnock and Newlands Synagogue.

The Jewish encounter with Scotland is essentially a product of the past two centuries, and during this time there has been considerable reflection on the questions of Jewish identity in Scotland and the Scottish identity of its Jewish citizens. A new short essay on this subject is accompanied by a number of extracts from books by well-known Jewish Scots.

This edition has been published by the Scottish Council of Jewish Communities, with the aid of a grant from the Scottish Government. The Council is the umbrella organisation representing the Glasgow, Edinburgh, Aberdeen, and Dundee communities, as well as the Jewish Network of Argyll and the Highlands, and Jewish students studying in Scotland. The Council has actively engaged in the many issues that Scotland has addressed since the establishment of the Parliament and devolved government at Holyrood, and has had much success in ensuring that Jewish concerns are understood in a positive manner. Much of the credit for this success is due to the Council's Director, Ephraim Borowski, whose vision for the Council was rewarded with the recent award of an MBE. His work is ably supported by the Council's Public Affairs Officer, Leah Granat, whose drive, energy, and attention to detail have ensured Jewish input into all the vital areas of contemporary concern.

DR KENNETH COLLINS

SCoJeC delegation
meets Church of
Scotland Moderator
Sheilagh Kesting, 2007

office of the
CHIEF RABBI

ב"ה

I have long been impressed by the Jewish communities of Scotland. They have combined strong loyalty to our Jewish faith and way of life, with a deep attachment to Scottish culture and identity. They have honoured the classic principle set out twenty-six centuries ago by the prophet Jeremiah, to 'seek the peace of the city to which you have travelled and pray to God on its behalf, for in its peace you will find peace'. That combination of integration without assimilation has been the delicate balance Jews have striven to achieve, and Scottish Jewry has done just that.

It is an enthralling story to read of how Jews came to Scotland, settled and built communities around synagogues, welfare institutions and educational facilities. The first arrivals and successive waves of newcomers had to struggle against great difficulties, learning the language, finding jobs, and braving sometimes hostile attitudes. They were able to do so not least because of the way Jews helped one another, through friendly societies, welfare boards and other communal institutions. The principle of *kol Yisrael areivin zeh be-zeh*, collective Jewish responsibility, made a real difference to people's lives, easing the inevitable pains of adjustment.

This latest edition of the by now classic Guide to the history of Jews in Scotland is a wonderful, informative introduction to a community that has had outstanding spiritual leaders, lay people who have achieved distinction in many fields, and synagogues of great architectural beauty and human warmth.

Scotland's Jews have written a notable chapter in the history of our people. May they, and the institutions they have built, continue to flourish, and may the Divine Presence continue to bless all you do.

In admiration and with my warmest good wishes,

Jonathan Sacks

CHIEF RABBI SIR JONATHAN SACKS

Chief Rabbi Sir Jonathan Sacks meets the then First Minister Jack McConnell on a visit to the Scottish Parliament, 2007

Rt Hon Alex Salmond MSP
First Minister of Scotland

The Scottish Government

I am delighted to introduce this timely new edition of *Scotland's Jews*. The story of how Scotland's Jewish population succeeded in establishing communities across the country is a fascinating part of the rich tapestry of Scottish history. It is a helpful illustration of how Scotland truly has been, and remains, a country of many cultures, faiths and beliefs.

But this book does far more than look to the past, it also provides practical information about Judaism and the issues affecting Scotland's Jewish communities today, which I am sure will prove highly useful to local authorities, schools, hospitals, other public bodies and the wider public who may not be aware of the contribution Scottish Jews have made to the development of our nation.

Scotland is a rich mix of people of diverse backgrounds, and everyone has their part to play in weaving the tartan of Scottish society. As the Declaration of Arbroath famously states *cum non sit Pondus nec distinccio Judei et Greci, Scoti aut Anglici*, which translates as 'there is neither bias nor difference between Jew or Greek, Scot or English', a sentiment which demonstrates our shared past and provides inspiration for the future for all of Scotland's communities.

One of the founding principles of my Government is the resolute belief in a One Scotland of many cultures, faiths and beliefs – a belief that all of us, regardless of background, have our pride in being Scottish woven into the complex make up of our individual identities. *Scotland's Jews* will undoubtedly help to reinforce this important message. It will also help us to understand the need to achieve a Scotland where diversity is celebrated and seen as a strength not a weakness.

I am confident that Scottish Jews will continue to build on the foundations of this impressive legacy of which they, and our nation, can be rightly proud.

Alex Salmond

First Minister Alex Salmond
learns about Chanukah during
a visit to Calderwood Lodge
Jewish Primary School, 2007

Jewish Identity in Scotland

INTRODUCTION

David Daiches once commented that many of his readers misunderstood the title of his stirring evocation of an Edinburgh Jewish childhood. He pointed out that his book is entitled *Two Worlds*, and not *Between Two Worlds* – he never considered that there was any dichotomy between the Jewish and Scottish. Indeed he felt that his family, led by his father's life-long search for a synthesis of the best of Jewish and Scottish thought and practice, inhabited both worlds simultaneously.

That synthesis was assisted by the fact that Jews and Scots share many of their attitudes to life: a strong belief in education, a reverence for the Hebrew Bible, and the struggle to maintain distinctiveness in a sometimes unfriendly world. As a result the Jewish contribution to the professional and cultural life of Scotland has been widely admired and appreciated.

Scotland has eschewed the American model of the melting pot in its approach to the assimilation of its minorities. In a melting pot all diversity is stirred away; pattern becomes sludge; everything becomes the same, as all difference is dissolved. Often the only alternative suggested is a society of segregated communities, isolated and ghettoised minorities each incommunicado in its own silo, as they are aptly termed, fermenting resentment.

That is the model of multiculturalism that the Chief Rabbi suggests in his latest book, *The Home We Build Together,* may well have run its course. Policies that regard all beliefs as of equal validity and so immune from criticism cause harm by dissolving the glue that creates society. Scotland has adopted a different and more durable model of multiculturalism, and its diverse communities have joined with politicians of all parties in uniting behind the campaign for *One Scotland – Many Cultures.*

That is what is increasingly recognised as the Scottish model – the tartan, with its intersecting pattern, each thread visible as itself against the background, but all holding together, not despite their intersections, but because of those intersections. A tartan is a design made with two or more alternating bands of colour that combine, vertically and horizontally, to form a chequered pattern. It is the very design of the tartan, with its divergence, difference, even disagreement, that holds it together, enabling the different colours and different directions to combine to form a single whole. A cloth of parallel threads, by contrast, is no cloth; it simply falls apart.

During Glasgow's year as European City of Culture in 1990 the local community mounted a very ambitious Festival of Jewish Culture. In our *Jewish Arts Anthology,* we attempted to examine what is Jewish about Jewish culture in a Scottish context, and concluded that there could be no simple definition. There is only a polychromatic mosaic of which the Jewish community is as much a part as any other. For example, the Glasgow Jewish Lads and Girls Brigade has long been proud to have the world's only Jewish bagpipe band, and the late Dr Arthur Shenkin, a well-known and respected psychiatrist, committed his own somewhat heterodox 'Arthurised Version' of the Bible to broad Scots:

> 'Ye see, Goad wis a novice when She makt oor heaven,
> She'd contracted tae finish and rest on day seven;
> Fur a start it wis dark and got Her a' worried –
> It wisnae a job that wis meant to be hurried.'

Thus have Scotland's Jews been proud to adopt Scottish themes as their own.

The Jewish Lads and Girls Brigade Pipe Band leading the annual Jewish ex-servicemen's parade, Armistice Day, 2007

Expatriate Scottish Jews in Israel host an annual Burns Supper complete with the toast to the (kosher) haggis, accompanied by copious quantities of Irn Bru, which the *Jerusalem Post* solemnly assured its readers a few years ago was a kind of Scottish champagne! Jews in Israel are also very aware of the Scottish presence in the Holy Land, though aware too of the reasons why that presence began – in a usually futile attempt to convert the Jews.

The Jewish presence in Scotland has never been great in numerical terms, always less than half of one percent of the population, and although individual Jews have lived in Scotland for a little over three hundred years the largest Jewish communities in Edinburgh and Glasgow are less than two hundred years old. Now the community is aging, and with few younger people around, the problems of providing a Jewish environment for those still here will become acute. The key issue today for Jews in Scotland is the maintenance of Jewish identity in an open society where antisemitism has rarely been a feature of Scottish life.

The Scottish encounter with Judaism has had many points of contact. Mission was at the heart of the earlier relationship between Scots and Jews, and missionaries at home and abroad attempted to use the Jewish desire for medical care and a modern education to evangelise and proselytise. While unsuccessful as a project, this missionary activity created a belief in the Jewish community that Scottish Christians were attacking the very core of Jewish identity, the glue that had held together a people scattered through generations of diaspora.

Nonetheless, Jews and Scots have both gained from their interaction during the past two centuries. Out of our many shared traditions have come tolerance and mutual respect, and the years have brought each a better understanding of the sensitivities of the other. One remarkable achievement of the Jews is in maintaining a distinctive identity and vision of the future, surviving as a people scattered across many countries, with their common language, Hebrew, used mainly in prayer.

The Jewish time line has been remarkably persistent, and Jews in Scotland have good cause to be proud of the twin strands of their identity – the mosaic in the tartan!

DAVID DAICHES

David Daiches

DAVID DAICHES'S MEMOIR OF HIS FATHER, RABBI SALIS DAICHES, RABBI OF THE EDINBURGH HEBREW CONGREGATION, 1919-1945

He was, however, a Scottish rabbi, more and more regarded as the Scottish rabbi, and his loyalty to Edinburgh was part of a larger feeling for Scotland. He knew the Fife coast from his annual summer holiday there; he knew about the cities because of his lecturing there. But what about the Highlands and Islands? He once recited to his children Tchernichowsky's Hebrew version of

My heart's in the Highlands, my heart is not here,
My heart's in the Highlands a-chasing the deer,

and finally, in 1934, he decided that the family should take their annual summer holiday in the Highlands instead of the East Neuk of Fife. So they rented a cottage just north of Kyle of Lochalsh, from where they visited Skye. And the following year they took a small house in Glenluig, almost inaccessible except by boat up Loch Ailort into the Sound of Arisaig and Glenluig Bay or by walking a seven-mile path (there was no road then) from Lochailort station. Here the rabbi would sit by the romantic western shore and watch the sunset; or he would walk up the glen with a book in his hand so that he could sit on the grass or on a rock when he felt tired and read. On the Sabbath he would sit by the water and read that day's portion of the Law from his Hebrew Bible, and as the sun set, sing quietly to himself a Hebrew song about Elijah the prophet returning one day to his people, a traditional song to accompany the end of the Sabbath on Saturday night. For some years henceforth the rabbi and his family were annual visitors to the Highlands. Somehow the Highlands scenery and Jewish feeling came together in his mind easily and spontaneously. His feeling for Edinburgh derived originally from his student researches into David Hume and the Scottish Enlightenment. For the Highlands he had no such literary preparation. But he did buy a tartan-bound copy of *The Lady of the Lake* on a visit to the Trossachs in 1921 and read it aloud to his children. He liked poetry with a strong and regular metrical beat and firm lines.

So the rabbi who was to give his name to Daiches Braes had trodden the Road to the Isles. It is strange perhaps to think that David

Hume and his fellow thinkers of the Scottish Enlightenment had no interest in the Highlands and considered the Gaels to be a wild and primitive people (although one of them, Adam Fergusson, was himself a Gaelic speaker). This view, however, was modified by Macpherson's *Ossian*, regarded as genuine by some if not all the Edinburgh literati, who believed it showed the simple nobility of a primitive people. The rabbi probably took an Ossianic view of the Highlanders. His personal experience of them was limited to brief practical conversations with shopkeepers and boatmen but his European education had left an Ossianic residue. He was rather taken aback to discover in a remote corner of Wester Ross a Jewish tailor who catered to the needs of the locals, and spoke Yiddish and Gaelic with virtually no English. This represented a synthesis he had never bargained for. No solitary Jew living apart from a Jewish community could lead a full Jewish religious life, so this was not really an example of *Torah im derech eretz* [the synthesis of Judaism with everyday life]. And the repudiated ghetto language preserved in Gaelic-speaking Scotland! He told the story as an amusing oddity.

From the essay 'Promised Lands' in *Two Worlds*, Canongate Classics, Edinburgh, second edition, 1997.

David Daiches (1912 - 2005) was a Scottish literary historian and literary critic, scholar and writer. He founded the English Department at Sussex University, and from 1980-1986 was Director of the Institute for Advanced Studies in the Humanities at Edinburgh University.

RALPH GLASSER

Escape from being a Jew was of course an immature idea. Identity was in the marrow, in the veins. I refused to believe it. Flight from it was to seek a special anaesthesia of the spirit, an erasure of sensibility, a kind of death. No wonder many traditional Jews believed that, if a son or daughter married out, the mourner's prayer, Kaddish, would be said. I would understand that in later years when I had begun the road back.

For that return journey I would have to learn a special understanding all over again – and learn it differently. In ritual or observance almost every word, every symbol, would be deeply interfused, and are so still, with bitter-sweet memories of childhood days when I clung to my mother's long black apron – even now my fingers remember the feel of the shiny worn cotton, warmed by her body, wrestling with the darkness of life, with shadows that prefigured the menace of the future; sadness that would not be put to rest. I still remember father telling me, his voice full of pride mixed with sorrow, how at the first Seder, or Passover feast, after my birth, when I was only a few weeks old, he laid me on a pillow beside the table, so that I should absorb the atmosphere – the food scents, the brilliant starlight of the candles, the prayers and the chanting, the family united in dedication. Slowly I would learn to placate memory, allow it to come and go, lessen its grasp.

Bits of the Gorbals were forgotten, truths it had taught me, which would have made life easier, or less likely to hurt, if I had taken them to heart.

They returned in unexpected form and caught me unawares. Since, in the Gorbals, everyone I knew lived on the insecure margin between sufficiency and starvation, no-one possessed anything worth coveting, or even noticing, so the only thing of value a person possessed was himself. You had to value him for his qualities – there being nothing else – and that 'value', the proper respect for himself alone, was his due. Foolishly, I had forgotten, or chosen not to notice, that this new world did judge you by your possessions.

Here, self enquiry has taken me deeper than I ever imagined, to show me that nothing, no perception, no vision, be the light however powerful and the images hard-edged and seemingly unambiguous, will ever answer the questions that possessed me when I left the Gorbals to cycle to Oxford long ago. Yet the ineluctable pursuit remains in command, intransigent as always, and of course no settlement, no halting place will ever be found. And Gorbals works on the spirit implacably – how could it be otherwise? – still kneading the original clay, continuing its questioning, the Sphinx constantly changing the terms of the riddle, never to be solved. The temptation grows – more dangerous than all the others – to create my own, and usurp her sovereignty once and for all.

Ralph Glasser was born and grew up in the Gorbals in Glasgow. As a psychologist and economist he campaigned against the destruction of traditional communities. His Gorbals trilogy tells of his flight from its constraints; his search for the values it represents is described in the final volume, *Gorbals Voices, Siren Songs* (Chatto & Windus, 1990).

CANTOR ERNEST LEVY OBE

Over the past few years mankind has made great steps towards international peace. Yet a lot more needs to be done. In modern society we continue to witness xenophobia – that unfounded fear and resentment of the stranger and the minorities that live among us. This fear arises from the fact that the stranger challenges our supremacy. His hard work brings success of which we are envious, resentful of the fact that his existence challenges our status.

Minorities are not completely blameless. Sometimes they do not easily integrate into society; my own family in Bratislava was guilty of that. Self-segregation enforces unfounded fears and hostility within the greater community. Each person must be part of society, without giving up his identity, values and traditions. And each person must recognise the validity of each other's beliefs and religions. There is a fundamental human right to be as different from each other as we please – each human being is unique. Instead of seeking conformity, we must turn the whole thing upside down and recognise that differences can be wonderful in adding colour and spice to our lives.

Diversity should be the norm. If you want a rich and full society, then everyone should have the right to their own little peculiarities. The more colour there is, the more beautiful the world becomes. Different people learn from each other, and their lives are enriched. In Glasgow I have learned many things from the Scots, and I hope that they have learned something from me. Only together can we build a brighter and safer world. Bratislava was a diverse community but the differences were feared, not celebrated. Instead of being enriched, it was degraded and people became bestial.

In the middle of July 1961, I arrived at Glasgow Central Station. For a moment, when I saw Glasgow with its grey, low-flying clouds, I thought I had made a mistake. But as we drove into Giffnock suburb I fell in love with the entire area something here had clicked, I liked the people and the city. For the

first time it looked as though I had a good and secure future ahead of me. I had found a 'home' and settled in Scotland for good.

The Single Light – launch of Rev Ernest Levy's memoirs at the Scottish Parliament, 2007

I am still in love with Scotland and its people. Scotland is like a sleeping beauty: there is little openly expressed prejudice here compared to other places, and the people lack cynicism and sarcasm – a trait from which other Europeans suffer an overdose. I once read somewhere that happiness can be measured by the number of friends one acquires. Making friends is not always easy, but here in Scotland it seems easier and on the basis of the number we have, our happiness is well secured.

From *Just One More Dance*, Mainstream Press, Edinburgh, 1998.

Ernest Levy (b.1925) is a survivor of Birkenau, Bergen-Belsen, and other extermination and labour camps. He is the Emeritus Cantor of Giffnock and Newlands Hebrew Congregation in East Renfrewshire, and was awarded an OBE for services to Holocaust education in Scotland.

CHAIM BERMANT

Scotland and Israel are both about the same size with about the same population. Although there is much to be said for being small, both have seen in their smallness something like a proof of excellence, and, as if it is not sufficient proof, both point to the Diaspora behind them to show that they are less small than is generally believed. 'Wha's like us?' the Scots will ask. In Israel they don't even ask; they already have the answer. What is often maddening to outsiders is that the good conceit which both have of themselves is not entirely unjustified.

I was born in a part of Lithuania which was then Poland and is now Russia. When I was three my family moved to Latvia; when I was five I was sent to school in Poland; at eight we all moved to Scotland; at twenty I first went to Israel. In Latvia I was known as a Polack, in Poland as a Lett, and in Scotland as foreigner. In Israel, however, I was known as a Scot. In a sense I had come home.

During my first year in Scotland I was in Glasgow but not quite of it. Outside of school hours I divided much of my time between home and synagogue, and was perhaps more in the latter than the former, possibly because I found comfort in what I thought of as God's presence, but mainly, I suspect, because the synagogue, though a modern and stately edifice, provided lingering echoes of the old country, and it was, I suppose, a way of escaping Glasgow.

Our first address was the Gorbals where Father had lodgings with distant relatives, and the Gorbals, somehow, was less intimidating than other parts of town, for it reminded me vaguely of Dvinsk. There were Yiddish posters on the hoardings, Hebrew lettering on the shops, Jewish names, Jewish faces, Jewish butchers, Jewish bakers with Jewish bread, and Jewish grocers with barrels of herring in the doorway. The herrings in particular brought a strong whiff of home. One heard Yiddish in the streets – more so, in fact, than English – and one encountered figures who would not have been out of place in Barovke. It was only when we moved into our flat in Battlefield Gardens that I began to feel my exile, for Battlefield – the area was named after the Battle of Langside – was certainly, in the late 1930s, posh, even elegant. In the Gorbals one ascended to one's flat up a dark stairway smelling of urine. In Battlefield all was light and cleanliness with a slight touch of Dettol in the air.

Chaim Bermant was a journalist, novelist and shrewd commentator on Jewish issues, both within Glasgow and beyond. These extracts are taken from his memoir *Coming Home*, George Allen & Unwin, 1976.

CHIEF RABBI CYRIL HARRIS

LATE CHIEF RABBI OF SOUTH AFRICA

My bris, circumcision, was in the synagogue on Yom Kippur, and the *Beth Din* allowed my non-Jewish nurse to carry me to the synagogue for the ceremony. I was born in Camphill Avenue in the district of Langside in Glasgow – the business magnate, Sir Isaac Wolfson, at the halfway stage of his illustrious career, lived next door at the time – and I was to be named after my grandfather who had died the year before, and who had been the spiritual leader of the Langside Hebrew Congregation.

As Yom Kippur is a fast day and as the benedictions at a circumcision are always recited over a cup of wine, there is of course a problem: who is supposed to drink the wine? Answer: the baby! I have it on the good authority of several persons who were present that when I was given the wine to drink, I took my week-old arm and pushed the cup aside, as if to remonstrate at the very idea of expecting me to drink on a fast day. 'One day this boy will be a rabbi' one of the onlookers joked.

Our family are direct descendents of the famous Vilna Gaon. Of course every *Litvak* [Lithuanian Jew] claims this honour, but unlike most of them we can prove it. My mother's maiden name was Bloch and our family is descended from the Gaon's youngest daughter, Tova. Incidentally, we, the Scottish branch of the family, are known to our cousins in other climes as 'the Blochs from the lochs'.

Chief Rabbi Cyril Harris with
South African President
Nelson Mandela

In Primary 3 (in Ayr) every Friday afternoon before school finished for the week, our teacher would tell us a long and exciting story. He was a marvellous raconteur and made the content, whether cops and robbers or cowboys and Indians, come to life. In the Scottish winter, *Shabbat* begins before school finishes, and I still remember having to put up my hand in the middle of the story to ask permission to go home. I used to wonder how those stories ended. My little mind thought how wonderful it would be if only there could be Jewish schools one day – at my school there were only three Jewish pupils out of 170 – so that we did not have to interrupt the routine and would not have to miss the end of a good story.

Chief Rabbi Harris was born in Glasgow and grew up in Ayr and Glasgow, before embarking on a distinguished rabbinic career in London and subsequently as Chief Rabbi of South Africa from 1988. His criticism of apartheid and his support for the white population's participation in the transformed South Africa enabled him to build bridges with the new leadership under Nelson Mandela. This extract is from his memoirs *For Heaven's Sake*, published by Vallentine Mitchell, 2001.

Jewish History in Scotland

JEWISH IMMIGRATION

The first Jews in Scotland came from Germany and Holland, but gradually, from the 1860s, Jews from Russia and Poland predominated as more Jews from Eastern Europe passed through Scotland on their way to America. Besides the growing merchant element there were the first Jewish professionals: Louis Ashenheim in Edinburgh and Asher Asher in Glasgow, the first Scottish-born Jewish university graduates. However, while some Jews were attaining prosperity, others, who had left Russia fleeing from poverty and antisemitism, formed a poorer section of the community.

Jewish Immigrant Family
in Glasgow, c1900

In the middle of the nineteenth century, the Jewish communities in Edinburgh and Glasgow were of equal size, but gradually the growing commercial economy of Glasgow attracted more Jewish traders and merchants. The burgeoning industries of Victorian Glasgow provided workplaces for the Jewish newcomers, and Jewish efforts aided the rapid development of production particularly in the manufacture of clothing, furniture, and cigarettes. The concentration of Jews in the tailoring trade from the 1880s led to accusations of sweated labour, charges which community spokesmen were able to rebut. Significant numbers of Jews from both Glasgow and Edinburgh were involved in peddling, selling goods to the mining communities within easy travelling distance.

From early in the nineteenth century, many Jewish companies in Hamburg with an interest in textiles, set up offices in Dundee; a community was established in 1874, and for a short time supported two synagogues. In Aberdeen the new Jewish community was the centre of national attention just weeks after its founding in 1893, when it successfully defended a case brought against *shechitah* by the local branch of the Society for the Prevention of Cruelty to Animals.

The growth in the communities was reflected first by the opening of new synagogues. In Glasgow an imposing synagogue was opened at Garnethill in 1879, when there were barely a thousand Jews in the city. This synagogue replaced the smaller George Street Synagogue opened some 20 years earlier with room for 200 worshippers. Though most of Glasgow's Jews lived in and around the city centre, the beginnings of a Yiddish-speaking community in the Gorbals, just south of the River Clyde, could already be seen. In Edinburgh, the synagogue in Park Place near Edinburgh University, dating from 1868, was replaced by a converted chapel in Graham Street that was opened in 1898. The Graham Street Synagogue was enlarged in 1913 and remained the main Edinburgh synagogue until the present synagogue in Salisbury Road was opened in 1932. A smaller but separate community existed for some years in the Dalry district of Edinburgh, where a group of Jewish waterproofers had settled in 1880.

Migration to Scotland in significant numbers did not really get under way until the 1890s. There were about 2000 Jews in Glasgow in 1891, and this number increased to about 7000 a decade later. Scottish shipping companies became increasingly involved with transporting emigrants from Europe across Scotland to America from the 1890s. Travelling conditions could be difficult; migrants passing through Leith were sometimes unfit for onward travel, and many travellers decided to end their journey in Scotland, joining family and friends already settled here. Some sick travellers also had to remain in Glasgow until they were able to meet American health requirements, and poor and sick Jews became a charge on local Jewish and parish welfare. Although the 1905 Aliens Act limited the number of poorer immigrants, more Jews continued to arrive in Scotland in the years before the First World War. About 10 000 Jews passed through Glasgow in 1908 alone on their way to America, and by 1914 there were about 12 000 Jews in Glasgow and about 1500 in Edinburgh.

Some Jews arrived from other parts of Britain, often from London, attracted by local employment prospects or by official attempts to reduce the numbers settling in the capital. The London Jewish Board of Guardians returned some 50 000 Jews to Eastern Europe between 1880 and 1914 to try to reduce tensions produced by the immigration. In Glasgow repatriation was seen as controversial, and was only arranged in a few instances in order to re-unite families divided during the upheavals of mass migration.

Outside the four major Scottish cities, smaller Jewish communities were also formed in Greenock (1894), a port city on the transmigration route to North America, and later also in such regional centres as Ayr (1904), Falkirk, Inverness (both 1905), and Dunfermline (1908).

HEALTH AND WELFARE

• Jewish Welfare and Self-help

The Jewish response to the arrival of poor and sick newcomers was the formation of a network of charitable and welfare institutions. The established community saw it as their duty to cater for specifically Jewish needs such as the observance of *Shabbat* and other holy days and the requirement for kosher food. Familiarity with Jewish customs and the close-knit nature of the community made it easier, and more appropriate, for welfare provision to be provided by the Jews themselves. Philanthropy was seen as an important activity in Victorian times and it was felt that decreasing Jewish reliance on parish relief would reduce any potential antisemitism.

The first Jewish welfare charity in Scotland was founded in Edinburgh in 1838, and a Glasgow welfare body was in existence soon afterwards. The Glasgow Hebrew Philanthropic Society was already functioning, with its own medical officer, in 1858. The increasing number of Jews settling led to a considerable increase in charitable activity, much of it led by the immigrants themselves. Self-help societies such as the Glasgow Hebrew Benevolent Loan Society (1888) were founded by the weekly penny subscriptions of their members, and provided benefits in times of need.

Self-help was also promoted by the Jewish friendly societies in Glasgow and Edinburgh. These served a social purpose, as well as providing visitors for the sick, medical and welfare services, and financial benefits during times of illness, bereavement, and unemployment. Medical and welfare facilities that met religious and ethnic needs were further enhanced when Jewish refugee shelters were opened in Glasgow (1897) and Edinburgh to provide temporary accommodation for newcomers, and to provide hostel facilities for onward travellers.

As the number of Jews increased, the local authorities made efforts to welcome the newcomers. In Glasgow they provided English language classes and supported a *mikvah* within the Gorbals Bathhouse when it opened in 1886. Local Jewish welfare provision also increased. The Edinburgh Jewish Board of Guardians was reconstituted in 1899 to co-ordinate and give support to the various Jewish welfare bodies in the city, and similar bodies were also formed in Dundee and Aberdeen. In Glasgow the Jewish Board of Guardians, still based at Garnethill, provided medical and social support in the paternalistic fashion of the day. Despite the need for a welfare centre in the Gorbals, where the Board clients were concentrated, it did not move south until 1911. This encouraged the proliferation of many small Gorbals-based charities. In 1891 and 1892, the level of immigration swamped local resources, and, although the considerable sum of £2432 had been raised in Glasgow alone, money had to be sought from the Russian Jewish Relief Fund in London.

Jewish welfare provision was a valuable addition to the sums provided by the local authorities. However, welfare was not the only call on Jewish communal resources as synagogue building, Jewish education, purchase of burial grounds, and the supply of kosher food also had to be funded. With many new charities being formed, there was always a concern at the Board of Guardians that their precarious income would be affected. There was also concern that wider Jewish considerations, such as support for the Zionist movement and for distressed Jews abroad, whether in Russia or elsewhere, might hinder local welfare efforts. Welfare provision for disadvantaged Jews has always been seen as a community priority, and although in the smaller communities support was usually confined to temporary financial assistance, by the early 1960s the Jewish welfare services in Glasgow covered such areas as housing and comprehensive residential care for the elderly and learning disabled.

• Christian Missionaries

Paradoxically, one of the stimuli to the better provision of Jewish welfare services was the activity of Christian missionary groups. Many Jewish social and welfare organisations were formed to provide direct competition for missionary facilities targeted at vulnerable newcomers. There was much Jewish poverty, misery and disease, and the missionaries dangled the carrot of financial support and medical aid to entice needy Jews into the mission halls. Christian groups devoted considerable sums to Jewish medical relief, providing well-equipped dispensaries and Yiddish speaking apostate doctors throughout the 1930s. Missionaries blamed their lack of success with conversions on the Jewish attitude to Christianity brought over from Russia. However, they remained determined to persist in their work despite the distress and hostility that their activities provoked. In Edinburgh, the Medical Mission to the Jews was run by the apostate Leon Levison whose attempts to pose as a benefactor to the Jews caused considerable resentment, and his award of a knighthood for services to Russian Jewish relief was widely condemned.

In Glasgow, the Jewish Hospital Fund and Sick Visiting Association was founded in 1899, countering missionary efforts, providing money for Jews requiring hospital care, and maintaining community links with poor isolated Jews in institutions. A Jewish Dispensary opened in the Gorbals in 1910, offering free medicines to counter similar missionary provision. It was popular from the start, quickly attracting 500 members who paid a weekly penny contribution.

• Jews and the Hospitals

Despite the poverty of the Jewish immigrants there were very few Jews in the local authority poorhouses. In 1908 there were only 75 Jews receiving statutory poor relief in all of Scotland.

Visiting hours in hospital were strictly enforced before the First World War, and relatives were not allowed to bring in food. This caused problems for the many observant Jewish patients who required kosher food and were unfamiliar with the Scottish diet. They felt that eating non-kosher food would be a hindrance to their convalescence and resented the restriction on their religious observance.

The Victoria Infirmary and the Merryflatts Poorhouse, on the South Side of Glasgow, dealt with the majority of Scotland's hospitalised Jews. In 1910 the Victoria Infirmary turned down a request to provide kosher food, because they did not want to establish a precedent which might commit them to offering additional facilities to the Jewish or other communities in the future. However, Merryflatts, now the Southern General Hospital, run by the Glasgow Corporation, agreed to the opening of a kosher kitchen in 1914 which functioned for many years.

The provision of hospital kosher meals has continued to remain a Jewish communal priority.

•   Jewish Institutional Care

Given the small size of most Scottish communities, it was only in Glasgow that residential Jewish institutional care was a possibility. The first to be established was the Gertrude Jacobson Orphanage, which opened in 1913 with support from the Glasgow and Govan parish councils. Some parents had died young from diseases like tuberculosis, and there were inevitable family disruptions during the upheavals of immigration. There was therefore a need for a home for Jewish children where kosher food would be provided, and the children could take their part in the life of the community. After the First World War, the Orphanage moved to larger premises in the Battlefield area, housing refugee children from Belgium and Hungary, as well as local Jewish children. Increasing numbers from Europe necessitated the opening of a children's hostel beside Garnethill Synagogue in 1938, and a Farm School at Whittinghame on the Balfour Estate for 160 children in 1939. In 1945, hostels were run at Cardross in Dunbartonshire, and at Polton House in Midlothian, to provide rehabilitation for a group of teenage boys who had survived the horrors of Nazi concentration camps.

A small home for the elderly was opened in 1913 in a rented Gorbals apartment, but it did not survive the war years. Another unsuccessful attempt to set up a Jewish old age home was made in Dixon Avenue in 1929. It was not until 1949 that the Jewish Old Age Home for Scotland, later known as Newark Lodge, was opened in Pollokshields, serving all the Jewish communities of Scotland. A Jewish convalescent home, primarily for tuberculosis sufferers, supported by the Jewish friendly societies in Edinburgh and Glasgow, operated during the 1920s at Slamannan, near Falkirk. In recent years further developments in sheltered housing and supported care have augmented the Jewish residential and hospital care provision.

•   Housing and Health

The slow pace and relatively small numbers of Jewish immigration, and its concentration only in the heavily populated Gorbals area in Glasgow, did not provoke the same popular clamour for alien immigration control in Scotland as happened in other areas of Britain. However, the Jewish community was upset by reports that exaggerated their numbers and gave false information about Jewish housing and health matters. There were concerns in the early part of the twentieth century that frankly antisemitic attitudes were noticeable in the rented housing market, but Jewish leaders maintained that there was no evidence of Jewish overcrowding and that Jewish housing conditions were better than those of their neighbours.

In Glasgow the traditional small overcrowded tenement flat was blamed for the city's poor record with tuberculosis. However, it was noted in immigrant areas throughout Britain that the incidence of TB and other contagious disease was lower in the Jewish population. Even so, the cost of regular grants to TB sufferers was a heavy burden on the Jewish community, and the Glasgow Jewish Board of Guardians launched an ambitious Jubilee Fund appeal in 1916. It was hoped to raise funds to send sufferers and their dependents to countries like Australia and South Africa, where the climate might help effect a cure, or to pay for treatment for patients at home or in sanatoria in England.

In the 1960s the Glasgow Jewish Housing Association was established to improve the accommodation of Jews affected by slum clearance from the Gorbals by buying good tenement property near Jewish facilities, and it has extended its activities in recent years to provide sheltered housing and supported care to an ageing Jewish population.

RELIGIOUS LIFE

• The Synagogues

The opening of the Garnethill Synagogue in Glasgow and the Graham Street Synagogue in Edinburgh did not end the need for synagogue provision in the two major Scottish cities. Shortly after the opening of Garnethill Synagogue in September 1879, the first small Gorbals synagogue opened in a converted workshop in Commerce Street. This move had become inevitable given the distance from the Gorbals to Garnethill. Further small prayer-houses opened in the Gorbals during the 1880s, but communal unity was preserved by a synagogue union in 1886 between Garnethill and the Gorbals.

The early Gorbals synagogues were small, informal prayer-houses, but major places of worship were opened in a hall in Main Street, Gorbals in 1887, and in a converted Baptist church at the corner of Oxford Street and Buchan Street in 1897. Despite a major extension to the Main Street Synagogue in 1891, the growth of Gorbals Jewry required a larger building, and the Great Synagogue was opened in South Portland Street in 1901.

The Great Synagogue was the largest in Glasgow and housed many of the city's religious institutions, including the *yeshivah* and *mikvah*. This was the last Jewish building to remain in the Gorbals, and closed in 1974. Other Gorbals congregations came into being in the first years of the twentieth century as the result of various schisms in the Oxford Street Synagogue. There were also a couple of Chassidic prayer houses, while other synagogues reflected the places of origin of the newcomers.

The synagogue union of 1886, and the formation of the United Synagogue of Glasgow in 1898, gave effective leadership of the community to Garnethill, despite its only having a small proportion of the total synagogue membership. The United Synagogue broke up in 1906 with disputes about *shechitah* and the cost of burials for poor immigrants. Gorbals Jewry appointed Rabbi Samuel Hillman, from Russia, as community rabbi in 1908, and his traditional stance balanced the more moderate style exemplified by Garnethill and its minister, the Rev. E.P. Phillips. In the interwar years, traditional religious leadership was provided through a Glasgow *Beth Din* by Rabbi Lurie and Rabbi Atlas. Phillips, minister from 1879 until 1929, had acted as the spiritual leader for all of Glasgow Jewry and was involved in many of the new welfare bodies. He took a high personal profile in the Oscar

Slater case, when a foreign Jew was falsely convicted of murder, subsequently reprieved, and eventually pardoned. Phillips also represented the community with regard to Sunday trading, an important issue for Jewish traders whose religious convictions prevented them opening on *Shabbat* (from Friday evening until Saturday night).

In Edinburgh too the immigrant period was marked by the formation of a number of small synagogues, in Richmond Street, Roxburgh Place, and South Clerk Street, where the newcomers could feel more comfortable than in the Graham Street Synagogue where the more assimilated community members prayed. When Rabbi Salis Daiches answered a call in 1918 from the various synagogues, his aim, achieved in 1932, was to unite all of Edinburgh Jewry within the new synagogue in Salisbury Road in the Newington district.

Former synagogue in Graham Street, Edinburgh

The Garnethill membership gradually grew as Jews moved from the Gorbals and settled in the Garnethill and Hillhead areas. Garnethill maintained its leading position for many years, although new synagogues were being formed in areas to the south of the Gorbals where Jews were settling in much larger numbers. Queens Park Synagogue was founded in 1906, and moved to a substantial new building in Falloch Road in 1926. About the same time, Langside Synagogue, originally founded in 1915, moved to Niddrie Road. In later years synagogues were established in Pollokshields (1929), Giffnock and Newlands (1934), Netherlee and Clarkston (1940) and Newton Mearns (1954). A Reform synagogue opened in Pollokshields in 1931, and later moved to Newton Mearns. A short-lived community was also established in Hillington, Mosspark and Cardonald (1937). Queens Park eventually closed in 2002, but Langside will be retained within a new housing development (2008).

In the post-war years the Edinburgh community consolidated its activities within the large synagogue in Salisbury Road although the community dispersed round the city, while in Glasgow population movements led to the concentration of the bulk of the community on the south side of the city. The last of the Gorbals synagogues, in South Portland Street, closed in 1974, by which time the largest communities in the Glasgow area were based in Giffnock and Newton Mearns.

Gradually, levels of religious commitment declined, often due to pressures of work and society, and the declining influence of the immigrant generation. Some regarded emigration to Scotland as their escape, not just from persecution and economic hardship, but from Judaism itself.

•   Burial Grounds

The provision of Jewish burial grounds was always a major concern. The first Jewish burial grounds in Scotland were in Edinburgh, where the eighteenth century dentist Heyman Lion purchased the first plots for himself and his wife on Calton Hill in 1793, and a cemetery at Braid Place, Causewayside, was opened in 1820. During the main period of immigration, the community's cemetery was at Echo Bank, and when this was closed before the First World War, the present grounds at Piershill were inaugurated and operated by an independent Burial Society.

The first Jewish cemetery in Glasgow, with room for about 50 plots, was opened in 1831 in a small but picturesque corner of the Glasgow Necropolis, near the Cathedral. A further cemetery was opened in Janefield near Celtic Park, and in 1895 Garnethill Synagogue purchased burial grounds at Maryhill that were later shared with some of the Gorbals synagogues. During the nineteenth century and early twentieth century, the Jewish communities in Dundee, Greenock, Inverness, and Aberdeen established their own cemeteries.

Consecration of a memorial bench in Dundee Jewish Cemetery, 2007

When the first Gorbals synagogue was formed in 1880, a burial ground was obtained in Craigton, and South Portland Street Synagogue opened its own cemetery in Riddrie in 1909. There were, however, continuing problems with the costs of pauper burials. With adult poverty and the large number of infant and child deaths, there were many who could not afford the funeral expenses, and communal institutions such as the synagogues, the *shechitah* bodies, and the Board of Guardians were often asked to help. The Glasgow Hebrew Burial Society was formed in 1907 as a mutual aid society whose members contributed a regular sum to meet the cost of funerals for themselves and their families. At first they obtained a small cemetery at Sandymount in Shettleston, and in the 1930s bought a substantial 10 acre plot at nearby Glenduffhill. By 1937 the Society had 1700 members and its growth continued in the post-war years.

The Reform Synagogue established its own burial grounds in Cardonald. A cemetery in the Cathcart area was established by Queens Park

Synagogue in 1927, and supported by Pollokshields Synagogue. When these synagogues eventually closed arrangements were made for the Cathcart Hebrew Cemetery to continue to function through an independent trust.

JEWISH EDUCATION

The first Hebrew classes began in the early years of the nineteenth century within the Glasgow and Edinburgh synagogues. As the communities grew, additional provision had to be made. While the Garnethill Synagogue had its own religion classes meeting two or three times a week, gradually the Gorbals synagogues made their own arrangements. The main provider of Jewish education in Glasgow was the Talmud Torah, founded in Clyde Terrace in 1895. At first the boys and girls were taught separately, with Yiddish as the language of instruction. These classes met at first for 3 hours every evening, except on Friday, and also on Saturday and Sunday. By 1899 there were 400 pupils at the Talmud Torah, and classes were accommodated at the Glasgow Corporation school in Buchan Street.

The language of teaching in the Talmud Torah was changed from Yiddish to English in about 1908, indicating how successfully the community had integrated. During the First World War, the hours of instruction were reduced to two hours nightly. With many children attending classes for upwards of 12 hours weekly, many of the new generation grew up familiar with the Jewish way of life, Hebrew language, and the sacred texts. This was usually reinforced by the traditional pattern of religious home life. As time went by the number of children committing so much time to Jewish education dropped, and by 1914 it was estimated that only half of Glasgow's Jewish children were receiving any Jewish education. The Talmud Torah with over 700 pupils moved to its own premises in Turriff Street in 1918, and in 1922 a Hebrew College for teenagers was established by Dr Nathan Morris, an acknowledged expert in teaching Hebrew. This provided its pupils with Hebrew language and Jewish culture, and encouraged them to become Hebrew teachers themselves. Despite competition from synagogue Hebrew classes, the Talmud Torah maintained its leading position in Jewish education in Glasgow well after the Second World War.

For some boys the regular Hebrew classes were supplemented with attendance later in the evening at the Glasgow Yeshivah. This was founded in 1908 to provide a more intensive learning pattern along the lines found in Eastern Europe, with an emphasis on teaching of the Talmud. With the high concentration of children in just a few Gorbals schools, it was suggested in 1909 that a Jewish school could be established. Another suggestion was that Jewish pupils begin their school day at 9am with an hour of religious instruction, while Christian children had their religious studies. An attempt by Glasgow Zionists to found their own Hebrew language school in 1911 foundered because of problems of funding and accommodation.

The Glasgow Jewish Representative Council took the lead, soon after its founding in 1914, in attempts to establish a Jewish school. Its aim was to provide Jewish tuition during school hours, and to extend Jewish teaching to all the children in the community.   However, negotiations with the Glasgow School Board broke down, as did further negotiations in the 1920s and 1930s, over the Board's insistence that Jewish and Hebrew teaching be limited to one hour a day.

Jewish education was clearly a priority if a new generation was to resist assimilatory trends, and grow up sharing the customs and mores of their parents and grandparents.   Unfortunately, in the early years, some of the Hebrew tuition was unsatisfactory because teachers had an imperfect grasp of English.   Thus Jewish education was compared unfavourably with the standard of secular teaching in the local schools.   Some parents were happy with their children's exposure to traditional Eastern European teachers, but many children were alienated by the experience.

A Jewish primary school, Calderwood Lodge, was finally established in Glasgow in 1962, under the joint auspices of the Glasgow Zionist Organisation and the Glasgow Board of Jewish Education.   This was intended to improve standards in the provision of Jewish education, integrate the teaching of Hebrew and Judaism into the curriculum, and provide the basis for further Jewish learning in the teenage years and beyond.

The opening of a Jewish day school in Glasgow and the gradual concentration of the community's children there, as well as demographic changes, led to the gradual weakening of the synagogue Hebrew classes through the 1970s.   There was competition also from Lubavitch, an outreach based Chassidic movement, which had recently established itself in Glasgow, and their Sunday morning Hebrew Classes eventually became the main source for out-of-school Jewish education in Glasgow.   The synagogues in Newton Mearns, both Orthodox and Reform, however, continued to maintain their own education classes.

In Edinburgh, the main classes were held in the basement of the Graham Street Synagogue until 1914, and subsequently moved to Sciennes School, where they continued to meet for 2 hours daily.   When the synagogue moved to Salisbury Road, classes operated there.   Similar classes could be found in the smaller communities such as Dundee and Aberdeen.

POLITICS

The community was active in the political sphere.   A number of Jewish immigrants had been active in the Bund, the Jewish trade union in Russia, and many were strongly committed to socialism, carrying on Bundist activity in Scotland.   There were Jewish trade unions in the Glasgow tailoring and cabinet-making industries, and many Jews took part in wider union activities.   Jews were also active in local politics, and Michael Simons, a leading member of the Garnethill community and director of a major fruit importing business, was elected a Bailie in the 1880s.   It was widely believed that Simons's prominent position within the Glasgow Council had assisted in the acceptance of the Jewish community in the city.   Another early Glasgow

Jewish Town Councillor was Manny Shinwell, then local secretary of the British Seafarer's Union, first co-opted as a member of the Fairfield Ward in Govan in 1916. He later was elected Independent Labour MP for Linlithgow, held ministerial posts under Ramsey Macdonald and Clement Attlee, and was created Baron Shinwell in 1970.

Jews were to be found in all the political parties, and there were even a few in the Communist Party and in a small anarchist group in the West End of Glasgow. A few Jews returned to Russia after the Revolution in 1917, although greater numbers left to settle in the United States. However, it was the Labour Party that received most of the community's political support in the interwar years, especially with the rise of fascism in the 1930s.

The major political activity, particularly after the Nazis seized power in Germany in 1933, was aiding Jewish refugees and organising a boycott of German goods. The republican movement in Spain also attracted some active support in the 1930s. During the 1930s there were Jewish socialist societies and left wing Jewish friendly societies, such as the Unity Lodge and Workers' Circle in Glasgow, with both a political and welfare message. In the post-war period Jewish political activity centred mainly round support for Israel, but Jews were still also active in the main political parties. The traditional Jewish prominence in the Labour Party was balanced by growing involvement with the Conservatives and the Liberals. Sir Myer (later Lord) Galpern, the first Jewish Lord Provost of Glasgow, and Maurice Miller were elected as Labour MPs in the 1960s and 1970s, by which time Malcolm Rifkind had become Conservative MP for Edinburgh Pentlands. At one time Secretary of State for Scotland, he later served as Defence and then Foreign Secretary in Conservative administrations in the 1990s.

• Zionism

The 1890s saw the beginnings of Zionist activities in Scotland, and this eventually developed into the dominant Jewish political ideology. Branches of *Chovevei Zion* ('Lovers of Zion') were formed in Edinburgh (1890) and Glasgow (1891) to help Jewish settlers in Palestine. There were delegates from Scotland at the Second Zionist Congress in Basel in 1898, and political and fund-raising activities quickly followed in both cities.

Zionist groups organised social and sporting activities to improve the physical condition of the Jewish community. Meetings in Glasgow regularly attracted audiences of over 1000, and new Zionist groups catering for women and youth were founded. Zionist reading rooms provided a place for the community to meet, to learn about the early pioneers, and to study the Hebrew language.

Pogroms in Russia that left a trail of death and destruction, especially a particularly brutal one in Kishinev in 1905, gave a considerable impetus to Zionist efforts. However, some Jews, impatient with the difficulties in organising instant mass settlement in Palestine, supported the idea of finding another territory where the Jews could form a national majority. A heated debate followed, lasting for many years, with the traditional Zionists, who saw Palestine as the only natural Jewish homeland, ultimately emerging successful.

Zionist groups also founded a network of friendly and self-help societies. In 1909 a co-operative society was founded aiming to settle Glasgow Jews on the land, showing the importance placed on practical Zionism. The Balfour Declaration of November 1917, indicating British Government support for a Jewish homeland in Palestine, was greeted with much enthusiasm in Scotland. This gave considerable impetus to Zionist political activities, especially in Glasgow, but also in Edinburgh, Dundee and Ayr, and to increasingly successful fund-raising for Jewish settlement in Palestine.

The founding of the State of Israel, and Israel's victory in the 1967 War channelled the enthusiasm of most of the community, and there was a small but significant trickle of immigrants to the Jewish state. Fundraising for Israeli institutions, whether welfare, religious, educational, or environmental, was an important communal priority, and many of these funding bodies became some of the largest and most successful communal groups, attracting a dedicated and effective leadership. The women's organisations, Emunah, and especially the Women's International Zionist Organisation (WIZO), were involved in continual fundraising activity, WIZO established many different groups, mainly in Glasgow but also in Edinburgh and the other communities.

During the 1970s and 1980s, Dr Albert Jacob led the Dundee community's response to local outbreaks of antisemitism, some of which related to the anti-Israel policies of local politicians who had twinned the city with Nablus.

BUSINESS AND PROFESSIONS

Much of the early economic activity of members of the Jewish communities in Scotland was based on production and merchandising of goods. New Jewish entrepreneurs set up businesses manufacturing a wide range of clothing, including the ubiquitous cloth cap. They were also active in warehousing, entertainments, and whisky. Most of the working members of Scottish Jewry were heavily concentrated in just a few trades and industries, such as shop-keeping, tailoring, shoe and slipper making, and the manufacture and distribution of furniture and picture frames.

Callendar's Jewish Bakery, Glasgow Gorbals, c1930

In the years before the First World War, many Jews began their businesses peddling to mining communities. Jews travelled from Glasgow to Ayrshire and Lanarkshire, from Edinburgh into Fife, and from Falkirk to Stirlingshire. Eventually, many of these new immigrants set up successful businesses of their own, often aided by loans and credit from the Hebrew Benevolent Loan societies. However, despite the success of some individuals, much of the Jewish community, especially those in the Gorbals in Glasgow, remained trapped in poverty, and there was a continual call on the funds of the Jewish Boards of Guardians for relief. In the 1930s it was not uncommon for over 10% of the community to be receiving such aid.

Despite financial difficulties, the opportunities offered by the Scottish educational system, supported by Carnegie grants to university students, proved increasingly attractive. Encouraged by parents who hoped to see their sons attain educational standards and financial security which they themselves would never achieve, increasing numbers of Jews entered the universities of Glasgow and Edinburgh, especially in the years after the First World War. Higher education was for many the means of escape from the old ghetto trades. Medicine was the most popular career choice, offering status and income. Prof Sir Abraham Goldberg became a respected and world-renowned figure. Many Jews also went into teaching, but law was less popular as it was hard for Jews to break into the conservative Scottish legal profession. Nonetheless, there have been three High Court Judges, Lord Kissen, Lord Caplan, and Lady Cosgrove, who was the first woman to be appointed to the High Court, and later to the Inner House of the Court of Session, and Prof Sir Gerald Gordon is recognised as the leading expert on Scottish criminal law.

Hazel Cosgrove wearing the robes of a Senator of the College of Justice

A considerable number of foreign Jewish medical students studied medicine in Scotland in the 1920s and 1930s. Many Jewish Americans came to Glasgow, Edinburgh, Dundee and St. Andrews, having been denied medical school places in the United States because of discriminatory entry quotas. Many German Jewish physicians found the Scottish qualification regulations much simpler than those in England, and studied in Glasgow and Edinburgh in preparation for examinations prior to British medical practice.

After the war, the most popular subjects for Jewish students were medicine, dentistry, teaching, law, and accountancy, but gradually media studies, computing, and information technology changed the form of Jewish professional life, and the economic base of the community widened to include many new professions while the traditional businesses in furniture and clothing manufacture declined.

SOCIAL AND CULTURAL ACTIVITIES

The development of the cultural life of the community was considerably enhanced by the newcomers. Jewish Literary Societies were formed in Edinburgh (1888) and in Glasgow (1893), and these kept their members informed on a wide variety of Jewish and general topics. They sponsored English language classes and helped the newcomers to adjust to their new life. The Edinburgh Society, still active today, continues to provide a platform for matters of Jewish interest and also attracts members not affiliated to the synagogue.

Choral and dramatic societies were formed in Glasgow and Edinburgh, and the Zionist groups had a wide range of cultural and social activities. The friendly societies also had an important social function. Masonic Lodges were

formed in Glasgow (Lodge Montefiore, 1888) and in Edinburgh (Lodge Solomon). Jewish drama flowered in Scotland with the arrival of Avrom Greenbaum in the 1920s, and with the formation of the Glasgow Jewish Institute Players in 1936 new standards in local Jewish dramatic art were set. Greenbaum wrote many of the plays himself, reflecting his preoccupation with man's fight for freedom.

Benno Schotz with the sculpture of his wife Milly

In the visual arts Benno Schotz and Hannah Frank were major Jewish figures. Schotz arrived in Glasgow from Estonia in 1912 and his outstanding talent was rewarded by his appointment as the Queen's Sculptor-in-Ordinary in Scotland. Frank's Art Nouveau sculptures and drawings have delighted generations of admirers over her long lifetime. Glasgow was also briefly home to such distinguished refugee artists as Josef Herman and Yankel Adler.

Illustration by Hannah Frank, c1928

Yiddish newspapers appeared irregularly in Glasgow around the turn of the century, but serious Jewish journalism did not begin until Zevi Golombok started the *Glasgow Jewish Evening Times* in 1914, and later a Yiddish monthly, the *Yiddishe Shtimme* (Jewish Voice). In 1928, recognising the local decline in Yiddish, he founded the English language *Jewish Echo*, which was published every Friday in Glasgow and served all the Jewish communities of Scotland. After the paper closed in June 1992, the Manchester *Jewish Telegraph* set up a Scottish edition.

Youth groups were formed from the first years of the twentieth century with youth sections of Zionist and Jewish literary groups, as well as Scouts and the Jewish Lads' Brigade. The Brigade, based on the Boys' Brigade, aimed to make loyal British citizens out of the immigrants, and its Glasgow branch dates back to 1903. Later it accepted girls as members and now boasts the only Jewish bagpipe band in the world. The first Jewish sports club, the Bar Kochba, was set up in the Talmud Torah building in 1933 and formed the precursor of the successful Glasgow Maccabi. Zionist youth groups such as Habonim and Bnei Akiva, which linked Jewish education, love of Israel, and youth club activities, also prospered in the post war era.

Jewish Institutes were established in Glasgow and Edinburgh from the turn of the century, with regular social and cultural events in the winter and sporting activities in the summer. The Glasgow Jewish Institute achieved its greatest success as a community centre when it moved into premises in South Portland Street, next door to the synagogue, in the 1930s. The Institute supported a theatre which was home to the Jewish Institute Players, later the Avrom Greenbaum Players.

Boys' Choir,
South Portland Street Synagogue,
Glasgow Gorbals, c1961

REPRESENTATIVE BODIES

Jewish Representative Councils were formed in Glasgow in 1914, and a year later in Edinburgh, to act as a unifying force in the community and to provide representation on matters of national and international importance. The Glasgow Council grew out of the committee set up to protest about the false accusations in the Beilis 'blood libel' case in Kiev. There had been no single community-wide structure in Glasgow since the collapse of the United Synagogue in 1906, and leadership had been provided mainly by the Garnethill Synagogue.

In Edinburgh, the first concerns of the Representative Council were with alien Jews interned under wartime regulations. In Glasgow too, support for alien Jews was a priority, and affidavits were provided for all the 2000 foreign Jews in the city. After the War, the Edinburgh community gradually centralised its activities within the synagogue, and all the representative functions were assumed by the Edinburgh Hebrew Congregation.

In Glasgow, the Council involved itself in trying to provide a communal structure for *shechitah*, supporting moves for a Jewish school, and co-ordinating Jewish support for the war effort. To illustrate to the wider community the presence of Glasgow Jews in the armed forces and to show the community's support for them, a major service was held in the South Portland Street Synagogue in October 1916.

During the 1930s, the Council continued to act to protect and represent the Jews of Glasgow, to fight antisemitism, and to support the economic boycott against Nazi Germany. While there were no clashes with fascists as happened in London, the Council had to steer a cautious role while mounting defensive action against anti-Jewish activities. In the post-war years the Council became the leading Jewish body in Scotland, dealing with civic and religious bodies, and providing a lively debating forum for community issues, as well as resolving issues arising within the local community. The Council took the lead in interfaith dialogue, beginning with the Church of Scotland, in order to promote Christian understanding of Jewish sensitivities. It also worked closely with the new ethnic and religious communities, mainly from the Indian sub-continent, which settled in Glasgow after the War.

In 1982, the Glasgow Representative Council and the Edinburgh Hebrew Congregation, with the communities in Dundee and Aberdeen and the informal grouping in Argyll and Bute, formed the Scottish Jewish Standing Committee, to provide a formal link between the Jewish communities of Scotland and to co-ordinate policy in its dealings with the wider Scottish society. With the establishment of a Scottish Parliament after the devolution referendum of 1998, this was renamed the Scottish Council of Jewish Communities, and it has been this Council which has linked the scattered Jewish communities of Scotland while providing an effective and comprehensive representative body widely recognised by Government and civic bodies.

CONCLUSION

While the growth of the Scottish Jewish community had been considerable, its numbers at its peak between 1935 and 1960 never exceeded 20 000. It was estimated that there were about 15 000 Jews in Glasgow in 1939, and over 2000 in Edinburgh following the influx of Jewish refugees from Nazi terror. However, the strength of Scottish Jewry derives in the main from those Jews who arrived in the country in the two decades leading up to 1914.

Glasgow in the twentieth century has been one of the major Jewish communities in Britain, exceeded in size only by London, Manchester, and Leeds. Its Gorbals community was still at its peak in 1945, but the movement of Jews south to the suburbs was accelerating. While some Jews moved to the West End, and reinforced the membership at Garnethill, most Jews were settling in areas such as Govanhill, Battlefield, Langside, and Shawlands, whilst many moved further south to Giffnock and beyond. This population shift was accompanied by a move of some of the institutions out of the Gorbals, beginning with the Zionist Centre to Queen Square. However, the Jewish Institute, the Jewish Board of Guardians, the majority of the synagogues, kosher butchers, bakers, and grocery shops remained in the Gorbals, which was still the centre of the community. Here also, Geneen's Hotel, run by the legendary Sophie Geneen, dispensed charity as well as food.

The opening of the synagogue in Salisbury Road gave Edinburgh Jewry a cohesion which made it the envy of many larger communities. With its scholarly rabbi, Salis Daiches, they attempted a synthesis of the best of Jewish and Scottish life, but had to accept a drift from traditional observance while showing a Jewish vitality which belied their numerical strength. The smaller Jewish communities around Scotland declined in numbers as their members migrated to Glasgow and Edinburgh, where the Jewish facilities were concentrated. In essence Scottish Jewry became a 'tale of two cities'.

In the immediate post-war period Jewish communities throughout Scotland were at a numerical peak, but numbers began to decline from the 1960s as increasingly well-educated young people left for careers in London. Others settled in Manchester or left for Israel, North America or Australia, while assimilation and intermarriage also reduced the size of the religious community, and continue to pose serious demographic questions for the future.

The challenge to Scottish Jewry was to survive beyond the immigrant generation and to establish new institutions to foster communal cohesion and to maintain Jewish identity. These years showed considerable economic and educational advance, and there was little serious antisemitism. Jews had become an established part of the Scottish scene with achievements in many areas of community, local and national life.

The Contemporary Community

From their first beginnings, the Jewish communities in Scotland have built up a network of organisations to cater for their needs. These cover the area of communal provision for religious, welfare, educational and social activities within a structure adapted both to the modern community and contemporary Jewish life.

REPRESENTATIVE BODIES

All the Jewish communities of Scotland are represented on the Scottish Council of Jewish Communities (SCoJeC), which was formed in 1998 as a democratic umbrella body in the wake of the establishment of a devolved Parliament and administration. During the past ten years, SCoJeC has taken the lead in identifying Jewish concerns, flagging up incidents of antisemitism, co-operating with other faith and ethnic communities in promoting good relations, and defending the rights of members of the Jewish community. It was successful in obtaining legislation at Holyrood to ensure that Jewish requirements are taken into account when a couple have a civil divorce, and has provided the Jewish voice on a wide range of issues, not just those with a specific religious interest. The Council also organises activities for the smaller communities and isolated individuals living outwith any formal community, and maintains an Enquiry Desk to help callers make contact with Jewish organisations and answer questions about Judaism. SCoJeC has been praised by senior members of successive Scottish administrations as an example for other communities of how to engage effectively with the civic and political process.

Rabbi Moshe Rubin and Cardinal Keith O'Brien plant a tree on the 40th anniversary of Nostra Aetate, Edinburgh, 2006

The Jews of Edinburgh are represented by the Edinburgh Hebrew Congregation which is Orthodox, and the smaller Liberal community Sukkat Shalom, while in Glasgow the Jewish Representative Council co-ordinates the activities of almost 50 Jewish organisations. The Council has taken an active role in defending the rights of Jews to observe their religion and in fighting discrimination, working closely with local religious and civic bodies in Glasgow and East Renfrewshire. The Representative Council, like SCoJeC and the synagogues in Edinburgh and Glasgow, is affiliated to the Board of Deputies of British Jews. The Council has often taken a lead in interfaith and anti-racist activities and has played a major role in developing Christian-Jewish understanding. It aims to promote greater awareness of contemporary Jewish issues, organises annual meetings for *Yom HaShoah,* and supports Armistice Day commemorations. It also provides speakers for any organisation about Judaism, organises synagogue visits, and gives presentations to school groups and other interested bodies.

RELIGIOUS ACTIVITIES

There are about ten synagogues in Scotland. Edinburgh has an Orthodox synagogue, and a Liberal community which does not have its own building. There are small synagogues in Aberdeen and Dundee, while in Glasgow there are five Orthodox synagogues, organised in a Council of Synagogues, and one Reform synagogue, while Lubavitch provides regular religious services in one of the community care homes. *Shabbat* and Festival services are held in all the main synagogues with a smaller number holding the traditional thrice daily prayers.

The synagogues provide a wide range of social, educational and cultural activities expanding the religious life of their congregations. Some synagogues have ladies' groups, Friendship Clubs for their older members, and mother and toddler groups.

A wedding in the recently restored Victorian Garnethill Synagogue

Garnethill Synagogue, built in 1879, is a listed building, and its fine Victorian architecture has recently been beautifully restored. The Giffnock and Newlands Synagogue, the largest in Scotland, has a *mikvah*, a *kollel* for advanced rabbinical studies, and a Community Centre within its complex, the latter providing a wide range of Jewish educational facilities for the youth and adults of the community. When Queens Park Synagogue closed in 2002, its magnificent set of modern stained glass windows, designed by John K Clark and rich in colour and symbolism, were relocated in the Giffnock Synagogue.

In Edinburgh the synagogue was reconstructed in 1981 to provide a community centre as well as 500 seats for religious services. The building is the focus for a wide range of social, cultural and educational activities. The Aberdeen Synagogue is located in a Georgian listed building and provides accommodation for both religious services and community activities, as does the purpose-built synagogue in Dundee erected after the previous building was demolished in the 1970s to make way for the Tay Bridge approaches.

Many of the synagogues have their own burial grounds. In Glasgow and Edinburgh there are Hebrew Burial Societies, but, despite close links with the local synagogues, they remain independent of them. In Glasgow there is also a Kashrut Commission which supervises the local kosher facilities including a restaurant, bakers, caterers and East Renfrewshire Council catering facilities at Calderwood Lodge and Jewish Care, while in Edinburgh the rabbi approves a number of local establishments, including a vegetarian Indian restaurant, as being kosher.

EDUCATION AND CULTURE

In Glasgow there is a Jewish day school, Calderwood Lodge, founded in 1962, which caters for the majority of Jewish primary schoolchildren. Initially an independent school, Calderwood Lodge was taken into the state system in 1982. The school is now run by East Renfrewshire Council, though Jewish studies at the school are funded and managed by Calderwood Jewish Education. The Edinburgh communities and the Glasgow Reform Synagogue have their own congregational Hebrew classes.

Within the last few years the United Jewish Israel Appeal (UJIA) has developed a Renewal Division which aims to renew Jewish life in Scotland. From its base at the Jewish Community Centre in Giffnock, it organises Jewish Assemblies in schools with a significant number of Jewish pupils. It maintains a Resource Centre with a library of Jewish books and videos and provides lectures and discussion groups as well as courses in Hebrew and understanding Judaism. UJIA Renewal also supports Jewish youth activities and has built up close links with Jews in Edinburgh.

Educational activities are enhanced by a *kollel* with around 10 postgraduate rabbinical students, which runs classes of a more traditional nature for children and adults. So too does Lubavitch which also aims to reach out to Jews who have become estranged from their faith, organising a variety of religious and social programmes. Jewish students in Scotland have the support of the Northern Region Jewish Chaplaincy Board, which encourages student educational and religious activities and provides a Jewish student chaplain who is available to provide individual counselling for Jewish students in the various universities and colleges throughout Scotland. Adult education meetings are provided by a wide range of communal organisations, including the religious bodies, the Jewish Archives Centre and the Glasgow Jewish Educational Forum.

The Scottish Jewish Archives Centre, based in Garnethill Synagogue, preserves, catalogues, and displays the records of the history of all the Jewish communities of Scotland. Its growing collection is on display within the synagogue building, in a recently redesigned visitor centre. This incorporates a timeline of Scottish Jewish history, and an exhibition on immigration entitled *A New Life in Scotland*. The Glasgow Friends of Yiddish hold regular classes and meetings to learn the language and to preserve Yiddish culture. There are a number of organisations that seek to provide meetings of a cultural or political nature, often bringing speakers to Glasgow from England or Israel. In Edinburgh this function continues to be provided by the Jewish Literary Society, and the *Edinburgh Star* magazine is published quarterly with articles of general and local interest and community activity listings.

There have also been Jewish choirs. Over the years Jewish Choral Society concerts have raised many thousands of pounds for Scottish charities. The Glasgow Jewish Singers perform regularly at synagogue services and weddings, and at concerts both within and outwith the community. The Edinburgh Synagogue male voice choir also performs regularly at services and weddings.

ISRAEL

The Jews of Scotland have traditionally had strong ties with Israel, and these are fostered by a network of organisations based mainly in Glasgow but also in Edinburgh. Fund-raising groups collect money for universities in Jerusalem and Tel Aviv, and for Israeli medical services. A number of women's groups affiliated to WIZO collect funds to provide facilities for disadvantaged women and children of all races and religions in Israel, and also support some local social and cultural activities. Similar activities are offered by Child and Youth Aliya and the religious women's group Emunah.

The United Jewish Israel Appeal (UJIA) raises funds to rescue Jews from countries of distress, such as in the former Soviet Union, and bring them to Israel, as well as to improve the Israeli social fabric. The Jewish National Fund, (in Hebrew *Keren Kayemet LeYisrael* or KKL), raises funds for specific projects related to the environment and social welfare in Israel.

Support for Israel has generally been steady and loyal, and the community holds an annual event to mark Israel's Independence Day. However, its support is not always uncritical. Organisations such as the Glasgow Zionist Federation and the Scottish Friends of Israel hold different views, and arrange public meetings addressed by Israeli and other speakers. Glasgow Friends of Peace Now maintain close contact with the Israeli peace movement and have held regular meetings with Palestinian representatives and the Israeli left.

WELFARE

During the past two decades there has been a complete transformation in Jewish welfare services in Scotland as agencies have become more professional and institutions have moved to be nearer their client groups. Jewish Care

Scotland works in partnership with East Renfrewshire Council as a recognised care provider, delivering care and support to members of the Jewish community according to the religious and ethnic needs of its members. It also co-ordinates a remarkable number of welfare activities from its centre at the Maccabi complex in Giffnock where it operates in conjunction with other bodies such as the Jewish Blind Society and Cosgrove Care.

The Glasgow Jewish Sick Visiting Association has a group of voluntary workers who visit Jewish patients and residents in long stay hospitals and residential institutions throughout the West of Scotland, and the League of Jewish Women assists with hospital transport and home visiting, and runs a small club for the elderly.

The Jewish Housing Association, now called Arklet Housing, has become a major social housing provider. It provides sheltered housing and augmented care for the Jewish elderly on two sites within the Giffnock area. Cosgrove Care, which looks after Jews with learning disabilities, has also considerably expanded its client base, and has moved its residential and support services to Giffnock. Newark Care, founded in 1949 as the Jewish Old Age Home for Scotland, has relocated from Pollokshields and now provides residential and nursing home facilities in Giffnock and Newton Mearns.

YOUTH

There are Jewish youth organisations operating in both Glasgow and Edinburgh, and there are links between the youth groups in the two cities. In Glasgow there is an informal Jewish Youth Forum, supported by a youth worker based at the Jewish Community Centre, who seeks to co-ordinate activities and run special events. Most of the youth groups receive financial and operational support and professional assistance from UJIA Renewal.

Most of the Jewish youth groups have regular weekly meetings often supplemented by additional activities around the time of the Jewish festivals. Thus the Jewish youth movements have a strong educational and cultural influence on the life of the community. Bnei Akiva is a religious Zionist youth movement adhering to Jewish religious tradition with a strong Israeli orientation. Habonim-Dror is a Zionist youth movement with close links to the Israeli kibbutz and labour movement, while the Federation of Zionist Youth runs regular educational meetings for teenagers. RSY/Netzer is the Zionist youth group of the Reform Synagogue movement. There are also Jewish Brownie and Guide packs, and the Jewish Lads and Girls Brigade encourages disciplined participation in sport, drill, crafts, and social activities.

Glasgow Maccabi, whose aims include providing a Jewish environment and fostering Jewish identity and an awareness of Israel, provides youth, cultural, and sporting activities at its complex in Giffnock, which also houses communal welfare and other facilities.

Judaism: A Brief Account

PHILOSOPHY

The earliest of the three major monotheistic religions, Judaism believes in an incorporeal God who is the universal creator of all that exists. Orthodox Judaism believes that God revealed both the text and the oral interpretation of the *Torah*, the first five books of the Bible, to Moses, and has communicated with the Jewish people through inspired prophets, as recorded in the Hebrew Scriptures. Judaism does not distinguish between the status of ethical and ritual obligations, seeing both as mandated by God, and actions are regarded as being more important than personal beliefs. Judaism believes in a force of evil, generally conceived as an individual's 'evil inclination', but also that people have freedom of choice, and will be rewarded or punished by God according to the manner in which they exercise it. Unlike Christianity, Judaism does not believe in original sin.

The *Torah* tells of the Divine promise to the Jewish people of the land of Israel, and the restoration of Jewish sovereignty and the ingathering of the exiles to Zion are central to Jewish prayer. The modern political philosophy that underpinned the re-establishment of a Jewish state in its ancient homeland is known as Zionism.

Although not mentioned in the *Torah*, canonical Jewish belief includes an 'end time' or Messianic Age, when a Messiah will establish an era of global peace, and bring about the return of Jewish exiles to Israel and the resurrection of the dead.

Judaism accepts but does not seek converts, believing that non-Jews should follow their own path. Tradition identifies 613 commandments in the *Torah* for Jews to follow, of which only seven, including obligations relating to social justice, sexual morality, and animal welfare, are regarded as applying to non-Jews

TEXTS

The Bible, written in Hebrew, consists of three parts of which the *Torah*, the Five Books of Moses, is the most important. The others are the *Prophets*, and the *Holy Writings*. The word '*Tanach*' is an acronym for the Hebrew names of these three. It is obviously inappropriate to refer to the *Tanach* as the 'Old Testament' since this suggests that it is seen not in its own right, but merely in the context of the Christian 'New Testament'. (Jewish perception of Jesus varies: some think of him as a great teacher, and others view him as one of many false claimants to be the Messiah, but there his no disagreement that his teachings are not included in the Jewish Bible).

The *Talmud*, which was compiled in its present form between 100 and 400 CE in Babylon and Israel, is in many ways the central text of Judaism, as it is based on oral traditions ascribed to Moses. It is mainly a record of rabbinic debates on Jewish law and the interpretation of the bible, and forms the basis of traditional Jewish law. The *Shulkhan Aruch* is the main codification of this law, dating from the 16th century.

HISTORY

Jewish tradition counts dates from the Creation, so that 2008 CE is the year 5768. Since we cannot know the length of the 'days' of the creation described in Genesis, many regard this as being compatible with modern science.

As described in the *Torah*, Abraham left his family in Mesopotamia, and settled in Canaan, modern Israel, which he was promised in perpetuity by God. Abraham, his son Isaac, and grandson Jacob (also called Israel), are referred to as the Fathers of Judaism, and their wives, Sarah, Rebecca, Rachel, and Leah as the Mothers. The descendants of Jacob's twelve sons became the twelve tribes of Israel.

One of Jacob's sons, Joseph, was abducted to Egypt, and subsequently rose to the position of Viceroy. Jacob took the rest of his family to Egypt to escape famine in Canaan, but the Israelites were later enslaved by the Egyptians for 210 years, before being led to freedom by Moses. After receiving the *Torah* from God on Mount Sinai, Moses led them on a 40-year journey through the wilderness to the borders of the Promised Land of Israel. They then crossed the River Jordan under his successor, Joshua, who divided the land amongst the twelve tribes.

During the subsequent 300 years the Israelites were led by a succession of judges and prophets. These included Deborah, who defeated the Philistines, and Samuel, who anointed Saul, and later David, as king. David established his capital in Hebron. Later, some 3000 years ago, he moved it to Jerusalem, and it was here that his son, Solomon, built the Temple. After Solomon's death, the northern tribes seceded, establishing the kingdom of Israel with its capital at Shechem, while Jerusalem remained capital of the southern kingdom of Judea. Israel was overrun by the Assyrians in 722 BCE and the people were sent into exile. Judea survived a further 135 years until Jerusalem was captured and the Temple destroyed by the Babylonians in 586 BCE.

After the fall of Babylon a group of exiles led by Ezra and Nehemiah returned to join the small Jewish community that had remained in Judea. They built the second Temple, which survived until the Romans destroyed Jerusalem in 70 CE. To eradicate even the memory of the Jewish kingdom, the Romans renamed Judea 'Palestine' and dispersed the Jews around their empire. Large Jewish communities grew up in North Africa, Mesopotamia, Italy, and Central Europe, although significant numbers remained, especially in the Galilee.

Mediaeval Jewish communities in Europe suffered greatly during the murderous antisemitism of the Crusades and the Inquisition; Jews were expelled from England in 1290, France in 1306, and even from Spain in 1492, where an earlier 'Golden Age' had yielded many literary and scientific masterpieces. Some found refuge in Italy, the Ottoman Empire, and the Netherlands, from whence a few eventually came to Britain when Jews were formally re-admitted by Cromwell. However, most of the British Jewish community came from Germany or the

Russian 'Pale of Settlement' to escape the economic privations and pogroms of the late 19th and early 20th century, or fleeing the Holocaust during the Nazi era of 1933-45, in which six million Jews perished.

Small Jewish communities have always remained in Israel, principally in Tiberias, Safed, Jaffa, and Jerusalem, since pious Jews have always sought to end their days there. However political Zionism was only born in 1897, when the First Zionist Congress at Basle endorsed the proposal of the Viennese journalist Theodore Herzl for a state in the biblical Promised Land in which Jews could escape persecution and achieve self-determination. After the First World War, Britain was given the League of Nations Mandate for Palestine and, following the United Nations resolution in November 1947, which called for its partition into Jewish and Arab states, the modern State of Israel was founded when Britain withdrew in May 1948.

GROUPS

Despite their shared belief, the ethnic origins of Jews are diverse, and there are three principal groupings:

• Sephardim – properly of Iberian origin, although the term is often used to include those of other Mediterranean, Arabian and North African origin. Ladino is a Hispanic language with Hebrew admixtures which was common to many Sephardim especially from the Balkans and Turkey.

• Eastern Communities – sometimes also loosely referred to as Sephardim, with origins in Asia or the Arabian Peninsula and including smaller groups such as the Jews of Ethiopia, and the Bnei Israel and Cochin Jews of India.

• Ashkenazim – whose ancestry is in Central and Eastern Europe and Russia. Yiddish is a Germanic language with Slavic and Hebrew admixtures which was widely spoken by Eastern European Jews.

Although there are more Sephardic than Askenazi Jews in Israel, the reverse is the case worldwide, as the Jewish communities of the USA, Canada, and the UK are substantially Ashkenazi.

Cutting across these ethnic groups there are distinct denominations that have different understandings of the status of the Torah and of Jewish law:

• Orthodox – The principles of Orthodox Judaism have not changed significantly since Biblical times, since they presuppose that the *Torah* as interpreted in the Talmud was given directly by God. Within Orthodox Judaism there are two main groupings: the *Charedim*, or so-called 'Strictly Orthodox', and the Modern Orthodox. The latter participate more in secular activities than do *Charedi* Jews, but are nevertheless faithful to traditional religious practices. The *Charedim* are one of the largest and most conservative movements, with several subsections including various groups of *Chassidim*. They tend to reject many aspects of modern life, and, for example, generally wear traditional clothing, whereas the Modern Orthodox engage more with the modern world, for example by entering secular employment.

•   Reform – The Reform movement rejects much of Orthodox practice while retaining many of the underlying teachings of Judaism. Unlike Orthodox movements it allows women to be ordained as rabbis, permits men and women to sit together in the synagogue, and regards cremation as acceptable.

•   Conservative – known in Britain as Masorti (Traditional): This movement began as a reaction to Reform Judaism in the United States, and although based on a more Liberal understanding of traditional texts, it still retains many Orthodox practices.

•   Liberal – Liberal Judaism views the *Torah* as a product of its time rather than as the literal word of God, and therefore subject to change. Liberal Jews do not attach great significance to traditional codes for dress and diet but regard them as a matter of choice.

In addition there are a number of Jews who regard Judaism as having less to do with faith than with cultural identity, but many of these still identify very closely with the Jewish community and observe its cultural traditions.

SHABBAT AND FESTIVALS

•   Shabbat – the Sabbath is the weekly day of rest, beginning at dusk on Friday and lasting until it is completely dark on Saturday night. It commemorates the fact that God rested on the seventh day of creation, which Judaism regards as part of creation itself, and is observed with varying degrees of strictness by the different Jewish denominations.

In traditional Judaism there is a clear code that determines which activities are permitted and which are forbidden on *Shabbat*. Generally, creative work is prohibited, so that the Sabbath is a family and home based festival, free from mundane concerns. The prohibition on making fire includes turning on any electrical apparatus, such as lights, television, and telephone. The prohibition on cooking means that *Shabbat* meals are prepared beforehand and kept warm from Friday afternoon. Carrying, travelling, and writing are also prohibited. It is not permitted to ask a non-Jew to do anything one could not do oneself, except in an emergency, when any prohibition must be set aside if life is in danger. As individual levels of Sabbath observance vary, it is always wise to ask people individually, in order to determine their needs.

The principal festivals are also observed from dusk to nightfall, and are generally subject to the same rules as *Shabbat*. They are:

•   Rosh Hashanah – New Year is a two-day festival (usually in September). This begins a ten-day period of contemplation and repentance culminating in Yom Kippur. The centerpiece of the synagogue service is the blowing of the ram's horn (*shofar*).

•   Yom Kippur – the Day of Atonement is marked by an entire day spent in worship, contemplation, and fasting.

• **Sukkot – Tabernacles** is an autumn festival, five days after Yom Kippur, that, together with Shemini Atseret and Simchat Torah, lasts eight days (seven in Israel and for non-Orthodox groups). Orthodox Jews build a sukkah or tabernacle, a temporary hut roofed with vegetation, and eat in it during the festival, to commemorate the nomadic lives of the Israelites after leaving Egypt.

• **Shemini Atseret – the Eighth Day** and
Simchat Torah – Celebration of the Torah are the days after Sukkot, when the annual cycle of readings from the *Torah* is concluded and immediately recommenced.

Passover Seder in
Aberdeen Synagogue, 1950s

• **Pesach – Passover** commemorates the Exodus from Egypt. The calendar is adjusted to ensure that it falls in spring (March-April), and it lasts eight days (seven in Israel and for non-Orthodox groups). The ceremonial Seder meal eaten in the home on the first two nights includes many elements symbolising the escape from slavery and the foundation of the Jewish Nation. Matzah replaces bread for the entire week, and many Jews are more than usually meticulous about avoiding prohibited foods. Seven weeks, known as the Omer, are counted from the second night of Pesach leading up to Shavuot.

• **Shavuot – 'Weeks' or Pentecost** lasts two days in June (one in Israel and for non-Orthodox groups) and commemorates the giving of the *Torah* on Mount Sinai. Observances include studying throughout the night.

Other festivals on which the prohibitions of *Shabbat* do not apply include:

• **Chanukah** – festival of lights in December, commemorating the rededication of the Temple in Jerusalem by the Maccabees, following its desecration by the Greeks. It is marked by some by the exchange of gifts.

Chanukah lights in the
Dundee Synagogue, 2004

•   Tu b'Shvat – New Year for Trees is the beginning of the growing season in Israel (February) once the start of the tithing year, now often observed by eating fruit dishes.

•   Purim is in early spring, and marks the deliverance of the Jews in ancient Persia following the intervention of Queen Esther; celebrations include fancy dress, charitable giving, and exchange of gifts.

•   Yom HaShoah – Holocaust Day is observed a week after Pesach.

•   Yom HaAtzmaut – Israel Independence Day and
Yom Yerushalayim – Jerusalem Day – these are now established as festivals marking the anniversaries of these important events in modern Jewish history, in May 1948 and June 1967 respectively.

•   La'G b'Omer – the 33rd day of the Omer marks the date when the plague that killed most of Rabbi Akiva's students, who are mourned between Pesach and Shavuot, ended. It is a popular date for weddings, and is marked by bonfire parties.

•   Tisha b'Av – a mid-summer fast day commemorating the destruction of both Temples in Jerusalem, the first by the Babylonians in 586 BCE, and the second by the Romans in 70 CE.

In addition, there are several minor fast days each year commemorating significant historical events.

WORSHIP

Synagogue practice depends on the denomination of the worshipper. In Orthodox synagogues traditional dress code is observed and men and women sit separately, whereas in Reform and Liberal synagogues they may sit together. *Shabbat* services involve prayers, reading from the *Torah*, and generally a sermon. Orthodox Jews pray in Hebrew (with some Aramaic – the language of the Talmud), while Reform and Liberal Jews use varying amounts of English. The synagogue also operates as a community and education centre, and one of its roles is generally the teaching of Hebrew and *Torah* studies to children.

Home and family are central to Jewish life and are frequently regarded as being more significant than the synagogue. Traditionally women play an important role in raising children, giving them a religious education and creating a kosher domestic environment, but they often also have responsibility outside the home in both community activities and paid employment. Orthodox Jews place a *mezuzah*, a small scroll containing passages of the Bible, on all doorways (except the bathroom and toilet) in fulfilment of a biblical command, whilst others place them only on their front door.

Men are required to pray three times daily – morning, afternoon, and at night, but the obligation on women is more flexible. More generally, women are exempt from most obligations for which there is a fixed time.

Diet

Jewish dietary laws, *kashrut*, dictate what constitutes kosher food. There is a popular misconception that the production of kosher food requires the performance of some 'ritual'. This is false. Kosher food is simply food that is supervised by someone competent to ensure that it complies with Jewish religious law. Neither is kosher food 'blessed by a rabbi', as is sometimes thought. According to the *Torah*, meat is only kosher if it is from an animal that chews the cud and has cloven hooves. Domestic poultry and fish with fins and scales are also permitted. Meat and poultry must be killed in accordance with the Jewish Laws of *shechitah*. This is carried out by a skilled and ordained *Shochet*, who has an obligation to cause the animal the least possible distress. The consumption of blood is prohibited, and this is removed during *shechitah* and the subsequent process of salting and washing.

Notice issued by the Kashrut Board of the Ayr Hebrew Congregation, 1941

AYR HEBREW CONGREGATION

The Executive hereby notify the Jewish public of Ayr that KOSHER POULTRY will in future be sealed with a numbered label round the leg.

Meat Label.

KOSHER MEAT will have a numbered label stuck on the parcel, and they trust the public will make sure that all purchases are so labelled.

Poultry Label.

Other animal by-products are permitted provided they come from a kosher animal. Foods prepared for the general market, such as cheese made with animal rennet, cakes, jellies and puddings made with gelatine, and biscuits made with animal margarines are obviously not kosher. Some people may find vegetarian versions of these more acceptable in that the animal component is left out, but the more Orthodox will only eat food prepared under supervision since that is the only means of being certain that it is, in fact, kosher.

Meat and milk products are not eaten in the same meal, or even directly after one another. In Britain most Orthodox people wait three hours after a meat meal before taking dairy products, although the strictly Orthodox wait six. As meat and dairy products may not be cooked or prepared together, kitchens have separate preparation areas, utensils, towels, and cutlery for each.

LIFECYCLE

Jewish boys are circumcised at eight days of age. This is regarded by almost all Jews as a central assertion of their identity, and is almost universally observed.

Jewish girls become responsible for their own religious lives at the age of twelve and boys at thirteen. In all denominations, a boy's *Bar Mitzvah* is a time of celebration when he is called up in the synagogue to read from the *Torah* for the first time. Modern Orthodox, Reform, and Liberal Jews also celebrate a girl's *Bat Mitzvah*, and for Reform and Liberal Jews the ceremony takes the same form as a *Bar Mitzvah*.

Jewish Marriage is a voluntary contract between the parties, and need not be solemnised by a rabbi, although it generally is. It is marked by the husband giving the wife a ring, and undertaking to provide for her needs by accepting a formal contract, the *ketubah*. The ceremony takes place under a canopy, *chuppah*, representing a symbolic home, and concludes with the breaking of a glass to symbolise that no celebration can be completely joyful since the destruction of the Temple. In the UK and most other western countries, a Jewish marriage is recognised as simultaneously constituting a civil marriage.

Divorce is also a contractual matter between the parties, although it is supervised by a *Beth Din* because of the seriousness with which remarriage without divorce is viewed. In the absence of agreement between the parties, however, no court can impose a divorce, with the result that they are unable to remarry under Orthodox auspices. Consequently even after a civil divorce, a separate religious divorce or *get* is required. The Family Law (Scotland) Act 2006 recognises this necessity, and permits the civil courts to delay the completion of the civil divorce until after the religious divorce has taken place. Reform and Liberal communities have relaxed these rules to enable marriages to be dissolved and one party to remarry without the consent of the other.

Burial should take place as soon as possible after death, generally within 24 hours where possible. The human body must be treated with utmost respect, and most Jews do not permit cremation. Following the funeral, the parents, children and siblings of the deceased observe a week of formal mourning ('sitting *shiva*') during which they do not go out and prayers are held in the home. They say special prayers (*kaddish*, which is often described as a memorial prayer, but is in fact a hymn of praise to God) for the rest of that year and on the anniversary thereafter.

DRESS

Traditionally girls and women behave and dress modestly, and Orthodox women wear sleeves covering the elbows and skirts reaching well below the knees. Nudity may be an issue for Orthodox and Conservative

Jews, for example where public changing and showering is required, and some Jews do not approve of mixed swimming, or of revealing swimming costumes. Tattoos and piercing are regarded as desecrations of the human body, although many women wear earrings.

Orthodox men wear a square garment (*tallit*) with fringes (*tzitzit*) under their shirt, as well as a skullcap (*kippah* or *yarmulke*). *Charedim* generally wear rather formal clothes, including hats. The *Magen David* (Star of David) has no particular religious significance but has been associated with Judaism for more than 2000 years, and is often worn as jewellery as a statement of an individual's identity.

NAMES

A child is Jewish if his or her mother is Jewish, but the name used in most religious contexts is the individual's Hebrew name, followed by 'daughter/son of' and the father's name. Naming customs do, however, vary, and a less traditional family may choose to include the mother's name as well. Many Jews also have an 'English' name, which they use at school or work.

More about Judaism is available on the Scottish Council of Jewish Communities website at www.scojec.org/resources/resources.html

Jewish Concerns

INTERFAITH ACTIVITY

The Jewish community has been very active in the area of interfaith activity, and supportive of the many efforts in Scotland and elsewhere to further dialogue and understanding, while remaining cautious about some of its manifestations.

At the lowest level, interfaith activity serves a positive purpose in breaking down barriers and forming friendships. Even more important are symbolic or ceremonial public events that bring lay and religious leaders together. And yet such events, as well as meetings to exchange agreement on broad generalities about peace and love and the restricted pursuit of happiness, may give none of us any real understanding of the other's view of the world. And neither, unfortunately, does the simple fact of our meeting!

It is all too easy to agree on words without regard to their meaning. The same may be true of our readiness to sign up to a single prayer for peace, without probing what others understand by 'peace'. On the contrary, we need to embrace diversity, even while recognising that that diversity is set against a particular background. True dialogue, such as the conversations between the Church of Scotland and the Jewish community two decades ago, requires us to share and probe our disagreements, and not merely express our superficial agreements.

Joint Jewish Muslim dinner at Giffnock Synagogue, Scottish Interfaith Week, 2006

At some interfaith events, such as the launch of the Chief Rabbi's book, The Dignity of Difference, and the Respect project in Scotland, the provision of kosher vegetarian food enabled those of all faiths to eat together. At others, however, a table labelled 'Jewish food' has been set up in a corner. Inclusion is a better model for fostering cohesion!

The interfaith enterprise is fraught with difficulty because each of us, deep down, believes that the other is fundamentally, metaphysically, and perhaps even mortally wrong. Indeed, we cannot begin to understand one another's faith unless we understand that. To say that is not to say that we can only treat each other with contempt or disrespect; nor does it mean that our only interaction can be to seek to convince one another of our own unwavering view of the truth. But it does mean that we have to accept each other's scepticism, antagonism, and incomprehension. Not to do so is to be dishonest to ourselves, as well as disrespectful to others – dishonest to ourselves, because it would require self-deception about the uniqueness and exclusivity of our own belief system, and disrespectful to others because it would treat their views as mere re-expressions of our own.

Jews have no problem in recognising that Scotland is predominantly Christian in its history and perhaps its origin, and even today in its culture, but that does not oblige us to see it through Christian eyes. Moreover, we would expect that where the Jewish view is expressed, it must be our own voice expressing it. We have had too much experience of those who cull material from Jewish sources, but lack the Jewish knowledge or sensitivity to interpret the information correctly. Having learned the hard way that those who should know better sometimes put words in our mouths, we are jealous of our right to speak for ourselves.

DISCRIMINATION AND ANTISEMITISM

The Jewish community is understandably sensitive about the Holocaust, and is constantly vigilant about threats, particularly from right wing extremists and others who use antisemitism as part of their political armoury. While there are relatively few serious antisemitic incidents, there is increasingly a climate of hostility created in large part by the demonisation of Israel. Criticism of Jews collectively on grounds that are not applied to others is a form of antisemitism just as much as individual discrimination, and this provides fertile ground for more pernicious forms of antisemitism. The onus is on politicians, the media, trades unions, and churches to take action to counter this evil, and the Community Security Trust (CST) works closely with the police, local councils, and other authorities, to ensure that communal activities can take place safely and securely. In addition, the communal representative bodies work with other communities to promote good community relations and to enable people to practice their faith whilst playing a full part in Scottish society.

- Behaviour which may offend Jewish people:

  - reference to stereotypes of Jews as greedy, mean or dishonest
  - inappropriate use of terms such as 'Holocaust' and associated images
  - erecting obstacles to religious observance
  - emphasis on the alleged ritualism of Judaism while ignoring Jewish ethical teachings
  - failing to consult the Jewish community when devising policies or compiling material which impact upon it
  - expecting everyone to conform to a secular norm by, for example, failing to provide kosher food or scheduling events on *Shabbat*
  - describing Judaism in Christian terms by, e.g. calling the *Torah* the 'Old Testament', or using 'AD' and 'BC' instead of 'CE' (Common or Christian Era) and 'BCE' (Before the Common or Christian Era)

Naming ceremony for
Segal Place, in memory of
Dunfermline Synagogue's
last Minister, 2005

• Good practice

The Jewish community welcomes opportunities to explain its specialneeds to those involved in providing educational, employment, social or care facilities. It expects that employers, carers, teach-ers, and work colleagues will be sensitive to the needs of Jewish people, and accord them the opportunity to maintain their traditions while playing their full part in society. It welcomes initiatives to produce appropriately sourced material about Judaism and Jews in Scotland to further understanding of the Jewish community and its needs and concerns.

• Antisemitism in Scotland

There are fortunately fewer antisemitic incidents in Scotland than in the rest of the UK. It has, however, been documented that any media reporting of the Middle East, not just Israel or Palestine, results in an increase in the number of antisemitic incidents and, in turn, in Jewish people's perception of being threatened. The Scottish Jewish community has not curtailed its communal activities as a result of this perception, but significant numbers say they do feel more apprehensive about attending events at known Jewish locations and in particular about appearing visibly Jewish (for example, by wearing a skullcap). While the perception of attack is higher than the actual risk, the reality is that antisemitic incidents are increasing, and Jewish organisations in Scotland have been advised by the police to take measures to improve security.

Although most incidents are minor, for example, verbal abuse against visibly Jewish people, they do contribute to an increasing perception that Scottish society is becoming more antisemitic. Jewish students have reported that they feel persecuted and insecure on campuses, as they feel that criticism of the actions of Israel can be taken as criticism of Jewish people. The situation has worsened in recent years, for example, during the Glasgow University rectorial election in 2004, when supporters of the Israeli dissident Mordechai Vanunu were reported to have chanted 'Israelis are evil. Jews are evil.'

The horror of the Holocaust has inevitably shaped the way many Jewish people relate to the world. Many members of the Scottish Jewish community lost family members in the Holocaust, and many are themselves first- or second-generation refugees who may as a result feel more vulnerable and thus more sensitive to antisemitism when it occurs.

Inter-Christian sectarianism has been the most prevalent religious hatred in Scotland. However, the use of the term 'sectarianism' as a blanket term for religious hatred is unhelpful as all religious hatred cannot be subsumed into inter-Christian sectarianism.

· ## Antisemitism and the State of Israel

In common with Jewish people across the UK, members of the Scottish Jewish community hold a wide variety of views about current Israeli politics, from far right to far left and every position in between. Criticism of Israel as a state and of any particular Israeli government is entirely legitimate – as is criticism of the US, the UK or any other state. However, depending on the context, criticism of Israel may sometimes be antisemitic. For example, whereas criticism of UK government policy is not taken to imply criticism of the existence of the UK, that is often not the case with regard to Israel, and when Israel is criticised on grounds that equally apply to other states, that also raises suspicions of an antisemitic motive.

Graffiti outside Garnethill synagogue during Lebanon War, 2006

Antisemitism does not consist only in violence, harassment or discrimination against individual Jews, but in treating Jews differently from others, whether as individuals or collectively. When Israel is singled out in this way and the only thing that distinguishes its conduct or activities from other states is that it is Jewish state, then that is an example of political antisemitism.

There is clear documented evidence of this in Scotland when 'Israel' and 'Jewish' are conflated and used inter-changeably, so that what purports to be criticism of Israel becomes antisemitism, for example a man convicted in Kilmarnock Sheriff Court of painting Nazi graffiti and shouting anti-Jewish abuse claimed in mitigation that he was motivated by 'umbrage against Israel' (January 2005).

· ## Combating antisemitism

There is no simple answer to how antisemitism can be combated, and additional resources are needed to raise awareness, and develop appropriate responses, and promote religious equality. Antisemitism, Islamophobia, and sectarianism should be recognised as different facets of the same phenomenon, and should all be included by name when any one of them is being condemned.

Additional security is required for many communal buildings, which places a strain on the already overburdened resources of Jewish organisations.

Education is clearly a key contributor to preventing antisemitism but can only be successful if teaching staff have received adequate training and all materials employed are accurate and appropriate. It is essential that these should be prepared in co-operation with the Jewish community to ensure that they do not unwittingly introduce or preserve falsehoods or perpetuate myths.

It is vital that individuals have the confidence to report antisemitic incidents, but this will only happen if they see that reports are taken seriously and acted upon by the appropriate authorities. Legislating against religious hatred would send a strong message that it will not be tolerated and would enable the courts to respond more effectively than they are able to do at present.

JEWISH ISSUES IN HEALTH CARE

The *Torah* and other books of the Bible, together with the Talmud and its commentaries form the foundation for the codes which guide Jews in their religious and ethical behaviour to this day. One important Jewish custom is visiting the sick, and Jewish patients in hospital expect to be visited by family, friends, and representatives of the Jewish community. This may be the local rabbi, members of the synagogue, or, in the Glasgow area, the Jewish Sick Visiting Association, which has carried out this task for more than a hundred years.

Since the Jewish community in Scotland encompasses a wide range of Jewish observance and practice, religious and secular, Orthodox and Reform, Ashkenazi and Sephardi, Chassidic and non-Chassidic, all with differing outlooks and world-views, it is important that healthcare staff do not make assumptions, but ask individual patients about their own requirements. For example, whilst it is essential to accommodate the religious observances of Jewish patients, it may offend secular Jews to be expected to conform to a religious norm that they do not follow. However, staff should be still be alert to sensitivities on the part of secular Jews, many of whom regard Jewish health issues as imperatives, albeit ethnic rather than religious.

• Shabbat which commences at dusk each Friday and ends at nightfall on Saturday night, is the most important of all the Jewish Festivals. It is a day of complete rest from the normal working week; restrictions on writing, cooking, and travel enhance the unique character of the day and religious Jewish patients expect to be able to follow these observances. This would include, for example, not signing documents, attending an outpatient clinic, or being discharged from hospital and being expected to travel home. Areas of direct patient care may also be affected and, where possible, these should be explored sensitively in advance. Most of the same restrictions also apply to the other Jewish festivals. However, *Halachah* (Jewish Law) mandates that restrictions must be set aside whenever there is a risk to life, and patients may need medical guidance, for example, on their ability to undertake the fast of Yom Kippur.

• **Kosher food** is usually an important concern for Jewish hospital patients, and the Jewish community works closely with hospital dietary and catering provision to ensure the availability of meals prepared under rabbinic supervision. Many hospitals, such as the Southern General Hospital and Victoria Infirmary in Glasgow, which frequently treat Jewish patients, keep a stock of kosher meals, and other hospitals can easily obtain these on request. While vegetarian food may be broadly acceptable to some Jewish patients where no kosher facilities exist, not all vegetarian food meets kosher dietary rules. Guides to foodstuffs available to the general market which meet most kosher standards can be found in the *Kashrut Guide* produced annually by the Kashrut Division of the London Beth Din (the Court of the Chief Rabbi), and hospitals are advised to make a copy of this available to staff.

• **Women's issues** may require a particularly sensitive approach to understand matters from the Jewish patient's perspective. The attitude of religious Jewish women may often be very different from that found in contemporary sexual behaviour, pre-marital sex is frowned on, and abortion and contraception may be restricted. Many gynaecological procedures which affect menstruation could have an effect on traditional observances, especially those relating to monthly immersion in the *mikvah*, and although only a minority of Scottish Jewish women adhere to all these those who do should be able to expect understanding for their requirements. Again, attitudes to proposed procedures should always be discussed sensitively, where possible in advance, to avoid later misunderstandings.

• **Genetic Diseases,** such as Tay-Sachs and some other genetic disorders are much more common in the Ashkenazi Jewish community than in the wider Scottish population. Careful screening, support and counselling in recent years have reduced the incidence of such diseases but provision for ongoing screening and counselling is greatly valued.

• **Circumcision** of baby boys is normally carried out on the eighth day after birth, unless the baby is ill, and, despite campaigns against the practice, its observance within the Jewish community is virtually universal. It is carried out by a *mohel*, a trained circumcising practitioner who is often a doctor or a rabbi, licensed, supervised, monitored, and audited by the Jewish Initiation Society in London. This Society takes great care to ensure the high standards of all their *mohelim* both with regard to carrying out the procedure, and the safety and hygiene of instruments and dressings.

• **End of Life issues** are important in Judaism. Euthanasia is not permitted, but neither does Judaism condone extending the dying process in the final stage, and all measures to treat pain and suffering are permitted. Thus, families may welcome open discussion of these situations and their implications, and some may wish to involve their rabbi in the discussions. Living wills have been widely reviewed in Jewish law, and, to be religiously acceptable, these should include nomination of a proxy, usually a relative who understands both the family dynamics and Jewish law, to act for the patient when he or she is no longer able to make decisions.

• Death has its own customs in Judaism. Some Jews will wish to sit with the deceased until burial has taken place, and, where possible, a room where family may be present should be made available. The expectation is that the body should be buried intact and that no organs will be retained without due reason, information, and prior consent. Jewish funerals are held speedily, usually on the same or following day after death. No impediment should be put in the way of these arrangements as the formal week of mourning only begins with the burial, and delay can cause anguish for the family.

Organ donation is permitted but the complexities of the *Halachah* mean that families may wish to consult a rabbi before giving consent.

When there are clear clinical indications for a post-mortem, these should be discussed with the family and their rabbi, but in general these should only be done for legal reasons or where compelling medical reasons pertain, because of the imperative to bury the body intact. In some places the medical and legal authorities have approved non-invasive post-mortems using scanning technologies that are preferred by the Jewish community.

Caring for Jewish Patients, Joseph Spitzer, Radcliffe Medical Press, Oxford, 2003 provides a comprehensive account of how health issues may impact on Jews as patients, and its detailed bibliography suggests further reading. Every hospital library should ensure that a copy is available to staff.

More information is also available on the Scottish Council of Jewish Communities website at www.scojec.org/resources/resources.html

JEWISH ISSUES IN EMPLOYMENT

Jewish people work in every area and at all levels of industry, trades and professions, whilst still fully observing Judaism. However, since religious observance varies amongst Jews of different affiliations, employers should not make assumptions about the requirements of Jewish employees, but should discuss each staff member's needs on an individual basis.

Many employers, especially in the public sector, have adopted codes of practice providing that no employee can be refused leave on religious grounds. Since the introduction of the Employment Equality (Religion or Belief) Regulations in 2003 [referred to here as the R&B Regulations], all employers should have reviewed their policies and procedures in this area.

The law affords various types of aid to Jews who suffer discrimination because of their ethnicity or religion. The Race Relations Act 1976 defines race as 'colour, race, nationality and ethnic or national origins' and prohibits discrimination on these grounds. Although the Commission for Racial Equality (CRE) Code of Practice for the Elimination of Racial Discrimination and the Promotion of Equality of Opportunity in Employment (1984) is not legally binding, it is admissible in evidence in proceedings before an Employment Tribunal. This provides (para. 1.24) that employers should consider whether it is reasonably practicable to vary or adapt their work requirements to enable cultural or religious needs to be met. In 1976 the European Court of Human Rights held that the requirements of a practising Jew 'may not be deliberately or wantonly ignored', and that they 'should be accommodated unless there are overriding reasons to the contrary'.

Under the Human Rights Act 1998, all legislation must be interpreted in accordance with the European Convention on Human Rights, which must be taken into account by the UK courts, together with decisions of the European Court of Human Rights. The Scotland Act 1998, which established the Scottish Parliament, also effectively incorporates the Convention into the law of Scotland. Article 9 of the Convention provides that 'everyone has the right to freedom of thought, conscience and religion, includ[ing] public or private worship, teaching, practice, or observance, ... subject only to such limitations as are prescribed by law and are necessary in a democratic society.' This is a very high standard, and puts the onus on the employer to show that any limitation is necessary 'in the interests of public safety, for the protection of public order, health or morals, or for the protection of the rights and freedom of others'.

In October 2000 a Framework Discrimination Directive was agreed by the EU Council of Ministers to combat discrimination on grounds of sex, racial or ethnic origin, religious belief, age or sexual orientation. In 2003, the R&B Regulations made it unlawful to discriminate on grounds of religion or belief in employment and vocational training. An employer may only offer or refuse employment to a person on grounds of his or her religion where being of a particular religion is a genuine occupational requirement, or where the organisation has a particular religious ethos. Otherwise, the Regulations prohibit direct and indirect discrimination, victimisation, and harassment in the employment field, by reason of any religion, religious belief, or similar philosophical belief. ACAS has produced a very detailed guide to the application of the Regulations, and this and the CRE code should be followed in all cases. Employers should be aware that under the R&B Regulations any policy to refuse time off for religious observance might amount to unlawful discrimination.

Shabbat and festival observance (see previous section) falls within the ambit of the R&B Regulations. As well as not working on Saturdays and festivals, this may involve leaving work early on some winter Friday afternoons in order to be home in good time before dusk. However, it is extremely unusual for all the major festivals to fall on weekdays, and some often coincide with bank holidays (see page 78-79 for ten year calendar). These absences can be accommodated within the 20 days paid holiday required by the Working Time Regulations 1998, and in some cases, it may even be to the employer's advantage for a Jewish employee to make up hours on Sundays, or to cover colleagues' holiday periods, e.g. over Christmas.

While the importance of *Shabbat* and festivals cannot be overemphasised, some leniencies apply where life is at risk, such as in the health and emergency services. Health workers may wish to consult a Rabbi about which parts of their work may be carried out on these days, and they may ask for assistance with tasks not directly contributing to saving life, such as taking notes.

Interviewers should not ask personal questions, including about religious affiliation, unless these are relevant to the duties of the job. Prospective employers should be prepared to reschedule interviews scheduled for Friday afternoon, Saturday, on festivals, or on the afternoon before Festivals if requested by an observant Jew. Employers should make clear to all applicants what a job entails and what hours are required, to enable both parties to ascertain whether the applicant is able to meet the needs of the employer's business. The applicant should raise all relevant matters at the interview stage to permit constructive discussion as to whether it is reasonably practicable to vary existing working practices, and to prevent any later misunderstanding. Under no circumstances should an employee be expected to enter into a contract of employment containing terms that are inconsistent with his or her religious observance, nor should an employee sign such a contract. Failure to take into account the employee's requirements will result in either breach of contract, or a breach of religious obligations; clearly neither option is acceptable.

There are occasional instances when someone who has not been offered a job, or has been refused promotion, feels that he or she has been treated unfairly because of his or her religious requirements and beliefs. If such a person thinks he or she has been discriminated against when applying for a job, or in the course of employment, specialist advice should be sought promptly.

In general an employer should seek ways of being sufficiently sensitive and flexible to accommodate these needs of the employee. These might include wearing a skullcap (kippah) by Orthodox Jewish men and hair covering and modest dress by observant Jewish women. A restrictive dress code, not required for health and safety reasons, would amount to an act of racial discrimination, a breach of the Human Rights Act, and discrimination under the R&B Regulations, for which the observant employee can obtain redress in an Employment Tribunal. A prudent Jewish employee will check the availability of kosher food in advance of business lunches or other such occasions.

Since a Jewish funeral must take place as soon as possible following the death, if possible on the actual day of the death, Jewish employees may need to attend a funeral at short notice; a reasonable employer will treat attendance at a funeral and the Shiva (week of mourning for close relatives) as compassionate leave.

Employers should also take any necessary measures to facilitate the religious requirements of a newly observant employee, and refusal to do so could also amount to unlawful discrimination. In this situation the employer and employee should consider together how to adapt working practices to enable the new needs of the employee to be met.

If a person thinks he or she is being discriminated against, or being harassed or victimised by his or her employer or fellow employees, because of being Jewish, the employer has a duty to act to prevent or stop it. An employer is responsible generally for the actions of his or her employees whilst at work, and where an employer does not have a contractual grievance procedure, the employee should use provisions of the Employment Act 2002 (Dispute Resolution) Regulations 2004 in the first instance.

•   Further Information

An extended version of this guidance can be found on the website of the Scottish Council of Jewish Communities at www.scojec.org/resources/resources.html.

For further information or advice contact the Scottish Council of Jewish Communities, the Board of Deputies Trades Advisory Section, a solicitor, and/or Trades Union Official.

ACAS has a booklet that gives a detailed explanation of the Employment Equality (Religion or Belief) Regulations 2003. This may be found on their website, www.acas.org.uk or telephone 08702 429090.

The Commission for Racial Equality (CRE) has been replaced by the Equality and Human Rights Commission (EHRC), which can be contacted at The Optima Building, 58 Robertson Street, Glasgow, G2 8DU, 0141–228 5910, scotland@equalityhumanrights.com
The CRE Code of Practice is available on the EHRC website at www.equalityhumanrights.com/en/publicationsandresources/Race/Pages/Publicsector.aspx

Jews in Scotland

THE 2001 CENSUS   MARLENA SCHMOOL

The Scottish census of 2001 for the first time included questions on religion, and, uniquely, these questions were voluntary. The Scottish census was more sophisticated than that of England and Wales as it asked not only 'what religion do you belong to?'[1] but also 'what religion were you brought up in?'.

The Jewish community debated whether or not to support the questions. Some sections of the Jewish community were unhappy about including a religion question on the census, but supporters pointed to the utility of the data for communal social and educational planning and exhorted Jews to answer the question. Surveys of Jews in London and Leeds indicated that more than 80 percent of respondents chose 'Jewish' as their census reply.[2]

•   Response rates and census totals

In the event, in Scotland, 5.5 per cent of the total population ignored the question and a further 27.6 per cent responded that they had no religion.[3] From the viewpoint of communal institutions, the totals for all religious groups were therefore considered to be undercounts. Moreover, general comment and discussion prior to the census had made it clear that there would be Jews who regarded themselves as ethnically but not religiously Jewish.[4] These people are excluded from a population defined according to religion, and consequently from these analyses.

The census therefore enumerated only those who self-identified as Jews by religion and/or as having a Jewish upbringing: 6580 identified as currently Jewish[5] – where 48% were men and 52% women. They accounted for 0.13% of the Scottish population, and 7% of the non-Christian religious population. This represented 87% of the 7446 people (0.15% of the total population) who said they were brought up Jewish. Of these, 49% were men and 51% women. There were 5661 people who were recorded as both currently Jewish and brought up Jewish, 787 people who were currently

---

1. The question in England and Wales was simply 'What is your religion?'

2. Graham, D., M Schmool and S Waterman (2007) *Jews in Britain: a snapshot from the 2001 Census* (London, JPR)

3. Analysis of Religion in the 2001 Census: Summary Report 2005 (Scottish Executive). Data following are also drawn from General Register Office for Scotland (2003) Census Theme Tables on Current Religion (T25) and Religion of upbringing (T26).

4. See Patterns of Prejudice, (1998) Vol. 32, No.2, (London: Sage Publications).

5. Analysis of Religion in the 2001 Census: Summary Report 2005 (Scottish Executive).)

Jewish but brought up in some other or no religion, and 1785 people who were brought up Jewish but now had no (774) or another (620) religion or did not answer the current religion question (391).

- ### Ethnicity and birthplace

The census did not provide a pre-coded box for Jews to tick in order to class themselves ethnically as Jewish, and overwhelmingly (97%) Scottish Jews described themselves as white: 70% were born in Scotland and 16% in England; 3% each were from the USA and the Middle East, just under 2% came from EU countries, and slightly more than 1% were born in Eastern Europe. Scottish Jews are no longer an immigrant community and have recently been a community of emigrants (the census of England and Wales recorded 2782 Jews by religion who were born in Scotland).

- ### Presence, location and housing

The Jews of Scotland are concentrated (81%) in large urban areas. About half (49%) lived in East Renfrewshire, where they made up 3.5% of the population, and a further 17% of Jews were in Glasgow City, and 12% in the City of Edinburgh. The majority (6191) lived in a household where the Household Reference Person (HRP) was Jewish. A further 284 people were in a medical, care or other establishment, such as a student hostel. The Jewish group had the highest proportion of all religious groups (2.5%) living in medical and care establishments, reflecting its older age profile.

In the main, Jews live in unshared accommodation: 62% lived in a house or bungalow, and 38% in a flat, maisonette or apartment; 19% were in single-person households, and 71% lived in single-family households. These homes accommodated 1719 Jewish families, of which 37% (636 families) had dependent children. 42% of families with children had one dependent child, 43% had two children, and 15% had three or more. Lone parent families accounted for 15% of families with dependent children. Jewish homes are predominantly owner-occupied (77%), with 9% living in privately-rented homes, and 8% in local authority or other social-rented housing. This compared with national patterns of 67% owner occupation and 33% renting. Households with a Jewish HRP have the lowest level of overcrowding, with 70% of those households having an Occupancy Rating of +1 or more, and only 9% of Jewish households were below the occupancy rating standard.[6]

- ### Marriage

Of the 5615 Jews aged 16 years and over, 27% had never married, 45% were in a first marriage, and 6% were remarried. 2% were separated, 7% divorced, and 13% widowed. Of all religious groups, Jews were most likely to be widowed. For 55% of the 1807 married couples in which at least one partner was Jewish, the other partner was also Jewish – the lowest proportion

---

6. Occupancy rating relates the number of rooms in a house to the quantity required for the number of people in the household, taking into account their ages and relationships.

of endogamy for any non-Christian religious group. In 23% of marriages the non-Jewish partner was Christian[7], and in 13% the partner had no religion. The religion of 7% of partners was not given.

There were additionally 234 opposite-sex cohabiting couples in which at least one partner was Jewish. Fewer than one in ten (8%) were between two Jews, and for 32% the other partner was Church of Scotland. In 30% of these cohabiting couples, the non-Jewish partner had no religion. This high proportion where one partner does not have any current faith is found consistently for mixed partnerships in all religious groups. Jewish couples reported religion for 822 children, with 94% described as Jewish.

- ## Age

    While some 19% of the total Scottish population was of pensionable age, 30% of Jews were in this age group. For those aged 75 and over, the national proportion was 7%, as against 16% for Jews. There were 19% of Jewish women aged 75 and over, compared with 12% of Jewish men. The Scottish Jewish profile is more aged than British Jewry, where 12% of all Jews by religion were aged 75 and over, partly a result of Jewish emigration from Scotland over the past three decades. In contrast, only 23% of the Scottish Jewish population was aged 24 and under, compared with 31% nationally.

- ## Education and occupation

    71% of Scottish Jews (4593) were in the working age population, compared with 74% of the total population. Of this Jewish working population, 57% were economically active, i.e. working or looking for work whether full- or part- time, 13% were students8, and 29% were economically inactive. This last group were predominantly retired persons (49%), permanently sick or disabled (20%), or those at home looking after a home and family (18%); 78% of men were economically active, compared with 63% of women. Jews had the lowest unemployment rate at 5%, compared with the national rate of 7%.

    Of those working, 27% were self-employed either full- or part-time, compared with a national proportion of 11%, contributing to the 13% of all Jewish males aged 16–64 years who were small employers or workers on their own account. 36% of Jewish men and 17% of Jewish women in employment were self-employed, and of these 22% worked part-time and 78% were full-time. Of the Jewish self-employed, 46% did not have any employees, and 60% of Jews in employment work in organisations with fewer than 25 employees.

    While 13% of Jews aged 16 to 74 were students, the national proportion is 7%. 33% of the national total population aged 16 to 74 had no qualifications, but the proportion fell to 23% for Jews. 51% of Jews in the oldest age-group (pensionable age to age 74) had no qualifications, falling to 9% of Jews aged 16–29. Conversely, 21% of the older group had graduate qualifications, rising to 48% of those aged 30–49 years: nationally only 24%

---

7. 11% of partners were Church of Scotland, 6% each were Roman Catholic and Other Christian.

of 30–49 year olds had these highest level qualifications. 51% of employed Jews aged 16–74 were in higher managerial and professional occupations (compared with 23% nationally), 16% were in associate professional occupations (nationally 14%). Favoured industries were wholesale and retail trade and repairs (21%), real estate, renting and business activities (19%), health and social work (12%), education (11%), and manufacturing (10%).

- ## General health
For Jews of all ages, 64% assessed their health as 'good' and 23% felt it was 'fairly good'; 89% of Jewish men and 87% of Jewish women felt their health was 'good or fairly good' compared to the national figures of 71% of men and 68% of women. The levels of disability rose for both men and women through all age groups, so that 61% of Jewish men and 67% of Jewish women aged 75 and over had some disability or long-term illness, but these rates were still slightly lower than the national levels. 11% of Jews said they provided at least some form or care, with 7% providing between 1 and 19 hours per week, 1% giving 20 to 49 hours a week, and 2% providing 50 hours or more.

- ## How many Jews in Scotland?
Establishing that the number of Jews in Scotland differs from that given in the census must be based on assumptions that give rise to a range of estimates. Data from the Leeds community, which in age-profile and history is very similar to Scotland, indicated that 13% in Leeds did not self-identify as Jewish. If a similar proportion did not self-identify in Scotland, a Jewish population of some 7450 would be indicated.

A cross-tabulation of the two Scottish Census religion questions shows that 10% of those brought up as Jews said they currently had no religion, 8% had another religion, and 5% did not indicate their current religion. If those who were brought up Jewish but currently had no or another religion (1785) and those who did not answer the religion question (391) are added to the 6580 who identify as currently Jewish, then the Jewish population of Scotland would be 8756.

Editorial note: Other assumptions yield higher estimates: applying the finding of the Canadian Census that 27.6% more people described themselves as Jewish by ethnicity than by religion would give a maximum figure of 10 673; and the analysis of the Jewish Policy Research Institute (Times 5 Sept 2003) results in a figure of 10 791.

A fuller version of this study, with supporting tables and references, can be found on the website of the Scottish Council of Jewish Communities at www.scojec.org/resources/resources.html.

The 'Queens Park' Windows

CREATED BY JOHN K CLARK

One of the most significant works of art ever commissioned by the Jewish community in Scotland must be the Queens Park Synagogue Windows, now housed in the Giffnock and Newlands Synagogue.

John K Clark was already well known as one of Scotland's best contemporary artists, but this commission, to produce a series of 22 stained glass windows that would depict all the Festivals of the Jewish year, was to be one of the defining commissions of his career.

After a year of extensive study and research, it took him two more years to complete the project, and his willingness to consult religious authorities and sensitivity to the depth of Jewish tradition, although he is not Jewish, are unmistakable. He worked alone to design, cut, etch, stain, paint, lead, and install the windows. At every one of these stages, each window undergoes dramatic transformations, and it is only the will of the artist, expressed through his knowledge of the subject and facility with the materials, that brings the project to life.

The windows provided colour and illumination that had been lacking in the synagogue, and the magnitude of the commission provided the artist with a unique opportunity, to produce a large and harmonious scheme. The windows are significant, not only in terms of their scale and artistry, but also in terms of the scope of their educational merit, and their sensitivity to Jewish tradition. This is reflected in recurring themes: scales appear in a number of the windows, reflecting the Talmudic tradition that the world is judged at four different periods of the year, and hands are used to denote human agency while complying with the prohibition on depicting the human form.

John Clark's windows have attracted much positive critical acclaim and have been compared with Marc Chagall's windows of the twelve tribes at the Hadassah Hospital in Jerusalem. The style is abstract, but symbolically representational in that nothing is included for mere embellishment. As Linda Cannon wrote:

> 'hands and doves break free out of a pure white border in the Day of Judgement window; the Tree of Knowledge dances about a stormy sea; and the scales of justice are balanced precariously against a new moon. And why not? Why should an eagle not fly majestically over a golden city? Why should one tree not contain the fruit of many others? In stained glass, all things are possible.'

The windows were commissioned by Queens Park Synagogue in 1987 and completed in time to form part of the Jewish Community's contribution to Glasgow's year as European City of Culture in 1990. The project was proposed by George Barlow, and generously funded by members of the Congregation. When the synagogue closed in 2002, the windows were moved, with the assistance of Lottery funding, to Giffnock and Newlands Synagogue, where they can be viewed by arrangement. Contact 0141– 577 8250 for information.

Shabbat and Creation Windows

The first window to be designed was the Shabbat triptych, which represents the Biblical narrative of Creation. This is now on the eastern wall of Giffnock Synagogue, above the Ark containing the sacred scrolls of the *Torah*. The left-hand window depicts the first light and the separation of the waters on first two days of Creation, and the right-hand window shows the creation of vegetation on the third day, and of the sun, moon and stars on the fourth.

The large and dramatic central window is divided into three sections; the creation of birds and fish on the fifth day are depicted outside the circle, alongside symbols of the Exodus, which took place on a Thursday; the creation of animals and humanity on the sixth day is depicted inside the circle but outside the *Magen David*; and, in the border, God's first covenant with mankind after the Flood is represented by a rainbow and hands releasing a dove with an olive branch, which can also be understood as the dove of peace. Other hands shield the Shabbat candles, depict the blessing that parents give their children on the eve of Shabbat, wash before eating bread, and hold the candle for *havdalah*; hands also pick fruit in the presence of the serpent in the Garden of Eden, and catch fish to symbolise human dominion over animals. Shabbat ceremonies are represented inside each of the six points of the *Magen David*. These include wine being poured into a cup for *kiddush*, the two plaited loaves eaten at Shabbat and festival meals to commemorate the double portion of *manna* that fell before Shabbat during the forty years that the Israelites wandered in the desert after the Exodus, and an overflowing cup of wine, spices, and the braided *havdalah* candle mark the departure of Shabbat. Finally, the central panel shows three important symbols: the *menorah*, the seven branched candelabrum from the Temple; the *Magen David*, and the *Torah* scroll.

ROSH HASHANAH (NEW YEAR) SERIES

The first of these three windows depicts Rosh Hashanah as Yom Teruah, the day on which the *shofar* (ram's horn) is blown at the dramatic climax of the festival prayers as a call to faith and returning to God. This recalls the ram that was sacrificed in place of Isaac in the biblical account of the *Akedah* (the binding of Isaac). This story, which is central to Judaism as the final test of Abraham's faith in God, is read during the Rosh Hashanah service, and is represented in the window by two bound hands and a hand above holding a knife.

The second window shows Rosh Hashanah as the Day of Remembrance. The imagery, of a crown surrounded by darkness at the very top of the window symbolises the kingship of God, and comes directly from the *Machzor*, the festival prayer book. Since Rosh Hashanah is the anniversary of Creation, this is represented as in the Creation Window, by the separation of darkness from light. Once again the *Akedah* is depicted by a hand holding a knife, and other hands release a dove carrying an olive branch, as a symbol both of peace and of God's covenant with Noah. The window also refers to the Exodus from Egypt in its representation of the parting of the Red Sea.

The third window in this series depicts Rosh Hashanah as the Day of Judgement, when Jewish people examine their deeds of the previous year and resolve to improve in the year ahead. The scales of justice feature prominently, as do the heavenly books in which, according to tradition, the fate of mankind is inscribed. Other traditional symbols included in this window are apple and honey, which symbolise the hope for a sweet year ahead, and fish, which represent the *Tashlich* (literally 'casting') ceremony that takes place on the first day of Rosh Hashanah, when sins are symbolically cast into a body of running water. As the eyes of fish never close this is also seen as a reminder of God's eternal and merciful watchfulness. White birds represent prayers rising to heaven in purity.

YOM KIPPUR (DAY OF ATONEMENT) WINDOW

This solemn 25 hour fast takes place on the tenth day of the year. Yom Kippur is seen as the holiest day of the year, and much of the liturgy deals with repentance, introspection, and self-improvement, but also includes a detailed description of the service that used to take place in the Temple. The principal purpose of Yom Kippur is repentance, and the windows reflect this mood. White is used as a symbol of purity, reflecting the traditional white covers on the *Torah* scrolls and synagogue furniture, and the white *kittel* (robe) worn by some men during the synagogue service. The window depicts the Temple sacrifice and the scapegoat, which represents atonement for sin, both individual and national. As in the Rosh Hashanah window, birds are used to represent prayers, and the Book of Life and the *shofar*, blown once at the end of the day, also reappear.

PESACH (PASSOVER) SERIES

The first of these three windows represents Pesach and the Spring Season in the Land of Israel. This window shows nature coming back to life after winter, with new growth on the trees and from the earth under a hazy sun. As the Bible says in The Song of Songs. 'For Lo, the winter is past, the rain is over and gone, the flowers appear on the earth, the time of singing has come'. In the three agricultural pilgrim festivals of Pesach, Shavuot, and Sukkot, the seven types of agricultural produce of the Land of Israel – wheat, barley, grapes, figs, pomegranates, dates, and olives – are shown in different stages of development. Here they are blossoming and showing new growth, while in the Shavuot window they bear fruit. The focal point of this window is a composite fig, olive and pomegranate tree. The window also shows the *etrog* (citron), palm, and willow, that are used on Sukkot.

The onset of spring also symbolises dawn of national freedom: 'for the winter of bondage is passed, the deluge of suffering is over and gone.' (Song of Songs 2:11). So the second window represents Pesach as the Season of Freedom, when the liberation of Israel from Egypt marked its birth as a nation. This window depicts the flight from slavery in Egypt, represented by the parting of the Red Sea at the base and the eagle at the top. This represents the Angel of Death that passed over the homes of the Israelites on its way to destroy the Egyptian first-born in the last, and most devastating, of the ten plagues. But it also represents the liberation itself: 'You have seen ... how I bore you on eagles wings and brought you to me' (Exodus 19:4). This deliverance is a recurring theme throughout all the windows as it is in Jewish writings and prayers: 'He brought us forth from bondage to freedom, from sorrow to joy, from mourning to festivity, from darkness to bright light, and from servitude to redemption' (*Haggadah*). This theme is reflected in the chains of bondage round the border of the window, with the twelve stars and the twelve gateways through the sea representing the twelve tribes of Israel.

The third window in this series represents Pesach as the Festival of Matzot (unleavened bread): 'For seven days you shall eat *matzah*, as I commanded you, at the appointed time in the month of *Aviv* (spring) – for in it you came out of Egypt' (Exodus 23:15). This window represents the highly symbolic *Seder* meal, which takes place on each of the first two evenings of Pesach, during which the *Haggadah*, the story and songs relating to Israel's deliverance and freedom, is recited.

The symbolism begins at the base of the window with the ritual burning of any leaven left over in the house before the festival begins, and the methods used for cleaning utensils for Pesach use; fire and boiling water. Above this is the ceremonial Seder Plate, on which are three *matzot*, a roasted shank bone and an egg as reminders of the sacrifices that were offered in the Temple, a vegetable that is dipped into the salt water that represents tears, bitter herbs as a token of the bitterness of slavery, and *charoset*, a paste of apples, nuts and cinnamon, that symbolises the mortar used by the slaves. Round these symbols are the four cups of wine drunk during the *Seder* to represent the four expressions of redemption in the book of Exodus.

A fifth, golden, cup of wine is also shown. This is known as the cup of Elijah, and is designated for the prophet who will inaugurate the messianic age.

The *Leviathan* (great fish) and *Behomot* (great red ox) appear in both the Pesach and Sukkot windows, and also represent the messianic age. The scales in this window represent judgement for grain, and some barley has been added to the border of this window as an allusion to the counting of the seven weeks of the *Omer* till the harvest festival of Shavuot.

SHAVUOT (PENTECOST) SERIES

The first window focuses on Shavuot as the Festival of the Giving of the Torah, the climactic event on Mount Sinai when God taught Moses the *Torah* and all of Jewish tradition. This occurred exactly seven weeks after the escape from Egypt and is considered the fulfilment of the Exodus. The central image is the tablets of stone on which the Ten Commandments were written. The *Torah* records the Revelation on Sinai as being accompanied by the sounding of horns blowing, the flashing of lightning, and the sound of thunder. Tradition also records that mountainside flowered.

At the base of the window is the burning bush where Moses first encountered God, and was told by Him to lead the Jewish people out of Egypt. Above, surrounded by darkness, is the golden calf, the sin that condemned the Children of Israel to spend forty years in the wilderness of Sinai.

The other windows in this series show Shavuot as the Harvest Festival. Shavuot is the summer pilgrimage festival when people brought the first produce of the fields to the Temple in Jerusalem as thanksgiving. 'The choicest first fruits of thy land you shall bring into the house of the Lord your God.' (Exodus 23:19). This is represented by a palm tree and the seven biblical species, again growing on a single tree, but this time in fruit, and by scales representing judgment for the fruit of the trees. A sickle cutting wheat provides a link to the next window which depicts the Wheat Harvest.

This illustrates the story of Ruth, depicted here by a hand gleaning behind the sickle. Ruth is a daughter of a Moabite who returns to Israel with her mother-in-law Naomi after her husband dies, to be part of the Jewish people. This story is read on Shavuot as Ruth's acceptance of Judaism echoes that of the Jewish people at Sinai. At the top of this window, on either side, there is a representation of the festival sacrifices that would have been offered at the Temple in Jerusalem.

Sukkot (Tabernacles) Series

This festival is especially rich in religious symbolism, and it is represented by no fewer than four windows. The first reflects the main name of the Festival, Sukkot, the temporary dwellings that the Israelites lived in during their 40 years in the desert, and that are commemorated by eating, and in warmer climates, sleeping in decorated huts roofed with vegetation.

The arch of this window contains two palm branches that represent the roof of the *Sukkah*, while in the border area golden vine leaves symbolise the Temple where a great golden vine surrounded one of the doors. As the leaves move upwards they become the stars seen through the roof of the *Sukkah*. The Leviathan and Behemoth are represented here in the hope of a share in the great feast in the *Sukkah* in a future messianic age. The next window in this series shows Sukkot as the time of the Ingathering of Crops: 'on the fifteenth day of the seventh month, when ye have gathered in the fruits of the land, ye shall keep the feast of the Lord seven days' (Leviticus 23:39). The arched area of this panel shows another interpretation of the Sukkah, as the Clouds of Glory, cloud by day and fire by night, that accompanied the Children of Israel in the desert and gave them continual Divine protection. The window also includes a reminder of the Exodus in the form of the parting of the sea. Again the seven types of produce appear, as throughout the agricultural windows, now harvested and put in storage. Sukkot was considered the most joyful of the festivals, and was sometimes therefore called simply The Festival.

The third window is dominated by one of the main symbols of Sukkot, the *Arba Minim*, the four species – willow, palm, *etrog* (citron) and myrtle – that are taken together and shaken in all directions during prayers on the first seven days of the Festival. This window also represents *Hoshannah Rabah*, the seventh day of Sukkot, when the Temple ritual reached a climax with prayers for water, and a libation ceremony at the Altar accompanied by music on trumpets and harps, flutes and cymbals. In the synagogue the congregation circles the *bimah* (prayer desk) seven times with the four species before these are put aside and a bundle of willow twigs is beaten to symbolise expiation of sins.

The final window in this series depicts Shemini Atzeret, the Eighth Day of Assembly, when prayers are said for winter rainfall, and Simchat Torah (Celebration of the Torah) when the annual cycle of the reading of the *Torah* is completed and immediately recommenced. This theme is symbolised in the window, which focuses on the *Torah* – a Jewish community's most treasured possession: 'Let us be glad and rejoice with the *Torah*, for it is strength and light for us'. The *Torah* scrolls are adorned with silver ornaments and kept inside velvet covers, and are rolled toward their centre on two wooden staves, which are known as Trees of Life, also another symbolic name for the *Torah*. At opposite sides of the window, with the Tree of Knowledge between, are symbols of the first and last books of the *Torah*: the physical separation of light from darkness, and the light of wisdom.

The large *tallit* (prayer shawl) in this window represents the tradition of holding a tallit as a canopy over those who are called up to read the last and first portions of the *Torah*, and of calling up boys under *bar mitzvah* age. At the centre of this window is the Hebrew symbol for the number seven in a circle, to represent the seven times the *Torah* scrolls circle the synagogue in procession.

MINOR FESTIVALS SERIES

Chanukah, the Festival of Lights, commemorates the victory of the Maccabees over Syrian Greek rule in 175 BCE. The Greeks had defiled the Temple, and the Maccabean victory led to the rededication of the Temple and the kindling of the *menorah*, the Temple Candelabrum. Only a single small jar of undefiled oil could be found, but that miraculously burned for eight days until more could be produced.

To commemorate this miracle one more candle is lit in the Chanukah *menorah* each day, and the window alludes to this by depicting each flame in a different shade. Palm branches represent the victory over Hellenism, a laurel wreath in the darkness at the base of this window indicates the end of Greek rule, and once again golden vine leaves provide a reminder of the Temple. The window also shows a *dreidel*, a small spinning top used in a traditional Chanukah game.

La'G b'Omer is a joyous festival during the solemn period of the Omer between Pesach and Shavuot. In Israel many make a pilgrimage to Rabbi Shimon bar Yochai's grave in the Galilee. It is marked by bonfires and is a popular date for weddings, and it is traditional for young boys to have their first haircut on this day. The central image of the window is a bonfire, and there are also a chuppah (wedding canopy) and scissors for hair cutting. Above is the eagle from a Pesach window, and at each side is a sheaf, one of barley and one of wheat, representing the period between the two harvest festivals.

Tu b'Shevat, the New Year for Trees, is a time for planting and celebrating agricultural produce. At this time of the year, almond trees begin to blossom and birds return from their winter migration. The window reflects this and the tradition in the town of Tzefat of drinking white and red wine, signifying the coolness of winter and the awakening spring and regrowth. Since it is the day of judgment for trees, the window shows a set of scales.

Purim commemorates the Biblical story of Esther, when the Jews in Persia were saved from the hands of Haman who had plotted their destruction.

'Purim' literally means 'lottery', as lots were drawn to determine on which day the Jews would be killed. The window shows a silver-cased scroll of Esther, handwritten on parchment, which is read in the synagogue, the traditional triangular shaped cake, filled with poppy seed and honey, called *Hamantaschen*, and a Purim plate to symbolise the tradition of giving money to the poor and sending food gifts to friends.

Two circular windows depict Rosh Chodesh, the New Moon, which is important because the dating of Jewish festivals depends on lunar months. However, because Pesach is referred to in the *Torah* as the Spring Festival, the lunar calendar is adjusted by adding additional months when necessary to keep in step with the solar year. The first window depicts the new moon together with symbols of Rosh Hashanah (crown), Pesach (parting of the sea), Sukkot (palm) and Shavuot (fire).

The second Rosh Chodesh Window refers to the Blessing of the New Moon, which takes place in the synagogue on the preceding *Shabbat*. In the days of the Temple, the new month was declared when witnesses reported seeing the first sign of a new moon, and signals were then sent across Israel using hilltop bonfires. The window shows the moon surrounded by stars, and a bonfire, with the golden vine leaves, seen also in other windows, symbolic of the Temple.

Acknowledgments : This article draws on material in the *Giffnock and Newlands Synagogue Bulletin* of Passover 2005, from John K Clark's own website (www.glasspainter.com/synagogue/), and the article 'The Queens Park Windows – an appreciation' by Linda Cannon, Conservator of Stained Glass at the Burrell Collection, published in *The Jewish Arts Anthology* ,1990.

Scottish Jewish Resources & Services

- Scottish Council of Jewish Communities

  222 Fenwick Road, Giffnock, Glasgow G46 6UE
  Tel: 0141–638 6411   Fax: 0141–577 8202
  e-mail: scojec@scojec.org   www.scojec.org

This website contains information about all the Jewish communities in Scotland, and a Guide to Jewish Facilities in Scotland, as well as copies of the Council's newsletter Four Corners. The Scottish Council of Jewish Communities is the democratic representative body of all the Jewish communities in Scotland. It advances public understanding about the Jewish religion, culture and community, and develops and provides information and assistance to educational, health, and welfare organisations. It also works in partnership with other organisations and stakeholders to promote good relations and understanding among community groups and to promote equality. In pursuit of these purposes, it represents the Jewish community in Scotland to government and other statutory and official bodies, monitors the Scottish Parliament, and liaises with MSPs and others on matters affecting the Jewish community. It also supports the smaller Scottish Jewish communities with meetings, publications and events.

- Aberdeen

  Synagogue: 74 Dee Street, Aberdeen AB1 2DS
  www.aberdeenhebrew.org.uk
  info@aberdeenhebrew.org.uk

- Dundee

  Synagogue: St Mary's Place, Dundee DD1 5RB
  www.scojec.org/communities/dundee/index.html
  dundeehc@googlemail.com

- Edinburgh

  Edinburgh Hebrew Congregation
  4 Salisbury Road, Edinburgh EH16 5AB
  www.ehcong.com
  secretary@ehcong.com

  Edinburgh Liberal Jewish Community (Sukkat Shalom)
  www.eljc.org
  0131–777 8024

• Jewish Network of Argyll & the Highlands (JNAH)

Frank House: house.frank@gmail.com

• Glasgow

For all information about the Glasgow Jewish community, contact

Glasgow Jewish Representative Council
222 Fenwick Road, Giffnock, Glasgow G46 6UE
Tel: 0141–577 8200. Fax: 0141–577 8202
www.glasgowjewishrepcouncil.org
jrepcouncil@aol.com

The Council was founded in 1914 to speak on behalf of the Jewish community of Glasgow and West of Scotland. It fosters good relations between the community and other local religious and civic bodies and provides a democratic forum for almost fifty organisations including synagogues, and welfare, educational, social and cultural organisations.

• Welfare Services

A full range of welfare services, including day care and residential facilities, is available in Glasgow. A more limited range of services is available throughout Scotland; for information contact

Jewish Care Scotland
Maccabi Centre, May Terrace, Giffnock, Glasgow G46 6LD
Tel: 0141–620 1800 www.jcarescot.org.uk

• Universities

University Jewish Societies can be found on campuses all over Scotland. For details on Jewish students in Scotland contact the

Chaplain, Rabbi Dovid Cohen 07801–491 386
dovid@mobilechaplain.com

Union of Jewish Students: ujs@ujs.org.uk

Scottish Council of Jewish Communities 0141–638 6411
scojec@scojec.org

• Guide to Jewish Facilities in Scotland

Detailed information about Jewish facilities in Scotland is available on the SCoJeC website at

www.scojec.org/communities/guidebook.pdf

The Scottish Jewish Archives Centre

The Scottish Jewish Archives Centre was founded 1987, in the historic Garnethill Synagogue, 129 Hill Street, Glasgow G3 6UB, which opened in 1879. This listed building was the first purpose-built synagogue in Scotland and is the oldest Scottish synagogue still functioning. The Centre collects, preserves, catalogues and documents material relating to the Jewish experience in Scotland – religious, organisational, social, economic, political, cultural activity and family life. It also seeks to encourage the study of Jews in Scotland, publishing books and articles, providing a study centre for research using the Centre's large oral history collections as well as photographs, books, and articles and the magazines, journals and brochures of synagogues and other organisations. It has a full set of the Jewish Echo newspaper and copies of other newspapers. It also holds works of art by Benno Schotz, Hannah Frank, Joseph Ancill, and Hilda Goldwag, and has hundreds of religious and ceremonial artefacts from Jewish communities around Scotland.

The Centre has a Historical Database of Scottish Jewry with information on over 30 000 Jews who once lived in Scotland as well as cross-references to over 70 cemetery lists, synagogue registers, charity subscription lists and census records. This forms the most important starting point for those tracing their family history in Scottish Jewish community. The Centre handles family history enquiries from around the world and supports school projects, and undergraduate and postgraduate dissertations, and responds also to writers and the media.

A Life in Scotland, opened in 2008, is a new professionally designed display and historical timeline housed at the Centre. It is a unique educational and cultural resource for the Scottish Jewish and wider community, depicting the highlights of two hundred years of Jewish experience in Scotland, including various topics of Jewish religious, social, cultural, and political life, the Jewish contribution to Scottish life, etc.

Website: www.sjac.org.uk

Contact: 0141–332 4911 info@sjac.org.uk

Glossary

Note: because there is no standard transliteration from Hebrew, many of the terms listed have alternative spellings in English.

Names of festivals etc have not been included as they are explained on pp 40-42.

Aggadah: the narrative or homiletic part of the **Talmud** and other rabbinic texts.

Amidah: prayer recited standing and in silence as the central part of each of the three daily prayer services.

Bar Mitzvah: Jewish males are responsible for religious duties from 13 years. This is usually marked by being called to the reading of the Torah in the synagogue.

Bat Mitzvah: Jewish females are responsible for religious duties from the age of 12 years. This may be celebrated at a ceremony in the synagogue.

Berachah: (literally: blessing) any of a number of short prayers said on various occasions, such as thanksgiving before and after eating.

Beit HaKnesset: literally, house of assembly. A synagogue.

Beit HaMidrash: religious study and prayer house or room in a larger synagogue.

Beth Din: Jewish law court. It usually deals with matters of kashrut or personal status, eg religious divorces (**Gittin**).

Birkat Cohanim: traditional priestly blessing recited at weddings, by parents over children on Friday night, and by a **Cohen**, a Jew of priestly descent, on Festivals.

Birkat HaMazon or (Yiddish) **bentsching:** grace after meals.

Brit Milah: the circumcision of baby boys at eight days old.

Chag: a Jewish festival. The autumn festivals of Rosh HaShanah, Yom Kippur and Sukkot are sometimes collectively called the **Chaggim.**

Chazan: cantor or leader of the synagogue services.

Cheder: "Hebrew school". Religious elementary education classes.

Chesed shel Emes or **Chevrah Kadishah:** Jewish burial society. (Lit. "true kindness" or "holy society", as the care of the dead is done without thought of reward.)

Chuppah: wedding canopy: Jewish wedding ceremonies are conducted under the Chuppah either in the synagogue or in the open air.

Dayan: a Jewish judge, a member of a **Beth Din**.

Gemara: the debates amongst rabbis, from 3rd to 6th centuries, recorded in the **Talmud**.

Get: Jewish religious (bill of) divorce. (plural: **Gittin**)

Halachah: Jewish religious law in general, or a legal ruling.

Havdalah: the ceremony at the end of Shabbat, recited over wine, spices, and a candle.

Hechsher: a certificate from a recognised authority, usually that food is kosher.

Kaddish: prayer of praise of God recited during synagogue services, and by mourners during the year after the death of a parent and on their **Yahrzeit**.

Ketubah: Jewish religious marriage contract.

Kiddush: the ceremony at the beginning of Shabbat and festivals, recited over wine.

Kippah: skullcap worn by men at prayer and by the Orthodox at all times. (also **Yarmulke** or **Kappel**)

Kollel: college of advanced rabbinic studies (c.f. **Yeshivah**).

Kosher: prepared in accordance with Jewish religious laws, especially of **shechitah** and the separation of milk and meat products. Kosher products often have a **hechsher** from a kashrut authority on the packaging.

Ma'ariv or **Arvit:** the evening prayer service.

Matzah: unleavened bread eaten on Pesach.

Mezuzah: small parchment with the text of the **Shema** fixed to the doorpost of every room except the bathroom in a Jewish house.

Mikvah: ritual bath used monthly by married women, by converts to Judaism on their acceptance into the faith, and by Orthodox men before Shabbat and Festivals.

Minchah: the afternoon prayer service.

Minyan: prayer quorum of 10 males over **bar mitzvah** age.

Mishnah: the central text of Rabbinic Judaism compiled by Rabbi Yehudah the Prince in the 2nd century CE. See **Talmud**.

Mohel: skilled religious official who performs **brit milah**.

Mussaf: the additional morning service on Shabbat and festivals.

Pikuach nefesh: literally saving of life. Because life is so precious, all religious observances, except the prohibitions against murder, apostasy, and immorality, must be set aside when life is threatened.

Rabbi: teacher and spiritual leader of the community. The rabbi answers questions on Jewish law, gives sermons, and performs the duties of a minister of religion. "**Rav**" is the preferred title of Orthodox rabbis, with religious rather than pastoral connotations.

Seder: the ceremonial meal eaten on the first nights of Pesach.

Sefer Torah: scroll containing Torah, hand written by a scribe, and read in weekly portions on an annual cycle on Shabbat, as well as on Mondays, Thursdays, Festivals, and Fast Days.

Shacharit: the morning prayer service.

Shechitah: Jewish method for the rapid and painless killing of animals for food, carried out by an ordained **shochet**.

Shema: declaration of faith. "Hear, O Israel, the Lord is your God, the Lord is One" (Deuteronomy, Ch. 5) recited during the morning and evening prayers, on retiring at night, and on one's deathbed.

Shiva: (literally: "seven") the week of intense mourning and prayer at home after the death of a close relative. Family and friends visit to comfort the mourners.

Shochet: highly skilled ordained religious official who carries out **shechitah**.

Shofar: ram's horn blown during the morning service on Rosh Hashanah.

Shul (Yiddish), **synagogue**; a building used primarily for Jewish prayers, often also housing other communal facilities.

Shulchan Arukh: one of the most definitive codes of Jewish law, governing every aspect of Jewish life. Compiled in Safed, Israel in the 16th century.

Tallit: shawl with fringes (**tsitsit**) worn by men during prayers; the **tallit katan** (small tallit) is worn as an undergarment during the day.

Talmud: the main authoritative source of Rabbinic Judaism, compiled in 6th century CE, based on oral traditions, some dating back to Moses. Consists of the **Mishnah** and its commentary, the **Gemara**.

Tanach: abbreviation for Torah (Five Books of Moses), Nevi'im (the Prophets), and Ketuvim ("Writings", including Proverbs and Psalms), which together make up the Hebrew Bible.

Tefillin: small leather boxes containing the **Shema** and other biblical passages, worn by men above the forehead and on the arm during morning prayers.

Torah: the Five Books of Moses (Pentateuch), and by extension the entire body of Jewish religious tradition.

Tsitsit: the fringes on a **tallit**.

Yahrzeit (Yiddish): the anniversary of a death, when close relatives say kaddish.

Yarmulke (Yiddish): skullcap. See **Kippah**.

Yeshivah: religious school, often full-time for boys beyond the age of bar mitzvah. Those who qualify as rabbis often continue postgraduate study in a **Kollel**.

Yom Tov or **Chag:** a Jewish festival.

Bibliography of the Jews in Scotland

HISTORY

Braber, Ben:	*Jews in Glasgow 1879-1939 Immigration and Integration*	LONDON 2007
Collins, Kenneth E (ed.):		
	Aspects of Scottish Jewry	GLASGOW 1987
Collins, Kenneth E:	*Go and Learn:*	
	the International Story of Jews and Medicine in Scotland	ABERDEEN 1988
	Second City Jewry:	
	the Jews of Glasgow in the Age of Expansion	GLASGOW 1990
	Be Well!	
	Jewish Immigrant Health and Welfare 1860-1920	EAST LINTON 2001
Hutt, Charlotte and Kaplan, Harvey L, (eds.):		
	A Scottish Shtetl - Jewish Life in the Gorbals, 1880-1974	GLASGOW 1984
Kaplan, Harvey L:	*The Gorbals Jewish Community in 1901*	GLASGOW 2006
Levy, Abraham:	*The Origins of Scottish Jewry*	LONDON 1958
	The Origins of Glasgow Jewry, 1812-1895	GLASGOW 1949
Livingston, Harvey M:	*From Strength to Strength – 100 Years of Service, 1903-2003*	
		GLASGOW 2004
Phillips, Abel:	*A History of the Origins of the First Jewish Community in Scotland:*	
	Edinburgh, 1816	EDINBURGH 1979
	Serving Their Country: Wartime Memories of Scottish Jews	GLASGOW 2001

MEMOIRS

Bermant, Chaim:	*Coming Home*	LONDON 1976
Calder, Jenni:	*Not Nebuchadnezzar – In Search of Identities*	EDINBURGH 2005
Glasser, Ralph:	*Growing Up in the Gorbals*	LONDON 1986
	Gorbals Boy at Oxford	LONDON 1988
	Gorbals Voices, Siren Songs	LONDON 1990
Hofman, Ethel G:	*Mackerel at Midnight*	
	– Growing Up Jewish on a Remote Scottish Island	PHILADELPHIA 2005
Levy, Ernest:	*Just One More Dance*	EDINBURGH 1998
Schotz, Benno:	*Bronze in my Blood*	EDINBURGH 1981

ART

Frank, Fiona	*Hannah Frank – A Glasgow Artist:*	
	Drawings & Sculpture	GLASGOW 2004
Grant, Marianne	*I Knew I was Painting for My Life:*	
	The Holocaust Artworks of Marianne Grant	GLASGOW 2002

FICTION

A number of fictional works are set in the Jewish communities of Scotland, mostly in Glasgow.

Bermant, Chaim:	*Jericho Sleep Alone*	LONDON 1964
	Ben Preserve Us	LONDON 1965
	The Second Mrs Whitberg	LONDON 1976
	The Patriarch	LONDON 1981
Cowan, Evelyn :	*Portrait of Alice*	NEW YORK 1976
Taylor, CP:	*Bread & Butter*	1967
	Walter	EDINBURGH 1992
Ronder, Jack:	*The Lost Tribe,*	LONDON 1978

Set in Dundee and Edinburgh, and serialised on television.

GENERAL

Gilbert, Martin:	*The Holocaust: the Jewish Tragedy*	1986
	Israel: a History	1998
	The Routledge Jewish History Atlas	1995
Jacobs, Louis :	*The Jewish Religion*	1995
Jewish Year Book:	Produced annually by the *Jewish Chronicle*	
Johnson, Paul:	*A History of the Jews*	1998
Chief Rabbi Sir Jonathan Sacks:		
	Faith in the Future	1995
	The Dignity of Difference	2003
	The House we Build Together – Recreating Society	2007

USEFUL WEBSITES

• library.thinkquest.org/28505/judaism/intro.htm
General information site on Judaism.

• www.icteachers.co.uk/resources/resources_re.htm#Judaism
A range of resources developed by teachers to teach Jewish Festivals through drama, assemblies and other activities.

• www.Holocaust-trc.org
One of many sites dedicated to teaching the Holocaust, with lesson plans etc.

• www.scojec.org
Information about the Jewish Communities of Scotland, and the work of the Scottish Council of Jewish Communities.

Calendar 2008–2012

	2008 / 5768	2009 / 5769	2010 / 5770	2011 / 5771	2012 / 5772
Purim	FRI 21 MARCH	TUE 10 MARCH	SUN 28 FEBRUARY	SUN 20 MARCH	THU 8 MARCH
Pesach Passover	SUN/MON 20/21 APRIL	THU/FRI 9/10 APRIL	TUE/WED 30/31 MARCH	TUE/WED 19/20 APRIL	SAT/SUN 7/8 APRIL
Pesach Passover (Conclusion)	SAT/SUN 26/27 APRIL	WED/THU 15/16 APRIL	MON/TUE 5/6 APRIL	MON/TUE 25/26 APRIL	FRI/SAT 13/14 APRIL
Shavuot Pentecost	MON/TUE 9/10 JUNE	FRI/SAT 29/30 MAY	WED/THU 19/20 MAY	WED/THU 8/9 JUNE	SUN/MON 27/28 MAY
Tisha B'Av	SUN 10 AUGUST	THU 30 JULY	TUE 20 JULY	TUE 9 AUGUST	SUN 29 JULY
	5769	5770	5771	5772	5773
Rosh Hashanah New Year	TUE/WED 30 SEP/1 OCTOBER	SAT/SUN 19/20 SEPTEMBER	THU/FRI 9/10 SEPTEMBER	THU/FRI 29/30 SEPTEMBER	MON/TUE 17/18 SEPTEMBER
Yom Kippur	THU 9 OCTOBER	MON 28 SEPTEMBER	SAT 18 SEPTEMBER	SAT 8 OCTOBER	WED 26 SEPTEMBER
Succot Tabernacles	TUE/WED 14/15 OCTOBER	SAT/SUN 3/4 OCTOBER	THU/FRI 23/24 SEPTEMBER	THU/FRI 13/14 OCTOBER	MON/TUE 1/2 OCTOBER
Simchat Torah	TUE/WED 21/22 OCTOBER	SAT/SUN 10/11 OCTOBER	THU/FRI 30 SEPT/1 OCTOBER	THU/FRI 20/21 OCTOBER	MON/TUE 8/9 OCTOBER
Chanukah	MON-MON 22-29 DECEMBER	SAT-SAT 12-19 DECEMBER	THU-THU 2-9 DECEMBER	WED-WED 21-28 DECEMBER	SUN-SUN 9-16 DECEMBER

Calendar 2013–2017

	2013 / 5773	2014 / 5774	2015 / 5775	2016 / 5776	2017 / 5777
Purim	SUN 24 FEBRUARY	SUN 16 MARCH	THU 5 MARCH	THU 24 MARCH	SUN 12 MARCH
Pesach Passover	TUE/WED 26/27 MARCH	TUE/WED 15/16 APRIL	SAT/SUN 4/5 APRIL	SAT/SUN 23/24 APRIL	TUE/WED 11/12 APRIL
Pesach Passover (Conclusion)	MON/TUE 1/2 APRIL	MON/TUE 21/22 APRIL	FRI/SAT 10/11 APRIL	FRI/SAT 29/30 APRIL	MON/TUE 17/18 APRIL
Shavuot Pentecost	WED/THU 15/16 MAY	WED/THU 4/5 JUNE	SUN/MON 24/25 MAY	SUN/MON 12/13 JUNE	WED/THU 31 MAY/1 JUNE
Tisha B'Av	TUE 16 JULY	TUE 5 AUGUST	SUN 26 JULY	SUN 14 AUGUST	TUE 1 AUGUST

	5774	5775	5776	5777	5778
Rosh Hashanah New Year	THU/FRI 5/6 SEPTEMBER	THU/FRI 25/26 SEPTEMBER	MON/TUE 14/15 SEPTEMBER	MON/TUE 3/4 OCTOBER	THU/FRI 21/22 SEPTEMBER
Yom Kippur	SAT 14 SEPTEMBER	SAT 4 OCTOBER	WED 23 SEPTEMBER	WED 12 OCTOBER	SAT 30 SEPTEMBER
Succot Tabernacles	THU/FRI 19/20 SEPTEMBER	THU/FRI 9/10 OCTOBER	MON/TUE 28/29 SEPTEMBER	MON/TUE 17/18 OCTOBER	THU/FRI 5/6 OCTOBER
Simchat Torah	THU/FRI 26/27 SEPTEMBER	THU/FRI 16/17 OCTOBER	MON/TUE 5/6 OCTOBER	MON/TUE 24/25 OCTOBER	THU/FRI 12/13 OCTOBER
Chanukah	THU-THU 28 NOV-5 DECEMBER	WED-WED 17-24 DECEMBER	MON-MON 7-14 DECEMBER	SUN-SUN 25-31 DECEMBER	WED-WED 13-20 DECEMBER

Acknowledgements

The Scottish Council of Jewish Communities would like to thank the Scottish Government for financial support in the production of this booklet.

We are grateful to Canongate, Mainstream, Vallentine Mitchell, and Chatto and Windus for permission to print extracts from David Daiches, *Two Worlds;* Ernest Levy, *Just One More Dance;* Ralph Glasser, *Gorbals Voices, Siren Songs;* Rabbi Cyril Harris, *For Heaven's Sake;* and Chaim Bermant, *Coming Home.*

The help and support of Harvey Kaplan and the Scottish Jewish Archives Centre is also gratefully acknowledged.

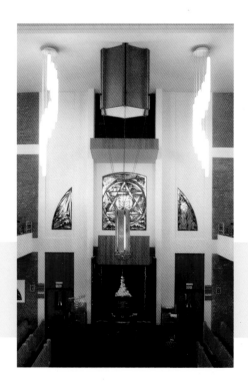

The Shabbat triptych from the Queens Park windows by John K Clark in their new location above the Ark in Giffnock Synagogue (see pp 60–61)